BLUE SONG

BLUE
SONG

— *A Novel* —

Nancy Rhodes

LUMINARE PRESS
WWW.LUMINAREPRESS.COM

Printed in the United States of America

Cover design by Melissa K. Thomas
Cover photo by Nancy Rhodes

Luminare Press
442 Charnelton St.
Eugene, OR 97401
www.luminarepress.com

LCCN: 2021904428
ISBN: 978-1-64388-479-0

For Mom, who believed in me as a writer long before I did, and for my son, Brian, kind and wise beyond his years.

"Someday, somewhere—anywhere, unfailingly,
you'll find yourself, and that, and only that,
can be the happiest or bitterest hour of your life."
—Pablo Neruda

CHAPTER 1

ighting a gag reflex from my boss's pungent habit of nuking broccoli florets for lunch, I stretched my arm across Ms. Baker's gargantuan oak desk. With a steady hand, I delivered my resignation notice.

"What's this, Allie?" she asked, with that phony signature smile I loathed more than the job itself.

Ignoring her question, I looked away, just long enough to release the poisoned air inside my gut.

My soon-to-be ex-boss unfolded the sheet of bond paper and read the first sentence. Her painted lips quivered slightly but soon steadied. As she read or pretended to read the three typed paragraphs, I looked beyond her head and that strikingly ugly ponytail of thinning, black hair. Through the smoky Plexiglas, I watched as the gang continued—some working hard, some hardly working, with newspapers strewn about like faux carpet.

Soon I'll be done, I mused. Nineteen years of deadlines, nineteen years of playing the game, fighting the fight, rolling from high to low and back again—time wasted, time I wanted back.

"This seems sudden," she said, absent of emotion.

"I've thought about this a lot."

Truth was I had dreamt of this day for nearly half of my tenure with Dunesberg Media Corporation. I wanted to say this but decided against it. That bridge just might need to remain intact.

When I returned to my desk, Jeff—my best friend and closest

office companion—asked if I wanted to sneak out for a short walk. I would never have lasted as long as I did had it not been for Jeff and our walks. He arrived at Dunesberg several years after me, but for close to a decade we had shared frustrations over pointless meetings, inexperienced managers, and impossible revenue goals.

No one else knew why I'd been in Baker's office. And I knew that if Jeff didn't have a wife and two kiddos, he'd have been out long before me—pursuing something to invigorate his creative juices instead of a pointless sales position for a doomed daily.

"Sorry," I answered with equal measures of guilt and sadness. I knew he was dying to hear how it went. "I have to finish these ads. Maybe later if I get done before you go."

I reached for my ruler and Sharpie, hating myself for being so damned conscientious for a job and boss I'd just divorced.

He nodded affectionately with that lopsided smile I adored.

"You okay?" he asked, not giving a rat's ass how our inflated-ego, slave-driving boss took the news.

I raised my head and smiled, feigning confidence as if I had a plan.

I didn't.

I had an idea, but I didn't like it. Actually, I hated it. I'd prayed every morning for a better idea. So far it hadn't materialized. I just knew that I could no longer live with the stressful pace of my job and the constant strain of knowing that no matter what I did, it was never enough. And something else was gnawing into the recesses of my soul. That other thing. Like an unwanted anchor, a piece of dark history that, even after twenty-eight years of denial, held me captive in some kind of muck-hole filled with guilt and fear.

"Yeah, I'm good. But I'll be a hell of a lot better in a couple of hours."

<hr />

THE NEXT DAY I CALLED IN SICK. WE WERE APPROACHING NEW Year's Eve, and things were slowing down. Not that I felt guilty.

After scanning the local yellow pages, I called a property management company. Three hours later I signed some papers, promising to have my house ready to lease within a week. Downing two more cups of coffee, I logged on the computer and gave in to that really bad idea.

I purchased a ticket to Chile. A one-way ticket. I would fly out on the first Saturday of 2012—a new year in a new place. Sometime later—a day, a week, or a month—I would take a train to Puerto Montt. I had lived in both cities a long time ago, about a year and a half in Santiago and an eternity in Puerto Montt.

I thought about calling Jeff but didn't. I would tell him eventually, probably after I'd left the United States. If I told him before my departure, he'd talk me out of it. Or try to.

Jeff knew more about my past than anyone. I'd even shared a little about Miguel Aguirre, the dashing and dangerous creature who had kept me away from Chile and a lot of other things for more than a quarter century. But to Jeff, Miguel—the object of my dark history—represented only some generic act of betrayal. Early in our friendship, he'd asked me to fess up, to fill in all the juicy details, but I made it clear he knew what he needed to know. Period.

The day after a lonely New Year's, I called my boss at five in the morning and left a message that I wasn't coming back. I expelled a few pink lies and apologized profusely for the inconvenience that I might be causing her or the company. Breaking my no alcohol before noon rule, I opened a bottle of champagne, blasted a CD of Andean flute music, and danced like a butterfly with new wings.

Being single and childless has its advantages. It took less than a week to wrap up the final contents of my life. On January 7 of the great New Year 2012, I checked in my two oversize suitcases. Two hours later I crammed my six-foot-three body into the window seat of a fully booked 767. Coach.

Staring out at a gray quilt of fog, I inhaled a shallow breath and expelled a small giggle. When I told my older sister, Sarah, that I'd quit, she called me reckless and irresponsible, questioning why I left such a good job. The irony was almost funny. All my adult life she had enjoyed comparing our jobs and our incomes, constantly reminding me of her successes and my failures. Sarah had followed our dad's footsteps in overachievement mania, becoming an investment banker and working seventy-hour weeks. She'd been married for fifteen years to an orthopedic surgeon and chose careers over children. I wondered why suddenly my low-ranking sales position was considered a good job.

Sarah. Older by six years, which she loved to remind me ever since she learned to verbalize those sentiments. After a certain age, she found a way to ensure her superiority without being quite so direct. We'd never been really close. It didn't help that she was the pretty one with wavy, auburn hair and natural blond highlights, a slender nose, and a healthy bustline. She might envy my height, but the rest of me was plain Jane: thin, straight, brownish-gray hair, a nose too wide for my narrow face, and boobs small enough to fit in a ten-year-old's training bra.

Our history post-Miguel was no less rocky than the jagged peaks along the Chilean/Argentinean border in Southern Patagonia. In all my pain following the Miguel trauma, I made the unfathomable yet desperate decision to move in with my big sis. I had no money, and the tips I earned waitressing at a chain diner would not afford me private housing. Immediately I knew I'd made a crazy-ass mistake. The discord and tension began on day one. It didn't help things when three weeks later I started dating a guy she met first. When she caught us in bed one afternoon, I was told to move out.

After near-daily anxiety attacks, I resolved to fight pride and ego and ask my parents if I could move back home. I dreaded it like hell. Mom was newly sober and crankier than ever. Dad was more manageable, when he was around. As the days ticked by, I couldn't seem to find that perfect moment to ask. In some act of uncharacteristic empathy, Sarah gave me two weeks, one of which had passed.

One day Mom called to tell me she and Dad were going to Monterey to celebrate their thirtieth anniversary. Without hesitation, I offered to house-sit. I didn't tell her it could be a permanent arrangement. No reason to put a damper on their holiday.

On their departure day, Mom spent three hours going over her ridiculously long menu of to-dos and don't-dos. I remember slamming the door behind them when they finally left. I might have cursed. Badly. I also remember thinking my life couldn't possibly get any worse.

It did.

They never made it to Carmel. Six hours after I'd slammed the door, two police officers arrived on Sarah's doorstep. They told us that something—a deer, perhaps—caused our parents' car to veer off Highway 1, down an embankment, and straight into an old giant cypress tree. Officer Richards made it clear there were no skid marks. It happened fast, he said, as if that was supposed to provide comfort.

Sarah and I grieved separately. Our grief didn't bring us together.

HEARING THE ANNOUNCEMENT THAT BEVERAGES WOULD SOON be coming down the aisle, I shook my head in an attempt to shake those memories up, up, and away.

I'd forgotten the agony of long-distance flying. I stared at all those fortunate souls who can sleep on airplanes. Through bouts of yawning and squirming, I closed my eyes to count either black widow spiders or fuzzy yellow Labs, both equally ineffective in putting me to sleep. When the plane began to dance in the air, I wondered if anyone besides Jeff would be sad if I died in a horrific plane crash. I imagined Sarah flying back to California and stressing over who to invite to my memorial and what music to play.

"Can I get you anything?" the sexy male flight attendant asked. I thought of several answers, none of which would be very appropriate.

"Orange juice, no ice. Thank you."

Maybe the acid would calm my stomach. My body embraced such contradictions. Coffee at bedtime, dinner for breakfast, breakfast for dinner, and back in my smoking days, cigarettes before sex.

Hours later when sunlight filled the cabin and people began sliding up the window shades, I saw the familiar outlines of the Andes Cordillera speckled with patches of old snow on the higher peaks. As the plane descended, a chill passed through my body—a chill that had nothing to do with the recycled air blasting against my disheveled hairline.

So why was I returning? Was it to find Miguel to learn what really happened all those years ago? As my ears crackled from the cabin pressure, I wondered if I could even find him again. If I did, would I learn the truth? And the worse fear ever—would I regret it? Not good thoughts after leasing out my home, quitting my job, and leaving my best friend.

The wheels screeched across the tarmac.

For better or worse, I was back.

CHAPTER 2

⊷⊶

A taxi delivered me to the same hotel in Santiago I'd stayed at more than a dozen times during the numerous childhood trips with my parents. The changes that occurred since the eighties unnerved me. Once a hotel with two floors, now it was a towering skyscraper with no less than twenty floors. The lobby had been redone, the old Santiago and European flare replaced with contemporary lounge seats appropriate for either the Jetsons or the next space shuttle.

Absent was the grandiose, five-tier crystal chandelier where, at age seven, I was standing when a 6.0 earthquake sent everyone, including my inebriated mother, scrambling for cover. So absorbed in the awe of phantasmal patterns of light swirling across the high ceiling and walls, I didn't let fear overrule my inquisitive nature. When the shaking subsided, an old woman pulled me aside and helped me locate my hysterical mother.

Now, a mustard-colored ceiling hosted a dizzying array of recessed LED lights. Also absent was the two-sided marble staircase with the slippery wood banisters that once provided endless entertainment hours after the hotel staff retired and Mom finished off a bottle of pisco. In lieu of the grandiose stairs, a monochromatic elevator bank with two glass elevators shuttled guests to the floors above or the expensive cocktail lounge on the top floor.

Ignoring the stalking bellhops, I approached the mahogany counter lined with a row of mostly male attendants, all matching in their starched maroon shirts and shiny black pants. Several cast their eyes upon me, offering smiles reminiscent of newly trained grocery checkers. With no one ahead of me, I approached the least threatening in the group, a lad about twenty or twenty-five with a neatly groomed ponytail and eyes as enticing as Johnny Depp's—minus the pirate eyeliner.

"*Una semana*," I said, figuring a week would be long enough while glancing at Latin-Johnny's nameplate. I extracted my Visa card and placed it, gently, very gently, into the hand of Rolando L. Rolando's hand somehow managed to delicately brush across my ringless left hand. As I felt his warm flesh touch the sensitive hollow of my palm, I scorned myself for lusting over a boy half my age.

After a restless night, thanks to sweltering January temperatures on the bottom half of the globe, I ate a small breakfast. Then, anxious to see Santiago again after so many years, I left the hotel and walked downtown. Although the city had changed considerably, some things were the same: the smell of fresh-baked bread from various *panaderías,* the statue of the Virgin Mary on top of Cerro San Cristobal, and the smog that hibernates below the Andes Mountains, creating an unappealing grayish hue across the skyline.

Even though it was barely eight in the morning, the day was getting warm. On top of jet lag, trying to adjust from a northern California winter to a Santiago summer was harder than expected. With the big five-oh behind me, my body didn't accommodate change like it did in my twenties.

I turned onto Avenida Bulnes out of curiosity. I should have realized everything would change drastically in twenty-eight years, but the differences startled me. Avenida Bulnes, once a main thoroughfare for buses and cars, was now a beautiful promenade lined with mature oaks and renamed Promenade Bulnes. A sudden rush of nostalgia compelled me toward the building where I had worked as a secretary for an import company.

For some reason, I remembered where it was, but now, of course, that company was gone. I had no clue what existed behind the locked doors of my old office space: perhaps a private apartment, or a company too small to afford signage.

My footsteps slowed as memories pulled me back to some of the happier years of my life. Don Antonio had been my favorite boss, a man so patient and kind he'd listen attentively to my ill-fated attempts at speaking Spanish. The other two bosses at Repuestos del Mundo Ltda had clout over Don Antonio—a sad thing since their decisions were too often driven by testosterone and ego. Despite the two ogres, I loved the job and adored my coworkers, especially a couple of young women who took me under their wing. They didn't address me as Allison or even Allie. They called me *gringuita,* like the term *gringa* but used (affectionately) in the diminutive form. It meant small American, hysterically inaccurate considering my height.

I left the building, leaving the promenade to a side street I used to frequent during my lunch breaks. The cool air lacked the city bus exhaust known to cling to the streets like black Tule fog. Crossing the second block, I looked between some buildings toward the peaks of the Andes mountain range. Every year when the first snowstorm blanketed the eastern peaks, I'd gaze in wonder at how the mountains took on a new dimension, suddenly so much larger and strikingly close to the city.

I chuckled silently, remembering my first southern hemisphere skiing experience. My egocentric boyfriend at the time brought me to Portillo, a famous and longtime ski resort known to avid skiers in both South and North America. I'd only skied a few times before that, never enough to get the hang of it. But Cutie Pie lured me onto a slope way too advanced for my skills, resulting in a long walk down the mountain, skis on my shoulder, and no boyfriend in sight.

A sudden screech of tires halted my passage down memory lane. I turned to see a dark-gray sedan fly past me. A police car followed from several car lengths away at speeds more appropriate for the Indy 500. I tucked my body into an alcove. I didn't trust this new Santiago. Whatever was happening, I wanted no part of it.

The car in front started to turn right but swerved back at the last second. Failing to shake the police, it made a sharp turn left, nearly scaling the curb. When it was only a block from where my vulnerable body stood frozen against the wall, the car slowed. I imagined the window lowering and an automatic weapon poking out, aimed at my heart. Feeling like I'd stepped inside an episode of *Cops*, I couldn't move. Suddenly, a young man parachuted from the moving car. His body tumbled into a ball before landing in the gutter. As my hands rose to my face, I couldn't believe that he stumbled back to his feet within seconds and darted behind a cigarette kiosk. Turning my head, I watched the sedan continue down the side street with the police following closely behind.

Time to get my ass back to the hotel! I turned toward La Moneda Palace, the state government office. I figured three blocks to La Moneda and four to the hotel.

I glanced back long enough to see that the same man who flew out of the sedan was coming after me.

I fought to calm the fireworks inside my chest. And then I ran.

His footsteps outpaced me two to one.

"*¡Ayudame!*" he shouted. I had no intention of helping this dude. If the cops wanted him, I didn't. I increased my stride, my backpack bouncing painfully across my back.

"*Por favor,*" he shouted, gaining distance.

Turning, I saw he held a small package, something wrapped in brown paper.

"*No te hará daño,*" he said from less than ten feet away. "*¡Tome esto!*"

He wanted me to take the package and was claiming he wouldn't harm me.

The slapping of shoes against concrete startled me. I searched ahead for help, my heart thumping irregularly under my sports bra. I made it around the next corner, praying that someone would appear soon. I didn't want to think what he might do to me, but some gruesome ideas were unwittingly forming in my head. I struggled for breath and continued to run, feeling like I had just fallen onto a treadmill spinning in the wrong direction.

I began to regret my plane had not crashed. At least that death would be quick as opposed to whatever might happen next.

When his breath prickled the hairs along the back of my neck, bile rose to my throat. Then his sweaty, warm hand grabbed mine. I jerked it back as he tried to hand me a brown package, which subsequently fell and landed in front of my left foot. When he turned to face me, I screamed. My thoughts spiraled into darkness. *Would he take me out with a gun or a knife? Would he kidnap me, rape me?* Taking a deep breath, I stared into his eyes to memorize his facial features just in case I was lucky enough to survive the assault.

"*¿Habla Español?*" asked my soon-to-be attacker with a strong accent.

What an odd question considering the circumstances. I shook my head, thinking perhaps he'd let me go if there was no hope of communication. Not that my Spanish was that great.

"English?" he asked.

Hard to lie on that one. "Yes," I replied with fifty shades of reluctance.

"Take package," he said. "Please. Address is inside. Bring soon to señor. Much necessary. Very important. Please do this."

Just as I opened my mouth to respond, a taxi appeared from around the corner. Before I could jump in front of my assailant to hail the cab, he took a step forward, pointed to the package, and brought his hand over his heart in a silent plea. Then he ran, waving for the taxi to stop. My taxi. The door opened, and he disappeared. I wanted to scream a multitude of profanities, but my throat had closed nice and tight on my vocal cords.

CHAPTER 3

I collapsed to my knees. Tears gushed down my face, landing like raindrops on the sidewalk.

By the time my middle-aged knees began their protest, the relief over not getting beaten to a bloody pulp wore off. Now I was pissed. Determined to grab the package and toss it in the nearest waste can, I reached toward the brown paper bundle. Pulling it to my lap, I noticed an oil stain on one side, the word *musica* on the other. I wondered why a package of music would be so damn important for someone to run from the police, jump out of a moving car, and entrust whatever these contents were to a middle-aged gringa he had never met.

I looked around. Maybe the package contained drug money or, worse yet, drugs. I opened my backpack, removed my camera, and stuffed the package deep inside. Maybe I would dispose of it, but in the meantime, I didn't want anyone to see me with it. Obviously there was some voodoo associated with the damn thing, which is why I kept looking behind me as I raced back to the hotel.

After locking the deadbolt inside my room, I closed the blinds and moved to the bed, package in hand. I carefully pulled back the taped edges and removed the brown wrapping. Inside, a thick manila envelope contained about sixty sheets of paper, bound together with intersecting rubber bands. The top three sheets were untitled music scores.

I thumbed through the next dozen pages, all written in Spanish. Many of the pages contained lists indicating dates and names of places I didn't recognize. Some pages resembled nautical charts. This package was a waste of my time. I didn't give a shit why some crazy young man begged me to take it off his hands. Tomorrow I'd dispose of it in the large dumpster near the service entrance of my hotel. The sooner I dumped it, the sooner I could leave the hotel and proceed with my plans to find Miguel.

Two hours later I found myself rethinking the dumpster plan. *Maybe I should turn it in to the police. Tell them what I saw.* But since there were no drugs, money, or evidence of pornography, I feared they would consider me crazy. Besides, I didn't exactly trust the Chilean police, despite the end of Pinochet's dirty dictatorship.

I stayed in my room for the rest of the day. After wrapping the papers in my sweatshirt, I put it on a chair in the far corner of the room. I grabbed my laptop and a large bag of cashews. Time to do some people tracking. Find old friends. I had no real reason for connecting with people from my past, but it felt like a good place to start even if none of them ever met Miguel. Besides, this would provide more entertainment than watching soaps I couldn't understand. I should have started with a search for Miguel, but after the morning chase episode, reality had me suffering enough excitement for one day.

I'd forgotten the last names of my old coworkers but hoped I might find my best Chilean friend, Mariela Munoz. Of course, her last name may have changed once or twice since we had said our goodbyes.

Mariela and I had met through our boyfriends, two handsome soccer jocks who had been buddies since the first grade. We were a crazy foursome with pastimes that mainly consisted of drinking and disco hopping. When we realized the boys enjoyed the alcohol aspect of our adventures more than the companionship, we dumped them. Not long after that, Mariela moved to Iquique. For the first time in my life, I fell hostage to loneliness and depression. I wore my desire for companionship like a wetsuit, my desperation ever so revealing.

"Ripe and ready," Jeff once said during one of our many confessional conversations. But he was right. I had that history and couldn't have been more ready for someone like Miguel. Someone who knew just how to grab, use, and abuse my heart. For nearly thirty years I blamed Miguel for squashing my happy-ever-after dreams of life in the southern hemisphere and for my lack of commitment in about every aspect of my life. But now I knew better. I could only blame myself.

I found only one Mariela Munoz—some jockette who sought adventure through rock climbing, skiing, and mountain biking. Not my Mariela, a girl who could not cross over a log without crawling on all fours. Apparently, Mariela didn't exist in cyberspace.

After raiding the minibar for chocolate and chardonnay, my thoughts returned to the danger zone. I typed in his name. Miguel Aguirre. There were twelve of them. Hell. One was bad enough.

Something about my second mini bottle of chardonnay pushed my curiosity to an all-new level of stupidity. I narrowed the search by entering the town of Puerto Montt with Miguel's name. Only one Miguel Aguirre came up, this one containing the middle initial T. My stomach did a reverse somersault, and it wasn't the wine or chocolate. I slammed the laptop cover down and yanked the plug from the wall. I threw off my tank top and jeans and crawled into the cold, starched sheets. Fortunately, the chardonnay worked like magic. I passed out before the sun dropped behind the Cordillera.

When I left for breakfast the next morning, I stumbled over the paper outside my door. I bent down to pick it up, and a wave of nausea rushed to my throat. Perhaps it was the sulfates from the minibar wine, but the headline of the *English Daily* didn't help. It read:

MUSIC CONSERVATORY BREAK-IN LEADS
TO HIGH-SPEED CHASE

Over black coffee and scrambled eggs, I picked up the paper again,

Nancy Rhodes

briefly noting the photograph of a familiar taxi missing its front bumper. The byline under the photo read:

A suspect, Christian Montero, was detained yesterday after-noon after his vehicle crashed into a parked bus. Another suspect remains missing. No serious injuries were reported.

I read and reread the three-paragraph story. Nowhere did it say what was taken from the conservatory. I returned to my room, threw the newspaper on the bed, and picked up the package. If this was important and I tossed it, could I become someone's target? Maybe it was time to rethink my reluctance about con-tacting the police so I could move on to more touristy endeavors like nursing pisco sours on the beach in Viña del Mar. Why not have some fun before I start searching for that self-absorbed possible murderer?

After returning to my room and stripping off the black jeans that were already too suffocating for the day, I looked at the phone sitting next to the Gideon Bible. I couldn't do it. Not yet. I opened the envelope. This time I removed all the contents.

A few minutes later I found a small, white envelope tucked between some pages. It wasn't sealed well, so I slid my index finger gently under the lip and found a wad of US dollars—drug money! Just like I had imagined. I picked up the phone to call the *carabin-eros* but then hung up, deciding I should count it first. A stack of fifties adding up to $2,850. And attached to the bills was a note in Spanish that indicated something like he wanted to donate more but that was the best he could do. This unidentified writer wrote: *Es para producir la cancion.* Money to produce a song?

The money left me curious. What was so important about a song? I started scanning some of the other pages, the ones contain-ing data such as dates, locations, and—oddly—sea temperatures. Near the bottom half of the stack, a few pages referred to *La Ballena Azul.* Blue whale?

I fanned the pages, checking for more envelopes or cash. One page didn't move like the others. It was thick, somewhere between construction paper and cardboard. I held it toward the window for better light. In the center was an outline of a square about three inches wide. Using my Swiss Army knife, I slit the page until the tip of the knife touched the insert. I carefully extracted what felt like tissue paper. After unfolding it, I saw a name and address: Carlos Costanera, 226 Avenida Torres, El Toyo, Chile.

Who the hell was Carlos Costanera? And where was El Toyo? Was this where I was supposed to deliver the package? Why was the name hidden so secretively?

Desire, fear, and curiosity are emotions likely to erode logic and reason, but I prayed I wouldn't be stupid enough to run off to some town I had never heard of to deliver a mysterious package that had been thrown my way after a high-speed chase in downtown Santiago.

I returned to the bed, read the note again, and stared at the music sheets. I thought about the young man's face, so desperate. This didn't help my indecision. Was he a thug or a victim?

Okay, Allie, forget the police. The idea of a military-controlled police force wasn't comforting. I was back to either tossing the papers into the garbage so I could leisurely visit Viña or going to someplace I had never heard of to deliver some mysterious package, to some person I didn't know. It should have been an easy choice.

It wasn't.

What about that cash? I certainly could use two grand. But my Pollyanna conscience shot that down. Maybe if this stuff was important enough for some guy to risk his life and/or liberty, there could be a little reward involved. Clean conscience and money. *Nice!*

With my pants and top removed, I moved to the hallway mirror and scanned my cellulite-speckled thighs, scrawny arms, and drooping breasts. Looking at my puffy bloodshot eyes, I spoke to that familiar face.

"Allie, we're going on an adventure. Warm sand, single men, and mouth-puckering toddies will just have to wait."

I rolled my eyes, shrugged my shoulders, and signaled a thumbs-up before disappearing from the mirror's silent reflection toward the shower.

CHAPTER 4

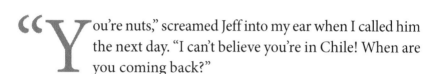

"**Y**ou're nuts," screamed Jeff into my ear when I called him the next day. "I can't believe you're in Chile! When are you coming back?"

Immediately regretting my after-shower decision to call him, I held the phone a foot away while taking one long, exaggerated deep breath.

"Allie?"

"Yeah, I'm here. Are you at work?" Distraction. Works fifty percent of the time.

"No, I'm on my way," he answered. "It's eight thirty, and I'm sitting in bumper-to-bumper traffic. You're avoiding my question, Allison."

"Don't call me that, and maybe I don't have an answer for you."

"You snot-ass. What does your return ticket say?"

"What ticket?"

"Oh God, don't tell me. You purchased a one-way ticket to memoryville? Why?"

"Don't worry. I'll be back. I just don't know exactly when. I can buy the return ticket just as well from here—"

"Tell me you're only staying in Santiago."

"For now." I knew he didn't want me going near Miguel. "But there's something I do want to talk to you about. Do you have a few minutes?"

"Yep. I'm driving, but I have my coffee balanced between my

thighs, my breakfast bar between the steering wheel and my left hand, and one hand free and clear just for you."

"I'm honored. Okay, I'll get to the point. Yesterday I came upon something that doesn't belong to me. Some guy handed me this strange package. He asked me to deliver it for him. He seemed pretty desperate, but yet—"

"Wait a minute. Listen to yourself. I thought you went down there to rest or take out the ex-lover. You haven't been there but three days, and you're already on a rescue mission! If you want to rescue someone, you could have stayed here and found me a better job. What's in the package? Cocaine?"

"It's a stack of papers. It's in Spanish. I don't know why he gave it to me, but it seemed important."

"I thought you spoke Spanish."

"*Poquito*. Besides, this is too detailed. I understand enough to know it's some kind of a report, something to do with whales."

A horn blasted into my ear like the car had entered my hotel room, followed by Jeff yelling a few expletives. Then the line went dead. I waited for him to call me back. Since he didn't, I redialed his number. It rang twice and went to voicemail. When I put the phone down, I stared up at the ceiling. I counted four sprinkler heads. Considering the size of the room, I found this excessive, but at least I wouldn't become a hotel fire statistic.

I gave up on Jeff and called the concierge instead. The young woman, Jessica, advised me that El Toyo was approximately twenty-five miles south. She said it would be easiest to take a taxi, but a bus would be leaving the Tobalaba Metro Station around 3:00 p.m. if I wanted a more economic option. The bus, she explained, would put me within walking distance of my destination. Despite memories of buses so overloaded that bodies hung off stairwells precariously close to the street, I opted for the bus. I didn't want to shell out my limited funds for a journey that might end up a total waste of time.

Knowing I had to hurry if I wanted to get to the station by three,

I threw on some khaki shorts and grabbed a lightweight sweatshirt. I expected a hot day, although I had no idea what microclimate might exist in the unknown town of El Toyo. I hid my camera under the mattress. No photos on this adventure.

The bus was hot and smelled like a boys' locker room. Getting out of Santiago seemed to take forever. Feeling my nails etching deeper into my palms, I looked between the buildings at shadows, wondering what in the hell I was doing. I might have been crazy enough to return to Chile to look for Miguel, but taking a bus to God-knows-where to hand off some who-knows-what package truly showed a severe deprivation of brain cells.

Once the bus left the highway and moved toward the foothills, my shoulders fell from my ears, and eventually my breathing settled from frantic flurry to slow and steady. Searching unsuccessfully for comfort on the hard plastic bus seat, I stared out my hazy window at the countryside. The tall, ancient trees and farms with their rundown barns felt so familiar, echoing memories from decades past. Whiffs of dried grasses and distant eucalyptus trees drifted through open windows. The bus noisily shifted gears as it started an ascent up a narrow and steep incline. The stops became fewer as the bus gradually emptied of day laborers and women shoppers, large bags hanging heavily off their arms and shoulders.

My eyes must have closed. I was startled by the driver's raspy voice just as my seatmate, a dark-skinned, well-weathered old man, jabbed his elbow into my side.

"*Señorita, hemos llegado a El Toyo*," the driver said, pointing out the window toward a tiny sign declaring my destination point. I nodded a silent *gracias* and stood up. I felt several sets of eyes upon me as I walked down the aisle, tilting my head so my hair wouldn't act as a dust mop on the ceiling. When my feet hit the road and the bus shifted gears and disappeared, I wondered if I looked as out of place as I felt.

The town was quiet. Deathly quiet. The main road was asphalt, but after a few minutes my sandaled feet cruised over narrow gravel streets in search of Avenida Torres. After two dead-end roads, I found Carlos's street. Fortunately, the number 226 was painted on a scrap of wood and nailed to a tree in front of his home.

The house, a small, gray stucco shack, was tucked behind a tall iron gate. The windows, like most I'd seen in Chile, had thick prison bars across them. I glanced down the street and saw a scruffy, brown dog licking an ice-cream wrapper. Sweat ran down my back, tickling my skin. I pushed the gate forward. As I walked across the gravel entrance toward a small porch, the insanity of what I was doing left me feeling like I'd tied my body to the tracks just in time for the train.

I turned around and walked toward the road. Glancing down at the package in my hands, I heard laughter. Across the street, two young girls of identical size and cuteness were playing in a small yard. They didn't notice me, which was good. One of them crawled onto a milk crate, trying to tie a Superman cape around her thin shoulders. After she finally got the cape tied, she jumped to the ground as if expecting to fly. Tumbling onto her knees, she then looked up and saw me.

"*Hola*," she shouted from across the street. "¡*Hola!*" the other echoed.

"*Hola*," I said, waving back with my free hand.

When I turned around to face house 226, a man close to my height appeared on the front porch. My eyes dropped to his legs. Couldn't help it. Something about his cutoff shorts, with those dangling frays of white fabric swaying against his mocha skin, pulled my eyes in that direction. Then I noticed he didn't have a shirt on. No beer belly. Toned abs. Curvy biceps. Lots of eye candy.

Good grief, Allie! Focus.

I approached the steps and in garbled Spanish asked if he was Carlos.

"Yes, I am Carlos." He spoke perfect English, no trace of an accent. I wondered if he was American. His arms dropped to his sides. "What can I—?"

I held out the package and approached the stairs. He stepped forward. I caught a quick movement from his lips, like a one-sided smile.

"My name is Allison Bennett, but I go by Allie," I said, nervously handing him the package, oily side up.

He shook my hand with a certain intensity without overdoing it. Besides killer green eyes, his features were handsome in a rugged, authentic way. His long hair, mostly black but with touches of gray, hung in tight curls around his face and down his shoulders. He had to be younger. No one this hot could be my age. Besides, lately, everyone seemed younger.

"Come in, Allie," he said, holding the door open.

Wondering if entering a stranger's home was wise considering the events that occurred two days ago, I hesitated.

"Or not," he said calmly.

CHAPTER 5

I stepped inside.

Pointing to a well-worn blue armchair, he told me to make myself comfortable while he grabbed a faded gray T-shirt off the counter. While he slid it over his head, I couldn't help but notice his movements carried a level of ease, somehow graceful despite a muscular physique.

"I just made some cold tea. Can I get you a glass?"

"That sounds good. Thanks."

"I'll be right back."

I planted myself on the edge of the seat. An enormously plump cat jumped from a nearby table onto my lap.

"*Gordito feo,* behave yourself," said Carlos, clapping his hands together.

"It's fine. I love cats." Slight exaggeration.

"And Gordito loves people, as I'm sure you've gathered."

When he went into the kitchen, I tried to shake the cat off my lap. Failing, my eyes then wandered around the small room. A large conga drum and a guitar occupied one corner. No TV. No boy toys. The furnishings were simple and minimal: a small, round table in the open kitchen across from the living room, a brown sofa tinted gray with a layer of Gordito's hair, and a coffee table barely visible beneath a blanket of nature magazines.

On the wall closest to me hung a cheaply framed poster of two whales breaching high above a tumultuous ocean. Opposite of where I sat, I saw a framed photo of an enormous whale next to a diver swimming precariously close to the whale's belly. A contrast like that of a flea resting on the back of an elephant.

Carlos returned. Handing me the tea, he asked if I lived in Chile.

"I'm just visiting this time, but I did spend a lot of time here when I was young. My father used to bring us to Chile once a year. He had business partners in Santiago. We'd always stay at least a couple of weeks. But after I turned fourteen, I stopped coming. Came back when I was nineteen and stayed for about four years."

Geez, was I rambling or what? I did not need to give this stranger a *Reader's Digest* version of my life.

"*¿Habla Español?*"

"*Poco,* but I'm rusty. Real rusty."

After Carlos sat down, I gave him the package, and a sense of relief instantly flooding my veins. I was so happy to be rid of it. As much as I dreaded my mission, I felt more determined to hunt down Miguel, deal with him in whatever way I could, and return to the States.

Carlos opened the package and inspected the contents.

"You're kind for delivering this," he said finally. "How did you end up with it?"

"Kind of a long story."

I hoped one I wouldn't have to share. But then again, he was nice to be around. For all the wrong reasons.

"There's some cash in here," he said with mild enthusiasm.

I held on tightly to the sweating glass, watching ice cubes bob on the surface. I was dying to pull one out and drop it down the back of my sweaty T-shirt.

"Yes, I know," I admitted. "I wasn't sure what it meant or what to do with it. I thought about giving it to the police, but—"

"I'm glad you didn't do that," he said, looking in the direction of the whale and diver picture.

"Someone gave me the package. Well, gave isn't exactly the word. But anyway, he begged me to give it to you."

"Who was that?" he asked casually.

"Don't know. But there was an article in the paper. Well, let me back up." I took a breath, wondering how to begin and how much to share.

First, I had to get this fat cat off my naked legs. Faking a cough, I shook my legs until the feline got my message.

While the cat disappeared down a hallway, I gathered my courage.

"A couple of days ago," I said, trying to hide my attraction, "I was walking in downtown Santiago. Suddenly there was this car chase—involving a police car—and the guy who ended up giving me this package rolled out of the car. I couldn't believe it. And then it got worse. He started chasing me."

"He chased you?" Carlos shook his head.

"Yes! I was scared to death. Well, he caught up to me. I thought he was going to stab me. But as it turned out, all he wanted was to give me that damn package. It didn't make sense. Not only am I a total stranger but a gringa."

"Maybe that's why he trusted you. So what were you saying about a newspaper?"

"Oh, right. This morning I saw an article about a break-in at the conservatory—around the same time as my incident. It said one guy got away. It did mention the name of who was caught, but I can't remember now who it was."

"Ha. Interesting."

"What is this is all about?"

Carlos sighed. Returning to the sofa, this time a bit closer to me, he nodded. "Now that's a long story."

His tone was difficult to read. I wondered if I should go, but then he offered more tea.

"Okay, half a glass," I answered.

"I'll fill you in. I owe you that."

Tempted to tell him he owed me nothing, I sunk my top incisors into my bottom lip. Surely a few more minutes wouldn't make a difference. Just enough time to settle my curiosity. I mean, really, I had been chased by a stranger! I could have been killed.

"Missing whales. That's what this is about."

Whether it was my inappropriate attraction to Carlos or a sudden interest in large mammals I knew nothing about, I wanted to know more. But I had to be careful. There was only one bus back to Santiago, leaving at six thirty, and I had no watch or cell phone.

"Huh? I mean, oh. I did see something about *ballenas*. I know that means whales. But missing whales? How would someone know that whales are missing?" I tried hiding a smirk when my brain suddenly pictured whales lining up along the coastline for an annual whale census.

"There are people across the globe who track whales. And like other species, the blues are still endangered. We almost lost them entirely before the 1970s because of all the whaling. And although they became one of the protected species, their numbers are still low. Scientists believe there are fewer than two thousand left in the southern hemisphere."

I knew nothing about whales but hoped to hide my ignorance. Truth be told, I didn't know much about anything in the animal kingdom. Apparently I missed the animal gene. My mom never allowed us to have pets. In my thirties I adopted a cat—only because I was suckered into it—but it was hit by a car less than a year later, and I swore never again. Why connect emotionally to something that nine times out of ten you're going to outlive? Okay, so telling Carlos I loved cats was a stretch.

"So," he continued while the menacing feline circled his feet. "Locally, a few of us started tracking the blues in some of the popular feeding grounds. There weren't many to track, but the numbers kept dropping every year. Enough to make us suspicious."

I nodded, curious what kind of numbers he was talking about. He paused. I wondered if this was the time to ask him what the package had to do with missing whales. I looked at the report he'd just placed on the table.

Nancy Rhodes

"This report," he said, "identifies a small population that has stayed within a forty-mile radius all year round instead of following the usual migration pattern to Golfo Nuevo and Golfo San Jose, where they breed during winter months. Four years ago, after noticing the numbers of blues decreasing, we set on a mission to tag as many as possible. We got tags on fifteen. Would've liked more, but it's not an easy task."

He paused to take a sip of tea. A gnawing fear of potentially missing my bus peeked into the forefront of my mind, but I couldn't break away, not yet. Surely I still had lots of time.

"Since then, we've been watching the blues closely. Three years ago, four of our fifteen disappeared. The following year we lost six, including the largest of the group. Often the transmitters fail after several months, but generally, we know enough about their whereabouts to find them on our own. It'd be a lot easier if they were coastline huggers."

"They don't come in close?"

"No, they're too large. Usually, they're at least four or five miles out."

"I know they're the largest mammals on earth. Aren't they the size of a school bus or something?"

"Well, at birth perhaps, but a full-size blue whale might be the size of three buses. We have an older blue that we suspect is ninety feet long! Anyway, over time we knew something outside of Mother Nature was involved. It was incredibly disturbing since some of our team thought the whales were within sighting range when their signals stopped. But after scouring the seas for weeks, we found nothing."

Gordito jumped back onto my lap. He sank his claws through my shorts, and I flinched. He purred. I felt it was intentional. This cat wanted me gone. I considered leaving to avoid further abuse from this oversize feline so intent on massaging me with built-in daggers. But didn't I still have more time to kill? It was too hot to wait outside for a bus that would probably show up late.

"Initially, we thought the whales might have divided up since blues are more apt to travel alone. So we spent months checking satellite feeds and scanning the area where the signal dropped. Last year we lost the remaining five. All the signals disappeared conspicuously close to the same location where they'd gone missing previously. And most alarming, four of the five transmitters stopped within an hour of each other."

"That doesn't sound good."

"We were devastated. But then, not that long ago, we found something that elevated our concern."

"I'm afraid to ask."

"We found a fluke."

"What?"

"The tail. Neatly severed too. Washed ashore with the tide. Later we found evidence that other cetaceans, including dolphins, had been slaughtered."

"That's horrible! Why would someone want to kill whales?"

"Maybe for meat. In the old days, they also used the blubber for oil and oil by-products including cosmetics. Even after the International Whaling Commission's moratorium on commercial whaling that began in the late eighties, slaughtering continues across the globe. First the Russians, then the Japanese and Norwegians, and now it seems we have a band of poachers in our backyard. Some of us believe that these men are part of an organized clan hiding out somewhere near Chiloé. Perhaps they're shipping whale meat to Japan or somewhere with looser controls."

The mention of Chiloé sent instant pain to my gut. Miguel and I had talked about visiting Chiloé when we were on that fateful Pucón trip. I remember the conversation. It was probably one of the nicest we had on the trip—perhaps ever. He spoke about us like we were a couple. I remember feeling hopeful that we might have a future together, an exciting, adventurous future.

Carlos refilled my glass. At this rate, a two-hour bus ride might present me with one hell of a challenge.

"This report may contain enough evidence to identify who might be killing the blue whales or at least lead us in the right direction."

"Really?" I asked, quietly congratulating myself for doing something right. Good thing I never told Carlos that I'd considered throwing it in the garbage. It was nice thinking that my small part in returning the package might actually save some whales. Who would have imagined? I couldn't wait to tell Jeff.

"If it's so important, why did that guy throw it at me? And why were the police chasing him?"

"Was the man who gave this to you about five foot five with straight, black hair cut above his ears, a small nose, and no facial hair?"

"Sounds pretty accurate."

"Mmmm. Well, that sounds like Jorge. He's been helping us and was supposed to bring this last week but never did. I don't know why he was being chased though. That alarms me."

"Why?"

"Well, for one, we have to make sure this doesn't get into the wrong hands. And then there's the concern about why he was being chased."

"You're afraid that the police shouldn't see it?"

"At this point, we don't know who we can trust."

"Why?" I asked, looking at the cat and hoping to somehow message him off my sweaty lap.

"Until we know who's at the core of this slaughtering ring, we can't take chances. It could be anyone, someone working inside the police or even inside the Whaling Commission—although I'd be surprised if that was the case."

Uncrossing my legs and losing the cat, I turned my gaze to the remnants of red polish splattered beneath my dirt-covered toes.

Carlos scratched the back of his neck. The cat began circling his feet.

"Not now, Gordito," he said. "Jorge studied at the conservatory in Santiago a few years ago. I met him through mutual friends at a political rally back in the Pinochet days. He was interested in whale research and invited me to join him on a couple of his outings. I was busy at the time and got the impression that Jorge was the kind of guy who flips interests like flapjacks. I never did join him, mostly just talked on the phone a few times. You said the paper mentioned a break-in at the conservatory?"

"Yes."

"Maybe he trusted the wrong person. He had a new friend, someone named Octavio. Whether true or not, I heard that Octavio invested in underwater probes, the kind used for monitoring and recording whale sounds. Jorge wanted to record whale sounds to put them into some song he was working on, or so he told me. I'm wondering if the whole thing at the conservatory was a setup."

I nodded my head like I understood what he was talking about. "That's crazy. Did you say something about recording whales? What do they sound like?"

"Depends on the whale. They can communicate with a series of clicks, pulses, moans, and even whistles in some species. Humans can't hear the pitch of a blue whale. It's too low. But the blue whale's call is the strongest underwater sound of any mammal. They can hear each other about a thousand miles apart."

"I remember years ago when some guy recorded the sound of humpback whales."

"That was probably Lucas Payne. He helped increase awareness of the plight of whales by popularizing their mating calls. But it was his work as a researcher of long-distance communication between whales that made him a legend."

Looking at the instruments in the corner, I said, "Speaking of songs, are you a musician?"

"Mostly for my own amusement. You?"

"*Nada.* I won't even sing in the shower. The tiles would crack."

He laughed heartily. Gosh, he was a looker. Even had nice teeth, straight, naturally white, not bleached. I always felt that one can tell a lot by a guy's teeth. Wished I'd realized that when I met Miguel, a man with incisors the size of dinosaurs and enough gold fillings to replicate a Golden Buddha statue.

"I saw a song sheet in that pile," I said.

"I can't tell you how grateful I am that you brought this. It probably took a leap of faith, especially after the frightening way you ended up getting it."

Faith, guts, or maybe just stupidity.

Based on the shadows creeping across the room, it had to be getting late. I needed to go.

CHAPTER 6

⸻

Wﬁhat should have come out of my mouth next was "What time is it?"

Instead, I asked more questions. Because Carlos was nice to look at, nice to be around, and I liked his energy.

"So you think Jorge and the other guy were set up and that the cops thought they'd broken into the conservatory?"

"I don't know. But Jorge was a pretty straightforward guy. A little reserved perhaps. But he'd have no reason to be breaking into the place."

Gordito Feo was now licking the hell out of my toes. What was I—a fricking Rocky Road ice-cream cone? I jerked my foot, sending Gordito flying at least two feet across the room.

"Oh gosh, I'm sorry," I said, trying to look ashamed.

Carlos shifted in his seat. I probably pissed him off. Fortunately, kitty seemed unfazed by his recent flight.

"He can be pesky."

Understatement.

What a twisted sense of fate. I'd left a newspaper job in California to fly to Chile in hopes of finding resolution and peace. But in less than seventy-two hours, I'd gotten myself mixed up in a strange conspiracy that made no sense whatsoever.

"Why did he give me the package? Why didn't he just return it directly to you?"

"Maybe he was afraid he'd still be caught and thought you were his only hope."

"I've got to be honest, Carlos. He scared the shit out of me."

"Like I said, maybe he was desperate. I'm just glad he had my address inside and that you found it."

"He hid it pretty good. I almost didn't see it."

Rubbing his stomach, Carlos looked at me. "Can I repay you for all that you've done? Are you hungry? I have some leftover *arroz con pollo*."

"No, I should go. Do you know what time it is?"

"No, but I can go check. I've got a small clock in my bedroom. Since there's no car out front, I presume you came by taxi or bus."

"Bus. And it might be leaving soon."

"Good call. The Santiago taxi drivers rarely want to come up this far. Even harder to find one to take you back. Shall I walk you to the bus stop?"

"It's close. I'll find it."

Carlos got up, walked to the bedroom, and returned. "It's about six twenty."

"Uh-oh. I have to run then!"

"Sorry I talked your head off."

"It's okay. I needed answers. Thanks for the tea."

Carlos walked me to the door. "Thank you for bringing this back."

"Well, glad it worked out," I said, nearly tripping over the small lion.

I reflected on what I'd just said. *Glad?* The only thing I was glad about was getting rid of that package.

"*Chao*, Allie."

With a full bladder, I ran down his steps, waved, and made a run for it. Before rounding the block, I turned around. Carlos was still on the porch. He waved again, which I thought was kind of sweet. He had some manners.

I picked up my pace trying for a sprint, but that proved impossible in flip-flops. After a couple of blocks, the bus stop finally came into view. What I saw stopped my heart. There was the bus, my bus, pulling away from the curb, a black spit of smoke heading straight for my lungs.

CHAPTER 7

⁂

The bus stop consisted of a small slab of concrete and a lop-sided wood bench. I looked around. The bakery, one of only three buildings in town, was closed. Noticing the clouds shifting to dark shades of gray, I knew that all too soon the town's only streetlight would leave me vulnerable. I was happy to spot a small store two blocks down the road and prayed it was open so I could order a taxi.

After fifteen minutes of waiting at the stop as if some second bus would magically appear, I got off the bench and stretched my arms toward the sky. I thought I heard footsteps behind me, but when I turned around, the street was empty.

Sighing with relief, I saw a hand-painted sign declaring the store *abierto*. As I entered the shop, a small chain of bells clanked and clamored against the wooden door. Three aisles and one register completed this little *almacén*. Behind a small counter were two very precisely stacked rows of cigarettes and one stack of Super 8 candy bars. The latter brought a wave of nostalgia as I remembered plenty of Super 8 binges after an excess of vino. A musty mix of damp wood and cigars filled my lungs.

"¿*Hola*?" I croaked.

No response. I could have taken twenty packs of Viceroys and the entire row of Super 8s. Walking into a completely unattended store was a new experience for me. Not one I particularly understood or appreciated.

"*¿Hola?*" I said a hundred decibels louder, my voice reflecting every ounce of impatience brewing inside of me.

After a moment, a hoarse voice called, "*Momento ya voy.*"

My shoulders fell back into place with the anticipation of a phone and, hopefully soon, a taxi. A man well into his golden years appeared, hobbling like one of his legs couldn't keep up with the other. His bushy gray hair and furrowed eyebrows reminded me of Einstein.

"*Buenas tardes, señorita,*" he crackled, moving slowly toward the counter.

I tried asking for a phone. My Spanglish sucked.

"*Si, tenemos telefono,*" he said, pointing past the toilet paper aisle. "*Pero,* so sorry, *señora, eso telefono no funciona.*"

Great. He had a phone, but it didn't work. I decided that I'd make a purchase. Perhaps if I gave him some business, he'd be more apt to help a stranded gringa find a ride back to Santiago. I cruised the aisles staring at hair dyes, toothbrushes, and colorfully packaged feminine hygiene products. I stopped at the chips and cookies aisle. When I reached for a giant bag of Lay's, the jingle of doorbells echoed across the store. Einstein had to be thrilled to have two customers in one night.

With no phone, no plan, and no bus, I decided one bag of chips might not be enough nutrition for however long it might take me to find a way home. Turning into the last aisle to peruse the fruit and vegetable bins, I saw the new arrival—a stocky, short man wearing a red cap with layers of crusty paint streaked across the brim, a testament to his profession. He entered the cracker aisle, but when he saw me, he did a swift about-face. I grabbed a vine of grapes and made my way to Einstein's counter. Along the way, I rehearsed my questions in Spanish—ask if he has a bus schedule, ask where there's a phone that works, smile a lot, and don't forget *por favor* and *gracias.*

"Bus?" the storekeeper responded. "*Ya no, no hay...ya es muy tarde, señorita.*"

He confirmed there were no more buses at this hour. I prayed for better results when I asked him about a phone.

"*No,* he responded, shaking his head. "*El único público es aquel pero no funciona.*" He pointed to the only public phone, explaining it was out of order.

"Taxi?" I asked, throwing my hands up pathetically.

Einstein looked outside, shaking his head. My choices were limited: sleep on a three-foot wooden bench or go back to Carlos's house. I didn't recall seeing a car at his house, but hopefully he had a motorbike tucked away somewhere. At least, I knew he had a phone. Purchases in hand, I left the store.

The unlit streets looked smaller at night. A few stars made their appearance in between patches of white and gray clouds. I walked a few blocks and turned on what I hoped was Carlos's street. The houses looked so similar in the fading light. Most contained barred windows, modest or no gardens, and colorful curtains aglow from interior lights. Smells of baked fish and sweet corn exacerbated my appetite. All I remembered of Carlos's house was the gate and front porch, but nearly every house had both.

In the distance a baby wailed, followed by a man yelling words I more or less understood by the tone. Dusk abandoned by darkness, a cool breeze swept across my face and over my bare arms, while an eerie silence filled the night.

As I walked up the unfamiliar road, I recalled the other time I had missed the last bus of the night in Chile. It happened a few weeks after I'd met Miguel. We'd only been out together a couple of times when he invited me for a picnic and hike. He didn't know it, but that day was my twentieth birthday. I said yes without hesitation. We took an early bus up the Maipo Valley, home to many seductive varietals of cabernet. Then we climbed up a steep trail, a hike that felt like twenty miles but was probably less than five, stopping where a secluded patch of grass lured us off the trail.

Two glasses of wine and a few strawberries later, we abandoned our clothes, our bodies entwining like a giant pretzel. Our first union felt free from the common awkwardness I'd experienced with prior lovers. Even as we lay naked, our eyes, arms, and legs beginning to explore each other, he didn't jump to the obvious. His hand found my face, tracing my eyes and forehead before running his fingers down to my breasts, where he lingered and played. As I felt the tightening of my desire, he slowed things down, moving a strand of hair from my face before dropping his hand to massage my ear lobe, pulling and tugging as I squirmed and pushed my mouth to his. Our lips met, and our tongues swirled wildly around as if lost in each other's forest. My anticipation almost unbearable, I pulled him on top, where finally his patience waned. I felt his warmth inside me and exhaled like a lioness, my pleasure echoing throughout the valley. He was gentle until the anticipation of climax pushed us both over an arbitrary cliff of passionate insanity.

I was content to stay where we were, but Miguel insisted we continue hiking to some spectacular waterfall he thought was nearby. We must have walked another five miles. Despite my painful quads, it was worth it. Reaching the thundering waterfall, he led me across several large boulders to a place where we stood below the cascades until our feet felt like blocks of ice.

Afterward, we thawed ourselves in the sun and fell asleep. By the time we got back to the road, the last bus was long since gone. We walked another hour, stopping when we found an old shed that offered protection from the wind and cold, our home for the night. We slept little.

⋯⋯∞⋯⋯

A BARKING DOG JOLTED ME BACK TO MY PRESENT SITUATION. Frustrated that I'd gone up the wrong street, I turned around and confirmed my previous suspicions were correct. Not only did I have someone following me, but he was close enough to impale a knife into any one of my nineteen upper vertebrae. Before I could scream, the potential assailant disappeared.

Cursing myself for allowing useless Miguel memories into my consciousness, I increased my pace, praying I'd find Carlos's street soon. My pulse pounded so violently against my chest I wondered if I might have a better chance of dying from a heart attack than being killed by a crazed stalker.

Ten steps later, my flip-flops hit the edge of something soft laying on the asphalt. Leaning over, I reached out and grabbed a crusty red painter's cap.

Nancy Rhodes

CHAPTER 8

ecreasing my stride, I considered my options, none of
which excluded risk. Either I headed back toward town to
find the house, risking the possibility of the stalker hiding
and pouncing on me or continued walking the opposite direction
in the pitch dark through an area I'd never been. The latter could
give the term *dead-end* an unfortunate, yet literal, significance. I
chose civilization.

I wanted to run, but my blisters wouldn't allow it. The slap
of my sandals flapping against pavement was about as subtle as a
handful of coins tumbling inside a dryer. I passed the parked truck.
No attacker. I exhaled. I veered as far away from the hedge as possible. I'd almost made it to the main road when a short whistle, the
kind that comes through a man's teeth when he wants a woman's
attention, broke the town's silence.

"Gringa *bonita*," yelled my pursuer. "¿*Dónde están los papeles?*"

He was looking for some papers. His tone reflected urgency.
Fight or flight? Kicking off my sandals, I chose the latter. To hell
with my blisters and all the jagged rocks lying on the gritty asphalt.

"¡*Ándate a la puta!*"

Sadly, I understood his obscenities. I could have told him I
didn't have any papers, but I preferred distance over conversation.
A small rock hit the back of my calf. Then a rock flew past my waist.
I tried consoling myself that they were rocks and not bullets, but
these weren't fish tank pebbles coming my way. A huge stone sailed

past my head a few hairs shy from taking out my ear. I ran as if my life depended on it, because it did. After a particularly jagged rock pierced my skin above my elbow, I felt the trickle of blood run down my arm.

Despite my pain, or maybe because of it, I smiled when Carlos's house came into view. A dim light peeked through the front window. Inside, the sound of a guitar playing an unfamiliar tune, a silky blend of jazz tones and folk, escaped from an opened window.

I rang the bell outside his gate but didn't wait for a response. Climbing the first step, my right foot started to cramp, the middle toe contorting away from the others. Despite the impending desire to scream, I remained quiet. My assailant was still out there. The cramp traveled up my leg, one of the larger muscles feeling like it wanted to pop outside of my skin. I couldn't walk up the remaining two steps. I fumbled my hand across the ground until I found a small stone. I aimed for Carlos's front door. The music stopped. An outside light came on.

He opened the door, just enough to peer outside.

"Carlos, it's me. Allie. I've had some trouble."

"What happened?" Before I could respond, he was at my side lending his muscular arm for support. "Good God. Let's get you inside."

"I'm okay," I said, hobbling inside. "But yeah, someone was following me. He threw rocks. My leg wasn't hit—it's just a cramp. But, oh geez, I'm dripping blood on your floor! I'm so sorry."

Tears unwantedly cascaded down my face.

"No worries. It's just a floor. Here," he said, leading me to the sofa. "Sit down, and I'll clean you up. Then you can tell me what the hell happened."

After he left my side, I wiped away the tears and tried flattening out my frizzies. Carlos returned with a damp towel and bandages.

"Did you see who it was?" He reached for my left arm and began wiping it gently with a soft towel. I noticed Gordito now wanted nothing to do with me.

"Not close up. I think he might have followed me from your house. I missed the last bus and went to that store looking for a phone. He came in right after me but kept his distance. From what I can remember, he was short, like five feet, kind of heavy, and wore this painter's cap." I was surprised the hat was still in my hand.

"Was he alone?"

"I think so. Do you know who he is?" I figured he would but wondered if this time he'd tell me the truth from the get-go.

"Not exactly, but it must be someone connected with the poachers."

I took a breath.

"If this is connected to missing whales, why me?"

"The package. He probably saw you or followed you when you came to my house with the package."

"Well, then he should have known I left it here. If I don't have it, why am I a threat?"

Carlos shrugged. "Yes, that's true, but maybe he thinks you know something you're not supposed to know."

"Holy shit, Carlos, do you think he wanted to kill me?"

"I wouldn't go that far. But you need to be careful and watch your back."

Shaking my head, I wanted nothing more than to get out of El Toyo. Maybe out of Chile altogether.

After a long silence, one where I silently wished he would offer to protect me and make this go away, Carlos stood up and asked if I wanted wine or something stronger.

"Wine, thanks."

After rumbling around the kitchen, he returned with a bottle of red and two glasses.

"Perhaps," I said, taking a generous swig, "they think I'm connected to the authorities. And—or—here to stop their exploits."

"That's a possibility. But he has to be an amateur. No offense, but threatening you with rocks?"

"So I should be happy he didn't have a gun?"

"I'm not saying that."

"Sorry, my nerves are kind of shattered. This wine is helping. Thanks."

Trying to speed up my recovery, I downed another sizable guzzle.

The wine hadn't made it down my trachea when a thunderous crash sent me flying. Hundreds of splintering, shattering glass fragments scattered across the floor. A rock the size of a baseball wobbled inches from Carlos's foot. We'd been sitting so close to the window it was some kind of miracle neither of us was struck by glass.

"*Mierda, concha su—*" shouted Carlos, scooting behind his chair. "Get down, Allie! Get away from the window."

Tucking my head and trying to crouch, I scooted onto the floor and waddled to the backside of the couch. Instantly, I felt a piece of glass penetrate my left foot.

"Shit," I yelled. Gimping my way along, I saw Carlos dart across the room, open a closet door, and return with a gun.

CHAPTER 9

"Is that necessary?" I said, trying to suppress my panic at the sight of a seven-inch metal of death.

"I'm not taking chances. I'll kill that bastard if he steps on my property. Here," he said, pulling off his shirt and tossing it my way. "Use this."

A small, red puddle had formed around the ball of my foot.

"I... I can just get a towel—"

"Get down!" Carlos shouted. "Just because he's throwing rocks doesn't mean he doesn't have a gun."

Trying to remain in a squat position behind his sofa was excruciatingly painful, but I couldn't move with all the glass shards around my naked feet. Been there, done that. So carefully I leaned to one side, and holding on to the back edge of the couch, I lifted my bloody foot to wipe off the glass with my free hand before wrapping his shirt tight around it to stop the bleeding.

My peaceful impression of Carlos was, to use an appropriate pun, shattered. The fact he had a gun was bad enough, but his actions reminded me of someone I didn't want to be reminded of. A shiver shot through my spine. *This isn't Miguel, Allie.* I consoled myself that Carlos's actions were not all that inappropriate considering our circumstances. After all, his window was destroyed, his front room looked like a glass factory after a seismic event, and small puddles of blood had turned his floor into a massive Rorschach test.

I wondered where Gordito had disappeared to. I wondered why the neighbors never came to check on us. I wondered what the hell I was doing in a stranger's house in a town with no phone, no transportation, and one really bloody foot. Most of all, I wondered about the man who had followed me and if I'd be safe anywhere. Maybe it was time to hightail my ass back to San Francisco.

"Wait just another minute," Carlos whispered.

Hunched low, he walked to the table and turned off the light. Then he moved toward the front door. The crunching of glass underneath his boots echoed across the room. As my eyes adjusted to the darkness, I noticed a flickering of light from the back of the house. I watched his silhouette edge closer to the door. Slowly he twisted the knob and opened it. I held my breath as he stuck his head outside.

When he returned, I stood up, my legs aching like I'd just completed two consecutive marathons.

"I think he's gone," he said. "How you doing?"

"I'm okay. I'm really sorry—"

"It's not your fault. If anyone's sorry, it's me."

"He followed me," I said sheepishly. "I should have been more careful."

"Nothing you could have done. If you'd confronted him, you could have gotten yourself killed."

"He was just throwing rocks. I didn't think he planned to kill me. He yelled a few things—"

"What did he say?"

"Obscenities mostly. But he did say *papeles*. At least I think that's what I heard."

"Did you say anything?"

"I was too afraid to open my mouth."

"That's probably best."

We looked around. The place was a disaster zone.

"I guess you're probably ready to go home?"

I wasn't sure if he meant home as in America or home as in

the hotel. Since either would evoke the same response, I nodded affirmatively.

As if reading my mind, he said, "I meant your hotel. Unfortunately, I don't have a car. I have a moped, but I don't think that'd be a good idea, especially at night. My neighbor will let me use his car, but we'll have to wait until morning." He glanced toward the couch.

"The sofa will be great," I said. "But let me help you clean this up."

"We'll work out the sleeping arrangements in a bit. Let's look at your foot."

After putting away the gun, he came back with rubbing alcohol and bandages. Removing his ruined shirt from my foot, he said, "This is a deep cut. Tomorrow you might want to get it looked at."

"I'll live," I replied, enjoying the sudden closeness. His hands were warm and slightly calloused. He smelled good. Manly kind of good. Not like a frou-frou cologne, more woodsy or earthy.

After cleaning and bandaging my foot, he moved to the kitchen, opened the refrigerator, and pulled out a large, brown casserole dish.

"I'm heating up a rice and chicken dish. I know you haven't eaten."

"I bought snacks but lost them along the way. So, yes, I'll take you up on that. Thanks."

Grabbing the wine, he looked my way.

"Yes, definitely," I said without hesitation.

After the meal, we started cleaning the front room. Because of the bandaged foot, I moved slowly, but it felt good to help.

Carlos didn't have a vacuum cleaner. His only cleaning tool besides a well-used broom was a retro floor polisher, obviously useless for our current situation. While Carlos swept up piles of glass, I picked up the throw rugs, shaking them into plastic bags. I found a small bristle brush and swept the glass that had landed on a few pieces of furniture. By the time I'd done all I could, Carlos had moved outside and was covering the broken window with plywood.

We finished sometime after eleven. For safety reasons, Carlos wouldn't permit me to sleep on the sofa or anywhere in the front room. I didn't argue, even though it meant I would sleep on his double bed while he'd have to cram his six-foot-something frame into a five-foot sofa. As soon as I entered his room and closed the door, I removed my jeans and crawled into the well-worn but soft cotton sheets. A faint trace of musk lingered on his pillow. I pulled the corner to my face, inhaling whiffs of his appetizing pheromones.

It took forever to fall asleep—so long I wondered if I'd be awake the entire night. But sleep came and, with it, a nightmare. A Hitchcock dream, one I'd had before, had me in a tall poster bed. I was watching Miguel undress, anticipating what would come next. When he silently lifted the sheets and I felt his warmth, I turned to snuggle as close as humanely possible. Watching him lift his arm, I anticipated foreplay. But what came was the cold end of a gun pressed against my temple.

My cry for help woke me.

Instantly, Carlos was leaning over me, staring with a look of great concern and a spatula in hand. "Are you okay?"

"Yes, why?"

"You were yelling. Screaming, actually."

"Oh…I just had a bad dream."

"Must have been. You sounded hysterical. For a second I thought someone snuck into my room."

Embarrassed at having Carlos hover over my crusty-eyed self, I shook my head. "No, nothing like that, but thanks for your concern."

"Well, I hope you're hungry. I'm making breakfast."

The combined aroma of fresh-brewed coffee and pancakes was intoxicating. After he left the room, I got out of bed, pausing to put on my pants and redo my ponytail. Carlos handed me a mug and pointed to one of two chairs by a wooden table tucked in the corner of his itsy-bitsy kitchen.

"Other than the bad dream, did you sleep okay?" he asked, handing me a ceramic plate loaded with a pile of thick, golden-brown

Nancy Rhodes

pancakes.

"The bed was comfortable. Thank you."

I saw no reason to elaborate on my restless night. After giving up his bed and having his house attacked, the man didn't need to hear a detailed analysis of my sleep issues.

"Whole wheat," he said, sitting beside me.

"They smell fantastic."

I reminded myself to breathe between bites. Even so, my plate was bare in under ten minutes.

CHAPTER 10

After breakfast, Carlos left to get his neighbor's Fiat. We rode in silence for the first ten minutes. I wondered if Carlos's quiet demeanor was reflective of the evening's events, or maybe he just wasn't a morning kind of guy. Not everyone bolted out of bed and planned their day before their feet hit the ground. In fact, most of the guys I'd befriended or dated were nocturnal, except Miguel, whose energy level excelled from early morning to very late at night. He often bragged how he could live on four hours of sleep a night.

"Are you okay?" Carlos glanced at me while shifting the Fiat into third gear.

"Yeah, I'm fine. I was just thinking how much the landscape reminds me of home."

Carlos nodded. "I haven't been to California, but I'm sure there are similarities since we are the same distance from the equator. Where in California are you from?"

"Northern, in a small town not far from the coast. I wasn't born there, but it's where I spent most of my life. I was born in Boston, then lived in Portland for a couple of years. I was six when my parents moved to California. Have you ever been in the States?"

"Yes, about fifteen years ago. I went to Washington."

"DC?"

"No, Washington State. I was there for almost a year. That was when I finally sought to do something about my passion for whales.

I started with a marine naturalist training program, then went on to work with the National Marine Fisheries Service and the Stranding Network as a researcher, collecting data on stranded whales and other marine mammals."

"That's why your English is so good."

"Well, it might have helped, but my mother was English. She grew up in London, met my father, a Chilean, on a summer vacation in the Lake District of southern Chile. They married three weeks later. She was only eighteen."

"How very romantic."

"Well, normally I'd say more stupid than romantic, but they stayed married. In their case, it worked. Anyway, even though she knew Spanish, she insisted I always speak English. She was very strict about it. I resented that for years, especially when I was a teenager. I even avoided bringing friends over because she wanted to speak English to anyone and everyone."

"Smart lady. She wanted to make sure you'd become bilingual. How about your dad?"

"Well, like I said, he was Chilean. He worked long hours at a lumber yard—wasn't home much. He'd speak to my mom in Spanish, and she'd answer in English except when they'd argue. Then it was straight Spanish."

"Are they still alive?"

"Dad passed about nine years ago. Mom last year."

"I'm sorry."

"Thanks. She was ready. After Dad passed, her mental health took a nosedive. A couple of years ago she finally spoke to me in Spanish and didn't even realize it. Near the end, she was calling me by my father's name."

Carlos cleared his throat. "How about you? Are your parents alive?

"No, they both passed a long time ago. I was in my early twenties."

"I'm so sorry."

I wished I had lied to him. I usually did. I didn't want to think about those years. Instead, I did the next best thing. I changed the subject.

"It is pretty here."

"Well, things are changing. Santiago is growing. The economy is stronger now."

"Isn't there an election soon?" I asked.

"Not until 2014. Sebastián Pinera is currently president. Rumor has it Michelle Bachelet will run again."

"It's amazing you have had a female president. I wonder if that will ever happen in the States."

"I've had mixed feelings about her. But if she supports the Corcovado Sanctuary, she'll get my vote."

"The Coco—what?"

"The Gulf of Corcovado. It's a special marine area, home to many blue whales because of the natural abundance of krill. It's near Puerto Montt."

Deciding to not share that I'd lived in Puerto Montt once upon a time, I stuck with politics. "If this sanctuary already exists, why does the president have to support it?"

"Several of us whale enthusiasts and a group of researchers want to see the government establish a larger protected marine area—much like the national parks you have in the States. This reserve has been talked about a lot, and now we just need it to happen. Once established all whaling would be banned—including, and especially, that done under the false premise of research. It'd be located within Chile's sixth-largest national park."

"That sounds important. I hope it goes through."

Carlos turned his eyes back to the road.

"Hey," he said, "How would you like to go out on a boat tomorrow? Maybe we'll see whales."

I nearly choked on my own spit.

"I don't do so well on boats," I said, feeling an arctic front pass over my shoulders.

Carlos laughed. "There's stuff you can take for the queasiness, you know."

Of course, he had an antidote.

"I've tried those," I said.

"Not mine you haven't. My pills contain a secret formula, specially designed for land-loving gringas!"

My resolve weakened. I couldn't dismiss the evolving attraction. Forget finding and facing Miguel. I could just jump into a hot fryer with this Carlos Costanera. Surely that would dissolve my funk. *Yeah, Allie, sure thing. Repeat old mistakes.*

"What kind of boat?" I asked just to say something.

I found myself staring at his lips. Something about them sent tingles to places that hadn't tingled in a while. Okay, he could have told me it was an inflatable kayak and I would say yes.

"She's a forty-two-foot fishing boat moored in Valparaiso. I'll be going to Santiago tomorrow to pick up some friends. You're welcome to join us. That is if you don't mind an early morning. I'm picking them up about five a.m."

"That is early!"

"I promise it'll be worth it."

Turning my head to look outside, I wondered if his friends were female. He hadn't said or implied any relationship. No rings on his hands.

I wanted to say something like "Good grief, Charlie Brown, that sure as heck is early," but what came out was "Sure, thanks. Sounds like fun."

Puking my guts out next to a bunch of cute twenty- or thirty-year-old bombshells. Fun. Yep.

CHAPTER 11

Despite a headache and the early hour, I was in the lobby fifteen minutes early. Carlos arrived promptly, pulling up to the hotel loading zone in a red Jeep. The car stopped, and just as I feared, a slender woman who might have been in her midthirties pushed her way into the back seat.

Carlos greeted me outside with a gorgeous smile before leading me to the passenger door. Once I got inside, he introduced me to Karina, the gal now in the back seat, and Juan Paul, who clearly hadn't hit thirty yet. Both, he said, spoke excellent English.

While driving through the deserted streets of Santiago, we exchanged brief bios of ourselves, mostly sharing how and when we came to Chile. Karina was a freelance writer and photographer, born in New Zealand but had been in Chile for ten years. Juan Paul was a native of Santiago who had moved to Puerto Montt when he was a kid. Without thinking, I announced that I too had lived in Puerto Montt.

"Nice Jeep," I said looking at Carlos and hoping to change the subject.

He checked the rearview mirror. "It belongs to Juan Paul. He's the only one with dough. But he hates driving. Go figure! "

"I heard that, old man," sneered Juan Paul.

I looked at Carlos and chuckled. "Old, huh?"

He smiled. "To those bambinos, I'm an old dude."

Karina leaned forward. "Hey *anciano*, I'm going to be forty next year. That's not exactly *un bambino*."

Carlos shook his head, grinning.

Decades had passed since I'd traveled the highway that runs from Santiago to Valparaiso. Once we left the urban sprawl outside Santiago and meandered through hills and pastures tanned from an early summer, my head stopped pounding.

"Take these now," said Carlos, handing me two small, white pills. "Trust me, you'll be glad you did."

"What about me, *compadre*?" demanded Juan Paul.

Carlos handed him the pillbox.

Karina laughed. "Isn't it about time you had your sea legs, JP?"

Juan Paul ignored the cackling and downed his pills with a swig of some yellow energy drink. I swallowed mine dry.

Juan Paul and Karina were talking in Spanish. I had a difficult time hearing them because of the traffic noise passing through Carlos's open window, but I thought I heard something about blue whales.

Carlos must have noticed my eavesdropping. He told them that they were rude, whispering between themselves in Spanish.

"That's okay," I said. "*Hablo un poco de Español y me gusta practicar.*"

Juan Paul asked how I learned the language. Suddenly I felt extremely self-conscious, stumbling over every word. I switched to English.

Three hours into our trip, Carlos pulled into a roadside restaurant for brunch. To my epicurean delight, the little *restaurante* specialized in *pastel de choclo*, my favorite Chilean dish made with a sweet and slightly glazed corn topping over a mixture of beef, onions, raisins, a signatory lone olive, and a slice of hard-boiled egg, baked and served steaming hot in a clay bowl. I was surprised but happy that it was available so early in the day. It's not exactly breakfast food, but because it was their specialty, we were told the dish was available from sunup to sundown.

After ordering, I tried masking my impatience for the food to arrive by sitting on my hands and asking the group benign questions about their educational backgrounds. When the waiter finally brought our plates, I stabbed the corn pastry with my spoon and dropped my head to the plate, inhaling the heavenly nostalgic aroma. As soon as the fork reached my mouth, sweet and savory flavors caressed my tongue. Lost in this appetizing orgasm, I disengaged from the group's conversation, stopping only to take sips of a full-bodied merlot that, despite the early hour, complemented the pastel.

"Allie, how long did you live in Puerto Montt?" asked Karina, the only person abstaining from wine.

Not particularly thrilled to have my attention pulled from my palate, I swallowed and replied, "About two years." *Two years longer than I should have.*

"Was that during Allende's regime?"

"Yes," I said, hoping she'd shut up. "It was in the early eighties—pots and pans clanging days, curfew. The antidictatorship movement was in full swing."

"Puerto Montt in the eighties," said Carlos. "Turbulent time. I was there also for about a year. Can't remember what year it was."

I hoped he wouldn't. It was time to change the direction of this conversation. Carlos looked pensive, his eyebrows wiggling like someone trying to recall something. Something like a major news event.

"I was eighteen, so it must have been around eighty-two or eighty-three. Hah! We might have crossed paths."

Carlos was a bit younger than me but not as young as I'd thought. I prayed he left Puerto Montt before December 1983. Hopefully, he missed the big event.

"Hey," he said a little too enthusiastically.

I had a feeling. A bad one. Time for a big swig of wine down my gullet.

"Wasn't that around the time of that horrible incident that was in the newspapers for weeks? Something about a young mom who disappeared with her two daughters."

Great. He not only didn't miss the event, he remembered the details.

"Before my time, old man," said Juan Paul. "Okay, I was born, but I wasn't reading the dailies at three."

Karina laughed.

I wasn't finding any of this funny. Second large swig of *vino tinto.*

My spoon fell from my hand, reverberating off the table and hitting the floor like a sledgehammer. Bending down to pick it up, I felt a major head rush. If I wanted to speak, I couldn't. My lips pressed into each other like forceps. Juan Paul and Karina exchanged nervous glances.

Karina broke the silence. "I'd just moved to Santiago, and even though I was a kid, I remember my parents talking about it. The girls were a lot younger than I was. But it sure upset them—especially Mom. They wouldn't let me out of their sight for months. What do you remember about it, Carlos?"

"Only that it happened on Christmas Eve. Everyone presumed the girls had been abducted. At least at first."

"That father must have been beside himself," Karina said, pushing her plate aside.

"Uh, that's not how I remember it," Carlos replied.

If there was any further conversation, I didn't hear it.

Someone touched my arm. A voice asked if I was all right. Another voice said something to someone about a stroke. Their voices were muffled.

I have no idea how much time passed, but I suddenly felt cold water splashed across my face.

"Shit," I yelled loud enough for every patron to jump from their seat. "Wha—?"

"Allie," shouted Carlos. "You scared me. I don't know what happened, but suddenly your head dropped and your face turned the color of ash. How do you feel?"

Awkward. They all were staring. They had stopped eating and drinking, and their faces were so motionless they reminded me of those freaky wax figures from Ripley's.

Wiping my face and neck dry, my brain gradually recovered. I remembered where I was, who I was with, and something about the conversation that doubled my heart rate and sent me spiraling to the tabletop. The ringing and humming faded to a small buzz, but the tension between my temples felt like someone had placed my head between two parallel jaws of a bench vice.

"Oh, sorry," I said. "I'm okay, just a little woozy. Probably had too much wine."

The others looked at my glass, half full. I thought I'd been guzzling it.

"Carlos, your pills!" shouted Karina. "I bet that's why she passed out."

"I'm a lightweight." I lied. "Maybe the pill had some effect, but I'm not used to drinking early in the day. Plus I bent down so quickly."

Karina said we should go. But noticing Carlos hadn't finished his meal, I told them I was fine.

"No problem here," said Juan Paul, staring down at his empty plate. "I'm ready."

"*Chancho*," chided Karina. "Are you sure, Allie?'

I nodded. After the waiter brought me a clean fork, I pretended to eat. I took small bites. Slowly. And then not at all.

Karina, who seemed to enjoy clinging incessantly to details and conversations, reminded Carlos about the pre-Allie-pass-out discussion. She asked him again about the event and what he remembered.

Carlos leaned forward to speak in a near whisper. "I saw that shithead three months after that *accidente*. He sure didn't act like a man who'd just lost his wife and daughters. Behind the cameras, he was always downtrodden with excessive grief, but he was a different *hombre* away from the limelight. That guy should have been locked up. But you know, money and good looks go a long way. In my opinion, that dick was another O. J. Simpson!"

Every bite of that pastel rose to my throat. Crap, not again, I thought as my head, face, and throat became instant solar panels. I reached for the water glass, hoping to avoid another face-plant scene.

While fighting to regain control of my stomach, I concluded that this outing was one of my worst decisions. In fact, the whole damn idea of returning to Chile was insane. Jeff was right. Hell, even Sarah was right! *If only I can get through this day. Then, well—maybe I'll just buy that other one-way ticket.*

Meanwhile, deciding nothing more could enter my belly, I waited for the others to finish their food.

"I'm pretty certain that he had a girlfriend at the time," said Carlos. "But *Dios mío*, let's change the subject."

Like now, I wanted to scream.

"Excuse me," I said, standing up a little too abruptly. "I'll be right back."

I steadied myself against another wave of vertigo. Searching for a bathroom, my eyes lost focus. I switched directions and managed to stumble outside before another wave of nausea flattened me to the gravel. I pulled myself to a curb and sat up, dropping my head between my knees. My only conscious thought was that I had to get away from Carlos and his compadres. But what would they think? Would they report me as missing?

I looked in my purse and found some antidepressants concealed in my lipstick case. The recommended dosage was one after a full meal with a warning not to take after consuming alcohol. I swallowed three dry.

CHAPTER 12

"Allie, wake up!"

Once again, Carlos was asking me if I was okay. Déjà vu. This time I couldn't lie.

I thought I was in my hotel room until I recognized Carlos's voice. A stream of air tossed the hairs on my scalp as a scratchy seat belt molded to my face. Opening my eyes wasn't easy.

We were on a busy street, presumably somewhere in Valparaiso. I was in the front seat, reclined as far back as it would go.

"No kidding you're a lightweight. You completely passed out," Carlos said, patting my thigh.

"I thought we should have taken you to the hospital," said Karina. "But Carlos said you'd come around."

I struggled to shake away my drug-induced stupor. What happened? A few glimpses came back to me—flicks of memories like short film trailers—savoring that amazing *pastel de choclo*, looking for a bathroom, nausea. And then, like magic wipers clearing away cobwebs inside my head, I remembered Carlos's friends talking about Miguel. They didn't mention any names, but they were talking about Miguel's wife, Sandra, and those precious toddler twins—Michaela and Marissa. They didn't know that three innocent lives ended in the depths of the Pacific Ocean. Ended. Because of me.

Spasms twisted inside my gut. I sure hadn't been prepared to be reminded of the horror, guilt, and confusion I suffered after learning about his family's disappearance.

The car slowed as we approached the hilly streets of Valparaiso, the touristy yet eclectic seaport located seventy-five miles from Santiago.

Carlos asked if I was up for a boat ride.

"No, but thanks," I said patting my stomach. "I think I'll just spend the day here in town. It's been so long since I visited Valparaiso."

"Would you prefer to go home? If you don't feel good, we could—"

"No, I'll be fine." I said, not wanting the additional guilt of ruining everyone's plans. "Maybe I'll ride one of those trolleys. They still have them, right?"

"You mean the funiculars? Yes, there's at least seven or so of them still running. I can stay back and show you around. The others can manage without me."

"No, absolutely not. You go on. I know how important this is."

"What are you two whispering about?" Karina asked.

I turned my neck to respond. "I was just saying that I'm not going on the boat."

"And I wanted to play tour guide," said Carlos, "but she won't let me."

"How about a rain check?" I asked, noticing his disappointment. "I need to stay landlocked today. Maybe have a strong cup of tea or coffee. But you all, please go ahead. Have fun, and take your time."

"Too bad," said Juan Paul. "The weather's perfect. The water is silky smooth."

"Silky?" Karina laughed. "Hey, Steinbeck, would you hand me my flip-flops? I think they're under Carlos's seat, on your side."

As we drove down a steep, narrow street, I caught sight of the ocean. Juan Paul was right. The ocean looked like a glassy lake, the surface sparkling with dancing, diamond-like prisms.

A few minutes later Carlos dropped me off in front of a small coffee shop called Café Americana. After waving goodbye, I pulled open an old wooden door whose rusted hinges announced my entry.

But no one looked my way. I counted fewer than ten people, and, fortunately, none of them stood out as fellow gringos.

Finding a high-back upholstered chair with a perfect view of the harbor, I sunk my tired ass into it, feeling the tension of the last few hours fall into the cushions. I ignored the menu, allowing my eyes to scan the seaside, hoping to catch a glimpse of Carlos and his friends. But that would be unlikely, even with this view. I had no idea what their boat looked like.

The vast stretch of water was littered with military and cargo ships. Even the largest of fishing boats disappeared among their giant sisters. Far in the distance lay an enormous cruise ship pointed intrusively in my direction, waiting, watching—an ominous reminder of affluence over preservation. The noise pollution emitted by these enormous beasts had to be disturbing—if not downright harmful—for so many of the ocean creatures below.

A sudden movement outside the window broke my trance. Two pelicans with elongated white necks and gray plumage strutted their way across the weathered deck onto the sand below. They stared across the water, ignoring the gentle waves that continuously swallowed their feet.

I grabbed a newspaper from the table next to me and turned from the front page to avoid the graphic photos of a head-on collision resulting in a family of six now in the intensive ward. Turning to the entertainment section, my eyes locked on the date at the top of the page.

8 de enero. January 8.

Dear God.

It was on that day, almost three decades ago, I learned the horrible and disgusting truth about Miguel. The boating incident Karina mentioned occurred on December 24. At first, I knew nothing about it. I never saw the papers that day, the next day, or, conveniently, for the following week. I was too busy drinking champagne and fucking a murderer.

CHAPTER 13
(December 1983)

M iguel had planned our holiday getaway months ahead of time. "Escaping Christmas," he declared with over-exuberant enthusiasm. He had everything planned. I couldn't have changed anything or offered ideas if I'd wanted to. But back then, I allowed my lovers to boss me around. We were going to a very expensive resort in Pucón, a touristy little town in Chile's beautiful Lake District. It all sounded fabulous. Our flight left on Christmas morning. As agreed, I took a cab to the airport. We had plans to enjoy a dinner together at the airport, but he arrived an hour and a half late. So instead of a relaxed meal, we had to hustle to the gate, boarding after everyone else had filled all the overhead compartment space. Despite my fury, especially after he offered no apology or explanation, I smiled and kissed his neck after clinking our champagne flutes together before takeoff.

Usually Miguel was the image of perfection. A well-put-together guy who cared about clothing choices more than most women I knew. But on this first day of what I had hoped would be our most romantic trip ever, sweat dripped off his unshaven chin, his breath reeked of old beer, gunnysacks hung under his eyes, and his clothing was so wrinkled it probably came out of an old laundry basket.

He was unusually quiet during the flight, and by the time we checked into our hotel, he turned downright cranky. When the porter opened the door to our suite, Miguel ran ahead, leaving me at the door trying to find tip money. A few seconds later, he pulled me back to the hallway and yelled at the luggage boy, saying he didn't like the room. Despite the room looking perfect, I didn't complain or question his strange behavior.

Miguel had a tremendous ego. I learned early on not to bruise it, especially in public. I waited until we got settled into another room two floors down. Although still a suite, it felt smaller, and the view, if you could call it that, was a peek of the north side of the garden in the rear of the resort.

"The other room had such a wonderful view of the lake," I said.

"Trust me. This is better."

Reluctantly, I said no more. At least I'd have him all to myself.

We seldom left the room. We ordered in for breakfast and lunch and would only go out for late-evening dinners to small, intimate restaurants. On our second day, he handed me a little velvet box. Despite some disappointment that it wasn't an engagement ring, I was stunned. The eighteen-karat gold diamond bracelet fit perfectly.

By New Year's Eve, I was dying to get out of the hotel. I'd heard that Pucón offered an awesome fireworks display and pleaded with Miguel to take me out to see it. At first, he said he said he'd consider it, but by early afternoon, he reneged, saying the show was overrated and would surely be a meek attempt at pyrotechnics.

"I don't care," I moaned. "I want to do something, Miguel. We've spent so much time indoors. It's New Year's. I want to celebrate!"

"I have a bottle of Dom Perignon and ordered a special dessert to go with it. Besides, you've seen fireworks before. Instead of all that noise, let's take our champagne to the lake. We'll find a secluded place where we can skinny-dip and make love under the stars. We'll only be here a few more nights, so let's enjoy it alone."

The champagne meant nothing. We'd already gone through nine bottles. The dessert meant nothing as my once-flat belly was swelling from all the booze and food. Skinny-dipping meant nothing since the water would be freezing. But making love under the stars—that was just the bait I needed.

"Let's skip dinner," I said, cocking my head with nothing but lustful intentions.

"Ahhh, that's my girl. You won't be disappointed."

We walked past a couple of abandoned warehouses before trekking through the brush on some rough path that might have been a deer trail. A half hour later we arrived at a secluded beach. The trees surrounded us like a gigantic curtain. The sand was fine and soft on my bare feet, feeling more inviting than any mattress. I wondered how Miguel knew about this remote paradise, but as an ethereal silence fell between us, I dismissed all the little doubts and disappointments that crept silently into my head since we got on the plane.

After finishing the champagne and exhausting our bodies, we slowly walked back to the hotel. The fireworks had long since concluded, and people were off the streets, tucked inside their homes.

The next morning, I woke up at noon. Miguel wasn't in bed. Getting up slowly, my head throbbing from postbubbly bliss, I checked the rest of our suite. Gone. A bit odd, but then nothing with Miguel was predictable. Deciding he'd probably gone for a paper or food, I retreated to the shower.

By the time I had dried my hair and slipped on my hip-hugging, way-too-tight stretch pants, Miguel had returned. I found him in the kitchen, scrambling eggs.

"Hey, where'd you go?" I asked.

His eyes darted to the window and back, but without hesitation, he said, "Did you miss me, beautiful?"

I shook my head teasingly. "Not yet."

And suddenly we were naked again. This time on the couch. Miguel turned off the stove burner, the eggs settling into a cold, stiff blob.

Then he was on top of me. Teasing me until my nails left a road map across his back. All too soon a climax rippled throughout my body, a thousand volts of electricity firing into every atom or cell.

Undoubtedly, the best orgasm ever. I fell into a deep and peaceful state of unconsciousness.

When I awoke, Miguel was in the other room, talking softly. "I already told you," he said. "She told me she was taking the girls out fishing. I'm not sure what day they were going, but I haven't heard from her. You might want to see if her boat is at—"

His voice grew inaudible. By the time I walked into the room, he'd hung up.

"Who were you talking to?" I asked.

"Huh?" he said, dropping the handset of the phone onto the sofa. "Oh, that…that was my cousin. He was asking about his sister. No worries. Just a lack of communication between them."

Clenching his hands together, I noted him using his right thumb to massage the top of his left hand. Was he nervous or just reassuring himself about something? I wasn't an expert on non-verbal communication, but it struck me as strange. Usually Miguel exuded confidence. Too much at times. What happened next was even more disconcerting. It was brief, but I noticed it. His right eye shifted while his left eye blinked nervously. He was lying. I knew that without a doubt. I just didn't know why.

He ordered room service for dinner. We ate in silence. Then we watched a few Chilean game shows and went to bed sans sex. The next morning, he was gone. This time, really gone. No note, no goodbye. Every trace of the man I'd given my soul and body to for seventeen months had vanished.

I flew home a day early. And as soon as I entered my Puerto Montt apartment, I numbed myself with vodka. Day after day I lived on that clear poison along with a diet of canned sardines and stale crackers. When I could no longer hold that down, I stopped eating. I locked myself inside and did nothing but cry, drink, and puke for six straight days.

I don't recall what caused me to turn the corner other than I guess I wasn't ready to check into the pearly gates. On January 8, I crawled into the shower, put on the only clean shirt I had, and scrambled three eggs.

At the table, fork in one hand and newspaper in the other, I glared at the headlines on the front page. A tragic account of a woman and her four-year-old twin daughters who were reported missing somewhere near Puerto Montt. They were last seen on Christmas Eve. I wasn't certain if I wanted to read the rest of the story. I sure didn't need something else to bring me down.

But I did. I read on.

How odd the husband hadn't reported his family's absence for more than a week. The article quoted the husband saying that not hearing from his wife while he was on his business trips wasn't abnormal because of his varying schedules and time differences.

The whole thing looked shady. What an asshole, I thought.

The story continued on page A5. Taking my last bite of eggs, I flipped through the pages.

On A5 there was a photo. An older photo of the man's family, with a caption: *Deceased's husband has been identified as Miguel Desoto, 32 years old, of Puerto Montt.*

I leaned forward and grabbed the page. Bringing the photo closer to my eyes, my pulse ricocheted throughout my body. My fork somersaulted onto my lap.

The man was not Miguel Desoto. He was Miguel Aguirre. My Miguel, the very person who had just deserted me in southern Chile. He was standing in front of a boat with his arms smugly embracing his wife and twin daughters—a family I'd known nothing about.

Although it was obvious he'd lied to me about having a wife and a family, I refused to believe he might have played a part in their disappearance. I could not have fallen for a violent murderer. No. Not possible.

God help me if I'm wrong.

CHAPTER 14

When I was growing up, my mother frequently asserted that sooner or later our memories turn to fiction, because our interpretation of what we think we remember gets more and more skewed until, eventually, we land on a version that either feels comfortable or impresses our audience. I had spent a good part of my life trying to forget Miguel, and when that failed, I tried to figure out a better version of the story. But even after years of expensive therapy, that week in Pucón was as realistic and unforgettable as the collapse of the Twin Towers.

I stepped outside of the cafe, huddling under a small patio that failed to protect me against a bone-chilling breeze. I pulled the hood of my sweatshirt over my disheveled ponytail and began walking through the winding and narrow streets of Valparaiso. Turning my head around, I noticed a splattering of tall buildings, probably condominiums or apartments. The city, like Santiago, had grown since my last visit—more cars, more buses, and more people. Yet the clusters of houses along the streets and hillsides were unchanged.

At one end of the harbor, I could see a funicular with two moving trolleys scaling the hillside, one ascending, the other descending, passing in the middle of the slope like two estranged lovers. The trolleys resembled two square buses minus wheels, painted daisy-yellow but with copious swatches of rust marking years of use with little restoration. The cables and pulleys clattered and squealed. I tilted my head back, cautiously observing the steep topography that this ancient piece of machinery conquered and reconquered every few minutes.

Do I really need to risk my life for a view?

Thinking about a runaway trolley with me onboard kept my feet captive to the asphalt. I might as well have been standing in freshly poured cement. The descending trolley clamored its way to the bottom as a dozen brave souls shuffled past me to purchase their tickets. *People ride this thing every day. Even locals. What could go wrong in a four-minute journey?*

The ride was over before my heart rate dropped to somewhere under a hundred beats a minute. While most of the riders looked like commuters and residents, one couple in their midthirties stood out probably as much as I did. They spoke Dutch or some Germanic language. Many people were using cell phones to take photos. I chuckled, remembering the brand-new Kodak Instamatic camera with pop-on flashcubes that I insisted on taking with me the first time I rode a funicular. It was my first trip to Chile and the first time Dad took the entire family on one of his business trips.

I was seven, Sarah thirteen. My big sis refused to ride the tram, so Mom stayed back while I pulled Dad up to the first row. When we reached the top, we walked around, admiring the expansive view of Santiago and the Los Andes mountains. We climbed the endless stairs up to the base of the towering Virgin Mary statue.

I still have the fake-gold cross Dad bought me that day at the tourist kiosk. In retrospect, I find his gift a bit odd since Dad wasn't a religious man. I suppose he fell victim to a brief episode of spiritual consumerism. Regardless, I adored that little cross.

My hand reached toward my neck, where, underneath my paisley tank top, it still nestled against my skin.

After exiting the Valparaiso funicular area, I crossed a cobblestone path and continued up a steep street toward an area with sweeping vistas of the harbor. In the distance were several rows of colorfully painted houses, reminiscent of the homes in Castro, on the island of Chiloé. I wondered if any of the distant boats bobbing about on the dark-blue ocean might be Carlos and his friends. At one end of the harbor, my eyes landed upon the busy container cranes moving multicolored containers from the vessels to the harbor.

Slowly, I meandered my way back toward the coffee shop where I was supposed to meet the group at three o'clock. Walking through the historical city, a cacophony of voices, blaring TVs, and radios created an unusual urban serenade.

Carlos greeted me with a warm hug. Anxious to share their day, the others circled in close. Juan Paul dominated the conversation, going on and on about all the whales they saw. I felt relieved when Carlos finally suggested we get going.

Once in the car, Carlos asked about my day, and I did my best to smile and portray the part of a happy tourist. Of course, I left out the part about the café, the newspaper, and the memories.

⎯⎯⎯◦◦◦⎯⎯⎯

WHEN I GOT BACK TO THE HOTEL, I WAS EXHAUSTED AND ANXious to fill both my tub and my wine glass. With chardonnay in hand, I dragged my feet to the bathroom and turned on the water. I let my clothes fall into a heap on the linoleum floor and tested the water with my left foot. Perfect.

Just as I had immersed myself, the hotel phone rang. I considered ignoring it, but with my luck, whoever it was would continue to call, and I'd never enjoy my bath. I shimmied my dripping wet body across the room, simultaneously trying to wrap a small bath towel around my torso.

I answered curtly with a simple and firm "Hello."

"Allie, are you okay?"

Sighing with relief to hear Jeff's voice, I told him I was fine. "I'm just out of breath because I was getting ready to take a bath and had to hustle to pick up the phone. Why do you sound so…so agitated?"

"I've been trying to call you all afternoon on your cell. I left you a message."

"Uh, oh, sorry about that. I was out all day, then my battery died. And, of course, I didn't bring the charger."

"You need to plug in your cell phone and call me back. I don't want to talk on this line. It's kind of urgent."

After I said goodbye and put on my robe, I grabbed the wine bottle and moved next to the bed so I could use my phone while it was connected to the outlet. Jeff had left three messages. I ignored them all and called him back.

He picked up before I heard any rings.

"Hi. What's so urgent?" I asked with equal measures of curiosity and annoyance.

"You need to come home. Right away."

"Uh, like Jeff, um, yeah...my day was fine, how about you? Now tell me what the hell you're talking about. Wait—are your kids okay? Did something happen?"

"The kids are fine. But, well, remember when we talked last? You might recall we were talking and our call got disconnected. Did you ever wonder why I never called you back?"

"I figured you were just busy or on your way to work, so I didn't call back. Come on, you know me better than that. You and I don't abide by the typical rules and regulations of proper social etiquette. So you urgently had to call me so you could chew me out?"

My emotional dial soared to super annoyed. My bath was getting cold, my wine warm.

"I was in a car wreck..." Jeff's voice dropped three octaves.

"Oh my God, Jeff. I'm so sorry! Are you okay? What happened?" Not only did I feel horribly guilty about being my usual judgmental self, but now it appeared that my phone call caused an accident.

"You don't need to apologize. It wasn't your fault. It was a hit and run. I suffered a little whiplash, but I'm fine. I didn't get the license plate number. I thought maybe it was an unlicensed teenager or someone who'd gone through one too many fender benders."

"They got away?"

"Yes, hit and run."

I took a breath. The bathtub had lost its appeal.

"There's more. Two days later my house got broken into and was totally ransacked. I discovered the disaster zone on my own. Maggie had taken the kids to the movies. "

"Shit. You really did have a bad week. What did they take?"

"Believe it or not, just my computer and my address book. They were obviously looking for something. They didn't take any of Maggie's jewelry or even the cash I'd left on my nightstand."

"What could they have been looking for?"

"At first I thought it was a case of identity theft. But I was wrong. The third strike came yesterday—"

"Car accident, break-in…there's more?"

"I found a typewritten note in my mailbox." I heard him exhale. "It said that you need to leave Chile by Friday. That—" He cleared his throat. Then silence separated us.

"Jeff, what?"

"The note said that if you didn't return immediately to California, my kids and wife would disappear. That's what they wrote. It was in English. No typos. Clear as shit."

CHAPTER 15

"I can't believe what you're saying! Oh my God! You've contacted the police, right?"

"Not yet. I haven't even told Maggie—"

"Dear God! You haven't told your wife? Man, you've got to tell her. Maggie isn't fragile. You know that, right?"

"Got that right."

"She needs to know—at the very least for her own safety and the safety of your kids." I stopped to catch my breath. "This is totally insane."

I looked at my foot. The one with the fat bandage on it. Was there a connection? Was this somehow connected to that package? As I massaged my calf, debating whether to fess up about the attack, I understood one thing. I had to return. I had to buy the other ticket. Immediately.

Jeff's voice dropped to a whisper. "What about Miguel? You never told me exactly what he did to you. Is it possible—?"

"Miguel? No, this isn't about him. I'll come back, Jeff. Don't worry. I swear, as soon as I can get a flight, I'll head back."

"Maggie and the kids should be coming back to the house in an hour. I want to get them out of the house before I risk getting the cops involved. She can go to her mom's or her sister's. I need to think things through first. Look, it's apparent whoever this is, they're serious. The car wreck, then the break-in. If not Miguel, then who do you think is behind this?"

With every minute, I grew more certain. This threat had to be tied to the whale thing, whatever the hell the whale thing was. I tried to remember how much I'd told Jeff about the package. If it was the whale poachers that Carlos had told me about, the less Jeff knew the better.

"Let me see if I can get a flight after this weekend. I promise you, I'll be there no later than Tuesday. We'll get through this, but you should let the cops know. Maybe they can send someone to patrol your neighborhood."

"Uh, I don't think so. At best, they might do one perfunctory drive-by at two in the morning. The police here don't have time for speculative fearmongers. Allie, you didn't answer my question—you know, the one where I asked you who could be behind this."

"I'll fill you in later. I have an idea but no proof. Can we leave it at that for now? Can you trust me?"

I heard his sigh. Loud and clear. "I've always trusted you. But I wish you could at least give me a hint."

"Okay, okay. This might have something to do with whales. I know that sounds crazy. But please, Jeff, don't ask me anything else."

"Got it. Sort of."

It worried me that Jeff wanted to take this into his own hands. He was a smart guy but stubborn as hell. I wondered if he still had the old Colt .45 he'd bought at an antique auction. He'd said he bought it for historical value and had no plans of trying to see if it worked. At the time, even I appreciated the artful craftsmanship, despite my intense feelings of revulsion around killing machines of any kind.

Long after Jeff had said good-bye, I let go of the phone cradled in the crook of my neck. After rolling my head around, I let the water out of the tub and collapsed on the bed, still wrapped up in my damp towel.

I don't know when the tears stopped and when the nightmares began, but there seemed to be little time between the conscious and unconscious world of pain.

The only flight I could get on such short notice was a red-eye that cost double. As soon as I found my seat, I took a sleeping pill. Miraculously, I slept a whopping four hours of the twelve-hour flight.

Once through the arduous and slow process of customs, I spotted Jeff standing halfway behind a column, wearing his favorite Dodgers ball cap. When I was at his side, I wrapped my arms around his shoulders, feeling every ounce of strain and fear through his long embrace.

We spoke little as we made the long trek to his car. San Francisco was gray, thick fog clinging to the roads like termites to wood. I'd been gone less than two weeks, but it felt like a decade—a century—a lifetime. I didn't tell Carlos or anyone in Chile I was leaving, even remaining vague when my limo driver in Santiago asked cursory questions about my trip.

Jeff looked ten years older than when I'd last seen him. I cleared my throat.

"Are Maggie and the kids staying at her sister's?"

He checked the rearview mirror but then returned his gaze to the road. "Yes, that part worked out well. Her sister is on a three-week vacation in Australia, so Maggie's got the Tahoe cabin to herself—well, with the kids."

"Are you staying there?"

"I still got to work. But I go there as often as I can. I was thinking you could stay with them. I know your house is rented, so you must need a place to stay."

"May I remind you that I'm the reason your family has been threatened? No chance in hell I'd do that. Drop me off at the West End Motel in town. I'll figure something else out after a few days."

"Are you sure?"

"Dead sure. Besides, I've got a slew of points. Maybe I can get a free upgrade. View of Mt. Tamalpais or the bike trail with all those skinny minis running by."

"Very not-funny, but I know better than to argue."

After checking in to the motel and dropping my purse on the miniature desk near the door, I pulled back a thin curtain framing the only window in my room. An overflowing dumpster and a near-empty parking lot dampened my already exhausted spirit. Not only was the room lacking a view of the noble mountain towering above Mill Valley, but I had to turn on a light to find my way to the bathroom. The walls were paper thin, which I discovered around eight o'clock when my neighbors decided to argue about who should pick up their Chinese food. The only plus was a scenic walking path that snaked around the hotel and, depending on whether I headed east or west, led to Mill Valley's neighboring town, Tam Valley, or the tourist-populated city, Sausalito.

The next morning I chose the latter, only because it was a longer trek and I needed to clear cobwebs and stimulate brain cells. For a mid-January morning, the day looked pleasant—clear, windless, and absent of fog. The local TV weather report indicated mild temps in the low sixties—a serious contrast to Santiago's summer temps hovering around ninety. Except for the parka Jeff lent me, I didn't have winter clothes. My first order of business after my walk and breakfast would be renting a car and visiting my storage unit. I'd also have to figure out somewhere else to stay, since $150 a night was not congruent with my dwindling savings account.

Decisions about cars, housing, and clothes would depend on how long I planned on staying. I didn't want to be in California. Of course, I'd rather be in the southern hemisphere in January, but it was more than that. I wanted to continue my journey in Chile even if I wasn't sure exactly what that journey would look like. But I had to stop acting selfishly. I couldn't return until I knew Jeff and his family were safe. This wasn't the time to figure out my life even if I was slightly past fifty with no career, kids, or partner.

As a herd of twenty-year-old runners with zero body fat and florescent Nikes sailed by, I exhaled an exasperated sigh. The only way I could ever return to Chile would be if I could figure out who had threatened Jeff and why.

I quickened my walking pace but slowed my breath. Somewhere around a half mile from the hotel, my mind cleared. I knew what I needed to do. And although it was a risk—a huge risk—I didn't care.

CHAPTER 16

Carlos's cell number wasn't stored in my contacts, but I found it by looking at my recent calls. I added the appropriate international digits before entering it as a new contact. *Might as well*, I mumbled to myself. *If things go according to plan, I'll be calling him frequently in the coming weeks or, God forbid, months.*

"Hi," he answered, sounding way too cheerful. "What a coincidence."

I cranked my head back as a large flock of noisy geese passed overhead in perfect alignment.

"We were just talking about you," he said. "I'm downtown having lunch with Juan Paul. Well, how are you? How's your foot?"

"Oh, that…It was only a superficial cut. I'm fine. Hey, can I call you later, or can you call me when you're alone? I need your help. It's kind of personal."

"Um, okay…well, sure. Actually, I'll be driving right by your hotel. Do you want me to drop by? Maybe we can go up to that swanky place at the top and have a drink?"

"Thanks, but no, that won't work. I'll explain later. Do you want to call me after you get back home?"

"I'll call you in an hour or two, but I won't be home. A good thing since I have no coverage there."

"Any time is fine, but call my cell number. Carlos, call me when you aren't around anyone."

"You said that earlier. This sounds serious. Should I be worried?"

"No."

"That doesn't sound convincing. But sure, I'll call you soon—probably in an hour to an hour and a half."

When I got to Sausalito, I found a trendy coffee shop that wasn't packed. I wrapped my hands around a soup-sized bowl of coffee while picturing Carlos at home in El Toyo, guitar or naughty cat on his lap, the serenade of crickets and frogs outside. I hated to admit it, but I missed the guy. He had said he wasn't going home. Was he off to a girlfriend's perhaps? Did he have one?

After paying close to five bucks for the oversized mocha, I walked through town, stopping at the small plaza that paid tribute to Sausalito's sister city, Valparaiso. After looking at my watch, I decided I should have enough time to walk back to the hotel, shower, and maybe even check out. It'd be more private chatting with Carlos outside on one of the benches near the bike path.

On my walk back, I wondered exactly what I'd say to him, how I could present my ideas. Would he be upset that I returned to the States without telling him?

He picked up on the second ring.

"What's the big secret, *gringita*?"

"That was fast. Are you alone?"

"Yes, except for some cows, a few llamas, and a dozen or so chickens. I'm at a friend's *parcela* in El Monte, caretaking his place for a week or two. But hey, what's up with you? Where are you? I called the hotel, and they said you'd checked out."

He said 'his' place. *His*. Nice. So he was not at a girlfriend's house. *Immature thinking Allie.*

"Yes," I said. "I checked out. I'm back in California."

"Whoa! I didn't see that coming. I got the impression you were going to stay here for a while."

"That was my plan. Well, the reason I'm calling is I need some help. I hate to impose—"

"Allie, excuse me for being blunt, but cut the formalities. It's me. Carlos. Remember? You and I shared that lovely assault together?"

I spent the next forty-five minutes telling Carlos about Jeff. I shared my suspicions about the whale poachers and how they'd been threatening Jeff. Carlos listened attentively, but when I stopped talking, he didn't respond.

"Carlos?"

"I'm here. I just need a moment to think."

I waited, but the sounds of silence were anything but melodic. My patience waned, so I kept talking. "I was so worried about Jeff, but now that he's okay, I think it'll be fine to go back to Chile. I just wanted to let you know and to warn you. They're probably watching you too."

"They are."

"What?"

"I'll fill you in later."

Instead of respecting Carlos's request for time to think, I continued to ramble—a bad habit of mine when insecurities raise their ugly head. "Well, anyway, I really want to head back to Santiago. I like it there and thought I might stay a few more months. Maybe learn more about the disappearing whales."

"Not now. No, you can't."

Carlos's tone reflected a level of assertion, harshness, that yanked my angry inner child strings. *I mean, really, who is he to tell me what I can do?*

"Carlos, what is this all about?" I growled.

"Your suspicions are spot on. This is about the missing whales and the report. Unfortunately, the wrong people know that it's back in my hands. And they're not too happy about that. I may have to leave. Hide somewhere."

"Oh my God. Tell me what's so damn important about whales that someone has to threaten innocent little kids on the other side of the globe. Whale blubber? Oil? Whale fin soup?" I wasn't trying to be funny, but the sarcasm that spewed from my lips might have been layered on a little too thick.

"Money and power," Carlos replied. "The root of all evil, as they say."

"So true. You know I don't understand any of this, but I feel it's important I return to Chile. Maybe I can help somehow. But don't worry. I'll figure this out. I shouldn't have called you."

"*Dios mío*, you are one stubborn woman! And impatient. If you really want to save your friend, his kids, and especially yourself, you damn well better hold off at least a month or two. These blokes are surely watching your every move right now. So get a job, find a place to stay, and lay low. A few months from now you can start planning a road trip."

"Road trip?"

"I can't smuggle you into the country on a private jet. If you want to come without anyone finding out, I'd recommend driving to Central America and flying out of Panama, Honduras, or even Costa Rica. Before you begin your trip, buy a throwaway cell phone with limited data. Turn your own cell phone off completely, and don't use it. When you get across the US border, I'll hook you up with some friends of mine who should be able to help you get through Mexico and Guatemala."

"Seriously?" I snarled. I'd never driven south of Los Angeles, and he thought I was going to drive across multiple borders to sneak into Chile like I was the criminal!

"The men behind this aren't to be messed with. And they won't go away. I'll do my best to help you, but I have to tell you we've been trying for years to find these guys. I really don't know what you expect to accomplish by coming back."

"Jeff's my best friend, Carlos. I've got to figure this out, and I'm not going to do it from the northern hemisphere."

After listening to another lecture on the importance of waiting at least a few months before attempting a return, I said goodbye and turned off my phone.

My insides felt colder than the granite bench under my ass. Why did conflict seem to find me, sting me, poison me? Over and over. Year after year, no matter what side of the equator I lived on. I wanted this to go away. I wanted to experience fun without fear.

Maybe have a little adventure, or romance, without life-threatening daggers screwing it up. Shoot, at this point, I happily would have returned to the crappy newspaper job if it would guarantee a life without all this damn uncertainty.

CHAPTER 17

C hecking out of the hotel without having a plan may have
not been my best move. But I managed to get a rental car, a
red Ford Focus, which doubled as my lodgings for the next
five nights. I called the HR department at Dunesberg Media to ask
if they had any open positions. They did, but it was for an online
interactive media specialist. I hung up.

I didn't want Jeff worrying about me, so I lied and told him I
was staying at an old acquaintance's house. Jeff and his wife were
planning a getaway for ski week. Fortunately, I saw a handwritten
index card hanging from a corkboard near the entrance of a small
independently owned market offering a room to rent. It turned
out that the landlady, Mrs. McKenna, had posted the card the day
prior, and I was the first to respond.

Mrs. McKenna, or Mrs. K as she told me to call her, was a
quiet woman, probably in her mid to late eighties with a long, gray
braid that hung motionless along her slender back. Over cups of
dark tea, she explained that her husband had not only been the
love of her life but had been her only trustworthy friend. He died
from a massive stroke three months prior, and she'd been feeling
quite uncomfortable living alone. After she agreed to give me a try,
which she did without asking for references, she explained that our
rental agreement could be terminated by either of us with a week's
notice. Perfect.

After sitting in my new abode for forty-eight hours, exiting only to purchase sandwiches at a dingy deli two blocks away, I realized that Mrs. K didn't really want company. She just liked the idea of someone being in her house. She rarely spoke to me. If I asked her something, she ignored me or simply grunted some monosyllabic word I couldn't understand. I didn't know what to do with my time, so I did nothing but read and stare at the hospital-green walls of my bedroom. The days were long and the nights longer.

Mrs. K watched a lot of TV but never once invited me to join her. I grew weary of the secondhand sounds of daytime soap operas and nighttime game shows and anxiously awaited the silence that occurred at 10:10 every evening when she'd shuffle herself to bed.

As days passed, even though my rent was a bargain, I grew less tolerable of Mrs. K, the TV, and the house. It didn't help that I had to use her bathroom, one so cluttered with adult diapers and plastic vials of prescription meds that finding a spot for my toothbrush proved challenging. There was another bathroom, but she told me it had been her husband's, and since she didn't want to clean it, she kept it locked and off limits.

When I explained that I'd clean up after myself, she shook her head and replied, "No, no, it just won't work." I prayed she wasn't storing his body in there, but since the only predominant smells were Chanel No. 5 and urine, I figured I was safe.

I knew I couldn't stay there much longer. I had to do something, but I didn't like my options. Either I'd have to forget returning to Chile and let Carlos and his friends save the whales on their own, or I'd have to change my identity and move forward with a scarier-than-hell road trip. Locked inside the musty room with cotton packed tightly inside my ears, I started picking at a crusty scab on my knee. I watched a slow trickle of blood run down my leg. It wouldn't matter if it hit the carpet. The stain would blend just fine with all the others.

Staying or going involved risk. If I did nothing and continued to hide and escape my past, I'd probably find another mundane job, stay single, and turn into a lonely and bored old maid who spends her retirement years planted in front of a TV set. Returning to Chile, however, not only had its share of emotional risks (especially if I let myself fall for Carlos) but might include the risk of death from some shit-ass group of whale poachers.

It should have been an easy choice.

Some people in my past considered me a risk-taker. "How can you go live in a Third World country and leave California?" my sister argued when, at age nineteen, I told her I was moving to Chile for a while. She and Mom both thought that I was just going through a phase and would be back in a week.

Sarah's visits to Chile were limited to two brief family trips back when we were still a family. After the second visit (I was nine, she fifteen), she refused to travel with us ever again. She loved America and felt no need to ever leave it.

The blood on my knee dried. Sometime later, I fell asleep—without a decision.

After two weeks of enduring life at Mrs. K's, I treated myself to dinner at a posh Italian restaurant. I started at the bar with an appletini and a plate of oysters, blowing my budget for the month. The dent in savings was worth it.

While sitting at the bar nursing my second appletini, a brief news clip caught my attention. The news anchor read the story without any signs of an emotional connection. Of course, I reminded myself, that's her job. She reported a two-minute story about a seventeen-year-old girl who hid five days inside a Porta Potty with just two bottles of water and three granola bars. She'd run from her rapist stepfather, some well-known and highly respected banker from a small town in the heart of Mississippi.

The girl, going by a pseudonym of Molly, was petite but outspoken. Her reddish-brown hair had been chopped short, apparently with a dull pair of scissors. With a strong commanding voice (and no tears), she said that she'd finally reached a point when she knew nothing could be worse than her current situation. There was no other option. She decided to do whatever it took to escape, including cutting her waist-length blond hair and stealing a package of hair dye from Walmart. After her interview, the newscaster added that Molly hitchhiked across three states, finally seeking help through a crisis intervention center, which notified authorities. Two days later the jerk was arrested.

At some point between the last slimy oyster and a large plate of mushroom ravioli, I had my answer. I wasn't going to run anymore. Screw emotional and physical risks. I was ready. I would do this. I would fight back. Even if it meant returning to Chile.

CHAPTER 18

I didn't have to steal the hair dye.

After advising Mrs. K that I was going to move in with my boyfriend, I purchased a one-way train ticket to Austin, Texas, using the name Annie Larine. My departure was two days away—perfect since I had a shitload of things to do before I left.

When I walked into a random hair salon, I explained I was having a midlife crisis and wanted a whole new look. Two hours and a hundred bucks later, I exited with what the hairdresser called sunflower blond, cut into a bob and emblazoned with red highlights. It was a bold choice for someone with thin hair, but I was embracing the change.

Buying new clothes to match the new me was the best shopping experience I'd ever had. I was told by a hip sales gal that my new clothes would accentuate my shabby chic hairstyle, which made me suddenly add a pair of obnoxiously large silver hoop earrings to my purchases. My favorite item was a black-and-white vintage houndstooth cloche hat that I found at St. Vincent de Paul. Besides fitting perfectly, the late-twenties-style hat hid my large forehead and, more importantly, the one-inch scar above my right eyebrow—a gift from Sarah who, at age seven, thought letter-openers were fun objects to toss at her defenseless one-year-old sister.

To avoid being traced, I destroyed my credit cards. I started visiting different ATMs and bank branches to withdraw nearly every penny from my savings. My money belt gave the appearance of a lopsided baby bump if worn in the front or, if I twisted it to the back, a really lumpy and unattractive derriere. On the days I wore loose-fitting blouses, I let them hang across my belly.

I didn't tell Carlos that I was preparing to make my way south since I hadn't exactly followed his recommendation to wait three months, but I hoped to hell I'd been away long enough to fool my stalkers. If he tried to call me, his messages were going to a phone located in the murky depths of Lake Sonoma.

Before returning the rental car, Jeff and I met for lunch. If anyone was following me or him, I felt it important they see us together. Seeing him again, I realized how lucky I was to have such a good friend in my life. Over burritos, he recounted stories about his time in Tahoe, filling me in on the joys of parenting two youngsters. He shared how six-year-old Kira was already trying to write her own stories and how little Sammy got into Mommy's tampons and decided that they looked cool inside his nostrils. After drying the laughing tears off my cheeks, I told Jeff that I was going on a little trip.

"Please don't tell me you're returning to Chile," he said, leaning across the table so he could look deep into my eyes. I hated the way he did that. Jeff could spot my lies before I even finished composing them.

"Okay, I'm not going to Chile."

"Don't know if you're being a smart-ass or not, but I'm not buying it."

I cocked my head just slightly to one side, took a shallow breath, and said, "You don't need to buy it, but you do need to believe it. At least for now. I'll be back soon. If anyone—and I mean anyone—asks about me, tell them I decided to go on a road trip to Portland."

"What about Sarah?"

"What about her?"

"Have you spoken to her since you came back?"

"I've only been here like three weeks. But yes, I let her know that I'd returned to California. Even told her that she'd been right…that

I never should have gone in the first place. Told her I was thinking of going back to work for the paper. If anyone contacts Sarah, they'll have no problem believing I'm back for good. Sarah loves to let people know just how right she is. But if you're asking if I'm telling her about my upcoming road trip, no—most definitely not."

"When will you be back?"

"Can't say."

"Will you stay in touch?"

"No."

Jeff dropped his head into his hands. "What about the threat? What about my kids?"

"Have you had any more since I've been back?"

"No...but—"

Without hesitation, I looked him straight in the eye and replied, "You'll all be fine. I'm sure of it."

I wanted to say something like "watch your back" or, better yet, "take long vacations away from home and lock up your kids," but I couldn't. It was essential that he trust me. If he was being watched, the perpetrators would know immediately if Jeff began acting differently. If they saw any signs of fear, they could suspect I was returning to Chile.

On the train, I found an info leaflet all about Austin. It said that Austin's early spring temperatures could be in the sixties to seventies range—perfect time to visit. The writer warned not to fall for the allure of spring without checking out the other seasons. But I wasn't there to buy a home. I wasn't even there to partake in the music scene. I would have loved to stay another month to check out their South by Southwest festivities, but I was on a mission.

Despite my plans—or mission—I was scared shitless. The haircut and new clothes were fun at first. On the train, I got to practice being someone else. Annie. But now that I was in Austin, away from everyone and anyone I knew, the fun and games were over.

As I walked away from the Austin train station, all I could think was *what the hell do I do now*? I could continue farther by train, but eventually, I would need a vehicle, and for that, I'd need a fake ID. I couldn't risk anyone tracing Allison Bennett on her way south. Deciding that I would have more options for both the ID and a car in Austin, this had to be my next priority. *But how?*

I started to call Carlos but hung up. I had a cheap throwaway phone I'd purchased before I got on the train and had memorized his number. But for some reason, once I heard the ring tone, I lost my nerve. I wasn't ready to tell him what I was doing or ask for help. I don't know why. I knew I had trust issues, especially after what happened with Miguel, but not trust Mr. Save-the-Whales? Despite all his philanthropic activities and gentle demeanor, I couldn't forget the fact that if it had not been for Jorge and Carlos and whoever else, Jeff's house would never have been broken into, his car bashed, or his kids threatened.

My nonplan plan was to start going out. A lot. Mix with the locals. Groove with the hipsters, the musicians, and maybe even a few druggies. If I found the right person, I could concoct some story to support my need for fake papers. *My dear auntie in Bolivia is dying, and I need to bring her hashish for pain.* Well, I'd have to do better than that.

Things didn't go so well. I soon realized I was too old for the hipster hangouts. And the one time I got the courage to ask a young gal at some dive where I could get some *supplies* (did I actually wink?), she looked me up and down, shook her head in disgust, and walked away saying something about stupid motherfucking female cops.

When I found a street that contained several instant-cash houses and bail bondsmen, I thought if I hung around long enough, I might find the right shady character to help me in my quest for a fake ID. But in the first hour, I was approached by three different men asking me about my rates and services. Number one was some white kid who looked twelve. The second scumbag was at least seventy with arms tattooed up and down with dozens of different female names. The last guy was a slender and somewhat attractive

Nancy Rhodes

African American. He looked clean. Too clean for the neighborhood. I wondered if he was a cop, so I hightailed myself out of that barrio as fast as I could.

I would swallow my losses, my fear, and my ego and call Carlos. The call went straight into voice mail, but I didn't think it wise to leave a message. The following day my phone rang at three in the morning. When I finally collected it off my Motel 6 nightstand, I'd missed the call. No one left a message, and the history only showed "unknown caller."

The next morning, while grabbing an egg salad sandwich from a 7-Eleven, the phone rang again. I prayed it was Carlos. I hoped he would figure out that his missed call was me.

"Hello?" I answered with equal measures of hope and caution.

The line went dead. Temporarily forgetting I was in a public location, I screamed "what the fuck" before tossing the phone into a trash can filled with failed lottery tickets, half-emptied Slurpee cups, and a thick layer of coffee grounds.

CHAPTER 19

⁂

"**D**on't drive at night" had been the most consistent advice I got on a brief internet connection using my recently retrieved, foul-smelling phone. I'd been searching for info on driving to Central or South America. The free Wi-Fi at Burger King was spotty, the cheeseburger slightly better. Without fail, whenever I happened upon something interesting, I'd either lose internet or the phone would die. Tossing it into the garbage was not one of my better moves—obvious by the fact that it no longer held a charge beyond fifteen minutes. My throwaway had become an unreliable beast of burden and was ready for permanent burial. Time to spend a little *dinero* on something that would work more than fifty percent of the time.

My toes and calves were not happy campers with the hour of asphalt abuse necessary to find an electronics store near the hotel. My stomach joined the growing number of unhappy body parts when two hours later, I was in the throes of weighing the pros and cons of tablets, iPads, and laptops. After choosing a tablet, the salesgirl, who oddly resembled my first Barbie, walked me to the pay center where four of my brand-new Franklins disappeared.

Leaving Gadgets Plus Electronics, I knew I needed food. Real food. And wine. Good wine. Whenever I start bouts of internal cursing, it's time to eat. Feeling the addition of blisters to my already-callused feet, I decided to spring for a cab. Tomorrow, I'd shop for a used car. No more trains, cabs, or blisters, thank you very much.

Understanding there was nothing I could do for Carlos no matter what could have happened to him, I feigned confidence. *I could return to Chile even without his help.* With my new computer, which I decided to call Barry, I felt empowered. Barry and I would drive across many borders. We would get to Chile. My confidence was nearing a perfect ten.

When I stepped inside the late-model Chevy posing as a taxi and directed the driver to take me somewhere near the restaurant district, he grunted before exhaling a large plume of gray cancer-causing agents into the sealed vehicle. I rolled down the windows to avoid puking, something I'd been prone to since childhood. Tobacco and cheap cologne mixed about as sweetly as overcooked sauerkraut and canned tuna. My cabbie's demeanor reflected someone who'd been hauling people across town far longer than he should have and resented every minute of it. He clearly didn't like chitchat.

"Will this do, ma'am?" he asked.

"Yes!" I answered a bit too enthusiastically.

Perhaps because of the aromatic abuse, my sniffer was on high alert for something that might taste as good as it smelled. When I passed an open patio, a wave or cloud of freshly sautéed garlic threw a lasso around my belly. I turned to scope out what was being served to a table of four sitting outside. I probably looked like a sheepdog picking up the scent of his herd. If eyes could drool, mine would have been sobbing. A steaming plate of stuffed mushrooms, a basket of thick slices of golden-brown-crusted garlic bread, and a huge bowl of plump calamari reeled me inside.

Happy hour was in full bloom, and the bar was packed. People looked happy. I carried Barry to one of the few empty tables, promptly kicking off my sandals.

An hour or so later, feeling satiated and sleepy, I returned to my hotel on foot. The night had been too perfect to risk ruining with another unpleasant taxi ride.

For the first time in a long time, the edges of my lips bent upward. While the lemon drop and chardonnay might have had something to do with my emotional state, strolling under the star-filled sky on a warm night and thinking of what I'd accomplished thus far empowered and excited me.

CHAPTER 20

A fter three days of checking online and newspaper want ads,
I found a car. A four-door Honda Accord, emerald green,
with low mileage. The engine sounded good, at least no
rumbles or belt squeals. The rather large dent on the rear bumper
didn't bother me. The owner, Mr. Thorsten, handed me a four-inch
folder containing pages and pages of receipts for tires, batteries, a
timing belt, air-conditioning repairs, and every service check since
its first six-hundred-mile checkup.

I couldn't bring myself to disappoint Mr. Thorsten, but I didn't
want or need such baggage. So I thanked him profusely for his
meticulous care and recordkeeping even though everything would
soon end up in a Texas landfill. After paying for the taxi and forking
over a very large wad of my cash, I drove my new-old car down his
driveway, watching in my rearview mirror as Mr. Thorsten waved
goodbye. When I stuck my hand out the driver's window and waved
back, the distinguished gent dropped his hand to his side and disappeared. Apparently, the farewell wasn't for me.

I thought about naming the car. I'd always done that in the past.
Blue Bomb for my first car, a three-year-old Vega hatchback, Mad
Max for the unreliable Camaro, and Johnnie F for the Ford pickup.
A few ideas came to mind: Hornet, Roxanne, and even GMT for
"Get Me There." But ultimately I decided that having one inanimate
named object was enough. The car was simply "the car." Fortunately,
it came equipped with a stack of maps. The East Coast road maps

got tossed, but the three Texas maps were keepers.

With Barry's help, I learned multiple border crossings existed in the great state of Texas. There were numerous opinions about which borders were best, but I kept my focus on reviews that touted seamless crossovers, barren of fake cops. I decided I'd go with Eagle Pass in Texas to Piedras Negras, Mexico.

I began my journey to San Antonio on a rainy Tuesday carrying five days' worth of nonperishable foods: canned fish, dried fruit, nuts, and granola. Not knowing what my water situation might look like, I bought a dozen gallon jugs and, at the last minute, a water purifier.

Despite traveling light from California, I pared down further on clothes and possessions, even opting to ditch my makeup. With my limited wardrobe of grunge clothes, wearing eyeliner and blackening my eyelashes made as much sense as rain gear in the Atacama Desert. I kept the houndstooth hat despite it not being climate appropriate.

Believing that San Antonio was close enough to the halfway point, I made that my first stop. And although I would have liked to have seen the Alamo and stroll along the River Walk, I limited my stops to the essentials—gas and bathrooms. Stretching my creaky legs out of the Honda, I gave thanks for what felt like midsixties temps, knowing that it could have easily been in the sweltering eighties or thirty degrees with pounding sleet.

The city was a lot bigger than I imagined. After getting lost and missing the exit to I-57, I ended up in a neighborhood where I stood out like someone from another planet. If I'd stuck around, I might have found the right character to create a phony ID, but I just couldn't muster the courage to explore that option.

After I got on the highway, thoughts of what lay ahead challenged my nervous system. An extremely discomforting mix of bloating, gas, uncontrollable belching, and a frontal lobe migraine overtook every cell. *Calm yourself, Allie*, I chanted.

I opened the glove box to check my passport. In less than two

Nancy Rhodes

hours, I'd be crossing my first border and would have to do so as myself, Allison Ruth Bennett. Bummer on many levels. I prayed the whale-poacher gang had no connections with the Immigration Department.

The one anomaly I hadn't prepared for was a flat tire. Since I'd never had one, it couldn't have been further from my thoughts. None of the blogs mentioned flat tires or any mechanical issues, except running out of gas. Flats were something that happened to my dad back when retreads were thought to be an economic solution to balding tires.

But there I was heading south on I-57, having just passed the intersection for US 83 in La Pryor, when the unthinkable occurred. I hadn't seen any of the numbered farm-to-market roads that had previously intersected the highway at regular intervals. In fact, I hadn't seen much of anything when my steering wheel suddenly jerked to the right. I rolled down my window, feeling the blast of dry and dusty heat waves, and listened to the uneven ca-chunk of a deflated tire thumping against the asphalt.

"Shit. Double shit," I yelled out the window. Geez. Even Barry couldn't get me out of this one, or could he? Maybe I could look up road service.

Unfortunately, Barry was on permanent disability. No battery. No power. No road service. And, of course, my cell phone had zero coverage. So I sat in my car, windows down, and waited for the sound of a car. I'd have to flag someone down. I didn't like the idea, but it was better than ending up like a roasted marshmallow slumped over my steering wheel.

Nothing passed. No cars, no critters, and no full-breasted Superman heroes on their way to my rescue. It was so quiet I started singing the only song that came to mind—"A Hard Day's Night." Where were all the Mexicans? The gringos?

The silence annoyed me. A lot. My singing wasn't helping. And to think how I used to *crave* silence. Working at the paper, I constantly yearned for snippets of time void of sound and stimulation.

That environment consistently roared with voices, telephones, and a variety of office machines. At one time we even had an older printing press that, while separated by Plexiglas, hummed an obnoxiously loud vibrato while the plates and rollers spewed out a hundred copies per minute.

Hearing a vehicle, my thoughts returned to the present. I got out and ran to the edge of the road, waving my hands like the grand marshal of the Rose Parade. A large blue car approached at a ridiculously slow speed. My hands danced in the air with more enthusiasm the closer it got. *They will stop. They have to. Who would ignore someone broken down in this desolate place?* Especially a gringa with an honest face? But the car picked up speed, sailing by me so fast I could not make eye contact with any of the male occupants. Men! If there had been a woman in the car, they would have stopped. Or so I thought until a few minutes later when another car passed with a young woman at the wheel, an old woman next to her, and a couple of kids in the back.

"Please stop!" I screamed. I might as well have been yelling at the yuccas and tumbleweeds.

I got back into the car to sulk. *How will I ever get to Chile if I can't even get out of the States?* While I doubted whether trying to sneak into Chile was the right way to go about things, I never once doubted my mission. Someone seriously threatened Jeff's kids. And Jeff was my only true friend.

When I moved to Chile, I lost contact with my few junior college friends. And after meeting Miguel, I lost touch with my Chilean friends. Barely surviving the Miguel ordeal, I had no desire for regular human contact. By then I understood that relationships always ended and were too damn painful or messy or both. Eventually, I became adept at keeping acquaintances as acquaintances and bed partners as bed partners.

After returning to California—post-Miguel—I'd occasionally meet people for coffee or a happy hour cocktail. But if anybody, male or female, asked one too many personal questions or called me more than three times in one month, they were nixed from my life with a shake of my internal Etch A Sketch.

I didn't want any relationships, even friendships. But I bent this rule with Jeff. Not sure why. I trusted Jeff from the get-go but still kept a few emotional fences in place. He knew which ones to approach and which to leave alone. Sex was never a consideration between us. Even if he wasn't married, there were no hot tamale trains running on our tracks.

Two more cars passed. I waved but was too late. Did all these people just think I was having a picnic out here? For one pathetic moment, I wished I'd hung onto my tight jeans and sheer V-neck top. Obviously, no one was interested in helping a filthy gringa dressed in baggy shorts and a faded gray T-shirt.

CHAPTER 21

⁂

A fter sitting on the side of the road for nearly three hours, I decided that if I ever got my flat fixed, I would throw in the towel and return to California. Who was I to think I could drive alone across multiple borders?

While pouting and kicking red dust over my tires, a yellow Ford Maverick pulled behind my car. Large splotches of rust had taken over most of the car's exterior. I wanted to run up and hug this Good Samaritan, but I refrained. The driver, perhaps thirty or thirty-five, spoke decent English and knew how to change a tire. Finally, my luck was changing. I even had a full-size spare tire! After twenty minutes, he had finished. I tried handing this kind angel a five-dollar bill, but he would not take it.

Despite my earlier resolve to return, I continued south. After passing over the murky Rio Grande, I saw two huge, wavering Mexican flags. Approaching the checkpoint, I slowed to a crawl and practiced looking like this was something I did all the time. Dozens of cops lined the sides of the road, none paying any attention to me or my car.

I still had to find the immigration and customs office, which according to my research, should be about thirty kilometers down the road. Just as I was beginning to think I'd missed the border patrol office and imagining Mexican police sending me to a dark underground cell without food, I saw the signs for *Aduana* (customs). I had to park and exit the car, shamefully tugging at my ragged shorts that had rolled up into the danger zone. I grabbed the original and three copies of my car registration, the pink slip, and the thick stack of driver's license copies. Not sure what I was thinking, but I had more than a dozen.

Walking into the immigration office made my nerves teeter between hot flashes and vertigo. I thanked God and the universe for not allowing me to obtain fake papers. The agent—a skinny man who looked around seventy-five—was the driest, coldest dude I'd ever met. He threw so many questions at me, one after the other, without eye contact or a pause. After asking for my name and birthdate, which of course were right in front of him on my driver's license, he proceeded with, "What is your destination?"

"Managua, Nicaragua," I responded without hesitation.

"Reason for your trip?"

"Visiting a cousin who lives in Managua." This, I prayed, would be my only lie.

"How long you stay in Mexico?"

"Not long. Probably for three days. Just passing through."

"Where will you be staying?"

"Motels. Don't know which ones. Any recommendations?" I tried smiling with a friendly giggle to lighten things up, but it went unnoticed, as did my question.

The questions continued—how much was I carrying (not much), was I carrying any drugs (does ibuprofen qualify?), and had I ever been convicted of a felony (not yet). I wanted to tell him to chill but opted to behave respectfully and answered his questions the best I could.

At least that was my original intention.

All I'd eaten in the entire day was an apple and a granola bar, and it had been a long, crappy day. When Señor Fuentes answered his cell phone during my interview, my emotions skyrocketed to Venus and back. Tired, hungry, and having to pee left me with zero patience. And that's when I did that thing that I do despite years of negative consequences. I made fun of him.

After all the questions, he began passing papers from one pile to another, stamping some, pausing on others—until he got that call. For some reason, I never imagined a customs agent owning or carrying a cell phone, at least not on duty.

I sat there and waited while he conversed with whomever using Spanish words that collided together so fast I couldn't understand the conversation. He could have been chatting with his wife about their granddaughter's baptism or with another agent needing advice. But after about seven minutes of staring at his sideburns and checking out the few boring framed photos and certificates, I grew restless.

Under my breath but loud enough to be heard, I mumbled, "No worries here, señor. I'm just loving the scenery." He continued talking. Apparently, I was invisible. Irrelevant.

"So, okay, since I don't have any hotel reservations for tonight, you got a bunk bed for me somewhere in the back? A pillow? A cold *cervesa*?"

By this point, I was convinced Fuentes was intentionally stalling to harass me. I pulled the tiny barrette from my bangs and shook my head like a horse dodging a swarm of flies.

Nothing. The more he ignored me, the angrier I got. I felt like I'd been there half a day. If I'd eaten or peed ahead of time, something I now regretted not doing, I wouldn't have succumbed to this slight rant of childish behavior.

"I really got to pee. I mean, seriously, does anyone even care how hot it is in here? Have you even heard of this modern device called an air-conditioner?"

He slammed his flip phone shut before placing it with excessive force on the desk. He leaned forward and in something close to a whisper said, "It is broken, *ma'am*. But if you would like to continue with your insults, you may take these papers, get in your car, and exit through that door. Follow the signs back to your country."

I was flabbergasted. And ashamed. I deserved that and probably more.

"I am so sorry, Señor Fuentes," I said in my most possible rendition of sincerity. "It's no excuse, but, you see, I am really tired and hungry, and, well, I really do need to use the facilities. But I'll wait. No problem. Please—take your time. You're doing a great job. I'm so, so sorry for being rude."

I poured it on, probably going a tad overboard. Eventually, he stamped my passport, returned the excess copies of my driver's license, and dryly told me to get on my way. Realizing I'd become the poster child for *The Ugly American*, I exited as quickly as possible. I didn't even stop at the bathroom.

When I was safely inside my car, I began a sobbing fest.

After the tears ran out, I got mad. Really mad. Mostly mad at Miguel. All of this, quitting my job, returning to Chile, the threats made to Jeff, this stupid trip. My entire fucking life was his fault. I wanted him out of the way. I needed to find him, face him, and move on. I would do everything I could do to help Carlos find the poachers responsible for threatening Jeff. But after that, I'd look for my poacher. I'd look for Miguel.

I turned on the engine, drove a few miles, and stopped at the side of the road to relieve myself and devour an orange and a piece of stale bread.

Not only would I do this, but I could do this. After a night's rest, I would begin the long drive through Mexico. I'd have to break it up, stopping at motels at least twice before reaching Guatemala. God willing, in a few days I could reach Guatemala. After that, one or two more border crossings before I could sit my ass down on an airplane.

CHAPTER 22

An hour later, I stopped at a sketchy diner. Despite the shabby interior and abundance of spider webs filling every corner, the burger met and exceeded all expectations. With a full belly, I continued driving through the barren desert plains without much to gander at except cacti, burros, horses, and bramble weeds. Having read that Americans should avoid lodging in border towns, I drove until my knees felt like a pair of rusted padlocks and my eyelids pulled downward with magnetic force.

I finally arrived in Saltillo and found a hotel that looked like it might be safe. When I stepped out of my car, I was stunned at the crisp, dry heat that sizzled across my skin. The hotel office had two fans, no air-conditioning. No one was at the reception counter. Not seeing a call bell, I took a minute to stretch out my back by twisting right and left and checking out the modest decorations.

After a few minutes, I heard voices from a nearby room. Within a minute, the faint whispers escalated. The man spoke Spanish, the woman English.

"Oh my God! How much?" she squealed.

I couldn't hear his response, but hers was loud enough to reach the Canadian border.

"Gordo, you know nothing about running a business! How will this hotel survive if you keep spending money on such stupid things? I can't believe you spent two thousand dollars on a vending machine! A used piece of shit that sells soda drinks. You think that will bring us customers? ¡*Ay señor!*"

Behind me, I spotted a slightly rusted vending machine leaning against a pale and peeling gray wall. Poor guy, at least he was trying. Despite their problems, my parents never lost respect for one another. Even when my mom was drunk out of her mind, she never put down my father like this woman. I coughed loudly to announce my presence.

They stopped talking, but no one came forward.

"*Hola*," I said, with a strong inflection on the second syllable. Normally I would have boldly asked or hollered if anyone was around with some snide comment about them not wanting my business. But with the customs incident freshly seared into my brain, I opted for crushing my lips together in complete silence.

The scowling señora, a gray-haired, stocky woman possibly in her late sixties, came forward and introduced herself in English. I could tell her mood wasn't conducive to chitchat, which served me just fine.

After handing Sra. Emmaline a cash deposit, she passed me the room key, curiously attached to a recycled coathanger with a gray rabbit's foot dangling from one corner. I suppose this was one way to assure patrons wouldn't lose the key. The gross-looking rabbit's foot looked disgustingly real. Struggling to carry it with all my other belongings, I doubted that the dead animal part would bring me good fortune.

Prior adventure seekers posting on the internet touted that it was best to avoid Mexico City. My plan after Saltillo was an all-day drive to the west coast, staying in or near Mazatlán. The following day, I'd try to endure another long drive to make it to the border of Guadalajara, where somewhere existed an airport. Then, depending on whether or not I could handle more road travel, my *autito* (little car) and I would trek through El Salvador and Honduras before reaching the big, busy airport in San Jose, Costa Rica. When I researched my road trip, it seemed the airport in San Jose was larger and had more flight options than the airport in Guadalajara.

For my safety, I felt San Jose would be better. But good to know if I grew tired of road travel, I had another option.

I liked Mazatlan substantially more than expected. I'd read that it was a touristy town with nice beaches that should be avoided because of the infiltration of various drug cartels. With the help of a kind taxi driver, I found a hotel only four blocks from the beach. Although we were driving in the dark, he took me through Old Town to see a little of the colonial architecture. Had I not been anxious to get to Santiago, I would have stayed at least a week and hired the young *taxista* to show me the sights and best beaches.

The farther I got from the States, the more I enjoyed my time behind the wheel. Although some of the roads were windy and overtaken with potholes, the changing scenery and peaceful surroundings left me feeling more relaxed since leaving Chile at the beginning of the year. I fell into a routine of departing early after sunrise. Usually I stopped between noon or one, depending on when I found a market or taco stand with more than one car in the parking lot.

Lunch was my one big meal of the day. Chips and tortillas became a staple part of my diet. The snacks I'd brought, namely granola and energy bars, provided my growling belly with in-between fuel, but I was growing tired of them. I bought fruit whenever possible: oranges, mangoes, and the cactus fruit they call *tuna*, known in English as prickly pear, which is a bitch to peel but worth the effort.

My khakis and shorts were looser, due to a combination of less refined sugar and no alcohol. I often longed for a cold beer, but between dwindling cash reserves and a necessity to be completely coherent, I resisted the cravings.

I did not fly out of Guadalajara. Except for filling up my tank, I didn't stop. What I saw of the city may not have been the best sampling, but between graffiti, bus pollution, and traffic, I continued driving despite being on the road for eight hours. The extra two hours of discomfort proved worthwhile. I found a small, quiet campground situated close enough to hear the ocean. Although the spots lacked privacy, I lucked out with my neighbors—a couple from Argentina traveling in an old VW bus covered in travel stickers.

They invited me over for beer and fresh fish they caught earlier that day. Despite my exhaustion, their company lifted my spirits. The two talked incessantly, but their stories were entertaining. Plus, I didn't need to contribute much to the conversation. When I did, I kept it vague. Long past midnight, after three beers and way too much food, I stumbled to the back seat of my car for the best sleep since leaving Austin.

The next morning I hit the road before sunrise but could not seem to find a place that felt safe to stop for breakfast. Thirty minutes into my drive, I grabbed an orange from the back seat and peeled it while driving. I was not as coordinated as I'd thought, because when I reached across the seat to grab a paper towel, I knocked over an open can of Mexican soda. In my unsuccessful attempt to catch it, soda soaked my crotch and the car seat. The few rags I'd brought were useless, already caked with grime from frequent attempts to clean the windshield.

I pulled off the two-lane road and jumped out of my car. The soda was flavored or colored with pomegranate juice, which didn't look great on beige khakis. I was less worried about my car than I was with the unsightly and sticky mess surrounding my thighs and buttocks. I opened the trunk and looked at my options for a change of clothes. Everything was dirty, but at least my cutoffs were neither damp nor sweaty. I walked behind the backside of the car and began to change. I kept my eyes on the road ahead of me, hoping no one would drive by.

Suddenly I felt the round tip of a pistol on the back of my neck. My body went rigid. My purple-stained khakis were laying in a heap by my feet since I had not yet pulled up my shorts. I prayed that the jerk behind the pistol only wanted money.

"*Dinero. Dame todo,*" he said. While relieved about his intentions, I wasn't exactly exhaling sighs of relief. I hardly had any money, and who knew what he might do when he realized he was robbing a near-cashless gringa.

"*Un momento,*" I said. Suddenly I couldn't remember if it was safer to speak in Spanish or English when one was being robbed. Hadn't I read something about that? I opted for my terrible Spanish, hoping he'd be impressed at my efforts and cut me some slack.

"Okay, okay. *No tengo mucho pero, no hay problema. Un momento.*" I hoped he got my point. I was telling him I would cooperate but not to expect much.

As I started to turn around, he yelled, "NO!"

"*El dinero esta en mi bolso,*" I explained, trying to point to the purse on the passenger side of the car so he could help himself to whatever money remained in my wallet.

"Lady, put on your damn shorts and hurry up. I don't have all fuckin' day."

Geez! My assailant spoke English! After pulling up my shorts, I leaned into the car, temporarily feeling a moment of relief that the gun had lost contact with my skin. I wondered if I could scare him off with my pocketknife. For a moment, I considered reaching into my purse and pulling that out instead of my money, but somehow a small knife against a gun didn't feel like great odds. I grabbed my purse.

"Don't turn around. I don't want you to see me. Hurry up, bitch!"

When I bent down to get the purse, I caught a glimpse of his face in the rearview mirror, noting a heavy ten o'clock shadow and narrow sideburns that reached his chin. He was only a kid. Maybe seventeen or eighteen. His face was narrow and gaunt, and he had really yellow teeth. Meth addict came to mind.

I didn't want to give up my driver's license, so I pulled out my cash, all of it, and held it out, behind my back. Thank God I'd stashed my only ATM credit card in a secret spot beneath the passenger seat.

"This is all I have. I swear."

It didn't take long to count.

"Sixty-two dollars! You kidding me! What else you got?"

My tablet was on the back seat. Could he see it? God, I really didn't want to lose Barry.

"Computer!" he shouted.

Damn! Too late. I handed it to him, trying not to grit my teeth. "It's broken," I said. "I dropped it last week, and it got wet. *No funciona. De verdad.*"

I waited and listened. I believe he was trying to turn it on. While I was grateful the battery was dead, I knew it would be a real long shot that he'd buy my cockamamie story. And of course, he didn't.

"What's that?" he asked.

Obviously, he wasn't exactly the brightest bandito on the block. How the hell did he expect me to know what he was talking about when I couldn't see where he was pointing?

"What's what? I don't know what you are looking at."

He opened the back seat and grabbed my houndstooth hat. I had no clue why he took that, but he did. And he didn't say a word. I wasn't expecting a thank you, but I expected he'd shout off something about not calling the police or not following him.

Just as suddenly as he appeared, he was gone. He had my sixty-two bucks, Barry, and my all-time favorite hat. But I still had my backpack in the trunk and my ATM card. I'd miss the hat and tablet but was walking away with my body intact.

I locked my doors and drove off, exceeding the speed limit by at least twenty kilometers an hour. I looked back but saw no one. There were tall bushes along the road where he must have been hiding, but I wondered how often people stopped there. Talk about being in the wrong place at the wrong time. I tossed the soda can out the window. The can tumbled and rumbled across the asphalt as I pushed the gas pedal to the floor.

CHAPTER 23

⁂

I crossed the Guatemalan border and finally got my phone working again. I called Jeff's cell, but it went to voice mail. I'd been feeling lonely. Needy. I am not sure what I would have said if he'd answered, but I took it as a sign we weren't supposed to speak. I hung up before the beep.

Between campsites, parks, and taco stands, I frequently met other Americans, Australians, and even a few Europeans apparently anxious to speak English with me. We shared travel stories, highlighting the highs and comparing notes on highways, food experiences, and border crossings. Only once did I reveal my border-crossing experience, thanks to too many tequila shots shared with a lively group of thirty-somethings from New Jersey.

Most people didn't have the horror stories I'd expected. I got good at avoiding questions about the purpose of my trip. Some travelers confirmed that the airport in Costa Rica offered the most flight options. Between the growing number of butt sores and the stressed vertebrae in my lower back, I needed to hear this.

⁂

TWO BORDER CROSSINGS LATER, I MADE IT TO THE CAPITAL CITY of San Jose. With great relief, I sold the car despite getting pennies on the dollar for it. From there I took a wild bus ride to the Juan Santa Maria International Airport. The fact I had gotten this far and was so close to Chile felt surreal. Only one six-and-a-half-hour flight, and I would plant my size ten soles on Santiago soil.

The exterior of the airport had a modern feel. It was massive, overflowing with people. I looked at my watch. Two and a half hours to departure—perfect. I might even order a glass of champagne to celebrate my success at traveling semi-incognito all the way from California. Sure it had taken about a month, but I never got arrested or raped and was only mugged once. I missed the hat nearly as much as I missed Barry. I envied all the travelers around me, checking their emails and text messages on their super smartphones or tablets.

I wasn't prepared for the masses of humanity. This airport looked like LAX on steroids. What the hell? This had to be the busiest airport in all of the Americas, perhaps the busiest anywhere. People of all sizes, colors, and shapes passing through the zigzag lines, shuffling their feet, shoelaces dragging across the tile floor.

I looked at my watch again. A few minutes past one. The plane, if on time, was scheduled to depart at 3:05 p.m. Maybe I had cut it a bit close.

Taking a deep breath, I moved forward until I reached a long security queue. A family of German-speaking towheads, in no rush to remove their shoes for the security check, stood in line before me. In front of them, a short, dark-haired, chubby man kept coughing into his sleeve. Behind me, a young Spanish-speaking couple argued about who was to blame for leaving their bag of gifts behind in the taxi. *Maybe butt sores are a small price to pay for avoiding all this airport chaos.*

Drips of sweat beaded beneath my turtleneck. I was dressed for the cold since it was midfall in the southern hemisphere, and normally I felt colder than shit once they started to depressurize the cabin, but something about sharing the terminal with several thousand travelers raised my core a few hundred degrees. By the time I reached security, it was 1:55 p.m. I caught a glimpse at the flight board to find my gate. Of course, it was on time.

The plane would board in twenty minutes. I hate running in airports as much as I hate seeing people run in airports, but I wasn't going to miss this flight. I broke into an awkward cadence somewhere between a walk and a jog. Trying to do this through the winding corridors with masses of people posed a serious challenge.

Most of the airport population didn't seem to be in a hurry, including an abnormal number of toddlers who frequently walked either backward or sideways. I bumped into one woman who cursed me in some language I didn't understand. Then I broke into a full jog, backpack bouncing against my back.

I finally made it to the departure gate. They were boarding families with small kids and the rich folks lucky enough to travel first class. I scooted toward the loading gate and planted myself strategically near the gate but not yet in line so I could cut into the queue as soon as they announced general boarding.

At least that was my plan.

Less than thirty feet away stood a man who, shockingly, resembled Miguel. I shook my head. Impossible. Couldn't be. But if it wasn't Miguel, why did he have the same stance, same tilted hips, and the same long neck framed by a ponytail? Not black, as I remembered, but light gray with streaks of brown. Was it a mysterious double? Or was it the man who cursed my soul and scarred my heart?

The man—whoever he was—couldn't see me. He got in line after the call for first class passengers. I backed up and hid behind a pillar. *To hell with optimal positioning.*

It had been close to thirty years since I last saw him. Time would account for the streaks of gray and the thin patches near the top of his head. *Was he that tall?* Why couldn't I remember? Beads of sweat cascaded across my forehead, across my armpits, and between my breasts. Basically everywhere.

I couldn't believe this. What were the chances? Not just the same airport but the same flight? I turned around to look for a bathroom. Maybe cold water across my face would clear my thoughts. Only I couldn't find the ladies' room.

I watched my nemesis hand his boarding pass to the ticket agent. As he waited for her to return it to him, he scratched his neck just below his ear. Not a significant gesture but a familiar one.

Proof. Raw, undeniable proof. A nervous habit I remembered. Miguel hated flying.

I shuffled toward the departure board to see if there were any other flights to Santiago. Nope. *Nada*. Shit.

Hearing another call for my flight, I considered my options—quit, stall, or proceed. Quitting wasn't my first choice. Stalling might work if I knew there was another flight, but I'd probably have to pay a fortune, and this wasn't exactly the best time to expand my already-blown budget. And what would I do if I ended up having to wait twenty-four hours? Sleep on the floor and risk death by human stampede?

My return to Chile wasn't just about protecting Jeff and his family. These whale poachers or mobsters had shown they were capable of doing some seriously shitty stuff. Besides what they'd done to Jeff, Carlos, and me, they were killing innocent whales. And while I might not be the biggest animal lover, that hit a nerve. If these creatures existed before dinosaurs, they had a right to continue into the twenty-first century.

Biting my nails as the last group of passengers moved closer to the ticket agent, I agonized over my decision. I was so close now… so close to doing something that wasn't just about me. I wanted to continue but didn't know if I could.

Maybe he wouldn't recognize me. Between my weight loss, funky attire, and the partially grown-out dye job, I didn't resemble the Allie of the eighties. But what if he did? What would I say? Could I still breathe if he started talking to me?

The line of passengers thinned out, only the stragglers were nearing the ticket agent. Fifteen people. Ten…five…and then I heard the final call for Flight 623 to Santiago.

The gate was absent of all passengers. Only the two boarding flight agents remained, ready to close the gate.

I stepped forward. I stopped. Then I took another step forward.

An image popped into my brain—something from the night I stayed at Carlos's house. He'd shown me a video of two blue whales at sea. I'd been moved, more than I thought possible.

"Wait," I screamed. "I'm coming!"

CHAPTER 24

⁂

There he was. Miguel. Nearly forgetting to breathe, I watched him put a fat duffel bag in the overhead. I prayed he would stay there so I could pass unnoticed. But he turned and sat down in the last row of first class. As I trod past all those premier passengers snuggled into their oversized faux-leather seats ready for their complimentary champagne, I felt his eyes upon me. I looked down at my boarding pass and looked away as if I didn't already know my seat was only a few rows behind his.

I prayed he wouldn't recognize me. I wasn't ready. I needed time to plan my dialogue, plan a strategy. But I could tell he was checking me out. Then again, Miguel—being Miguel—would be checking out any female passenger under the age of seventy.

Nausea spread through my core as I approached his row. He was in the aisle seat, legs extended into the aisle. When I passed, his right leg swayed out and tapped my knee. I looked at him and glared. I couldn't help it.

He responded with a quirky nod, followed by a sudden drop of his right eyelid. An exaggerated and obnoxious wink. That wink.

⁂

It was the dead of winter in Chile. June 2, 1981. I'd been in Santiago barely a year and was getting ready to celebrate my twentieth birthday. My friend Mariela and some other work friends wanted to throw me a party, and I had no problem being the center of attention. We met at an Italian bar in Providencia where we consumed more than our share of pisco sours and miniature empanadas. Later we took a taxi to a discotheque known for its infusion of American and European music and decor.

We hadn't been there long when I left the group at the bar to pee. On my way through the maze of dancers, drinkers, and dozers, I noticed a small table in the back where an extremely handsome man with long, wavy, dark hair sat alone, his hands hugging a frosted glass of beer. He looked pensive. I thought he was reading something on the table—but there was no book, no paper…nothing but his large hands, the beer, and a crinkled-up napkin.

Before I turned into the hallway toward the bathroom, he glanced up, and our eyes met. The solemn look vanished, replaced with a warm, infectious smile and…a wink. I felt my cheeks turn crimson, embarrassed that he caught me staring at him. When I exited the bathroom, he was right there at the entrance of the hallway, holding a sugar-rimmed pisco sour extended toward my chest.

"Hello, sweetness," he said. It was the corniest of pickup lines, but I didn't care. He then asked if I'd like to join him for dinner Saturday. I don't remember exactly what I said, but he handed me that crinkled napkin with his phone number scribbled in red ink.

Of course, I called him. He had me with that wink.

⁓⁓⁓

By the time I collapsed in my aisle seat, my hands were shaking so much I spent an embarrassingly long time fastening my seatbelt.

When the airplane left the runway, I held my breath, waiting for the sound of the wheels to rise and lock in place. This obsession had nothing to do with Miguel on the plane. I hated air travel. After reaching the appropriate cruising altitude, I heard the announcement that we were free to move about the cabin. I closed my eyes and concentrated on my breathing. After several minutes, I felt my heart rate drop to a safe level.

I dozed a few minutes. When I came to, I glanced at the young girl at the window seat of my aisle. Bob Marley seeped out of her headset. She seemed oblivious to my presence. I closed my eyes again, feeling the blast of air toss my bangs toward the ceiling.

A familiar voice shredded my Zen-like stream of consciousness. "Excuse me. Do you mind if I take that seat?"

I looked up, even though I knew who it was. He pointed to the empty seat between me and Marley Girl. She glanced at both of us and shrugged her shoulders like she didn't give a shit.

"Uh, yeah, sure…I guess," I said, berating myself for mumbling such an oxymoronic response. Fighting to recover some ground, I added, "Actually, why don't you take my seat? We can trade. You're up there a few rows, right?"

He cleared his throat. "Well, Allie, I was hoping to talk with you, so trading seats won't work out too well."

Allie. Oh Holy Mother of God.

The girl must have been eavesdropping. "Oh, you two know each other," she said all too sweetly. "Hey, mister, I'll trade with you so you guys can have some privacy."

I had no time to argue.

"That'd be great," he said. "You're a doll. Three rows up, aisle seat."

I tried to signal to Window Seat Girl that I really wished she wouldn't leave, but my silent eye language wasn't effective.

How in the hell could he recognize me? I had a different hair color (even if the dye job was a month old), no makeup, and was dressed like someone who'd just spent weeks camping in the woods.

"Miguel" was all I could say. My lips felt like they were suffering from a sudden neurological disorder. I swung my legs over the armrest to let the Window Seat Girl go by. Miguel stepped over my knees and plunked his tall frame into her seat.

Immediately he leaned his torso into my territory. "It's been a while," he said. "You…you look different."

Where was his accent? I remembered him having a Chilean accent. Now he sounded like someone from Iowa or Oklahoma.

I didn't know what to say. So I said nothing.

"*¿Regresando a Chile?*" he asked.

What a stupid-ass question. *Of course I'm going to Chile. That's where our flight is headed*, I thought, nearly chewing off a piece of my lower lip.

"Yes, Miguel, I'm headed to Chile as are you, along with the other three hundred other passengers on this plane."

"Ouch! Of course, I know where you're going. Just surprised that you're going there. I'm so surprised to see you, honestly."

"Honestly" is not a word I'd associate with Miguel. I let the silence sit between us. Great. Maybe he'd leave.

"Well, here we are," he said.

"Here we are. Yep. On a plane. Going to Chile. Here we are."

"Allie, *amorcito. ¿Qué pasa?* Why the attitude?"

"Don't call me that."

"What? *¿Amorcito?*"

"Yes. That. Don't."

"So how has life treated you? Do you live in Costa Rica now? Or Chile? Are you married?"

"Miguel, you know our past is our past. Let's leave it that way."

I grimaced at my own words. Hadn't that been the whole point of returning to Chile? To face Miguel and shove that nasty history into the past? Now the opportunity was staring me in the face, and I couldn't move forward. I didn't want to offer information about me. I wanted to hear him admit that he lied about having a wife and two kids. I wanted him to either confess to having them killed or offer me some logical explanation.

Anger boiled as I thought about his dead wife—some innocent, nice woman, whose only mistake had been to marry Miguel, and two daughters who would have been about the age of Marley Girl. Postcollege, maybe married, maybe with kids of their own. What had he done with *his* life for the last thirty years? How many other women had he fooled? Betrayed?

As I sank into a deeper cauldron of emotional rancidity, I realized my anger should be directed more toward myself than Miguel. When I quit my job and bought that one-way ticket, my goal had been to find this man, figure out if he was guilty or innocent, and understand what part I played. Why had I wasted nearly three decades of my life hiding from men and relationships because of this scumbag murderer? Why had I allowed myself to fall for such an unfaithful romantic?

If I didn't engage somehow with him now, I might momentarily feel some satisfaction for refusing his attention, but then I'd know nothing.

Change begins with change.

"I'm sorry, Miguel," I said, feigning some version of a smile. "Let's try this again."

CHAPTER 25

After our awkward start, I shared a few details to quench his curiosity and reengage his interest. I fed him a few truths and a lot of lies. I shared my interest in blue whales, telling him I'd seen several in Mexico. I even told him I might visit the Gulf of Corcovado to see the blue whale feeding grounds. I mentioned that because of the proximity to Puerto Montt, where we once lived together, hoping it might lead the conversation to what happened to his wife and daughters.

"Whales?" he said, seemingly picking invisible dirt from his fingernails. "Huh. I wouldn't have pictured you with that type of hobby."

"Actually," I said, "I'm meeting some friends who are involved with trying to protect the blues from being slaughtered by poachers."

"Oh, getting political, are we?"

"No, Miguel. It's not about politics. They're an amazing species, and they were almost wiped out in the twentieth century. We just want to protect the few that remain."

"Okay, I stand corrected. Well, sounds like a good cause, my sweetness."

"Miguel. Stop it. Please."

"You know, I don't know why you're so angry with me."

"Something about a wife and two daughters you never told me about. And I sure as hell am not your—your anything!"

Dropping his head, he grew silent. His cheeks turned slightly pale.

"I did lie about my family, Allie. I'm sorry. I'm sorry about a lot of things. It's no excuse, but it was a rough time for me."

My mind raced with things I yearned to say. Like *rough time— seriously*? I mean, the man was wooing me after his entire family disappeared!

"I really did love you. And for what it counts, my wife and I were already separated when I met you. And even though we weren't together, their disappearance shook me to my core. Not to mention, never having closure since their bodies weren't recovered."

"But you knew! You knew they were missing when we had that getaway in Pucón!"

"Oh, Allie, all I knew was they hadn't shown up when expected. I never thought they'd completely disappeared."

I didn't know what to believe. But regardless, he lied. He totally lied. I had no response, even if his magnetic eyes peered a little too close to my heart.

Two awkward minutes passed. The flight attendant passed by, offering beverages. Miguel ordered a beer. If poison was an option, I would have ordered it as a chaser.

After downing his beer, Miguel started talking about all the new breweries in Santiago—which ones had the best variety and how he was hoping to land a gig at his favorite downtown brewery. The color returned to his face. It was like a different person stepped into his body.

"I started playing the drums," he said, his chest inflating before my eyes. "I play with a few guys at some clubs in Santiago when I'm in town."

I nodded approvingly while secretly praying he wouldn't invite me. I asked him if he did something else for a living, and that occupied his vocal cords for another forty minutes. Something to do with importing machinery parts for industrial dairy equipment. I had a hard time pretending to be engaged when he sank into another monotone monologue.

As the plane descended, Miguel finally got around to asking what I did for a living.

"Real estate. Just getting into it." A lie for a lie I thought. Since I wasn't ready to accept anything out of his mouth as truth, I decided two could play that game.

"Guess you can make some big bucks doing that sort of thing."

"Well, the market is still recovering."

"Did you say you're living in Chile now?"

"No, just visiting," I answered as the flight attendant grabbed his empty can. "What about you?"

"I spend a lot of time there, but I've been living in Costa Rica. Just love it. Took up golf too. So between that, my work, and the music, I stay out of trouble."

Too bad you didn't have that regimen when we were together. Miguel in all his egotistical grandeur. Of course, he hadn't changed. People like that never do.

When the flight attendant announced we'd be landing in about fifteen minutes, Miguel decided to return to his seat. He did this quite abruptly. I'd expected an exchange of phone numbers.

"Good to see you again, Allie."

After taking a couple of steps down the aisle, he turned around. *Is he going to ask for my number? Do I want him to?*

"Good luck with the whales," he said, flipping his stringy ponytail over his shoulders.

Marley Girl never returned, so I sat back in my seat, staring at the swirls of gray outside the window while my ears adjusted to the descending altitude. When I closed my eyes, the whispers and sounds of nearby passengers annoyed me. A baby cried but fortunately was hushed. Perhaps a pacifier, a bottle, maybe a boob.

Then I heard a young woman laughing. Flirtatious laughter. It was Marley Girl. Then Miguel. His voice was low, but I heard enough—too much. Pheromones exuding like dandelions in the wind.

When the woman in front of me turned to look out the window, leaning into the man next to her, I had a line of visibility to Miguel and Marley Girl. He whispered into her ear, and then she turned to face him. And then they were kissing. Their lips lingered together until the woman in front of me straightened in her seat and I lost my view. *How does that happen when he's only known her ten minutes?* Then again, with Miguel that wasn't a hard question to answer.

After everyone exited the plane, I considered stalking him. Following him to baggage or waiting outside the men's restroom where he'd inevitably visit after the flight. Why had I been so nice to him? I'd wasted three decades of my life, suffering PTSD from a torrid love affair with a married man whose whole family mysteriously disappeared. And I did nothing. And now he'd vanished.

What a cruel destiny to be on the same plane.

Watching the carousel spin slow loops with everyone's bag but mine, I wondered why he'd approached me. By the time my tattered backpack came down the ramp and bounced onto the turnstile, I had my answer. He didn't want to hook up with me again. I was a forgotten chapter, a tired and useless piece of history. He didn't sit with me to start up an old fling or become new best friends. He wanted to make sure I was no longer a threat.

Well, obviously I wasn't.

I answered his questions, watched him make out with a girl half his age, and let him go.

CHAPTER 26

O ut of habit or laziness, I returned to the same hotel. This time my room was on a higher floor. I went straight to the fancy cocktail lounge and ordered a gin and tonic. Fifteen minutes later I ordered another.

When my fingers began to tingle and I felt a giddy light-headedness, I made the mistake of ordering a third. I knew two was my limit. But I was tired, angry, and really confused about what I was going to do in the morning. I wanted to put on my numbing blanket. At least I had enough sense to order a plate of fries and a bowl of soup—Chilean *cazuela*. Total comfort food.

After three G&Ts, I moved next to a single guy at the bar who looked no older than Marley Girl. Nice looking in a collegiate kind of way. As soon as he opened his mouth, I remembered why I don't stalk cute, young guys. He talked a lot about sports, especially American football. His claim to fame was going to a Super Bowl game and scoring seats at the fifty-yard line. He never asked any questions, which was fine. After twenty minutes of sports talk, I let him kiss me, but the second his tongue slipped inside my mouth, I pulled away, wiping the evidence off my lips with a cocktail napkin. Before he could try again, I excused myself to the ladies' room—which I passed on my way out.

Settling my head deep into the pillow, I breathed through the spinning walls around me. Images of kissing Miguel consumed my semiconscious state. I grabbed one of the ten pillows and stuck it between my legs, aching for something else to share the space. As the alcohol passed through my system, I forgot about Marley Girl. I forgot about Miguel's dead wife and daughters. I remembered the feel of Miguel's lips on mine, the commanding but gentle embraces, the way he used to run his hand across my face to tuck a loose strand of hair behind my ears, the arousing ear massages, the way he knew exactly what I liked, and how he read me, always knowing when to back off and when to bring it on. I'd had other lovers, but no one enraptured my heart or my body like Miguel.

I woke up close to three in the morning, having startled myself with a scream. My own, of course. I think the villain in my "nightmare du noir" was Miguel, but as dreams go wacky at times, he resembled the kid in the bar. This person's abnormally large hand was on the top of my head, pushing and submerging me underwater. I fought to get air while my lungs slowly, painfully began to close. Through swirling bubbles of H^2O, I looked straight into his face—a face that boastfully smirked with satisfaction.

Once I shook off the nightmare and the hangover, I understood I needed to do something. My first priority was to find Carlos. I grabbed the hotel scratchpad to write down a plan. After an hour, all I'd written was: 1) Rent a car. 2) Drive to Carlos's house. 3) Pray.

I hadn't had much exposure to religion except for when I was ten and attended my best friend's church for a whopping five Sundays in a row. I went because she was always boasting about how much fun she had in Sunday school. But just when I was beginning to enjoy it, she stopped going. She disappeared from the neighborhood without saying goodbye, which I didn't think was very godlike.

But with the crazy happenings of recent months, I decided to give the God-thing a chance. After I prayed, I got a good map from the concierge and planned the driving route to Carlos's house. *No more bus rides for me.*

I left after breakfast on a gorgeously sunny—but not too smoggy—March day. I walked two miles to a small car-rental place and got a nondescript, white Toyota. Cheapest rental they had, which meant inadequate legroom.

Arriving in El Toyo after lunch, I marveled at the subtle simplicity and beauty of this little barrio. Things looked so different in early daylight. Towering avocado trees were abundant, along with manzanita and laurel. I looked across the gravel road, hoping to see the young girls again. Maybe they were in school. There was an old Chevy parked alongside Carlos's house. I didn't recognize it. The front steps still groaned as I cautiously proceeded to his front door.

I knocked four times. My signature knock. Two fast taps, a pause, followed by two hard thrusts. I waited. And waited. Disappointed, I turned to leave. When I reached the bottom step, the door opened. It wasn't who I expected.

Nancy Rhodes

CHAPTER 27

"*Hola, Allie. ¡Que sorpresa!*"

Karina stepped forward extending her long, thin arms. Returning the hug, something felt very wrong. I remembered her as a petite woman, but now she was a lot thinner than when I saw her in Valparaiso. Her tank top hung loosely over her torso. And despite the heat of a late summer afternoon, her legs were hidden beneath a pair of baggy sweats that hung loosely off her protruding hip bones. Large half-moon circles hung beneath her eyes.

"Come in," she said, motioning me forward.

The furnishings were different. Someone had decorated the house with boxy, contemporary furniture, awkwardly grotesque and unfitting for the home. Gone were the photos of whales. Gone were all the photos. The walls were bare. And gone was the blue chair and the brown sofa. All signs of Carlos had disappeared including his guitar and conga drums.

I struggled to say something after hello. Suddenly, that familiar gigantic cat trotted from the kitchen, finding his way snug between my legs.

"Gordito!" My voice exuded far more exuberance than kitty could handle, sending him for safety beneath a glass table shaped like an oversized liver. Even I was surprised by my reaction, since I previously used kitty as a soccer ball. For some reason now, I wanted to hold him. He was familiar. Maybe he could channel Carlos.

Realizing I'd been more generous in salutations to kitty than Karina, I said, "It's great to see you again. It's been a while. This looks so different. So modern."

My dribbling attempts of conversation failed miserably. Karina avoided eye contact and acted unusually reticent. I waited in vain for an invitation to sit. Finally, I got to the point asking if Carlos was around and looking around like I expected him to pop out of the sofa cushions.

"Oh, I thought you would have heard," she said. "Carlos moved out a while back. He's down south somewhere—maybe Chiloé or farther south. I'm not sure exactly. I figured you'd been in touch."

"No, we haven't. Is he down there because of the whales?"

"Yep. I took over the rental. He sold most of his stuff except for the boat."

"Do you have his phone number?"

"Uh, sorry, I can't help with that. He ditched his phone after receiving a lot of threats. We all did right after those whaling records turned up."

Once again, she looked away. *That was it.* She must blame me since I gave the records to Carlos. No wonder she didn't want me inside her home. *Tough shit.* I had traveled a long way to see her and wasn't going to run off that easily.

"I thought things had calmed down."

She took a step back, her face expressionless.

"Do you want water? Tea? I don't have much else to offer."

"I'm good. Thanks. What kind of threats?"

"I don't know about Juan Paul, but I got a couple of phone calls. The basic message was if I valued my life, I better stop any meddling when it came to whales, although those weren't his words exactly. Whoever it was, and I believe he disguised his voice, told me to ignore the papers because they meant nothing. And—well, he said that you were dangerous and I better stay away from you."

"Shit. I'm sorry, Karina. I'll go. I had no idea."

"Of course you didn't. Hopefully you weren't followed. What about you? We never saw you after that outing in Valparaiso."

"Oh, yeah, that outing," I said, blushing at the memory of me passing out and bailing from the boat trip.

"*Esta bien,*" said Karina, feigning a smile.

"Just been busy. And a little out of touch," I said, realizing she didn't know anything about me returning to the States. Perhaps Carlos said little to protect me. "I would like to get in touch with him. Do you have an address or email perhaps?"

She rubbed her temples. "I don't have an address since he suggested we don't contact one another for a while. But he called me once. I wasn't feeling well that day, so we only talked a few minutes. I barely remember what we talked about."

I found that strange and almost unbelievable.

An awkward minute or two passed, both of us silent.

She stood up, the effort tiring her. "I'll check," she said, taking a deep breath. "I had his email address but don't know if it'll work. His computer was stolen before he moved out."

I watched Karina disappear into the bedroom. A dull ache was growing in my gut, and it wasn't food related.

While she was gone, I grabbed Gordito and held him against my chest. Large clumps of hair were missing as was probably a fourth of his body weight. If only cats could talk. At the sound of Karina's footsteps, Gordito jumped from my lap and dashed beneath the table.

"I found this. Don't know if works. I don't have internet service here."

I looked at the piece of paper. The shaky cursive letters were hard to make out. It reminded me of my grandmother near the end of her life.

"I'm sorry—can you make it out?" she asked, clearing her throat that suddenly sounded strained and raspy.

"Yep, this is fine. Thanks, Karina. I better get going. I appreciate your help. I hope everything works out."

She leaned forward to hug me. I returned the gesture, careful not to grip her thin body too tight. I wanted to ask if she was okay, but I knew she would have told me more if she wanted to. The hug lasted a few seconds longer than I expected.

Nancy Rhodes

CHAPTER 28

Using the hotel computer, I learned the email address that Karina provided was invalid. My hands fell off the keyboard and moved to the back of my head, fingers interlocked, elbows poking out like a pair of odd-shaped antlers. *What now, Allie?*

Eyes closed, I replayed everything Karina had said. She mentioned that Carlos might have gone south, possibly to Chiloé. It might not be a strong lead, but it was a direction. If Carlos had decided to follow the blues, he damn well might have gone to Puerto Montt or Chiloé. I vaguely remembered him saying something about blue whales residing in southern Chile all year.

Sitting at the one-computer media center, I made a decision. As soon as I could make the arrangements, I would head south. *Why the hell not?* The large island of Chiloé was only a ferry boat ride from Puerto Montt, so I could easily check out both.

Turning off the computer, I rose, feeling an unfamiliar lightness in my feet as I walked toward the elevator. The shrouded darkness from the stress of my long trip and visit to Karina was lifting, cautious optimism wanting to take its place.

The next day I used the computer again to finalize my trip to Chiloé. I fell into the online world of alluring tourist traps, enthralled by photos of Castro's wooden churches and brightly painted houses perched on stilts over the shoreline.

I booked a flight to Puerto Montt. From there I'd take a ferry across the Chacao Channel into Castro. I wasn't thrilled that I would have to wait two days for the flight. *More hotel fees and wasted time.* Returning to my room, I turned on the TV, flipping channels like crazy. I had no idea what to do with myself until my departure. Thinking I might as well go for a swim, I changed in to my one-piece swimsuit. *Maybe fresh air and cold water will change my mood.*

While many of the tourists had left, an end-of-summer heat-wave brought every possible child to the pool. After a dozen laps, I wrapped an oversized, plush towel around my torso and found a chaise lounge far from the banter of happy children and uptight parents. The water cleared my head, but the chlorine left my skin about as soft as a prickly pear. As a breeze from the east sneaked over the cordillera, the hairs on my arms stood tall above a scattering of goosebumps. I had no desire to return to my hotel room, so I cozied up to the bar.

"Black coffee, please," I said, looking back as half the pool emptied and white-lipped children ran for their towels.

"Sure. No problem, Miss Bennett, I'll get that for you right away."

Removing wet strands of hair from my face, I stared at the bartender.

"Excuse me—but—"

"Allie, it's me. Mar—Juan Paul. Valparaiso road trip...."

"Oh, I'm so sorry, Juan Paul. You look, well...different. I mean you look good, but didn't you used to have a goatee and long hair?"

"Welcome to corporate Chile," he whispered, motioning to his hairless chin. "What have you been up to?"

"Ha! Got an hour? Gosh, it's so bizarre to run into you! I just saw Karina yesterday. She—"

"Um, let's chat about this later, okay? I'm off at six," he said, repacking freshly ground coffee in the espresso machine. "Want to grab a bite? I know a decent Thai restaurant downtown."

"Sounds good. I'll meet you in the lobby," I answered. "It'll be nice to catch up."

"Yes, it will," he said, shrugging his shoulders while checking out the three bikini-clad young women who were obnoxiously giggling and flaunting their toned, tanned bodies on their way to the bar.

"Better attend to the guests," he said. "See you later."

"You poor thing," I said, offering an exaggerated motion of sweeping away tears.

When I got back to my room, I grabbed my backpack and dumped the contents on the bed. I had nothing to wear. One pair of khakis, two pairs of shorts, a few disgusting underclothes, and four battered T-shirts. And since I'd lost weight, everything I put on looked like living room draperies. After a quick shower, I found a boutique shop in the lobby that had an array of overpriced clothing. While I was tempted to buy an adorable green blouse adorned with daisy-style lace around the neckline, I settled for a polyester, made-in-China T-shirt with weird birds on the front.

We met in the hotel lobby and shared a cab. The small restaurant was crowded, but we only had to wait a few minutes for a table. After exchanging small talk, our conversation shifted to more serious topics like the economy, the construction boom, and the upcoming election.

After ordering, the waiter arrived with our wine, pouring a drop in Juan Paul's glass for tasting.

"I'd like a taste too, please," I said twisting my lips sideways. Juan Paul smiled.

After the waiter reluctantly dropped a minuscule sample in my glass and I nodded in approval, our glasses were filled.

"To old friends," I offered, watching the lines around his eyes soften.

"And whales," he responded, clinking his glass against mine.

"Speaking of whales, are you in contact with Carlos?"

"I was going to ask you the same thing. I saw him a couple of times a month after our trip to Valpo. We had talked about getting together after that, but I never heard from him. I tried calling and emailing him, but my emails bounced back, and the phone recording said the number was no longer in service. What about you? Have you heard from him?"

"A few times after the Valpo trip, yes, but not recently. I'd like to though. In fact, that's why I went to El Toyo yesterday. Did you know he moved out of that house?"

"He was talking about it, so I'm not surprised."

"Well, Karina's in his house now. And she looks terrible. I hope she's not sick."

"We all lost contact with one another. We kind of had to."

"What? I mean, why?"

Juan Paul stopped talking when the waiter appeared with our appetizers. I swallowed a large gulp of the sauvignon gris. *Damn, Chilean wine is good.*

After the wine warmed my throat, I tried to figure out which questions to ask first. As a person of no patience, I ended up blurting several at once. "What happened? Why did he leave? Why did you guys stop seeing one another?"

Juan Paul leaned forward, his voice dropping to a whisper. "Shortly after that Valpo trip, probably just after you left, Carlos and I met up one afternoon. He told me about the assault at his house, the threats, and that you returned to the States." He lowered his voice further. "Allie, I had problems too. About a week after I saw Carlos, they started targeting me. That's when we decided it'd be best if we all split up. We don't have any idea who's behind this, but if we don't associate with each other, maybe we can determine who they're after. And why."

"What did they do to you?"

"I received a threatening letter and ignored it. But two weeks later my sister's house went up in flames. She lost everything but her car and the clothes on her back."

"Oh my God! That's horrible! Was anyone hurt?"

"No, not physically anyway."

I shook my head before staring down at my hands clutching my napkin like a beloved baby blanket.

Juan Paul grabbed the wine bottle and refilled our glasses. Noticing the waiter approach with our food, he again fell silent.

Putting down his glass, he said, "I never understood why they considered you such a threat. The last time I saw Carlos, I wanted advice. I didn't know what to do after they burned my sister's house. He said we had to be careful. That's when he mentioned he might be leaving. But he was vague."

Juan Paul stopped chewing. Staring at his plate he said, "Whoever is behind this is hell-bent on scare tactics."

"Did Carlos tell you what happened to my friend—the car accident and the break-in?"

"He told me you'd been threatened but didn't share details. He said there were a lot of similarities."

"My friend, his name is Jeff. He got letters too. Those bastards threatened to hurt his kids. I have no idea how they figured out where he lived. This shit—sorry, this is insane. It almost sounds like mafia!"

Juan Paul shook his head. "That's actually possible, Allie. I've heard some of the Mediterranean fisheries are run by the mafia, but what that has to do with us or blue whales is a mystery."

Visions of men harpooning the largest animals ever to exist on our planet made me sick. Trying to wrap my head around any possible explanation but knowing it had to be for some form of financial gain annihilated my faith in the human race. I put my fork down. Eating another bite of anything was out of the question.

"Then," he said, "I got another letter."

"I'm afraid to ask."

"They told me to leave Chile. They said next time my sister would lose more than a house." He looked away but not before I saw his pupils darting nervously behind unwanted tears. "Sorry," he said, shaking his head.

"Nothing for you to be sorry about. I'm the one that brought this on. It is my fault. It started with that package."

I looked around. Everyone looked so damn happy. So much was screwed up in this world, and people just continued to eat and drink and laugh about stupid stuff.

"Maybe it feels that way," he said. "That's what these guys want. They want each of us to feel at fault and each of us to go away. But you know that's not true, right?"

"I don't know anything at this point. But you're still here. How come you didn't leave?"

"I had no choice. No money, no means. Instead, I changed my name and my appearance and got a different job. By the way, I go by Martin now."

"Martin? Oh, that's why you looked away when I said Juan Paul at the pool."

"No one at the hotel knows my real name."

"Understandably. I probably shouted it!"

"No one heard anything. Besides, I'm beginning to shake some of the paranoia."

We declined dessert. I grabbed the check despite his protest. It was the least I could do. Waiting for our cab, I asked him about Karina. He said he hadn't seen her since the day of our outing to Valparaiso.

The cab dropped me off first.

"Allie, I enjoyed tonight. It felt good to talk about all of this. Even if there's nothing we can do."

I disagreed but wouldn't push it with him. His sister lost her house. He had to be careful.

An awkward silence followed before he hugged me goodbye. "Well, I guess it's best that…"

He didn't have to finish his sentence. *Best to keep our distance.*

"Understood," I answered, nodding. I wanted to add something about how it would all be okay but couldn't. Nothing felt further from the truth. Instead, I told him if we ran into each other, I would remember to call him Martin. I wasn't sure why I said that. I'd be gone in the morning.

He turned to get back into the cab, waving goodbye.

Entering the hotel, I looked back to watch him leave, feeling more responsibility than ever to find Carlos and do something about the assholes who managed to incite fear with everyone I cared about.

CHAPTER 29

~~~~~~

T he flight to Puerto Montt was uneventful, a good thing considering who I ran into on my last flight. I slept for a whopping twelve minutes.

I took a cab downtown, casing out hotels that looked affordable. After two inquiries, I wondered if I might need to adjust my standards. *Like a tent, perhaps?*

Finally, I found a small motel offering decent off-season rates. I booked two nights. Since Puerto Montt had a population topping two hundred thousand, the odds of finding Carlos were slim to none. I ditched my original plans of going straight to Chiloé, so I could snoop around a bit.

Puerto Montt looked nothing like I remembered. The congestion and busy lifestyle frazzled my nerves. If I'd been a tourist with ample time and money, I would have split for Puerto Varas, an old German settlement boasting breathtaking views of the snowcapped Osorno and Calbuco volcanoes. But I wasn't there to sightsee.

My research began at Puerto Monte's library, a ten-block walk from my hotel. Along the way I passed several restaurants, a few pubs, and a yacht club. Carlos wasn't a yacht club kind of man, but maybe I'd check it out after visiting the library. If I wanted to find Carlos, I had to explore every option, even if it felt like a long shot.

The Puerto Montt library wasn't that different from the ones I'd visited in the States. I planted my butt down at a computer terminal and logged on, ignoring stares from bored teenagers.

After shifting in my seat for a good fifteen minutes, I came to the realization that I didn't know where to start. *Should I Google Carlos Costanera?* Past experience proved this to be a waste of time unless the person I was looking for had a million friends on Facebook or had done something newsworthy. I began with a general search for "blue whales, southern Chile." After scrolling past several YouTube videos and Wikipedia sites, I found a promising nugget.

Unfortunately, it was a scientific article that I couldn't read beyond the abstract. The one paragraph, however, looked promising. The authors discussed the detection of blue whales peaking from March to May in several southern Chile locations. Three university students wrote the article in collaboration with a scientific foundation I'd never heard of. While maybe a stretch, I wondered if this data was known to others, specifically Carlos. If so, any locations detailed in the full article could narrow my search.

I asked the librarian assistant, Lorena, how I might obtain access to the entire article. She showed me the link, but it was connected to a site requiring payment. Thirty-nine dollars later I had access to the full article and printed a copy. With a large manila envelope tucked under my arm, I left the library beaming with narcissistic pride over my acute detective accomplishments.

I skipped the yacht club but stopped at the Centro de Turismo and picked up two maps of southern Chile. Then I walked to a pub near my hotel.

After ordering a sparkling lemonade drink, hamburger, and fries, I spread out the maps so they covered my table and hung over the side like an ill-fitted tablecloth. Neither map showed oceanic longitude and latitude markings, but the scientific journal contained enough data to narrow down the proximity to specific coastal areas. Finally, after shifting my new tablecloth back and forth, I found three of the four areas mentioned in the article.

"*Su plato, señora,*" said a young waitress, anxious to deliver my plate. I yanked the map off the table. In my haste, the folds of the map twisted, making it difficult to refold. My effort turned into a battle of will with awkward acrobatics, coupled with the boisterous sound of cracking paper against air every time I tried to shake the map back open. Then, just in case I hadn't captured everyone's attention, my hand hit the lemonade glass, sending it flying to the tile floor. The room echoed with the sound of shattering glass. I looked down at what was left of my glass and became distinctly aware that my refreshing beverage had just cascaded over the sandaled foot of the man sitting near me.

As the waitress approached, I grabbed every available napkin to begin project cleanup.

"*Gracias*," I said, acutely aware that my face harbored enough heat to melt an iceberg. "I'm so sorry."

"No worries," she said, handing me my food. "I'll grab a rag. Do you want another drink?"

I wanted a double scotch but politely declined.

"*Lamento, señor*," I said to Sr. Sticky Foot. He shook his leg, before dotting it with his own supply of paper napkins. With ample passive-aggressive body language, the man communicated exactly how he felt about me. My apology meant nothing. When the waitress came back with a large cleanup cloth, I asked for a to-go container. I considered paying Groucho's bill but decided my money would be better spent on a couple of strong cocktails at the hotel.

Despite the nasty restaurant episode, it had been a successful day. The article in the scientific journal revealed a study of southwest Pacific blue whales, noting an increase of acoustical activity near the northwest of Chiloé Island and two locations within the Gulf of Corcovado. Before spilling my sticky-sparkling lemonade, I had circled three potential destinations: Castro, as previously decided, Quellón near the southern tip of Chiloé Island, and lastly—if necessary—I'd cross the gulf to Chaitén. The three locations formed an imaginary triangle around the popular feeding ground within the gulf.

While I knew these areas were too vast to find one lost soul, the anticipation of exploring thrilled me. I finally had a plan—a plan that might resurrect the adventuresome spirit and confidence that once upon an ancient time fueled my soul. A plan that required my own four wheels.

CHAPTER 30

I wired for more funds, noting my savings had shrunk to a dangerous three-digit number. After a couple of weeks and a fair amount of research, I found a car. The dealer agreed to buy my car back within six months for just fifteen percent less than my purchase price, a deal that seemed like a far cheaper option than leasing—as long as I didn't wreck the car along the way.

The next day I drove my fifteen-year-old black Nissan onto the ferry. As soon as all the vehicles were onboard, I scurried up the stairs to the deck. Puerto Montt disappeared behind us, and the blue stretch of the Pacific melted into the cloudless sky above, separated only by brightly colored fishing boats and ferries. It didn't take long to see the shores of Chiloé Island.

With a permanent smile stretched across my face, I stayed outside until the engines slowed and the port of Ancud grew close. Without even a hint of seasickness, I reveled in gratitude for the smooth and short voyage. A small wooden church came into view, with a welcoming red, white, and blue Chilean flag wavering near its entrance.

As the sky above darkened, I drove along Ruta 5 toward Castro, located halfway to the southern border of the island. The eighty-four kilometers took roughly an hour and a half on a two-lane road that was in great need of repair.

By the time I made it to Castro, sideways gusts of wind and rain attacked my windshield like miniature bullets. Despite the weather,

I got out of my car when I saw the famously photographed brightly colored stilt homes known as *palafitos*. A cluster of more than a dozen hovered over a shrinking tide, offering a rainbow of varying shades of reds, blues, yellows, and greens.

Castro, a city of narrow streets and hills, reminded me of old San Francisco. It wasn't hard to navigate my way around. Within the first half hour, I found an inexpensive motel with tiny, no-view rooms.

After a quick shower, I suited up in rain gear to explore Castro before dark. Not far from my hotel, I found Castro's Plaza de Armas. I walked past several of the early morning vendors, hoping to avoid their hopeful invitations. The plaza seemed typical of other town squares I'd seen in Chile until I looked across the street and saw a vibrantly painted church. I had read that Castro had sixteen wooden churches, but that church, Iglesia de San Francisco, was not to be missed.

As I stopped to admire the neo-Gothic architecture, I heard someone shout, "*Iglesia de San Francisco!*" Turning, I saw a vendor, an older man with a gentle smile, point to the yellow-and-purple church ahead. "You go see it, Miss, then come back here. I have this church. You take one back home. I have many!"

Taking a few steps to view his wares, I marveled at his colorfully painted, wooden churches resting on a red tablecloth. I felt the temptation to purchase one immediately but reminded myself that I barely had enough money to pay the hotel bill.

"Gracias, senor," I said, smiling before I stepped away.

Several people stood on the square, taking photos. I stepped off the curb and followed a group heading inside. Stunned by the intricate beauty of so much varnished wood, I froze at the entrance. I read that nearly everything was made from locally sourced wood, including the pews, walls, floor, ceiling, and intricately designed round pillars. The visual delight continued as I passed rows of stained glass windows.

Religious figures stood—so lifelike—in various depictions

throughout the church. A few I knew; most I did not. Jesus hung on a cross over the main altar. And another Jesus, cloaked in purple velvet, stood on top of a pillar, his thorn-covered head bowed, a large wooden cross on his shoulders. Farther down, a more peaceful image pulled me across the sanctuary. I stared at this Baby Jesus swaddled in the arms of Mother Mary. Ignoring the hurried tourists who passed me, some whispering, some talking, most dragging their feet in a shuffle across the wood floor, I stopped at the image of the Archangel Michael. The plaque near his feet indicated that he was considered a great victor of Satan. Taking a deep breath, I stepped backward until I could rest my hand on a pew.

I sat down on the wooden bench, casually closing my eyes. Suddenly the desperation and fear of my plan pushed me to do something I rarely did—especially in public. I prayed. I asked that God or whatever angel might be able to help send me enough strength to push past the evil forces burrowing into my life. I couldn't tell if my message was received.

Returning to the plaza, I strolled past several artisan stalls and shops. Despite an array of beautifully crafted baskets, blankets, and trinkets, my wallet remained intact. Cumulus clouds suddenly—but not unexpectedly—unleashed their contents, testing the water repellency of my ten-dollar rain pants. Within minutes, I clearly understood the difference between waterproof and water repellent.

By the time I found the harbor, the low tide sent stale whiffs of mud and algae to my nostrils. A few relics of fishing boats dotted the shore, but I didn't see any fishermen. Reminding myself that Castro was not exactly near the Corcovado Gulf, I wondered if this little excursion was a waste of time and *dinero*. Yet, as I stared across the mudflats and now-naked stilts attached to the *palafitos*, I didn't care. I had always wanted to visit this place, and whales or no whales, I was going to enjoy it.

The downpour continued, so I decided to seek refuge inside a small coffee shop. Before choosing a seat, I looked around hoping to find someone resembling a local fisherman. What that might look like exactly, I wasn't sure. I knew it wouldn't be someone holding a cell phone, or the woman with her head in a book, or the young girls engrossed in private chatter, their platform sandals exposing garishly painted toenails. I spotted three older men sitting at a table toward the back. In my mind, they didn't look like seamen. But what did I expect—a stout, heavily bearded Spencer Tracy?

The guys were my best bet, so I chose a table within earshot. They were past middle age. Two wore polo shirts, the other a gray T-shirt with sweat rings below his armpits. They could have been laborers, farmers, or even bankers on holiday. I tried to look disinterested during my eavesdropping mission. It didn't take long to realize they spoke Portuguese. I caught a few words, but nothing resembled Spanish words for fish, boats, whales, or poachers.

Finishing my *cafecito*, I was ready to pay my bill when I noticed two young men sitting in a covered patio area off the side of the building. Thinking it odd anyone would be outside, covered porch or not, I ordered a second cup and told the waitress I wanted to change tables.

A young man with short, dark hair glanced at me as I passed by but continued chattering in Spanish, unaffected by my presence.

"¡*Que suerte!*" (What luck!) said the one who'd glanced at me. I guessed both to be in their thirties.

"*Encontraron los azules tan cerca,*" said the other, who looked European or maybe American, with wavy, shoulder-length hair the color of dried wheat.

Even with my limited Spanish, I understood *los azules* meant the blues and *encontraron* from the verb *encontrar* meant "to find." Perhaps Archangel Miguel was working his magic after all. I couldn't have orchestrated this scenario if I'd tried.

"Perfect," I whispered, looking upward to thank whoever had intervened. I wanted to run to their table and ask a million questions. Maybe they knew Carlos. Slim chance, but blue whale talk was a big step in the right direction.

While I heard bits and pieces of their conversation, between the language barrier and street noise, it wasn't enough. When they asked for *la cuenta,* I decided to intervene. Fast. After the waitress took their money and left, I walked toward their table. Clearing my throat to get their attention, I tried—in the worst Spanish ever—to say that I'd heard them talking about whales and had a few questions. They nodded, but their faces reflected apprehension about my intrusion.

Suddenly wanting to hide my identity, I introduced myself as Sandra, explaining with my limited vocabulary that I wanted to see whales, particularly blue whales, and wondered if they knew of any whale watching tours. The odds were stacked against me, but my hope was if I found out where the greatest population of whales were, I might get closer to Carlos—or at least someone who knew him.

"You a gringa, right?" asked the blonde with an accent, perhaps Australian.

"Yes, yes, I am," I answered with relief. "Sorry, my Spanish isn't that great. I'm here on vacation."

"You're in luck. We have a boat," said the dark-haired fellow.

"We have a company," said the Australian, handing me a business card. "A tour company—whale tours, fishing tours, etcetera."

I took the glossy card emblazoned with CHILOÉ WHALE TOURS.

"Thanks. This is awesome," I said, studying the card and wondering if this fortuitous encounter was the real deal or a tourist abduction racket.

"My name is Ian," said the Australian. "And this is Lucas, my partner. We have a boat going out tomorrow. Only four others booked so far, so it won't be crowded. Our boat holds ten. We leave at six."

"Oh, wow," I uttered.

"Too early?"

"No, no, not at all. I just can't believe my luck! I just arrived today. But yes, this sounds great," I said, feigning an air of confidence. "Where do I meet you, and do you need payment now?"

They laughed. "Nah," said Ian. "You can pay on the boat. You know, in case you change your mind." Pointing to his left, he added, "Go to the harbor down past those *palafitos,* and you'll see a faded purple shack that's boarded up. That's where you'll find us."

"I think I can remember that. Do I need to bring anything?"

"Warm clothes, layers, maybe a snack if you want. We'll have water onboard."

"Okay, six. I'll be there." I put the card in my back pocket, making a mental note to buy snacks somewhere before I returned to my room. Getting up early wouldn't be a problem, but hopefully, I'd be able to get to sleep.

"Well, Sandra, we're glad you're coming. See you tomorrow. But if you change your mind, give us a call. Just in case we happen to run into a busload of tourists aching for a boat trip."

Lucas laughed. "Ah, *si, jefe*…like that's going to happen!" His English wasn't bad, but it was evident he lacked confidence.

"I don't think I'll change my mind, but yes—of course," I said. "Thank you both. I'll see you tomorrow then."

Walking back to my hotel, I realized I didn't have any Dramamine. There was no way I could get on a boat without drugs. Nothing in sight resembled a pharmacy. When I got back to the hotel, I asked where I could get seasickness meds. The clerk pointed to the tiny gift shop ten feet away. I bought the last five packets.

The next morning I arrived early. Approaching the harbor, I stopped and listened to the gentle hum of waves rolling upon the shore. I closed my eyes, feeling a salty breeze toss unruly strands of hair across my forehead. I have always felt a connection to the ocean. Its massive presence so abundant with life and energy, its contrasts of darkness and light, tidal fluctuations and volatile unpredictability, its timelessness, its history. And while the harbor was calm and bore no resemblance to the winter I'd experienced in the Pacific Northwest, I felt myself regress into a bliss of nostalgia.

I WAS EIGHTEEN AND RESTLESS. AFTER A SEMESTER AT A JUNIOR college, I decided I needed a road trip to clear the cobwebs, believing that salt spray and scenic vistas would magically provide me with a life purpose. One rainy morning between Thanksgiving and Christmas, I drove my Vega along the coastal highway to central Oregon. I passed many quaint and not-so-quaint towns, but after ten hours of driving, I needed a place to sleep. When I crossed over yet another iconic Oregon bridge and saw a small town off to my right aglow with streetlights, I exited the highway and checked into the first motel displaying a vacancy sign. I spent a couple of hours leisurely touring the river-lined old town of Florence. I didn't want to leave.

Before the sun had set, I located a vacation rental office and booked a one-month stay in a small cottage north of town. It was walking distance to a beautiful beach where I went every morning with a thermos of coffee. Sitting amid the smaller dunes and seagrass, I'd watch the tide deposit broken shells, rubbery strips of kelp, and driftwood onto the white sand. If it hadn't been for lack of funding, I would have stayed.

"SANDRA—SANDRA?"

I turned. Lucas was waving at me. Ian's back was turned, but he appeared to be pulling gear from the back of a rusted Chevy van. *Oh right, I'm Sandra.* I waved back, feeling both ashamed and embarrassed by my dishonesty.

CHAPTER 31

⸺⣿⸺

I hung around the shore while the guys prepared their boat, *La Estrella*. First to arrive were Bruce and Maureen, early retirees from the States. I paid little attention to their introduction but vaguely recalled it was one of the I states. They were on an extended vacation, visiting various destinations in South America.

Next onboard was a man named Gunnar, a stout Norwegian in his late sixties or early seventies. Gunnar was clasping a large pink bag, which we soon learned contained enough bakery treats to feed a cruise line.

At 6:40 a.m., Ian and Lucas, whom Gunnar affectionately called the boys, looked at their watches. Then Ian pulled out his phone. "Nothing," he said looking up and down the shore. "Guess he's a no-show."

Ian jumped back to the deck and started untwisting the stern line. Meanwhile, I popped another Dramamine, having already swallowed two an hour prior. I prayed they'd work without putting me to sleep.

"Wait," Lucas shouted just as Ian was about to toss the line on board. "I think that's him."

We all turned. Running toward us was a young man, maybe in his twenties, waving his arms. Maureen whispered a complaint to her husband, who shook his head. Minutes later, Mr. Tardy stepped aboard.

"Sorry, folks," he said. His accent was so thick he might as well have been speaking in tongues. "*Me* name is Duncan Craig, and I come *frum* Aberdeen, Scotland."

After a round of handshakes, Lucas threw the line onboard, and we gathered around Ian for a tutorial on rules and safety precautions. I listened for all of four minutes before my mind drifted. What a group—an older and quite chatty American couple, a friendly, humorous, middle-aged Norwegian, and a twenty-something Scotsman so loquacious I wished had brought earplugs.

Finding Carlos's whereabouts with this cast of characters around would be highly unlikely.

The rhythmic slapping of waves against the bottom of the fifteen-meter diesel cruiser was hypnotizing. My apprehension and nerves dissipated, replaced by an appreciation of the calm sea and vibrant blue sky. Like my fellow passengers, anticipation over our first whale sighting sent me to the bow the minute Ian completed his discourse. Above us on the third deck, Lucas stood at the helm, grasping the ship's wheel as the colorful *palafitos* gradually faded from our view. I closed my eyes, inhaling long, deep breaths through my nose.

After all evidence of land had vanished, the guests began moving about, some finding their sea legs for the first time. The married couple huddled around Ian, questioning him about whale encounters like a pair of news anchors. Gunnar seemed content standing at the bow with binoculars pegged against his eyebrows. Ian and Duncan hit it off instantly by sharing fishing stories. Beers replaced water, suddenly appearing from a cooler that'd been covered by a stack of scratchy wool blankets.

When Duncan finally exhausted his repertoire of tales, Ian joined the rest of the group. "Folks," said Ian, "I've got a real tale. And while it's sometimes met with disbelief, I swear on my great-aunt Tricia's soul it's the truth. I haven't shared this in a while, but you look like the kind of folks who'd appreciate a good story, whether you believe it or not."

After several minutes of moving about, the group settled in around Ian.

"The day started askew," said Ian. "My crewmate—this was before Lucas—canceled on the eleventh hour…said he came down with the worst case of food poisoning and couldn't leave the toilet. Having already chartered the fishing boat for a week, I didn't want to waste a day even if it meant going out alone, something I'd never done before. In hindsight, that was the stupidest move, especially on a day where whitecaps stretched across the ocean at six in the morning. But I was green and cocky and bent on catching a shitload of Chilean sea bass. I thought nothing could stop me, not swells or a darkening sky."

Ian knew how to tell a story. Enthralled immediately, no one spoke, no one interrupted, not even Bruce and Maureen. I grabbed a blanket from a pile left nearby and enveloped my body while he paused to collect his thoughts.

"Ten miles from shore, something snagged my line. Something big. When I caught sight of an enormous sea bass fighting for his life, the thrill of conquest overtook all logic. I estimated that beast was close to a hundred pounds. I started calling him *El Dragon*. Well, *El Dragon* suddenly shot above the water, landing with such force he took me with him! Yes, my friends, I actually flew out of the boat."

Duncan and Bruce roared, while Maureen guzzled her beer with unbridled enthusiasm.

Lucas, who I thought was too far to hear anything, looked back at us with a huge, lopsided grin on his face. Either he'd heard the story too many times, or he'd never heard it and didn't buy it.

"*El Dragon* shook himself free while the easterlies grabbed the boat. I floated in that frickin' freezing ocean with only an ice chest for a float, watching—in horror and disbelief—as my boat disappeared beneath a layer of fog coating the ocean like gelatinous layers of pudding."

"Reminds me of that movie *Cast Away*," said Maureen.

Ian smiled. "Well, I didn't have a Wilson soccer ball, but I did float for hours with that ice chest. My little float contained two cans of Miller Light and not a drop of water—not that I could risk opening it. But damn, was I thirsty."

"I would have slammed those suckers down," yelled Bruce.

"Oh, I thought about it! But if I'd tried opening the ice chest with my numb legs and frozen fingers, it would have filled with water faster than a teacup under Niagara."

The image of Ian alone at sea shook me. This wasn't a fable. Things like this really happen, and happen to good people. I wondered if Miguel's wife and daughters had to suffer for hours, waiting for help that never came.

Ian spoke frankly about his fears, sharing how he yelled desperate prayers to the sky and howled for no other reason than to hear his voice.

"How long were you in the water?" I asked, wondering about hypothermia.

"It felt like hours, but later I figured it was probably twenty, maybe thirty minutes. Fortunately, the area where this happened was known for warmer sea currents. Otherwise, I wouldn't be sharing this story. But I was worried. And angry."

"Angry?" asked Maureen, reaching for another beer.

"I thought that was it, and I was angry that I didn't have a chance to say goodbye to my girlfriend, or my brother, or my buddies back home. Eventually, I accepted my fate and decided to close my eyes, thinking maybe I'd just fall asleep and die without further pain."

I believe we all exhaled a cumulative sigh.

"But then I heard the sweetest sound on this planet. The roar of a boat engine close by. I lifted my head, which by then had gone somewhere between warm and numb. When I saw the Zodiac, I tried screaming, but nothing came out. When they waved at me, I started bawling like a banshee."

Maureen clapped. Bruce jabbed his elbow into her boob. Gunnar rubbed his hands along his beard, nodding his head. Most of us were speechless.

"Once they got me onboard the Zodiac, I met the men who aided my rescue. They were researchers who'd been at sea for about a week looking for blue whales. Later they told me that it was my ice chest, not my body, they spotted bobbing in the waves. When they saw my body, they thought they'd be pulling out a corpse."

"How long ago did this happen?" I asked.

"Oh, it was only about two years ago," Ian replied. He stood up, signaling the end of the story.

Gunnar asked who saved him.

"Well, one of the guys was Charlie, a slightly stout man with a great sense of humor. The other man was tall, nice looking, with long hair. I'm ashamed I don't remember his name now, because he was the one who actually pulled me out of the sea. On the quiet side but very smart. Knew a lot about whales."

I swallowed a mass of saliva accumulating in my mouth. I had an inkling who he was talking about.

"Oh yeah—I remember now. Carlos, Carlos Costanera. ¡*Dios mío!* How could I forget that name? He saved my life! He was—literally—my savior."

CHAPTER 32

After catching my breath, I leaned in closer to Ian. "I've met him," I said, trying to sound casual.

"Carlos? Seriously? The same Carlos?"

"Yes."

Unfortunately, Maureen heard me. "Well, isn't that an interesting coincidence. How would *you* know him?"

Struggling with my response, I was relieved when Ian interceded.

"I wish I'd stayed in contact," he said. "That guy knew more about whales than anyone I've met. But I was taken to the hospital, and—well—never saw him again. Never even got to thank him for saving my life."

"I'm sure he knew you appreciated their efforts. Besides, assuming we're talking about the same person, a thank you wouldn't have been necessary."

Clenching her gut, Maureen, whose face had gone grayish white, tapped Ian on his shoulder. "Do you have any crackers?"

"Uh-oh. Waves beginning to get to you," he said, handing her a small, cello-wrapped package. She nodded, thanked him, and dashed toward the stern.

Now I felt really shitty that'd I'd lied about my identity. Ian was the ally I needed, and we wouldn't get off to a great start if he couldn't trust me.

"How long has it been since you've seen him?" he asked.

"I met him about two months ago."

Since Maureen was gone and the others were distracted, I felt it was a good time to come clean.

"Ian?" My voice quivered.

"Yes?"

"Well, I wanted to clarify some—"

Interrupting my confession, Lucas hollered from the upper deck. I followed his hand motions past the starboard side of the boat. Amid the rolling crests of whitecaps were two distant plumes of water rising upward fifteen or twenty feet.

"Whales—two o'clock!" he shouted.

Everyone ran toward us. Everyone except Maureen, who had her head between her knees.

"They're blues! Looks like a mother and calf," announced Ian.

Staring at their bluish-gray backs that simultaneously rose and arched over the ocean's surface, chills ran down my spine. Ian said it was unusual for them to be so close to land. Usually only the larger boats made it out far enough to spot the blues.

We didn't see the fluke rise on the first spotting, but a few minutes later, the larger blue came up out of a deep dive, its back curving into a high arch. Then I saw its speckled gray fluke, water droplets cascading into the ocean as if in slow motion. Everyone stood transfixed. Quiet. Even Maureen had joined us, just in time to witness the giant's rise and fall.

"My first whale sighting!" I shouted, surprised at the level of my enthusiasm. Maybe it was just domestic animals that I didn't appreciate.

"That is special," said Ian. "And not only are they blues, but you get to see a mother and calf. Congratulations, Sandra!"

Sandra. I wanted to stick my head under a blanket.

Then two humpbacks breached completely above the sea, displaying their speckled flukes before disappearing. I appreciated the distraction.

I stood with my feet planted firmly on the deck, one hand on the railing, my head shaking in disbelief. Listening to the array of adjectives each time a whale spouted or rose, I thought I would never grow tired of this. We were like small children opening presents at Christmas, wanting and wishing for an encore.

I couldn't recall any living creature, man or animal, casting a spell of that magnitude. It was impossible to imagine how anyone wouldn't feel this passion, especially after witnessing the mother and calf. I was hooked.

Lucas switched to the trolling motor, cutting the throttle so our boat bounced over the increasingly large waves, circling and waiting for the next spotting. He joined us on deck.

"How big is a baby?" Maureen asked.

"At birth, a blue whale weighs roughly six thousand pounds. They gain two hundred pounds a day, living off milk for a year or so. Then they'll feed on thousands of pounds of krill. That calf might weigh anywhere from twelve to eighteen thousand pounds."

I did the math in my head and realized that would put her at about six weeks.

"The irony is how the largest animal ever to exist on our planet feeds on such tiny crustaceans," Lucas added.

We all stood in silence as several minutes passed without a sighting.

"Watch for the spray," said Lucas. "Okay, there we go. Look that way—four o'clock."

Again we observed the spray followed by the rise and fall of an arched back.

"Nice to have three sightings already," shouted Ian. "If that one comes up again, check out the dorsal fin. I believe I spotted a tag."

When the same whale rose again, I reached for my binoculars and saw something reflective clinging to her back. "I think I see it! Who put it there, and why?"

"Scientists, researchers—it's hard to say. But tags don't hurt them. Whoever is watching them has their best interest in mind."

"How can you be sure?"

"Interesting question. I'm not sure, but I can't imagine why anyone would want to go to the trouble. They're not easy to tag."

I learned that with whale watching, patience was critical. Whales had their own schedule. At times we went twenty minutes without a sighting. By early afternoon, we had seen a few more humpbacks. Then it got quiet. Others lost interest, busying themselves with booze and chatter as the surf grew choppy. I finally dropped my binoculars to give my shoulders a break.

Just as I thought they'd all disappeared, Ian yelled, "Eleven o'clock!"

"Ian," shouted Lucas. "Is that Millie?"

Even though the whale was a good distance away, it looked enormous.

"Millie?" I asked.

Ian smiled. "I think so. Millie is famous around these parts. Been around for years. The largest any of us have seen anywhere. More than twenty-seven meters—ninety feet."

Ian instructed Lucas to turn the boat, cut the motor, and move in closer.

Duncan joined us, wanting an update. As Ian filled him in, she crested from the water once again.

"Millie!" shouted Lucas from above, pointing again—this time to the opposite side of the boat.

"Unbelievable," said Ian. "Folks, gather around. You have no idea how fortunate you are! We've got our largest blue, less than a hundred meters away, giving us the show of a lifetime."

As the others gathered, I asked Ian, "Who named her Millie?"

"Don't know. But sure is good to see her. It's been a while. And never seen her in these parts."

He no longer finished his sentence when her enormous back rolled out from the ocean. Like slow motion, her body gently rolled farther and farther out of the water, curving, arching, before sliding gently back into the sea. Our boat rolled from side to side in her wake.

I dropped the binoculars, feeling a surge of blood rush from my brain to my toes. I didn't feel chills. I felt warmth like a different form of energy pulsing through my body. A stream of tears suddenly cascaded down my face. I didn't wipe them away. The power of this whale confirmed what I needed to do. I needed to find Carlos. And soon.

"Wow, she is spectacular," I said. "How old do you think she is?"

"Not sure. Could be seventy, could be ninety. This has been a most unusual day. Not only a large number of sightings but to see Millie—and to see her so close! I've never seen her on one of our whale watch trips."

I needed to tell him that I wasn't Sandra.

"What a day!" he shouted, laughter hanging between his words as he left to talk to the entire group. "Folks, you've been some of the luckiest passengers on any of my tour groups. And, no, I don't say that every time! But our time is up, and we'll be heading back in."

Duncan groaned, mumbling a whiny disappointment about stopping just as it was getting good. The others seemed relieved.

After Ian left the group to join Lucas on the bridge, I stopped him. "Sorry to bother you."

"Hello again," he said. "What's up?"

"I have kind of a weird question. If someone wanted to kill a whale, you know, illegally, could they use tracking devices?"

He shook his head. "I suppose they could, but why would they? Why not just spear it on the spot? Although frankly, I haven't heard of anyone killing blues in these parts—at least not since the whaling days. If someone tried killing a blue, they'd be putting themselves at risk. Especially if they hit a female. If a female is hurt, the males will circle her to protect her."

"And the females—do they protect the males?"

"Only their young, not their mate."

Interesting, I thought. Maybe true with some humans, although never having had children or a mate worthy of protection, I wouldn't know.

Whether or not Ian's battle of the sexes story was accurate, I disagreed about the tagging. If a ring of poachers was looking for patterns and opportunities to find multitudes of blues, tracking devices could be useful. From what Carlos told me and what I'd experienced, these poachers could have access to any number of high-tech gadgets. I wouldn't have even been surprised if they had fake IDs, posing as researchers or scientists.

I handed Ian the binoculars. *Keep it simple, Allie.* After all, he was a tour guide, not the poaching police.

CHAPTER 33

⌇

On the way back, we had one final sighting, another humpback. By that time, Bruce and Maureen had drunk a disgusting quantity of beers, noticeable by how their voices and behavior went from annoying to disturbing. At one point Maureen nearly fell overboard attempting to wash her hands and face with seawater after eating a half-melted Hershey bar. Ian flashed a smirk to Lucas, resulting in a bout of unrestrained hysteria.

Gunnar had been mostly silent. After consuming a plethora of pastries, he nodded off in an upright posture. Every time a wave slapped the bottom of the boat, his eyes opened, and he'd let out a grunt that, with my warped imagination, sounded like a constipated elephant.

Duncan was the only passenger who seemed interested in talking to me, but deciphering his brogue proved challenging. I kept my distance, feigning deep concentration over a map of southern Chile that I'd found inside the cabin. By midafternoon, thoughts of a shower and returning to the privacy of my hotel room had me checking my watch.

Dark clouds from the north sent ominous shadows across the sea. I grabbed my hoodie, zipping it to my neck. *La Estrella* began rocking and rolling. My motion sickness meds worked like pharmaceutical genies, even when I moved to the bow. We hit thirty- or forty-foot waves straight on, the hull splitting them in half, sending masses of water overhead. I gripped the railing tight as my legs bowed and bent to keep me vertical.

Ian's voice, faint behind the roar of the waves, startled me. "Hey, are you sure you want to be up here? It's getting nasty! You better hang on tight."

"I'm a bit wet, but I love this," I shouted.

Ian, also holding the railing, answered, "I don't hear that too often! Do you want an extra jacket? I've got one in the cabin."

"I'll be okay."

"A storm is coming, but hopefully we'll get back near the harbor before it catches us. Hope so, anyway. Tight fit inside the cabin."

Both of us glanced at the retirees from hell hunkering in and around the back cabin.

I laughed. "Guess you get all kinds on these tours?"

"That's for sure. Personally, I wish we could ban alcohol—but that would put us out of business."

"How many years have you been doing this?'

"What?" he asked.

"How long have you had this business?" My voice rose and fell as we crested over another wave.

"This is our seventh year. Before that, I worked for a tour company. One of many that didn't survive. It's a tough industry." After a pause, he continued, "I think you wanted to say something earlier before we saw the whales."

I'd been ready to tell him how I lied about my name, but my courage had faded. I'd gone on a four-hour boat ride as an imposter. I lied. I was a total phony. It would have been so much easier to stay quiet, but if I wanted to find Carlos, I needed to form some line of trust. I cleared my throat.

"I, well, I wanted to tell you that my name isn't exactly Sandra."

Ian studied me as if trying to figure out who or what I was all about. I wasn't a mind reader, but I saw a hint of a smirk. Either he thought I was psychotic or experiencing some adventurous midlife crisis as another person.

"So I'm sorry I didn't tell you earlier. My name is really Allison Bennett—but I go by Allie."

"And Sandra, apparently."

"Uh, yeah. That was a first. I can explain—"

"You don't need to. As we were saying earlier, I meet all sorts of people. Names mean nothing. People come, people go. What people do before they step on my boat or after is none of my business

"Only thing is," he said, refitting his fisherman's cap over his head, "I am kind of wondering why you decided to tell me now since the trip is almost over."

"Fair question."

"Which you don't have to answer."

"I will. I want to."

He waited while I collected my thoughts. The others were unusually quiet. I glanced toward the stern and saw Maureen leaning over the railing, puking again. Bruce rubbed her back with slow, loving caresses.

"I guess the chocolate didn't help her seasickness," he said. "Well, at least they've stopped quarreling."

"The reason," I said, "besides feeling terrible about my dishonesty, is that I need to ask for your help. I know that sounds terrible coming from someone who lied to you. But you asked. So here goes. I have come here, to southern Chile, to find the very man who saved your life. I need to find Carlos Costanera."

"That's an odd coincidence."

"Yes."

"And it sounds serious."

"It kind of is. You mentioned you'd like to see him again."

"I would, but Allie—I wouldn't know where to look. Can you tell me what this is about? I mean, if it's some torrid love affair gone south, I have to be honest—"

"God, no, nothing like that. It's about blue whales. Honestly, it's complicated and may be better if you don't know the details."

Ian looked before mumbling, "Uh-oh."

Suddenly, another massive wave crashed across the side of the boat, sending a strong spray over our heads. This one threatened to take me with it.

"Well," he said, grabbing my hand, "that is our warning. It's not safe out here. Can we continue this chat later, maybe after we get back?"

"Sure."

"Over dinner, if you're free. Don't know about you, but I'll be starving by the time we dock."

"That'd be nice. Can I go casual?"

He pointed to himself. "Definitely. This is a fishing town. No white tablecloths for miles. But hope you don't mind hanging around after everyone gets off. We have to clean and shore up the boat. It'll take fifteen to thirty minutes."

"I'm happy to help if I can. Least I can do after giving you a phony name."

"Don't worry about that. But no thanks on the help. We got it down to a system."

"Do you want to include Lucas?"

"Nah, he's got to get back to his wife and their rambunctious three-year-old."

"Okay," I said, trying to contain my excitement.

CHAPTER 34

I hung around for a while, watching everyone get off the boat. Of course, Maureen inquired why I was hanging around. I told her I was waiting to meet a friend for dinner, glancing at my watch as if my mysterious date was late.

It took half an hour for Ian and Lucas to clean the boat. Although not late by Chilean standards, eight at night felt more like bedtime than dinnertime. When we reached a restaurant called La Pescadora, Ian said it was a local hangout, and what it lacked in décor was well compensated by their seafood and pasta dishes. My stomach gurgled with anticipation.

We joined a small crowd waiting for tables, standing shoulder to shoulder. Whiffs of garlic and seafood permeated the locale while voices and cookware clamored in a kitchen so small I wondered how anyone could stand to work there. Inside the nine-table restaurant, guests seemed oblivious to the noise level, adding to it with their clinking of glasses and silverware, raucous laughter, and conversation.

Waiting for anything has never been my forte. But if food is the object of my impatience, especially near bedtime, I have been known to become a public menace. Here, the sound of too many people dining in a tiny space lacking acoustical cushioning had my nerves teeter toward insanity. At the risk of adding one more reason for Ian to feel complete contempt toward me, I was ready to suggest going somewhere else when a young lady led us to a table near the back.

About two seconds after we sat down, I asked for bread. As soon as those freshly baked rolls hit my palate, I was healed of all grumpiness. I didn't even care about the noise. Over a bottle of cab, we shared sketches of ourselves—siblings, careers, and travels. He casually mentioned a brief marriage.

"You? Ever been married?"

"No," I answered too quickly. "Came close once. But that, as the old cliché goes, is ancient history." I found rote responses generally effective in diffusing questions, especially on topics I preferred not to delve into. And, fortunately, it worked. By the time our meal arrived, we'd moved on to whales.

"You were very enthusiastic when we saw that first blue."

"That's got to be a normal reaction, right? I mean they're impressive animals!"

"They are, but you'd be surprised. People generally get excited, but I can sense when someone has more of a visceral reaction, something deeper than a momentary, passing excitement. Cameras and binoculars fall. Shoulders rise and bodies lean closer to the rail. Tears often enter the equation."

I couldn't help but laugh. "You nailed it. Especially when we saw Millie."

Sipping wine, he grinned. "I couldn't believe she was that far in."

Our food arrived just as I was going to ask him about Carlos. The *locos* (abalone) were so tender and the romaine leaves crisp and crunchy with only a mild hint of anchovy. I knew I had better get to the point despite my gastronomic ecstasy.

"About Carlos," I said, hesitating.

Ian reached for the wine, topping mine off first. "Yes, I'm curious to hear how you knew him and why you want to find him."

"I met him earlier this year, shortly after arriving in Chile. He taught me a lot about whales. I was impressed by his efforts to protect them."

"You mean as in ocean pollution, ship strikes, that sort of thing?"

"Actually, more like protecting them from pirate fishermen or poachers. He explained that the blues are disappearing rapidly off the southern coast. Maybe you already know about this?"

"We heard reports about fewer whales feeding and breeding around these parts, which we've attributed to the warmer ocean temperature affecting the food chain. But the idea of pirates and poachers seems far-fetched. If anyone was killing endangered species, it'd be major news. I've never heard anything about this, and I'm running a whale watching business. Besides, there are laws to protect them."

"I'm aware of that, Ian, but something is going on. And it's powerful. Carlos and some of his friends aren't merely speculating. And what's really scary is the poachers know someone's on to them," I said, pausing to collect my courage. "Carlos and his team haven't reported any of this because of the risks. They're trying to obtain sufficient proof. I don't know if I should even be sharing this, but I want to be upfront with you."

"Hence—Sandra, not Allie."

"Yes. I had to. I've been threatened. Others, including a friend of mine in California, have been too. I'll spare you the details, but it made me run. I actually returned home because of the threats. But eventually, I realized I had to do something, and I couldn't do much from the northern hemisphere. So I came back. Carefully. Through the back door, you might say."

"Back door?"

"Long story, but the trip involved a lot of driving. With all that's happened recently, it's hard to know who I can trust. That's why I told you my name was Sandra. Anyway, I need to find Carlos. He moved out of the house he'd been renting and has pretty much left without a trace. This probably doesn't make any sense."

I dropped my head to stare at the white linen napkin blanketing my lap, trying to stop an unexpected urge to cry. All of this seemed so pathetic. Me trying to find someone I barely knew, asking someone else I didn't know to help.

Nancy Rhodes

Ian looked around. "You're making sense. But it still seems crazy."

The waiter returned and asked if we wanted more wine or dessert. We declined both. After he brought the bill, I pulled out my wallet.

"I invited you," said Ian, grabbing the check.

"It's the least I can do, considering what I'm asking you to do."

Ian sighed. "The whales are my livelihood. I don't know how I can help, but I would like to see Carlos again. I'll do what I can."

"You got a boat. That's a start."

"That I do," he said, handing his card to the waiter before I could grab my wallet.

Outside, the salty air carried sour whiffs of brine as the tide receded, leaving ridges of mud amid rocks and driftwood.

When Ian said he'd start asking around to inquire if anyone had seen Carlos, I shook my head. "Not a good idea."

"How else can we find him?"

"By finding the blues."

"I thought we did that today."

"We need to head farther out. Away from the channels or at least south and closer to the Corcovado Gulf. I know they don't generally travel in big groups, but if we can find areas where they're feeding or breeding in great numbers, it might get us closer to Carlos. I know, it's a long shot, but that's where we should start. And I have another request."

"What's that?"

"I need, well, I want to learn more about whales and the sea. I'll pay you what I can."

"Allie, I'm a boat captain. I lead tours. I'm not a scientist."

"But you know whales."

"Yes. That I do."

After we walked a couple of blocks, Ian asked about my lodgings.

"Nothing fancy, but it works."

The wind had died down, and the evening felt unusually warm. Even a few stars twinkled in the distance.

"Ian," I said, "I know I'm asking a lot, but this is important. If you can help me, I'll pay for your gas and whatever else."

"I just don't want to get your hopes up. I'll take you out as much as I can, but of course I have to put my business first. I think we might be able to go out later next week. Wednesday or Thursday if the weather cooperates. Lucas is going to be out of town, so we haven't booked any tours."

"That'd be awesome," I said, resisting the urge to hug him or do a happy dance right there in the street. "Here's my cell number, but you may have better luck calling me through the motel. I don't know the number offhand."

"Which one? I can find the number."

"El Marino, I think it's called."

"I've heard of it. Shall I walk you there?"

"No, I'm good. But thanks."

The minute I got to my room, I made a beeline for the bathroom. While on the toilet, I looked across my shoulder at the mirror. Something seemed different. My eyes still had more lines and age spots than I thought possible for anyone under ninety, but they kind of looked soft and peaceful. Examining myself in a way one only does in private, I thought perhaps I had shed a few pounds of emotional baggage. Standing up, I leaned in close. Besides the lady whisker I should have plucked before dinner, I saw something in my face that damn well resembled hope.

CHAPTER 35

⋯⟨⟩⋯

The invite came a week later. I'd been growing restless, concerned Ian might have second thoughts about helping out some gringa who lied about her identity and claimed some badass conspiracy theory about missing whales. But when he called and invited me out the following day for our first adventure, I realized I was the one with doubts. How could I afford to pay him for private charters? What was I thinking? My little fantasy might not only be a waste of time but could zap whatever *dinero* I had left.

On our first outing, the sea grew cranky after only two hours, and we were forced to return without a single sighting. I tried, unsuccessfully, to hide my disappointment. Another two weeks passed before Ian had a free day to take me out again.

The third time we went to sea coincided with Earth Day in the States. I figured that had to count for something. Maybe the universe would appreciate even the lamest of efforts from some to save our planet by blessing me with a plethora of whales. Conditions were optimal; no breeze, no clouds to cast shadows, and calm water with only a few whitecaps.

Before long, Mother-Universe complied. We witnessed at least fourteen different humpbacks, providing hours of entertainment with their breaching, tail slapping, and spy-hopping activities. Ian explained the difference between the southern right whales and the humpbacks since they were close in size.

"Southern right whales don't have fins on their back," he said. "The humpbacks have a small dorsal fin." I figured that was all good and dandy, but unless the whale breached right next to us, I'd still be confused. Regardless, it didn't matter. I wasn't there for humpbacks and southern rights.

After lunch, while staring at the horizon, my mind strangely drifting between thoughts of Jeff and memories of my sister, at first I heard, but later saw, an enormous column of spray expel from a blue whale fewer than twenty feet away. I pointed and yelled to Ian, who'd been busy unraveling a rope.

"Woo-hoo," I screamed, renewed with hope.

"Woo-hoo is right!" he echoed.

We watched her blow two more times before disappearing beneath the surface. And although we saw no more, I couldn't contain my joy. "This is only the beginning," I said as we began to motor back to the harbor.

Ian nodded. "Hope you're right, gringa."

Within a matter of weeks, heavy rains pounded the earth and sea, sending a majority of tourists back to drier pastures and leaving Ian more available for private whale watch excursions. We fell into a routine of heading out two and sometimes three times a week. I was open about my finances, so we agreed that I would pay for his gas and treat him to dinner at least once a week.

We kept our adventures under wraps, except for Lucas. I would have loved to share my excitement with Jeff but couldn't risk it. He had been through enough. Since arriving on the island of Chiloé, I only talked to him once. I was relieved to hear he had not received any more threats, but I still wanted to be cautious in case his or my phone was bugged. He wanted to know where I was and what I'd been up to. I told him I was having a great time and not to worry. He probably saw through my vague responses but didn't push for more. I hoped my secrets were not wedging a greater space between us. Jeff was still my best friend. I didn't want to screw that up too.

At the end of April, Ian invited me to stay at his house to save on hotel costs, a no-brainer since my credit cards were dangerously close to their max. He offered the second bedroom, but while showing me the property, I noticed a small outbuilding that looked more private.

"There's no heat and no bathroom," he said.

"If you have a few blankets, that'll work. And for the other, well, it's not that far a jaunt up to the house."

He agreed, and we spent an entire day emptying and cleaning it before moving the second room mattress on top of a makeshift frame of cement blocks and plywood. The shed-turned-bedroom was tiny and not well insulated, with only one electrical outlet. But I loved it. In exchange, I offered compensation by doing light housekeeping, shopping, and occasionally making dinner.

His home was located on a hill seven miles from the harbor. We began using a couple of rusted one-speed bikes that'd been in the shed. Locks weren't necessary. No matter how long we were out at sea, the bikes, left at the harbor, were always there upon our return. Gradually, my calves and quads adjusted to the six-kilometer climb back to the cottage.

A week after moving in, I sold my car.

Ian was a patient teacher. Eventually, I became familiar with terms like "dry weight, beam, gunwale, and sag" and funny acronyms like PFD (personal floating device) and the not-so-welcome PWCs (personal watercrafts). I learned how to operate throttles and when to switch to a trolling motor. I replaced flip-flops with rubber boat shoes and never left the house without SPF-30. And I always dressed in layers no matter how promising the morning looked.

I kept a log, a simple blue-line, college-ruled, spiral notebook. I started each day's journal with the obvious—the date, weather, time, and longitude-latitude coordinates of areas covered. Often I filled the lines with extraneous details about stupid stuff like what we ate for lunch or how a visiting cormorant preferred chunks of tuna salad over stubs of a cheese sandwich. A separate, final paragraph was dedicated to whales. By the end of May, only seven of my sixteen entries exceeded the one-line note stating *no blues today*.

Why I continued to insert "today" was just plain superstition.

Every one of those seven sightings produced the same physiological shifts that I'd experienced the first time: a noticeable intensity or increase of heart rate, a feeling of goosebumps throughout my body, and an uncontrollable dispensing of tears. Nevertheless, after several weeks of only a handful of single sightings, discouragement and frustration threw blankets over my joy. I realized that these small populations would never lead me to Carlos.

May slipped into June, and before I knew it, I'd turned a year older. On my fifty-first birthday, I found myself sitting on my twin bed, staring at my journal. Nine blue whale sightings. Lots of whales, but in nearly five weeks, only nine blues. At this rate, I'd be lucky to find Carlos by my ninetieth birthday. It was time to move on, leave Castro, and head south to Quellón.

As I stuffed my mouth with an endless stream of Cheez-It knockoffs I knew that this would entail making two very challenging decisions. The first—asking someone for money—was something I despised to my core. I had avoided it since I turned seventeen and bought an old Vega with a million miles and a bad radiator. The car lasted about a tenth of the time it took to pay off the loan with my dad.

The second decision was whether or not I wanted to include Ian or try to do this alone. Since I stupidly sold my car, I could use his help. But it would be a long distance to haul his boat. Although it wasn't tourist season, we were entering the heart of winter, which offered its own challenges. But how could I ask him to leave his business and home when I didn't know how long we'd be gone? After an hour-long assessment of the pros and cons, I decided to ask. He could say no.

After eating the last of the fake-cheese crackers, I called Jeff. He agreed to lend me three grand, but I sensed some irritation when I didn't explain why I needed it. After hanging up, I sat quiet and motionless until my toes went numb and my knees felt like a pair of twisted licorice ropes.

A week went by until I saw Ian again. We headed out before sunlight on an unusually calm day. Finally, as we were approaching the Curaco de Vélez peninsula, I shared my plan. We'd reached our farthest-out destination ever and were giddy with anticipation of sightings. I'd barely finished explaining what I wanted to do when he commented how he'd love to accompany me—albeit if only for a couple of weeks.

"Awesome! What will we do about a boat? Can you bring yours?"

"No, we can't do that. I don't have a trailer. We'll have to find something there."

"I've arranged for a wire," I said, "so I'll have some funds. But it's going to be a challenge. We'll need lodging and food."

I hoped he understood that lodgings would be basic. Might even mean sharing a room. "We'll figure it out," I said, feigning some absurd level of confidence.

"Yup," he answered, sounding more gringo than ever. "How soon were you thinking of going?" Before I could answer, a whale's blow sprayed mist into the air only ten feet from our boat. It was a humpback. After the blow, it dived below and then rose again, this time showing off with a full out-of-water breach.

"Wow!"

"Yes," he responded. "¡*Espectacular*! As much as I love blues, I never tired of watching the humpbacks breach. They give some of the best shows."

"Maybe she's saying goodbye. Some kind of parting gift," I said, smiling at Ian. "And to answer your question—as soon as we can."

"Couple of days then," said Ian. "I'll need to settle some things with Lucas."

The whale never resurfaced. I grabbed a pen from the bottom of my pack and began writing. This entry would be a long one.

Two hours later we saw the familiar rainbow of *palafitos* on the

Castro harbor. Feeling nostalgic, I inhaled the salty air and stretched out my arms wide and high. Castro had brought me Ian. Hopefully, Quellón would bring me Carlos.

CHAPTER 36

⚬⚬⚬

We left the next morning before sunrise. Of course it was raining, but rain was something anyone living in southern Chile accepted. Back on Route 5, otherwise known as the continuation of the Pan-American Highway, Ian filled me in on what he knew about Quellón. He'd been once before. Nice place if you're into fishing but not a tourist destination. He'd spent a week there with a couple who he met hiking and was hoping they still lived there. They had a boat, he said. Not a big one, but adequate.

We stopped where a sign marked the end of the Pan-American Highway. Ian explained that the highway covered about thirty thousand miles within nineteen different countries. Our next stop was Quellón. Meanwhile, sheets of rain hit our windshield from every direction. The wipers couldn't keep up.

"Do you even remember their names?" I said as Ian drove us up yet another one-way street. I was getting annoyed. We'd driven more than half an hour trying to find their home. I wondered if Ian really had any idea where these people lived.

"Rodney and Parker. Can't remember their last name," he said, his nose practically touching the windshield.

"Are Parker and his wife retired?"

"Rodney is the guy and Parker's the woman, and I don't think they were actually married. I think they are retired. Parker's the one with the boat. She knew more about fishing than most of the fishermen I know."

We reached yet another dead-end street, this one unpaved. Ian was in the middle of a three-point turn when our front tire sank into a mud pit. The tire spun endlessly sending Pollock-like streaks on to the windows. We were stuck.

"FRACK!" I blurted to no one in particular but louder than intended.

Ian started laughing. And it wasn't a polite laugh. It had to be the loudest, most obnoxious laugh I'd ever heard. Exuberant bellows, like a deep chest cough, filled the car with every exhalation, followed by a brief silence before tilting his head backward to take in a new breath. After a few minutes, his hands dropped to his belly like his outburst might cause his insides to fall out.

"Well, crap, Ian! Are you just going to have a private party over there while we get swallowed up by a mile of mud?"

He shook his head, turning off the ignition. "We're stuck."

"I know that."

"And I don't know what to do."

"So your answer is to laugh?"

"Well, frack—yes!"

And while I was in no mood to laugh, I allowed a smile to creep across my face. "I guess I am kind of grumpy."

"Hell, yes! You must be hungry."

"I am. I'm so frigging…or fracking hungry my head hurts."

Then I was laughing too. He handed me a bag of cashews. "Here you go, Queen Bee," he said with a cynical smirk.

"Thanks. My favorite."

Looking around, I noticed a house down the road. "I'll go get help."

"No offense, gringa, but I better go. Stay here and eat your nuts."

I watched Ian disappear down the hill through a yard full of overgrown shrubs. And then I waited. And waited. I guess the nuts contained tryptophan, because by the time he returned with help, I'd fallen asleep. The two young men he'd found were carrying planks, which they wedged under the tires. I didn't envy them, especially when they emerged with legs and shoes coated with smelly, slimy mud.

It didn't take long to get out and on our way again.

"We're in luck," said Ian a few minutes later.

I couldn't imagine what he could possibly consider lucky at this point. Perhaps he saw a launderette, a hotel, or a giant hose? Perhaps a restaurant? Looking at—and smelling—his mud-stained legs, I doubted a food establishment was involved.

"Those two guys know Parker," he said. "I have her address, and we're close!"

"No way! And you tell me this now?"

"Yes, way."

"¡*Fantástico*!"

"Apparently, Rodney is no longer in the picture. They were kind of vague, so I don't know if he died or they split up. I'll clean up a bit at that gas station ahead, and then we can grab something to eat before visiting her."

Despite eight ounces of cashews sitting in my belly like a can of Crisco, I was thrilled by the thought of an actual meal.

CHAPTER 37

P arker Primrose lived in a two-story, wood-plank home ten miles from town. She bragged about her eighty-one years with good reason. Her mind and body were decades younger. She stood a little over five feet and, at most, weighed a hundred pounds. A blondish-white braid fell nearly the full length of her back. The only giveaway to her years was her well-weathered skin.

Parker remembered Ian immediately, inviting us in without hesitation. She'd been born in England but lived most of her life in Chile. She spoke English and Spanish perfectly with only a slight Chilean accent. After offering us a choice of hot or cold tea, she led us into her living room where a crackling fire filled the room with warmth. Ian scooted his chair closer to dry his soaked legs.

"How did you two meet?" I asked.

"One day," said Parker, "I was scheduled to take a group of chartered guests out fishing but woke up with a high fever. Knowing I wouldn't be able to do the trip, I went to the harbor before daybreak to find a replacement."

"And she found me," said Ian, grinning from ear to ear.

"He didn't hesitate for a moment," she said, looking my way. "And since his boat was on the smaller side and definitely not clean, he followed me to my boat and guests. Two hours later he was greeting them as if that was the plan all along. And that," she said, leaning forward to pat Ian's shoulder, "was the beginning of a splendid friendship."

"What a nice story," I said. "I'm not surprised. He's been equally kind and accommodating to me."

"Yes? In what way?"

"Oh," I sighed. "That's a long story." I glanced at Ian, wondering how much to share.

"Oh wonderful! I love a good story. But let me get you something to eat. I'm sure you're both hungry."

"We just stopped at El Pez Feliz, but thanks," he said.

"Never heard of it. Happy Fish seems like an odd name. Were the fish on your plate smiling?"

He laughed. "Well, not sure how happy the fish were, but they sure made my stomach happy. Allie had empanadas."

When Parker asked what we were doing in Quellón, Ian told her we were looking for whales.

Parker's eyebrows lifted. "Did all the whales suddenly leave Castro or wherever it is you came from?"

"I'm particularly interested in blue whales," I said. "Ian agreed to help me look for some large groups that might be feeding in and around the gulf."

I didn't need to tell her about Carlos. If things worked out, that would come later.

"This woman is serious about whales," said Ian, smiling. "We spent a lot of days during the past three months looking. Most of the time we couldn't get out far enough. Not sure if it was weather or water temperature. We didn't see many."

"I've heard there's been quite a few in the gulf recently," said Parker.

"That's encouraging," I said.

"I couldn't bring my boat here," said Ian. "Do you still have yours?'

"Oh, *mi hijo,* no. I sold *Mirabel* many years ago. My body just can't do boats anymore. But you can find someone down at the port. You will find plenty of hungry fishermen down there."

"Sorry, Parker. I bet that was a hard decision."

"Hell, nothing to be sorry about. I had all the years I ever wanted on that boat. And then some. I don't miss it. Well, maybe I miss the thrill of seeing the big whales like we used to or catching a big old Patagonian toothfish. Enough of this reminiscing. Do you two have a place to stay?"

Of course, we didn't. We hadn't even discussed it. I presumed we would bunk up in a hostel—if one existed. I waited for Ian to say something.

"No problem. You can stay here," she said, chuckling. "There are two rooms upstairs. Well, or one if you prefer," she said with an exaggerated wink. "I'm a lonely old widow and would love the company. You can stay as long as you'd like."

Dropping his head slightly, Ian replied, "We'll take the two rooms. Thanks, Parker. I won't be staying too long. I'll need to return in a couple of weeks."

I wanted to offer to pay for my room, but my less than three grand would disappear fast enough just paying for food, gas for the boat, and daily essentials.

Parker led us to our rooms, stopping to show us the bathroom and a small linen closet where she instructed us to help ourselves to towels and sheets. After the tour, she insisted we join her downstairs for some Chilean wine.

After several minutes of chatter about the weather, boats, and local gossip, Ian asked if her husband, Rodney, had died.

"Rodney? Hell, that bastard is still alive. He left me years ago, moved to England, or maybe it was Ireland. Don't know, and I sure as the Almighty don't care. He wasn't my husband, thank God!"

Ian looked over to me and grinned. I winked back.

"I did marry eventually. My Denny was a lovely chap. We'd only been married six years when his heart decided it was done. He collapsed right over there on the kitchen floor. One minute we were standing there laughing about a woodpecker trying to drill his way into a steel pole, and the next minute he was gone."

"Oh, I'm so sorry," I said, feeling the irony that the good one died while the scoundrel hadn't.

"Well, I wish I'd had found him sooner or that he could have lived longer, but I'm just happy I had him when I did. Never been happier. You know, some people never get to experience that kind of love. However short, I'm glad I did."

Painfully true I thought.

⤙∽⤚

"She's a character," I said to Ian, walking to a nearby store.

"I hope I'm half that sharp at her age," he said, zipping up his sweatshirt.

Parker's generosity and credibility merited complete openness from us. Eventually we'd tell her about our desire to find Carlos and why. She'd even offered to introduce us to a sea captain friend who might help us. After loading our shopping basket with the items on her grocery list, Ian grabbed a bottle of vermouth.

"For Parker?" I asked.

"Yep. I noticed a near-empty bottle on her booze cart."

"Nice," I said picking it up and looking at the price. "And generous!"

"No worries, AB. I'm getting this."

"AB? No one's called me by my initials before. Does that mean I should start calling you IT? Taylor's your last name, right?"

"Close. It's Thompson, you crazy gringa."

Walking back to the house, I asked about his parents. Ian's father was Australian, his mother Spanish and Irish. They both still lived in what he called "The Gong," which made me chuckle.

"Wollongong. It's in New South Wales, a seaside city less than an hour from Sydney. My parents met at the university there. I left when I was nineteen. It was too industrial, too crowded."

"Why southern Chile?"

"A woman. A Chilean woman."

"Didn't work out, huh?"

"Exactly. But worth the heartache. I was meant to live in southern Chile. *Quedare toda mi vida, si puedo.*"

"Got that. You'll stay all your life if you can," I said.

"*Muy bien,* gringa."

⁓

Two days later Parker introduced us to a couple of fishermen. Unfortunately, they needed their boats, because this was their livelihood. One lost day could mean no food on the table. I understood despite my growing disappointment.

The next day our luck changed when Parker introduced us to an old sea captain who went by Captain Jack even though his given name was Nicolas. His old-country Spanish proved challenging for me to understand. Parker helped translate, telling us he agreed to let us join him on his boat. We found this surprising since he was a serious fisherman, fishing six days a week, beginning at five every day. He made it clear he would not go out on Sundays. Ever. Sundays, he told Parker, were for family and God.

The Captain's English was limited to a few common greetings and an equal number of swear words, so Parker and Ian did most of the talking. Ian explained our interest in finding blue whales and that we needed a boat and a captain.

"*!Aaayyy ballenas azules, he visto muchas recientemente!*" Ian, underestimating my Spanish vocabulary, explained that the Captain had seen many blues recently. With outstretched hands demonstrating the enormity of a blue, the old man rolled his eyes, lifting his wiry, gray eyebrows into the weathered and dark creases of his forehead. "*Si puedo, lo hare.*" (If I can, I will.)

While it wasn't a resounding "no," I questioned if Captain Jack would be the right man. Later that afternoon, Ian asked Parker if she thought such a serious fisherman would really be willing to pull in the nets and cut the engine when we spotted whales.

"Without a doubt," replied Parker. "Despite his gruff exterior, that man has a heart of gold. And he loves whales and marine life more than anyone I know. You'll be in good hands with *El Capitán*."

Clapping my hands like an excited child, I turned to Ian. "We finally can get started! I only hope this will lead us to Carlos."

"Uh yeah, about that…"

"Uh-oh."

"I'll be able to join you if you head out this week, but I just heard from Lucas. I need to return to Castro no later than June twentieth. We've got a big group coming in."

"In winter?"

He nodded.

"That's less than two weeks away."

"I know. I'm sorry. But these guys booked us for a week. Can't turn that down."

I tried to look understanding. I didn't want him to feel bad even if I had no idea how I could make it without him.

"What about you, Allie? Any idea how long you'll stay?" he asked.

I had no idea. "As long as necessary," I said. *Or until my money runs out.*

The following Monday we joined Captain Jack for our first trip outside of Quellón. In typical Ian fashion, he started calling our host CJ. I thought it lacked respect, so most of the time I called him the Captain or *El Capitán*.

We didn't see blues but spotted some southern right whales and, as we were returning, a pod of humpbacks. I couldn't contain my excitement now that we had a boat and a captain. But soon I'd be on my own with an old man who barely spoke English.

"You'll be fine," Ian said over dinner one night at Parker's. I wasn't convinced, and, despite feeling some excitement about what lay ahead, I dreaded my friend's departure. My eyes dropped to my lap as I began a course of napkin origami to quiet my soul.

I wanted to believe him. Or look like I did.

"Yes, of course," I said, looking at the lump of one seriously crumpled napkin. "Today was perfect, so calm." *Focus on the positive, Allie.* "Can't wait to go out again."

"But no blues?" Parker asked.

"No, but we will. It's just a matter of time," I said, emphasizing the *we*.

A couple of hours later, while lying on my bed, reading through my journal, I heard a knock.

"Come in, Ian," I said.

"Hi, AB."

"Hi," I echoed. The ensuing silence felt ridiculous, but I didn't care. I was too sad to speak.

"I guess you're not too excited to see me leave."

"I knew this was the plan. But I'm just not happy about it. You're leaving in a week, right? So maybe one or two more trips?"

Watching him sigh before pretending to clear his throat, I knew more bad news was on the way.

"Uh, about that Allie, Lucas called again. They're coming early. I have to leave tomorrow."

"Tomorrow?"

I watched him inhale, hold his breath, and let out a long exhale.

"I'll try to come back in a few weeks. But I hope you understand this is how I make my living."

He was right. I knew I was acting selfish. But that damn me-gene was too powerful to be merciful.

"Who are these people? The king and queen of England?"

"There's no king of England, gringa. At least not yet."

I knew it was a stupid comment. I knew it, and I felt like shit for being so self-centered. Guilt rose to my chest like some highly charged electric probe, poking and pinching every inch of my heart.

"Smart-ass. I know that."

We shared another minute of silence—a minute that might have lasted the entire night had we not simultaneously turned to one another, our faces twitching from grimaces before melting to smiles.

CHAPTER 38

⁓⦾⁓

The next morning I followed Ian outside after he'd said good-bye to Parker. A friend of Parker's was driving him to the airport and had just pulled up in front of her home.

"Wait a minute," he said. "I forgot something." He disappeared into the house while Parker's friend, a young woman named Graciela, introduced herself before opening her trunk. I thought about telling her not to bother since at most he'd have a tiny backpack, but my emotions were so amuck I couldn't speak. I didn't want him to go.

"*Hola, Graciela!*" he shouted, coming out the door with a package in his hand. *"Ya voy, dame un minuto."*

Handing me the package, he said, "Open it quick, Allie. I've got a plane to catch."

"What? I'm the one who should be giving you something!"

I knew what it was before I'd shed the newsprint wrapping. It was the digital camera I'd seen when we visited a thrift shop in town. I never owned one before and knew little about how they worked. I remember admiring it until I saw the price tag. Ian must have seen me even though we had gone our separate ways inside the store.

"Oh, Ian, this is way too generous!"

"It is an Olympus E-5, which is a high-image-quality digital that came out like a year ago. I got a deal on it, but it is a high-end model. You can change the lens, although it didn't come with other lenses. It even has a water-repellent case. Anyway, I think it's time you start photographing your friends out there."

"This is awesome—I still can't believe you got this for me. Well, it'll take me a while to figure it out, but once I do, I'm sure I'll use it lots."

"Wish I could help you with that," he said, offering a final hug.

"I don't know how to thank you. I don't know what to say."

"Well, for now, let's just say *hasta pronto*."

And with that, he was gone. I prayed his departure was temporary and brief.

As FEARED, INITIALLY IAN'S ABSENCE CREATED A LANGUAGE challenge with Captain Jack. The first time we went out I tried talking ridiculously slow in English, adding a few Spanish words now and then. He was so quiet and indifferent I figured he either didn't understand me, didn't like me, or didn't like talking. Finally, I gave up and found a spot on the boat to perch my butt and stare at the sea. Watching, waiting, for whales.

After a couple of trips, I understood that old CJ probably just didn't talk much in any language, at least to women. Sometimes he nodded when I attempted a sentence in Spanish, but mostly he kept to himself. Eye contact seemed out of the question.

We met on Mondays and Fridays, weather permitting. But because we were in the heart of winter, several trips were canceled. June was typically the wettest month, and the last two weeks were no exception. July 2 and July 6 were also called off. Parker had told me that usually in July it didn't rain as much, although it could be cooler.

Mid-July, the rain eased, allowing us to venture out several times in the last half of the month. Sunrise was late, so I didn't have to meet him until about eight. I made sure to be there early every time, greeting him with a thermos of dark coffee and crustless egg salad sandwiches.

The weather gods blessed us for several weeks in a row. By the time August approached, I noticed that CJ showed signs of feeling more comfortable around me. On one occasion when he saw me throw bread crusts to the hovering gulls, I caught him smiling.

Eventually, the Captain tried speaking a few English sentences, like "How are you today, Miss Allie?" He gained confidence more rapidly than most, his sentences turning to paragraphs, his dialogue more complex. And meanwhile I began creating a photographic history, recording what I could when I could. Within weeks, I got so comfortable with the camera I no longer used the automatic setting. Within seconds, I knew the best aperture and speed to capture the sighting of the moment. A steady hand was critical, and I had been blessed with that.

One gray afternoon when we'd been out for hours without seeing any fish or whales, Captain Jack began sharing some local history. Talking more candidly than ever before, he explained how fishermen like himself had lived this lifestyle all their lives. They followed and copied habits and patterns ingrained by generations before them. He spoke with passion, not regret. It became obvious that this was a life he and others fell into and accepted. The only negative sentiment was how things were changing and the fear that his generation might be the last to provide for their families from the sea.

Chewing on the end of a toothpick, he explained that now most young men joined larger fishing outfits, companies that owned huge trawlers, disappearing for months on end. He blamed the large-scale fishing industry for emptying the seas of fish. One of the last things he said that day—in my mind, the saddest—was that the bulk of what they caught ended up in the mouths of people far, far away.

———

IN EARLY AUGUST, WE WERE BLESSED BY AN UNSEASONABLY warm and perfectly beautiful day. The calm ocean surface glistened with reflections of an occasional passing cloud. We experienced a record number of sightings, on par with numbers more common from December to March. My eyes and camera stayed glued to the sea. While the number of sightings thrilled me, it was the variety of whales that electrified my spirit. We saw humpbacks, orcas, and southern rights. Once when we traveled a good thirty miles from shore, we saw blues.

Other fishing boats dotted the marine landscape, but none were there for whales. But just as Parker had predicted, CJ had no problem forfeiting a day's catch despite financial consequences. I counted at least six different blues in one small area.

In his recently mastered blend of Spanish and English, Captain Jack explained the whale's diet. He described masses of tiny shrimp-like creatures swirling in large masses like pink clouds.

"Gringa, the blues swim toward this *comida* and open their large mouths to swallow tons of water and food, then using their…what you call *lengua*?" He stuck his tongue out for clarification.

"Tongue."

"Si, si. They use tongue to scrape krill off baleen plates. You know sticky like peanut butter?"

"Yummy!" I said.

"*Si, deliciosa*," he confirmed, laughing.

I pictured myself floating below the sea, looking up to observe this crazy phenomenon—the largest mammal in the world eating something so tiny. Like filling up on pomegranate seeds, I thought. All those little red jewels requiring tons of effort for so little reward.

Just as we finished our tuna sandwiches, a younger blue rose so close we saw the intricate speckling pattern along its back. The Captain also taught me that markings like these and patterns on the fluke were used to identify and keep track of specific whales. I managed to take at least a dozen photos before she disappeared.

Five minutes later, two more blues appeared.

"*Capitán*," I hollered. "*Mira allí, una enorme.*" Both were large, but the one I pointed to was enormous.

He turned the boat for a better view. Leaning forward, I saw his face break into a big grin. With an uncharacteristically joyful bellow, he said, "*Aha. ¡Eso es Millie! ¡Que suerte ya ha vuelto!*"

"Millie, seriously? I know Millie! I saw her once before—it was my first whale watch trip with Ian and Lucas."

"*Que suerte tuviste.*" (What good luck you had.) How long ago was that, Miss Allie?"

"Three, maybe four months ago."

"*Ella es muy vieja,*" he said with a heavy sigh. "She moves slow just like an old lady." He laughed at his own remark.

"Slow and steady," I added.

I knew blue whales could live up to a hundred years. Watching Millie rise again before taking a shallow dive, I marveled at her years—her history. She'd been born before the start of radio broadcasting or even, ironically, the invention of plastic.

We were within ten or maybe fifteen feet when Millie came up again for air. This time she rose higher than I've ever seen an adult blue whale breach, arching her back before heading down for a dive. With mouths agape, we watched as she slid back into the water, leaving only her fluke held high and straight. Then she did something even more unusual. She let that massive fluke slap the ocean surface with such force that our boat rocked heavily, taking on a couple of inches of water.

"Incredible!" said the Captain as I reached for the bucket.

I began bailing out water with an old, dented bucket, actually enjoying the effort. Even Captain Jack was impressed and surprised by Millie's behavior. Offering to take over with the bucket, he told me he'd never seen a blue behave like that. He didn't know what to make of it.

After months of boat trips, I learned that once I allowed myself to be fully present in the entirety of my experience—enjoying the sights and sounds of the sea…the slurping of waves against the boat, the gulls overhead…the way light came through clouds and made magical patterns on the ocean surface or over a sinking sun— time became irrelevant.

So I don't know if it was seconds after the breach or minutes, but my bailing activity came to a halt when out of nowhere came the deafening roar of a speedboat.

The Captain hollered my name, his voice reflecting such an uncharacteristic urgency I dropped the bucket that then hit my knee. With my heart drumming inside my chest, I was confused by this deafening foreign sound. *What the hell?* This was not exactly ski boat territory.

Twisting to find the location, I suddenly froze. Ahead was not one but two speedboats, their sleek frames traveling at ridiculous speed, both coming straight toward us from opposite directions. When I looked up, I saw Captain Jack waving his hands, motioning for me to get down. Lie down? I couldn't hear his words, but his widened eyes and open mouth signaled trouble. Real trouble.

Before I could lie down and before any logical thought or plan of survival had crossed my horrified mind, both boats were within striking distance. Had there been time, my life might have flashed before my eyes. One boat turned seconds before striking us, twisting into a hard one-eighty and sending a massive wave into our boat. My relief that we weren't hit was short lived. Cold seawater surrounded my ankles. I looked up just as the second boat came so close I was certain it would to take us out.

The boat didn't hit us head-on, but the wake did. We tipped sixty, maybe seventy, degrees. Far enough to capsize. But rather than gently sliding with the boat into the ocean, the force ejected my body. Airborne, my head hit something the consistency of a cement pillar before feeling the shock of fifty-degree water enveloping my body.

Tossing and tumbling underwater, I had no idea which way was up. Briefly, between moments of panic, I wondered if this was payback. Maybe this was what Miguel's wife and daughters felt in their final moments. But a combination of stubbornness and perseverance kept me alive.

I blew into the swirling mass of water, following the direction of bubbles to the surface. Once I took my first welcome gasp of air, I knew I wouldn't have long before hypothermia would take me down once and for all. Already my hands, feet, and lower legs were numb. Within seconds I wouldn't be able to stay afloat.

Twisting my body, I rolled onto my back, thinking a new position might buy me time. I caught sight of CJ's boat bobbing up and down against the waves. From my viewpoint, it seemed empty. Slowly swirling myself around, forcing my limbs to move, I scanned the sea, praying the Captain escaped his sinking boat without harm. For now, I was alone. I tried to scream, but no sound exited from my throat.

My legs transformed into matching anchors, pulling me down against my will. I had partial use of my arms, which I used to try to stay afloat. But soon my neck, then my chin, and finally my nose sank below the water's surface. A welcome warmth spread throughout my limbs.

CHAPTER 39

◆

S till in the ocean, barely conscious, I thought I saw a seagull or pelican, something that caused the light in the water to shift. Then, a strong force—be it God, angels, or Lucifer—tugged at my body, pulling my corpse from the depths of the Pacific. Who or what or even when were not part of my consciousness.

I spent five days in the hospital. I remembered nothing of my stay until the third day when I awoke to find someone who, in my delirium, looked just like Carlos, staring down at me with the most disturbing set of bloodshot eyes. I'd spent months looking for Carlos, and now his ghost, or some apparition, was at my bedside. Had to be the narcotics. Squeezing my eyes and attempting to take a breath, not an easy task with tubes inside my nose, I made my brain focus on counting. I would count to thirty.

But when thirty, then forty seconds had passed, I opened my eyes and this carbon copy version of Carlos Costanera was still at my side.

He reached for my hand. Those callused fingers felt so real. Familiarly real.

I tried to talk, to say his name, but when I moved my lips, nothing happened. I'd gone mute.

"Don't try to talk, Allie. Save your strength," he said.

Some time passed—maybe minutes, maybe hours—when a white-haired woman with a fair complexion edged her way between us. She was looking at a loud machine at my bedside, making notes.

My eyes zeroed in on her scrubs. Dozens of pink flamingos scattered in every which way across her ample breasts and thick waist. I found this funny and heard a hoarse cackle escape my throat.

"Good to see you awake," she said, removing the tubing from my nose. "I'm sure you won't mind this going away."

I nodded, trying to smile.

"So how are you feeling?"

"She can't talk yet," said the man resembling Carlos.

"That's the meds. Give her a bit. She's been through a lot."

"Yes, of course," he said. "I know that."

It was odd hearing them discuss me as if I wasn't there. I began to wonder if this was a dream—or perhaps I'd died and was having an out-of-body experience. I willed my eyes to move, taking in the beige curtain on one side and a window with blinds on the other. Green walls. A small table next to me. On it, a stained hourglass vase filled with a colorful bouquet. Do dead people see such detail in the afterlife?

"Your friend here brought you those," said Pink Flamingos.

"Thank you," I said, more surprised than anyone to hear my own voice.

"Aha! She's back! That didn't take long," he said.

That voice. It was Carlos! I wanted to ask how he'd so magically appeared but struggled to form words.

"Well, three days, but who's counting?" replied Flamingo, whose real name was Frances, according to a pink name tag.

"Three days?" I asked, my voice shrinking to a whisper. *Why is it so hard to talk?*

"Yes, Miss Bennett. You have been here since Sunday. You suffered minor frostbite to your feet, especially your toes. And your lungs were compromised from ingesting an unhealthy amount of seawater. But other than perhaps some permanent loss of sensation in your toes, you were fortunate. Had it not been for Sr. Costanera, I'm afraid we wouldn't be having this conversation."

Carlos looked embarrassed. "I just happened to be in the right place at the right time. But she gets all the credit. What a fighter."

I wanted to ask a hundred questions, but the heaviness inside my head drew me deeper into the pillow.

The next time I came to, I looked around the empty room, realizing what I thought had been a bad dream was an agonizing reality. Reaching to my face, I confirmed the tubes were gone. But tilting my head, I saw a noisy monitoring device flash numbers and graphs in harmony with a pattern of annoying beeps and hisses.

Looking at a window with closed blinds, several thoughts and memories began to seep, unwillingly, into my head. I felt my body immersed in the freezing ocean, tossing and fighting and sinking. Then, as if watching a movie in reverse, I saw a speedboat racing toward us. The Captain yelled a warning, so I turned my head and saw men wearing bandannas over their faces. These visions jolted inside of my body like lightning flashes, terrorizing every nerve.

I heard a scream, wretched and desperate, fill my room. A stabbing sensation pierced my ribs. I twisted to find the call button, and when I did, I pushed it three, maybe five, times.

Where was he? Where was *El Capitán*? My brain couldn't remember. I wasn't even sure if the vision of men in bandannas was real or something I'd experienced in my drug-induced stupor. Did the Captain make it? Maybe he did, or he was later found. Maybe he was in the same hospital!

Eventually, a different nurse, who also spoke English, entered my room. This young man looked tired and perturbed about something or everything.

"Yes? What do you need?" he asked curtly.

"I…I…I need to contact someone. I need to know…was someone else brought into this hospital? I was on a boat with this man. We were attacked. The Captain, his name is Jack. I can't remember his last name. Is he okay?"

"Miss, I just came on duty today and don't know anything about your case. Chances are no one else does either, but if they did, there are rules about discussing other patients. Our concern relates to you, to your medical condition. I am aware you nearly drowned, and you suffered a little frostbite. I've been told you will probably be released later today or tomorrow. Depends on when the physician on duty can see you for an assessment."

"Yes, yes, of course. Thank you. But can you just tell me if you have someone named Jack—"

"No, ma'am. I cannot. Now, if that's it, I've got four other patients to see."

"Oh, okay. But, but can you help me make a phone call?"

He sighed out loud and gave me a look that reminded me where I was. This wasn't a big city hospital. *Dorothy, you're not in Kansas!* No phones in the rooms, and this overworked chap was not about to offer me his cell phone if he had one.

"Never mind," I said, not wanting to hear another whiny, negative response.

The morning dragged on so long I began to plan my escape. I figured if I got up slowly, I could probably dress myself. I had no clue what was outside my door, and as the minutes ticked by, I felt every last bit of my courage sink into the bedsheets.

Around eleven, a doctor arrived. After reviewing the chart and my vitals and listening to my lungs, he said I could leave as long as I would commit to no physical activity for two weeks.

"*¿Desea que nos llamemos alguien para llevarte?*" He asked if I wanted them to call someone to pick me up.

"*Si, por favor, llamemos al Señor—*"

"That won't be necessary. I'm here." It was Carlos! Pushing a wheelchair, he said, "Sorry I couldn't get here earlier."

Tears blurred my vision. A vague memory of Carlos at my bedside returned. I thought that had been a dream. Carlos? I spent all that time looking for him, and he was here?

After trying to find my voice again, I cleared my throat and whispered, "Nothing to be sorry about. I can't believe it's you. I can't believe you are here!"

"Well, believe it, *mi amiga*. I'm here, and I'm taking you back to Parker's."

"Carlos, my head feels weird. And, and…I can't remember everything. But, well, I know we were hit by another boat. Wh-what happened to the Captain? Did they find him? Please, please tell me…."

"Allie, they're looking. When the paramedics came, you were mumbling his name. The authorities have been trying to contact his family."

"This is my fault. This can't be good. I mean, if they haven't found him, I don't know what I'll do if…if…well, you know."

"Stop it. It's not your fault, and there's nothing you can do. Besides, you never know. You weren't too far out when I found you. He probably made it back."

"Wait a minute…you saved me?"

"Yes," he said, nodding.

I didn't remember Carlos pulling me out of the ocean. I didn't remember lying on the sand with Carlos pushing hard onto my chest and covering my lips with his mouth to give me air. He told me all of this as we drove away from the hospital. My breathing had actually stopped, he explained.

None of this mattered. My initial joy to have him back in my life turned to resentment. Because of me, the man who'd given up feeding his family to entertain my search for whales was most likely dead, a lost corpse in the Pacific. I should have died. Carlos shouldn't have interfered.

By the time we approached Parker's house, my mind went to an even darker place. Miguel's family. Miguel's wife and daughters drowned while, or because, I was having an affair with him. Now the Captain might have drowned because of my selfishness. I was cursed. Innocent people died because of me. And although my eyes focused outside the window, I saw nothing. I was blinded by my sinful, selfish tears.

Late afternoon we finally arrived back at Parker's house, where she greeted me as soon as we pulled in to the driveway. It took both of them to help me inside. My balance was off.

After a brief rest on the bed, Parker helped me into the shower. Once I got steady, she left. She waited outside the bathroom door. I let the hot water run over me until my skin turned bright red. I felt nothing. *Where the hell had Carlos come from?* After turning off the water, I yanked the towel so hard the curtain rod bounced onto the floor.

"You okay?" Parker shouted.

I lied. "*Bien. Todo bien.*"

"Well, *mi hija*, when you're all done, come on out. You need to eat. Or would you like me to bring it to you so you can rest in bed?"

"I've had enough time in bed. Days, apparently."

After slowly pulling on baggy sweats and a loose shirt, I went into the kitchen.

"Smells good," I said, moving past the kitchen once I saw she and Carlos were in the living room.

Carlos sat on the sofa next to a small table with crackers, cheese, an open bottle of red wine, and two partially filled glasses. He handed one to Parker.

"Do you want a small splash?" Carlos asked me.

Parker shook her head. "Are you sure that's a good idea, Carlos?"

"Yes," I said before Carlos could respond. "More than a splash. Thank you. I'll be fine, Parker."

Carlos scooted over, making a space for me. After handing me a glass and pouring some for himself, he asked if I felt better.

"The shower felt good," I said. *Better?* Better than what? Better than being dead.

Parker pointed to the cheese plate. "Help yourself."

I went for the wine first. I couldn't remember the last time I'd had any.

"Tastes good," I said, swirling the velvety tannins across my tongue.

"It's one of my favorites," said Carlos. "But go easy. Parker's right. You probably should be drinking water, not wine. Can I get you some?"

"Later on the water," I said, grabbing my wine glass again.

"Be careful, my friend. Your body has been through quite a bit."

"Carlos, I'm fine." But I wasn't.

Parker shifted in her chair.

"I still can't even believe you're here."

"I was worried, Allie. I'm still worried. I never imagined they'd sink so low."

"Carlos, they set fire to a house. They attacked me. They threatened all of us."

He nodded.

"Where are you staying?" I asked.

"At a friend of a friend's—not far from here."

I smiled, hoping I looked more sober than I felt. "Where were you all this time? I kept trying to follow whales, hoping they would lead me to you."

"And they did. Sort of."

"That's not even funny," I said.

"I know. Sorry. I went to Japan."

"Whaaaat? God, I was sure on the wrong track. *Japan?* Why?"

As I waited for his answer, Parker got up. She told us dinner would be ready soon, so I laid off the cheese.

"Thanks, Parker. Need help?" asked Carlos.

"Nope, go on and fill her in. It'll be about ten minutes."

I grabbed the wine bottle. Carlos shook his head in disgust.

"So," he said. "A while back I joined an organization based out of California that's been trying to track down poachers. Someone got a report that there was a fish market north of Tokyo that might be selling blue whale meat."

"Were they?'

"Never found out for sure. We suspected one vendor in particular, but by the time we approached, there was only the usual eel, tuna, squid, and scallops. When we approached the table on our first day, we saw a bare spot on their table. That's highly unusual, at least if it's left bare for more than a few minutes. Table space is a precious commodity in those markets. Of course, an empty spot isn't proof they were getting ready to lay out whale meat. We returned the next day, but that vendor did not."

"Sounds incredibly frustrating, especially after traveling all that way."

"Well, it wasn't a total waste. I met some interesting people, and it's always good to have connections across the globe."

We talked more about his time in Japan. Just as my eyelids started to fall, Parker announced the meal was ready. Carlos extended his well-calloused hand to assist me off the couch.

Parker's *casuela* was better than I'd had at any restaurant. The broth contained the right amount of seasoning, the potatoes were cooked perfectly, and the beef practically melted inside my mouth.

"God, this is good, Parker," I said.

"It's my go-to food. Has a little bit of everything, at least what I can get this time of year."

We all grew silent for a few minutes, with only the clanking of forks against plates to fill the void. I couldn't relax. Enjoying a good meal, drinking wine—it all felt wrong. We should be out looking for the Captain. And I had so many questions. Serious questions. Where would I start?

When we finished, I told Carlos I needed to talk. We walked into the living room. Parker stayed behind, insisting she wanted to wash the dishes before joining us.

"I don't know where to begin, Carlos, but I have questions."

"Of course you do. But I don't know a lot. I'll answer what I can. Only thing is the doc told me to make sure you don't overdo it."

"I'm feeling better," I said, tipping the wine glass upside down to drain the last sip. "But I'm still grasping the fact *you* are here. And that you appeared from nowhere and pulled me from the ocean. I mean, if I wasn't here talking to you and someone told me that the man I'd been searching for months happened to be out on the ocean when I needed rescuing, I'd think they were *loco!*"

Carlos stared at me, his eyes compassionate. "Divine intervention, perhaps?" he said, smiling.

"Why were you there? Where'd you come from?"

"I had come down from Puerto Montt last week. Straight from Japan. Exhausted as hell, but I heard the krill were unusually heavy in the gulf and had to check it out. I'd been out the day before but didn't stay out long, because jet lag hit me hard."

Carlos paused to empty his glass. "That day, the day you were hit, I had set out early. When I later called in to register my coordinates, I heard a distress call. Since I assumed I could get there faster than anyone else, I turned around. As I raced toward the area, the same person called on the radio again—pleading for immediate help. That was the last thing I heard."

"Was it the Captain?"

"I didn't know that at the time, but it must have been. Unfortunately, the radio signal from his end went dead before I could respond. I had reported my coordinates, indicating to whoever might be listening that I hoped to get there in about five minutes. I got there in four. When I found the empty boat, my heart flipped. Then I saw an orange patch bobbing up and down not far from the boat. It was your sweatshirt or coat…I don't remember. But it was you."

He paused to exhale. "Allie, I thought you were dead."

"And you gave me CPR, right?"

"Well, I tried on the boat, but it was too difficult. Fortunately, I got to the shore quickly, and that's where I was successful."

"I don't know what to say. You saved my life. Thank you seems a little flat. But, well, thank you."

He seemed embarrassed. Whatever his feelings, he got quiet.

Dropping my head, the shame returned with tsunami force. How could I be here when the Captain was still at sea? When he might be dead?

"I need to ask. What do you know about the Captain? What have you heard in terms of a search?"

"As I told you, the authorities are looking. And many, if not all, of the local fisherman are searching too."

"He's a good man. A smart and generous man. God, I hope he

made it."

Parker appeared from around the corner. "I called Ian yesterday. He'll try to make it down in a few days. He said he'd be here tomorrow if he could, but he just can't. He was very worried about you. Give him a call tomorrow, early evening, since he'll be out on a fishing tour during the day."

"Thank you, Parker," I said. "I'm sorry. God, I feel so damn helpless."

"You have nothing to be sorry about, Allie," said Parker.

"I'll head down to the harbor tomorrow," said Carlos. "See if I can find out any more news. I'll give you a full report."

"I'm going with you!"

"No, Allie, you can't. Doctor's orders, and I'm enforcing them. By the way, speaking of the—"

"We'll see," I said, shaking my head.

Carlos rose to stoke the fire. Parker told him he could spend the night and stay as long as he liked, but he declined. The wood crackled and sputtered, sending out tiny sparks like fireflies onto the stone hearth.

Yawning, Parker excused herself and went to bed. Carlos and I sat side by side on the couch. I closed my eyes, taking in the comforting smell of burning oak.

"Can you hear that?" Carlos asked, motioning with his eyes toward the window.

I sat still to listen. I could hear the loud surf in the distance. I stood up, grabbing the side of the sofa for balance, and walked slowly to a window by the front door.

"Can you see the sea from there?" Carlos asked.

"No. Parker said she used to, but the trees grew too tall."

When we returned to the couch, Carlos sat close to me, his shoulder touching mine. He gently touched my overgrown bangs, moving them away from my eyes. It didn't make sense, but I wanted more. *Stupid. Selfish.* He may have saved my life, but it didn't mean he wanted to have sex with me. My timing was so off. How could

I feel sorrow and sadness one minute and lust the next?

The doorbell rang. Startled, I jumped to my feet.

"The doc," he said. "I started to tell you that he wanted to come check on you."

"Isn't it kind of late for a house call?"

"Not by Chilean standards."

I sighed. Soon I'd be undressing for all the wrong reasons.

CHAPTER 40

Other than minor frostbite on my toes and congestion hanging around my lungs, I was okay. But the doc said I should continue to rest. My immune system would be shot for weeks. He told me I was one small step from contracting pneumonia. He warned that alcohol and sugar were not my friends. Wondering if he smelled the wine on my breath, I refrained from talking.

When I awoke the next morning, I felt like shit. The combination of an intense headache and exhaustion kept me under the covers. I hadn't slept much, tossing for hours, flipping the small pillow over and over, and throwing my blankets off, then back on. I tried meditation, but ugly thoughts pushed their way across all that was good. Eventually, I fell asleep. Just long enough to have two horrific nightmares.

In one, I was in a boat with Miguel, his wife, and daughters. It was a bit like *Moby Dick* meets *Jaws*. All I remembered was clutching a little girl as I stared ahead at a giant whale that wanted us as appetizers. Miguel and his wife were at the stern, making out and oblivious to the threat before us. I kept screaming at them, but Miguel just laughed. I awoke just as the whale nudged our boat, causing me to let go of the little girl's hand.

In the other, Captain Jack was in the boat with Carlos. The former was throwing nets in the ocean, hoping to catch a blue whale. It would have been comical had it not turned morbidly gruesome with a sudden change of events that left Carlos dead and Captain Jack pulling up a net loaded with human body parts. My scream ended the nightmare. After that, sleep was impossible.

Doc wanted me to rest for a week. My compromise was three days. During that time, all I did was sleep. And eat. Carlos stayed away. Parker was the kind of mother figure I'd always wanted but never had. She doted but didn't annoy. She gave me space when I needed it. And she cooked. God, did she cook.

On my fourth day, I had enough. I pulled on the same old pair of baggy sweats from the night before. My legs ached. Everywhere. And my toes were developing a bluish-green hue. When I looked in a mirror, I saw a butterfly bandage on my forehead. I didn't remember the doctor working on my head, but when I peeled off the bandage, there were five tiny x's sewn above my right eyebrow, near the end of my bangs.

I meandered to the kitchen, happy to see a pot of coffee on the stove. Walking into the front room, I found Carlos in a chair, drinking coffee in a brown mug stenciled with white letters that said "Cold Hands, Warm Heart."

"Good morning," he said. "Sorry I woke you. I came by to see Parker but turns out she has plans today. She told me to help myself to breakfast."

"You didn't. Wake me, I mean."

"Why are you dressed? Shouldn't you still be in bed?"

"I can't, Carlos. I feel fine. I need to do something. I have to go down to the dock. I need to find out who's looking for CJ and if there are any updates. If not, I need to get on a boat."

"That's the last thing you should do."

"But…"

"You're grown, and you're smart. I get that you need to do something. I get that."

"Thank you." I started heading to the hall closet to get my coat.

"I'm also not going to risk losing you again. At least let me go with you."

"Fine."

"But can you wait a few minutes? I mean I just got here, and Parker told me to help myself to eggs. She's already eaten. You hungry?"

"No. But I'll eat. Let me help you cook."

"Nope. You sit down. If you insist on being a stubborn ass by going to the harbor, you should at least take it slow now and let me feed you."

"That's all I've been doing is eating."

"You need fuel."

I sat at the small kitchen table while he waited on me with fruit, toast, fried eggs, and more coffee. Rain pounded noisily overhead.

Turning his head to the window, Carlos asked, "Are you sure about this? It's coming down hard."

"I'm totally sure. I've got a good coat."

After he sat down, I devoured everything on my plate.

"So," he said. "When did you return to Chile?"

I detected a falter, a pause between words like there was more he wanted to ask. His right eyebrow drifted high near his forehead.

Slathering my toast with orange marmalade, I said, "Sometime in March, about five months ago. Wow. Can't believe I've been back here for that long."

"Time flies...."

"Uh. No comment."

"Sorry," he said, dropping his head to the floor. Poor Carlos. He looked as tired as I felt.

"Why did you return? Things were crazy when we last talked."

"You're thinking I shouldn't have?"

"Not necessarily. But I am curious."

"I know. Here I go again, creating chaos. I know you told me to stay back there for several months, but I couldn't."

Waiting for his response made me nervous. I figured the next thing out of his mouth would be to tell me it was high time I returned home. For good.

"Allie, I don't know what you mean. You haven't created this chaos. You were a victim. And a brave one at that. If you hadn't returned those documents, we wouldn't have had any hope for putting an end to the whale killing."

I stared outside, anxious to move, anxious to get out and look for CJ. Rain or no rain, we had to start looking. Victim or not, if my instinct about the Captain's fate was correct, then hopefully a lightning rod, whale poacher, or heart attack would take me down. For good.

I sat, twirling my ankle in circles.

When he grabbed my plate, I told him to sit down. "I need to answer your question about why I returned. You did save my life. I owe you that."

"You don't—"

"Carlos. Hush. Let me talk. I need to tell you this. I came back because I was tired of running. Tired of letting fear dictate my future. Tired of so many past mistakes. When I got back to California, things were okay but just okay. I rented a room in this terrible house with this old lady and tried to stay busy. But nothing I did had meaning. Besides, I didn't have a job."

"Okay, but why back here? I mean, I'm sure you didn't come here looking for work?"

"No, not paid anyways. I couldn't stop thinking about the whales. Not sure what Parker told you, but I've been out a lot lately. The more I was at sea and the more I learned about whales, the more I wanted to help them. It was like I couldn't stop. The experience made me look deeper into myself. And it may sound corny, but I felt like my life before was…well, kind of void of purpose."

Opening up was empowering but painful. None of the experiences I'd just shared would have happened without the Captain. I couldn't say this, but I wanted to. If I did, the tears would gush. I wasn't ready for that.

"So," I said, "I decided I had to do what I could to protect them. To help."

Taking a breath and finishing my coffee, I continued. "I know you get this. This is what you've been doing for years. But until I started seeing the whales up close, I didn't realize how vulnerable they were."

Nodding, he reached out to rub my shoulder. "I'm happy you understand, and I'm glad you'll help."

I tightened my lips. "Let's go to the harbor. See what we can find out. I have to ask, is there any chance CJ made it?"

Carlos bowed his head. "There's a chance."

He didn't believe it either. But for the moment, I needed to hold onto some thread of hope.

We heard the groan of water pipes as Parker finished drawing her bath.

"This newfound passion for whales—is that why you were looking for me?"

"Yes," I said. "Trying to find you by following a whale path. . . kind of a longshot."

"You were on the right path. I mean we did end up in the same place. Sadly, under tragic circumstances. Allie, we both understand how seriously dangerous these men are. More than ever we'll have to be more cautious."

"*Por supuesto.* I understand that. You don't need to tell me they're dangerous. But I will say they're not very intelligent. I mean, why do they think—still—that I had something to do with your investigations?"

Carlos stood up and grabbed our plates. He put them on the counter and started running water in the sink.

"Need help?"

"I got it."

He mumbled something else that I didn't make out.

"What?" I asked.

"The package. You delivered it. To these poachers, you're a problem because you gave me the reports, and they know enough about the content to be worried."

"But if Jorge hadn't given the package to me, or if I hadn't given it to you, the papers would have either stayed with Jorge or been given to the police. Wouldn't it all have been taken care of by the authorities? If Jorge cares about whales, why would he give them to me?"

Carlos turned. "I'm not sure. Perhaps he didn't want someone to know that he had this information. Someone he was afraid of. Maybe the group behind this is larger than we thought. There's even been speculation, by a few of the more extreme theorists, that the whale killings could be connected to one of the largest fisheries in South America. I'm not sure if I buy that theory, but there's a lot of mistrust between groups."

"I still don't understand why Jorge wouldn't have turned the papers into the police."

Carlos turned on the tap and began washing the dishes, making an unusual amount of noise. There was something he didn't want to tell me.

"Carlos, do you think it might be someone connected with the police?"

He didn't have to answer.

"You're saying they may have members inside the police force or the government? Please tell me this has nothing to do with some underground military or government supporters?"

Visions of being secretly swept off the street and imprisoned or tortured or worse suddenly sent a chilling tingle from my neck to my toes.

"The dictatorship is history, my friend. The Pinochet era ended long ago. I doubt if he even had a handful of supporters by the time he died. And while I wouldn't put it past certain officials to be in bed with the fishery operation, I don't suspect a government cover-up. Having said that, I'm not sure who we can trust. The problem is even if the cops aren't involved, they're not going to drop their current responsibilities to help a few whale-loving liberals."

A knock on the door sent my feet to the air. Carlos looked

equally startled. Whispering, he said, "The doctor wasn't supposed to return, was he?"

I looked at Carlos. "No."

Carlos walked to the door. "Can I help you?" I heard him ask.

Approaching the door, I saw a policeman. I knew why he was there. The coincidence of our conversation and the arrival of the police felt like a cruel twist of fate.

Carlos motioned him to come in, and within minutes, my worst suspicion—what I'd really known but tried to negate—was confirmed.

We wouldn't be going to the docks.

They had found Captain Jack's body.

CHAPTER 41

Forty or fifty townspeople packed into a small, wooden chapel to mourn Nicolas Sepulveda III. Like generational bookends, the Captain's father, Nicholas Sepulveda II, and son, Nicolas Sepulveda IV, sat side by side, a quiet bond of grief stretched between them. To the right of the younger Nicolas was the Captain's wife, Sra. Maria, her head shrouded by a black veil. I could not see her face but knew she was struggling to hold it together by the way her shoulders shook.

I felt sick, literally, figuratively, emotionally, physically. The reality of his death was now painted before my eyes, like oversized brush strokes marking an X against my existence. A family, his family, mourning. Dozens of others, some I recognized, many I didn't, staring at the pine box. No one had to say it. No one would say it, but I knew. They had heard what happened. His death was unnecessary. A death I caused. Had I not hired the Captain, his family would be together in life, not death. Instead of lying in that pine box, he'd be gathered with his family around a large table filled with barbecued meat and fish, wine, and bread. Rather than sniffles and sobs and whispers of condolence, sounds of laughter and love would fill the spaces of their hearts.

What am I doing here? I should leave.

As if reading my thoughts, Parker wrapped her arm around my back, affectionately rubbing my shoulder. I couldn't look at her. Ian sat on her other side. Carlos chose not to attend. He had never met the Captain and had an aversion to churches of any denomination.

I turned my gaze to the rows across from me, noticing a couple

Nancy Rhodes

dozen men—probably fishermen, eyes ahead. Many fidgeted with their ties and starched collars, clothing reserved for such occasions.

A priest spoke. I didn't understand much of what he said, and that was okay. When the procession stood up for the viewing, Ian and I remained glued to our seats. Parker got in the queue, slowly making her way to the front.

Some two hours later, after a full Mass, the priest led the funeral procession through a hilly graveyard lined with weeping, rain-soaked eucalyptus trees. I kept as far back as possible, wishing to disappear completely.

After the service we climbed back into Parker's old Renault, a rusty sedan with various cracks streaming through the front windshield. I insisted on sitting in the back. After a few miles of silence, I couldn't hold back any longer.

"I still don't understand," I said, staring at the space between their two heads. "Does anyone know the exact cause of his death? Have they started a murder investigation?"

"They say he drowned," said Parker. "I don't know if they started an investigation."

Ian asked Parker if they did an autopsy.

"I don't believe so," she replied, "which seems odd. Rumor has it there were bruises on his back and neck."

"What? Who told you that?" I asked.

Looking at Parker, Ian said, "Be careful about rumors. You should understand that more than anyone, having lived here as long as you have."

She didn't respond.

"That's fucked," I said. "They better do an autopsy. Someone killed him. They have to find out who before these assholes do something else."

Ian turned to look at me. "I'm sorry," he said. "I cannot imagine how you are feeling. What you went through. . .and I know you'd grown close. But things are different here. People will mourn for weeks, but most people will do so silently. The authorities will try to find out what happened, but I wouldn't hold your breath on any immediate results."

Parker drove so slow cars began to pass us on both sides. "Allie, I'm with you," she said. "We owe it to the Captain to find the truth. A couple of fishermen were the ones who told me about the bruises. I've known them close to twenty years, and while I don't know how they knew those details, they aren't the kind of men to invent stories or partake in gossip."

"Where's the boat?" asked Ian.

"Don't know," said Parker, her voice terse, "but doubt the boat would give anyone answers."

I hoped I was wrong, but I didn't like what I perceived as an undercurrent of tension between them. If I was right, there wasn't anything I could do about it. Besides, I had big mountains of guilt and pain to climb. I stared out the window, noting hints of green upon the hills. Visions of the Captain, full of life, filled my head.

Nicolas. The Captain. Captain Jack. *El Capitán.* One man, many names. A selfless, generous soul who didn't deserve to die like that. I wondered why the hell I survived and he didn't.

As we passed several run-down farmhouses, I just wanted to be out of the car and by myself. I was so angry. We needed to do something. We needed to demand justice. Every last one of these thugs, these murderers, needed to die. Hopefully in some long, slow, and excruciatingly painful manner.

Carlos must have heard us arrive, because he was outside waiting for us when we pulled onto Parker's driveway.

"You've had a visitor," he said. "Well, besides me. Hope you don't mind I let myself in."

"Of course I don't mind," said Parker. "Who else came by?"

"That same policeman. Sr. Telero, I think his name is. He brought something for Allie."

I staggered out of the car and followed everyone inside. Carlos grabbed a red plastic bag off Parker's hall table. "This is yours, Allie."

I knew what it was. I couldn't believe it…couldn't believe that the camera I had on the boat was recovered. It should have been on the ocean floor. *Amazing.* Other than water stains, it looked intact. I had stored it in the Captain's waterproof tackle box.

"Wow" is all that came out of my mouth. My heart lurched, knowing I had the last photos taken of the Captain.

I lost it. At first quiet, slow tears, then not so quiet.

Carlos leaned closer to embrace me.

"Don't!" Clutching the camera, I stepped back from the doorway and started running.

"Allie—wait!"

"Carlos, please," I said, turning around. "Don't follow me. I—I need to be alone."

I ran several blocks, wiping my face, leaving streaks of snot and mascara up and down my black dress. I don't know how long I ran but long enough to get completely drenched by the sideways sheets of rain. Long enough to stop crying.

I found a park. No one was there. Obviously. Only idiots who get innocent people killed would go to a park in a mad rainstorm. I sat on a hard, wet bench and began crying all over again.

As the wind turned tree limbs into windmills and the rain became hail, I smiled. I wanted to be punished. I wanted to stay on this cold-ass bench and freeze myself to death. And when my surroundings evaporated into the darkness and my body began to shake, I stopped crying. I'd exhausted the reservoir of tears. I had nothing. No tears. No feeling. No soul.

I walked for blocks, suddenly finding myself at the harbor. The streets were empty and dark. Apparently, no one else sought punishment from Mother Earth. My feet carried me down a long pier. Virginia Woolf had lined her pockets with rocks, but I was too impatient. I didn't even remove my shoes. When I reached the end, my fingers opened, dropping my purse onto the wooden slats. The railing was conveniently short. Easy to climb.

The ocean stirred as if Sedna, goddess of the sea, was calling my name.

CHAPTER 42

⁘

An arctic blast of wind from the north pushed my body sideways on the pier. If it'd come from the east, I would have been in the water. But while straightening my feet for the plunge, a pair of large hands grabbed my waist and pulled me from the edge.

"Good God, Allie! What the hell are you doing?" said Ian. I hated him for interfering with my plan.

I said nothing.

He turned me around and wrapped his arms around my back. I heard Parker. She was screaming my name.

"I got her," Ian yelled.

When Parker reached us, she hugged me so hard I screamed. Whatever she was saying got muffled by the noises in my head.

"Let's get her into your car before she freezes to death. She's shaking," said Ian, handing my arm over to Parker.

"I've got a blanket in the back," Parker said, leading me away from the water.

I felt like a captured stray on the way to the pound. When we reached the Renault, she wrapped me in a blanket that smelled like wet dog. A laugh escaped my throat. How amusing. She didn't have a dog. My senses were skewed. Or maybe just my brain cells.

"Get inside, dear," she said.

I sank into the passenger seat, my limbs twitching spastically while my teeth danced up and down in a loud chatter. Feeling the warm air from the vent opposite my face, I turned toward the window. They were discussing me—probably figuring out what to do with me. *Too bad*, I mused, *there isn't a pound for pathetic gringas whose selfish exploits kill innocent souls.*

Once inside, Parker turned, reaching her hand over to hold my quaking knee. "Allie, I understand how you're feeling, but you can't do this. This is not your fault. You have to believe me."

"Nope. You're so wrong. This is my fault. It is. Period. Don't try to tell me it isn't. Don't patronize me. And you know I really do not want to talk about this. Not now. Not ever."

Ian said something to her in a mumbled whisper. So be it.

Whether it was what he said or what I said, she honored my demand and said nothing more. I prayed Carlos wouldn't be waiting for us at Parker's. I didn't want to face him. I wanted to crawl under a blanket. Forever.

⸻

PARKER LEFT ME ALONE. SHE DIDN'T BABY ME. I STAYED IN MY ROOM for nearly forty-eight hours. At one point, I thought she knocked, but she hadn't. It was the wind pushing a spruce branch against the window. While I'd asked to be left alone, I began to resent her indifference. One morning I smelled muffins, so I spent an extra fifteen minutes in the bathroom, thinking she'd put some on my nightstand. She didn't. I decided she was mad at me. She had a right, considering the way I talked to her. Maybe she would kick me out.

But I didn't feel any regret. I didn't feel anything. While splashing water over my face, I stared with disgust at the dark circles below my eyes along with a whole new layer of wrinkles around my eyes and mouth. They weren't laugh lines. I couldn't remember the last time I'd laughed. I'd probably never laugh again.

By the end of day two, my stomach rumblings sent me sneaking into the kitchen near midnight. I ate three of the muffins, slathered with jam. In the morning, I smelled coffee and cinnamon rolls, so I threw on my oversized sweater and shuffled my way to the kitchen.

This time Parker was there, her back to me, washing a pan. I wondered if I should do an about-face.

"Good morning," she said. I didn't sense anger. Or judgment. "Help yourself. I just took them out."

"Thanks," I replied, staring at the plate of sugar-dusted rolls on the table. I forced myself to sit down, despite an urge to grab the entire plate and retreat to my room.

They weren't like the white frosted rolls I was accustomed to back home, but they were good. Damn good. After reaching for my third, I told her they were really good. I guess the sugar was softening my heart.

She nodded but said nothing more. We still hadn't made eye contact.

Picking up my plate, I walked to the small counter. "I'm sorry, Parker. I was rude. I know you were just trying to help."

Turning off the faucet, she wiped her hands on her brown apron. "*Querida*, you have been through a lot. You were right. I don't know how you feel. But I do understand what it's like to feel responsible for someone's life."

Her blue-gray eyes grew moist. "My daughter took her own life on her nineteenth birthday. We had an argument the day before. Something silly. A jar of marmalade. She'd dropped it on the floor, and I exploded because it was my last jar, and I'd planned to bring it to my friends for tea in the afternoon."

I reached for her hand. Together we returned to the table. Tears slowly rolling off her face, she raised her head. Looking straight into my eyes, she said, "It took me years—many years and lots of therapy—to let go of my guilt. Eventually, I accepted the fact that she'd been unhappy for years. She didn't kill herself because I yelled at her. It wasn't the marmalade. It was desperation. I think she had a hole in her heart. A hole that felt so enormous she thought it could never be filled enough to make living worthwhile. I wish I'd seen that." Parker paused, her eyes moving past me to a small table cluttered with at least a dozen framed photographs.

"I wish I'd known," she said. "I wish she'd given me a chance. What I want to say, Allie, is that after nearly starving myself to death in grief, one day I began to let go. It didn't happen overnight."

"Oh, Parker. I had no idea. I'm sorry."

"Of course you didn't. I don't like talking about it. But talking is what we must do to heal. I hope you'll consider talking to someone. When you're ready, I can recommend a counselor—or therapist. I'm not sure what her qualifications are. But she helped me."

I leaned forward to gently wipe her face with my napkin. "Thank you, Parker."

I wasn't ready to commit to therapy. Past experiences with therapy sucked my wallet dry and did nothing to help me with the Miguel crises. Besides, my chances that her counselor spoke English were slim.

Later that night, I lay on my bed, pondering what to do. Nothing came to mind. I sat up, my back against the headboard, staring at a simple bronze cross on the wall in a corner. Glancing around the room, I saw the camera. My camera. Parker must have left it there for my benefit.

I crept toward the dresser, feet heavy on the hardwood slats. My fingers touched the camera, and then I let go. *Allie, you're being ridiculous!*

After more self-loathing, I finally picked up the damn camera. Feeling the cold metal in my hand, I swear my heart stopped.

My right finger grazed over the power button. Did I really want to see photos of the man I'd killed? The very last photos of the man whose life ended prematurely because of me? One hand trembled, then both. Trembling gave way to shaking. I peeled my fingers open to let go of the camera, literally dropping it on the nightstand.

Not yet. Maybe not ever.

***

NEARLY THREE WEEKS AFTER THE BOAT ATTACK, A SHRINK showed up unannounced. Well, unannounced to me. She'd driven like a million miles, and between Ian and Parker's not-so-welcome encouragement, I grudgingly agreed to see her.

Her name was so unusual I couldn't remember it. I took to calling her The Shrink. She didn't seem to mind. The Shrink came every Friday, always wearing a loose-fitting skirt of some bright color and blouses that in my mind didn't match. She could have been sixty; she could have been eighty. Either way, I had more wrinkles than she did. Her straight, white hair hung in two tight braids over the top of her very flat chest. Lucky me…her English was perfect.

I didn't exactly cooperate. At least not at first. When she asked questions I didn't like, I shrugged my shoulders and stayed quiet. After three once-a-week visits, I had planned to ask her to stop coming. Just like I'd thought. It wasn't working.

But on that day, which oddly coincided with the one-month anniversary of the Captain's death, something changed. We had the house to ourselves and were sitting at the kitchen table with steaming mugs of black tea, ready to begin our session. She held up the camera. I wondered if Parker had prompted her in that department. I never noticed that it'd disappeared from my dresser. The Shrink did not try to give it to me. She held it for a long minute before placing it on the center of the table. A measuring tape could have confirmed it was exactly halfway between her chair and mine. Her hands and mine. Deliberate.

"I hear you're an excellent photographer."

"Novice. Nothing amazing."

"You took photos that day, right?"

"Maybe."

"I know this is painful, Allie, but I think looking at your photos might help. I'd like to see your whale photos."

"Sneaky."

"That's not my intention. And you don't have to if you're not ready."

"Whatever," I said, unable to take my eyes off the camera.

"Your decision, but it might be helpful to reconnect with something you're passionate about. Whales, nature, photos of whatever. This might be a good place to start."

"There are photos of the Captain in there," I said. "But you probably knew that."

"How do you feel about seeing him again?"

Geez. Typical shrink. "Well," I said, trying to ward off a sarcastic reply, "sad. I feel sad."

After too many minutes of silence, I reached forward and grabbed the camera. I was a little curious.

The camera was remarkably intact. Water hadn't even seeped into the case. I turned it on, relieved the battery hadn't died or corroded because it took some kind of special batteries that I didn't have. I looked through the viewfinder, and while I could see images, they were frustratingly too small and too dark.

"What's the matter?" she asked.

"I can't see anything. The images are too small. I need to download them and have no idea how to do that or what I need."

"My brother-in-law has a similar camera. He has a cord that hooks into a computer. I can bring it next week. Does Parker have a computer?"

"She doesn't even have a television."

"What about your other friend, Carlos?"

"I'll ask, but I doubt it."

"I'll bring the cord next week."

<hr />

I'D FORGOTTEN ALL ABOUT THE CAMERA BY THE TIME THE Shrink returned the following Friday. We talked a lot about processing grief. I even told her a little about Miguel. Not how he killed his wife and daughters during our tumultuous love affair, but how he was the first to steal my heart, and how, after he disappeared, I learned he was married. At the end of our hour, she told me I was making great progress.

"And," she said, opening her purse, "here is the cord for that camera. I will, of course, need it back, but keep it as long as you want."

"Right. Thanks. I'll ask Carlos if he has a computer."

"I hope you do. I understand if you're reluctant, but the sooner you start, the sooner you can begin to heal."

Thinking that was an inflated promise if I ever heard one, I agreed.

⌘

Two weeks later I finally asked Carlos if he had a computer or laptop. He confirmed what Karina had told me back in El Toyo—that his laptop had been stolen. Remembering the jerk who took mine, I shook my head. Something else we had in common. Carlos said he knew someone who could probably sell him an old refurbished one.

A few days later he invited me to a place he'd just moved to since he'd worn out his welcome at his friend's house. The new abode was tiny. Super tiny. A room and a kitchen—all in a space smaller than my garage back home. After dinner, he showed me how to upload the photos. We enjoyed slices of dried mango for dessert while 327 photos tried to upload.

"It's slow, I know," he said. "And I'm not sure there's enough storage capability but guess we'll find out."

"It's okay. I appreciate this. So," I said, looking around. "This place is kind of cute. Wish I could find something like this."

"Why? What about Parker?"

"I think I've worn out my welcome. Besides, I might be staying awhile."

"Really?"

"Yes, really. That is if you'll help me find those bastards."

I'm not sure who was more surprised by my comment. I hadn't planned on continuing the search.

I swallowed the last of my wine. "Oh look, the photos are up."

CHAPTER 43

A lot of the photos were blurry. After some two hundred photos I paused, taking a deep breath before reciting the Serenity Prayer Mom taught me in her sober days. I had to be getting close to seeing photos of Captain Jack.

Despite all my apprehension about seeing him, a part of me was grateful that I had something I could give his family. If they wanted them. Maybe not now, but perhaps someday after grief began to edge slowly from their hearts.

I'd never been much of a people photographer. During the past three months, my photography focused on whales, boats, mountains, and landscapes. I had taken some of Ian when he first gave me the camera. Parker, like many of the locals, detested cameras, computers, and cell phones. But I had a few of the Captain.

In the first photo, taken before we got on board, he was looking out at the sea. He had no idea I took the photo. Even from a slight side-angle shot, I saw concern etched between his brows. Or was I reading something into it? Why would he have been concerned? I tried to remember our conversation that morning. Nothing in particular stood out.

The Captain caught me taking the next photo of him. He looked up just as I was framing my shot. I hit the shutter release the exact moment he motioned to me to put the camera down, so all I got was a streaky blur of his arm. He was used to me bringing a camera to photograph whales, but things changed that day when I tried taking photos of him. He gave me a little lecture, saying it was crazy to bring a camera, because it would get wet. After that he patted my shoulder, looked me in the eye, and, in perfect English, said, "The ocean should be experienced through eyes, not machines. Miss Allie, God created eyes, not cameras."

Hence, I only had four photos of the Captain. I managed to take two after the lecture. Carefully timed, so he did not know. In one, he was standing near the bow after having untied the boat line from the dock cleat. Behind him were a scattering of other fishing boats—boats of all sizes and colors—rowboats, larger commercial boats, and middle-sized fishing boats like his. The shadows of the ebbing tide made for a well-composed shot, but it was the stunning snowcapped landscape of the Corcovado Volcano that pulled my eyes beyond the Captain's gaze.

Looking at that photo from behind, Carlos asked if he could get a closer look. His voice startled me. I'd forgotten he was there.

"Is that Captain Jack?" His words faded into silence, reflecting that awkwardness or fear people succumb to when having to say a deceased person's name for the first time.

"Yes. That's him. *El Capitán.*"

Carlos put his hands on my shoulders, trying to console me with a tender massage that extended into the tight tendons of my neck and shoulders.

I didn't have any tears left, but something about his touch deepened the pain, pulling me into another round of despair. I thought I was okay. I thought I could be strong. But now it didn't feel that way. I got up, and not knowing where I could hide, my feet led me to the miniature bathroom. I'm not sure how long I was in there, sitting on cold tiles with my feet tucked against my chest.

I tried deep breathing. I closed my eyes.

"Are you okay?" he asked, knocking gently on the door.

Unfolding my legs, I stood and flushed the toilet. "Yes, I'll be out in a sec."

"I heated some food," he said softly, "but before we eat, I want to show you something."

"Sure. Be right there."

I hobbled out as if I'd just had a double knee replacement surgery. Carlos was still on the computer.

"You've got to see this!"

When I approached, Carlos was still staring at the photo of the Captain with the mountains in the background.

"Here, sit down," he said, pointing to a stool he'd brought over during my absence.

"Carlos, I…I've seen this."

His hand pointed to one of the boats in the distance.

"Hold on," he said, playing with keyboard buttons to increase the image size. "You see this boat?"

"Yes. It's larger than the others. What about it?"

"I recognize this boat. She's not your standard fishing boat. This, my friend, belongs to someone with big pockets and big intentions."

"Is it one of theirs? The poachers?"

"Pretty damn sure. I suspect they were there when you got on the boat and that they were watching you."

He handed me a magnifying glass.

"Nice boat."

"If you look close, you'll see her name—painted there," he said, pointing to some minuscule lettering near the rear of the boat.

"¿*La Aguja*? What's that supposed to mean?

"*The Marlin*. Marlins are fast. And quite aggressive."

"Symbolic, no doubt," I said.

Carlos nodded. "She's a sophisticated and fast vessel. We'll need to come up with a careful plan."

"Carlos?"

"What?"

"I know I said—"

"Are you changing your mind? I get that this could scare you."

"But?"

"Well, if we head out without you, they'll be out of our sight before we know it. Without you, they'll have no reason to follow us."

"So you think with me onboard they're going to throw us a welcoming party?"

"No, not exactly. But with you onboard, they won't disappear. Remember they see you as a threat. I hate to say this, but it's you they are most worried about."

"Gee, that's comforting. So I'm bait."

"Sorry, but yeah—something like that."

I shrugged, shook my head, and looked away. He was right, but that didn't make me any more accepting of whatever scheme was spinning inside his head. I wanted to be fierce, but fear threatened all prospects of heroic grandeur.

"Sounds like you have a plan," I said.

"*Mas o menos.*"

I bit my lip. He wasn't exactly winning me over with the "more or less" response.

"We'll need two boats," he said, feigning confidence. "But that won't be a problem. And we'll put you on the first one so they will follow you. I'll be monitoring them within a safe distance away."

"Safe? Safe for whom?"

"For both of us. I won't let anything happen to you. I'll be prepared."

"Prepared?"

"Firearms."

"What the fuck! What are you talking about? You have guns? And you're talking about using me as a lure for some battle out in the middle of the ocean? Seriously? Congratulations, you've just managed to talk me out of it!"

"Yes, I have a couple of guns. Believe me, when you're dealing with these kinds of people, you're not going to scare them with a BB gun."

"Well, if they can outrun you, what's the problem? You won't need guns."

"Yes. Obviously. But you're forgetting—"

"No, I'm not. I know. The whales. The blues. I'm not forgetting. I just think there should be some other way, something else we can do."

I needed time to process this insane plan. A game of cat and mouse, with me as the mouse, was beyond anything I imagined when I decided to help save whales.

Carlos walked to his miniature refrigerator. "Beer?"

I wanted a gallon of whisky. But thinking the beer might relax both of us and help him come up with a better plan—like one that didn't involve me getting on a boat—I agreed.

"Okay. I don't need a glass."

"Good. I don't have one."

He wasn't trying to be funny. His mood had shifted. I tried convincing myself this wasn't about me.

I took a few swigs, hoping it would quell my angst. It didn't. I waited.

And waited.

His green eyes, once so appealing, darkened.

I tried to think of something to say. I wanted to prove myself, to show him that I did care about the disappearing whales. I cared a lot. Just not enough to be the bull's-eye for a group of men who might have ties to the mafia.

He got up, and I listened as he turned off the oven, opened the oven door, and closed it with a bang. Smelling something made with onions and cheese, I waited for the invite.

None came. The light from the kitchen dimmed. He returned. This was so unlike Carlos. Obviously, he was desperate to finish this—to catch the bastards, but he had no right to take this out on me.

"Well, I said. "I have to get back. Thanks for the use of the computer."

"Glad you got what you came for," he said, shaking his head. I was shocked. He'd never been anything but civil and kind.

I started for the door, anxious to slam it so hard I'd shake the little clapboard shack into a pile of firewood. I felt bullied. Old defensive habits are hard to break.

"Come on, Carlos. That's low. Why are *you* upset? I'm the one who was almost killed. I'm the one who is responsible for the death of a sweet old grandfather whose only mistake was to help a stupid gringa look for whales!"

"I thought you cared, Allie. And I thought you trusted me."

I did slam the door on my way out. But the building didn't crumble.

CHAPTER 44

When I got back, I was greeted by Parker and Ian, the latter clutching a mug tightly. His eyes darted nervously between Parker and the floor. They'd been talking about me. How nice. Carlos must have called them after I left. Why Carlos couldn't accept me wanting to avoid boats and poachers was incomprehensible. Didn't anyone have any compassion?

Parker asked if I wanted a cup of tea.

"No thanks. I'm exhausted. I'm going to bed."

Ian folded his arms across his chest. "Allie, we need to chat. Just a few minutes."

I scanned his face for clues. Had Carlos called him? Did he know I was bailing from further whale-rescue efforts? I crossed my legs, putting my hands on my thighs. I felt like a schoolgirl waiting for the principal's scolding after getting caught with cigarettes.

"So," said Ian, his Adam's apple bobbing up and down like a fishing lure. "I heard things got crazy over at Carlos's."

"My, news travels fast."

He stood up, walked to where I sat on the couch, and grabbed my hand. "We know you've been through a lot. We're not here to tell you what you should and shouldn't do."

"Good."

Knowing the escape to my bedroom wasn't an option, I sat on the couch. With Parker present, I decided to behave with a certain level of maturity. A small part of me was beginning to regret some of the things I'd said to Carlos.

Finally, Parker made an excuse about being tired and retreated to her bedroom.

Ian sat opposite me. "We need to put a team together by tomorrow."

"I've heard this already. And as I told him—"

"Please let me finish, Allie. *La Aguja* was spotted near the harbor today. So they're still around, but we're not sure how long they'll stay. Carlos didn't call me to rat on you. I called him, apparently just after you left, to tell him this news. We're running out of time. The whales are abundant but could be leaving soon, and we suspect that the cartel is getting anxious. Tomorrow Parker and I will call everyone we know who has boats. And I've contacted Lucas, who, fortunately, will come help us. He'll be here before daybreak tomorrow."

Why was Ian telling me this? To guilt me? Scare me? Convince me? Whatever his logic, it wasn't working. They could do whatever they were going to do just fine without me.

"Glad you have a plan," I said, feigning civility.

"There's one problem," he said.

It didn't take a detective to know what was coming, but I didn't want to hear it. I'd made up my mind. I wouldn't and couldn't go out there and be a sitting duck. Not after what they did to the Captain. *Allie once again disappoints. Ten lashes. Nine Hail Marys.* Continued quiet self-degradation fueled my resolve. Sure, I might wallow in certain pangs of guilt, but that was a better choice than getting dead.

"If we head out in our little boats," said Ian, "we'll never catch him. We need to surround him. Surprise him. Someone needs to lead him to an area where that can happen."

"Yeah, I heard that part. Carlos can do that."

"I'm afraid not, Allie. Carlos needs to attack offensively not defensively. If we can get *La Aguja* to move to an area, to one of the feeding grounds where we've seen a lot of blues, we'll disappear and wait at a distance to record their actions on video."

"Excuse me, but exactly what actions are you talking about? Because I'm thinking if these mafioso thugs see me sunbathing on some slow-moving fishing boat, they're not exactly going to come onboard for a social visit."

"You won't be sunbathing. I can assure you. I know the plan may have a few weak points. But if they believe you can lead them to a larger population of blues, they'll follow. And once we get to the islands where we've seen a substantial population feeding, we're confident they'll stop following you."

"You think they're going to simply wave goodbye once they see a few whales?"

"For whatever reason, you are a threat to them, but we suspect they want whales more than they want you. If the whales are there, and you're then out of sight, they'll want to get as many as they can. Their time here is limited, so they'll move fast. If we can make them believe you're not a threat, they'll stay in the area long after we get you out. If we're wrong and their crew goes after us, Carlos won't be far. He can intercept them."

"Right, I know. He has guns. Very reassuring." I shook my head. In my opinion, the plan was weak and lame. Carlos should have come up with something better.

"I get your apprehension. I haven't forgotten the Captain and what happened. I wish we didn't need to do this. If there was another way to end this and to save the whales, I'd do it."

I looked down at my knees, which were bobbing up and down like apples in a bucket of water.

"Gringa, you'll be safe. I've talked extensively with Carlos to make certain. Remember, I knew Captain Jack too. And I sure as hell don't want anything to happen to you."

"Thank you."

"I'm not sure if you know the extent of the equipment on Carlos's vessel. He can travel undetected. The boat has high-range sonar tracking, so he can find whales without being anywhere near. The whales will eventually be the true bait. Not you."

"You may be right, but if you're not…"

Ian ran his hand across his brow.

His desperation—and frustration—was more than obvious.

"Who are these guys? Do you know how many we're talking about?"

"Probably between six and nine. There are other poachers in different regions, at least that's what Carlos believes based on recent intelligence. Carlos knows the kingpin of this group, and that's who he's interested in. A guy named Armando Montero."

"Did you say Montero? Is that a common last name?"

"It's not exactly Jones, but yeah, it's fairly common. Why?"

"The Montero brothers—Jorge and Christian. They're the ones who got me into this."

"Well, the only one I've heard of is Armando. Doubt there's a connection."

"Hope you're right."

Closing my eyes, I took a deep breath, realizing that I couldn't do this. I had to tell Ian now. I would not, *could not*, let another night pass with this hanging over my head. They simply had to find another way.

"I…I'm sorry. I can't do this. I can't get on a boat again. I don't think I can even get near the harbor. I appreciate your explaining everything, but I just can't do it. Isn't there some other way?"

Rising to his feet, Ian said, "Allie, I wish there was." He wasn't angry, but I could see defeat in the slump of his shoulders and the slowness of his movements as he gathered his jacket.

I wanted him to say more. I wanted to hear how he'd figure something else out. How they had a Plan B to save what was left of the southern hemisphere blue whales.

While Ian put on his coat, a terrible image of Miguel's daughters swept into my head. Two beautiful, brown-haired girls who never made it to high school, never dated, never married, never got to have children of their own. They died because of me.

Why did I end up getting so damn involved with whales and

whale poachers? I'd completely ignored my reason for going to Chile. I'd come to face that demon, Miguel. To seek justice. And while I had no proof he had a role in their death, the coincidences and timing pointed in that direction. But was it right to assume that his omission about having a wife and kids made him guilty of their disappearance and death?

I shook my head. This was not the time to be rehashing burdens that had held me hostage for more than half my life.

Ian stopped before opening the door on his way out. He looked at me, and I thought I saw a twitch in his lower lip.

"Good night," I said, fighting with all my might to hold back the floodgates.

As he grabbed the doorknob, he turned back. "There's something else," he said, letting go of the door. "I wasn't going to tell you."

"Tell me? Tell me what?"

"Millie. She was spotted again last week."

Oh, dear God. Millie. I thought back to when I'd first seen her with Ian and then the day we were attacked and the Captain was killed.

"Is she near? Why didn't you tell me?"

"I haven't seen her, but that's what I've heard. About fifteen miles out when she was last seen. She was moving slow. Taking long, deep dives. She's not well."

"I'm pretty sure she was the whale that hit our boat."

Ian came back to the sofa and sat next to me. "I suppose that's possible, but she's never exhibited aggressive behavior."

"No, no, it wasn't aggression. It was a warning. I didn't know then, but I think she was trying to get our attention. I know that sounds crazy."

"It does, but they say whales have good memories."

"I hope she's okay," I said. "I really hope something hasn't happened to her."

The silence between us lingered, like an awkward and unwanted guest.

"I better go," said Ian, standing up.

"Right."

"Well, good night, Allie."

"Ian?"

"Yeah?"

"I'll think about it. For Millie."

"We'll be at the dock before sunup."

"Really?"

"Assuming the storm passes and assuming we can get the boats."

"Don't get your hopes up. About me, I mean."

"Of course," he said. A smile flickered across his face before he gently closed the door.

CHAPTER 45

Drained beyond exhaustion, I thought I'd fall asleep immediately. I was wrong.

A massive full moon brought streams of light through my window. Staring at the rose-colored ceiling, my conscience battled my heart. I tried telling myself I could decide in the morning. No pressure, Allie. Maybe I'd sleep in. Then the decision would be made.

I turned onto my side and wept, shook myself out of it, then lay on my back again.

Thoughts came and went, tossed and tumbled.

Millie. From the beginning, the massive whale had cast a spell on my heart. Although astonished by her size, it was also the beauty of the patterns etched across her fluke that got me. I'd seen her four times total.

Then I thought about the accident. There were two boats. Was one *La Aguja*? I couldn't remember what they looked like. Raindrops pounded against the aluminum roof. I wondered if the weather might delay their plans. I hoped it would. I needed more time.

Hours passed. Two, maybe three. It felt like ten. Finally, in a fit of frustration, I tossed the blankets off my legs, planting my feet on the cold, wooden floor. Moving to the window, I noticed the storm had fizzled out. Great. If they got boats, this half-brained trip to capture a possible murderer would proceed. With or without me.

I folded my hands together and did something I hadn't done in a while. I prayed. I didn't hear any thundering, God-sounding voice assuring me I'd be safe, but the tension that'd been pulling tight along my neck and shoulders receded. Staring out the window, I watched as clouds drifted past stars. Appearing and disappearing. Shapes and light dancing in mystical patterns.

Then, at some point when the clouds disappeared, I realized I didn't need to stress about this. I had my answer. The right answer. My brain and my heart agreed, erasing the strain of guilt and indecision.

Ian answered on the second ring.

"It's Allie. Sorry to wake you," I said in one quick breath. It was only a few minutes past two in the morning.

"I was awake. What's up?"

"I'll be there. See you soon."

I hung up before he could ask questions. Before I could change my mind.

At most I probably slept an hour. A glance in the bathroom mirror revealed a face I didn't recognize. Despite the lines and puffy shadows from sleep deprivation, I saw a hardness, something resembling confidence.

"Warrior!" I said, leaning into the mirror, my breath casting an oval shadow.

I thought about packing food but didn't want to disturb Parker. I tiptoed to the front door. Even though I hadn't put on shoes, my steps seemed to send howling cries from every floorboard.

Reaching the hallway, I heard my name.

"So you're going," said Parker. More of a statement than a question.

"Yes, I am."

"I'm glad you changed your mind."

"It wasn't easy."

"I'm sure it wasn't."

I didn't want her to say anything else. But as she reached to embrace me, I knew she wasn't done.

"*El Capitán* would be so proud."

"Really?"

"*Si, mi hija*. What you're doing will mean so much to his family."

I shook my head, looking at my feet.

"It's true," she said. "He talked about you to his wife. He knew how much you cared about the whales. She told me that he once said, 'This gringa is going to do something someday. She's going to make a difference.' He believed in you."

"He really said that about me?"

"Yes. Yes, he did." She paused as if embarrassed to share this personal information. "Now you better get going if you're going to catch the boys."

"Right, *me voy*." (I'm going.)

"Oh wait," she said turning to grab a small day pack off the hallway table.

"What's in here, coconuts?"

"There's a couple of energy bars but no coconuts. And your camera. I wrapped it up. You might need it."

I really would have preferred to never touch the camera again. But I took it, feigning appreciation.

"*Hasta pronto*," I said, giving Parker the customary kiss on each side of her face.

"*Si, mi linda gringuita, hasta pronto*."

CHAPTER 46

When I reached the harbor, I saw Ian. He was preoccupied with a small group of fishermen, so I searched the nearby boats for Carlos.

I'd have to apologize. Even if he did egg me on, I might have overreacted.

Ian called my name, motioning for me to join him. Once I was next to their boat, I saw that Lucas had come too.

"Welcome back, Lucas," I said, giving him a hug. "It's been a while."

"You look good, gringa. Sorry to hear about everything you've been through."

"Thanks."

"We are going to get these bastards," Lucas said, pumping his fist to the air.

I nodded, wondering if Ian had coached him to encourage me. I didn't believe we would catch anyone, because this plan was too damn far-fetched. But I was willing to try.

After Ian reminded Lucas we needed to leave soon, he led me down the dock to meet the other two fishermen who would join this great adventure. Their names were Pedro and Mateo, two brothers who looked so much alike I couldn't tell them apart.

They began loading supplies onto the boats. The amount of stuff unnerved me, especially when I spotted four camo bags that presumably held weaponry.

Nancy Rhodes

"Two boats total?" I asked Ian.

"These two and Carlos's, of course."

"Where is he? I haven't seen him."

"Oh, sorry. I forgot you don't know his boat. It's behind the red building over there. You can't see much of it from here. He wanted it that way. Walk down the pier, turn left, and before you reach the fueling station, you'll see a larger vessel with purple trim moored alongside some smaller boats."

"Thanks. Should I go now?"

"Yeah, of course. But here," he said, handing me a green parka ten sizes too large. "Wear this, and keep the hood up over your head. Better that no one else knows you're here for now. Try to get back here within fifteen minutes."

"Seriously? Who's going to see me at this hour? Especially from there," I said pointing in the direction of *La Aguja*, at least a mile away.

"Just because she's moored there doesn't mean the crew's onboard. We can't take chances. If they want you out of the picture like we suspect, they might have someone scoping the harbor, especially in these early hours."

The jacket practically fell to my knees. The sleeves were so long and thick, it swayed as I walked like a pair of enormous sea lion flippers. I rehearsed what I'd say to Carlos, debating whether to offer a clean, simple apology or explain my feelings so he knew why I felt so hurt. He had—after all—been rude.

Despite the darkness, once I rounded the corner, I saw the fueling station and Carlos's purple-trimmed boat. The vessel was about eighteen feet long, with two enormous motors, but no cabin or covering.

My stomach tightened.

Carlos turned when I approached the pier and froze. I had expected a wave or a smile but got nothing. Was this defiance? Anger? Revenge?

Maybe I'd made a mistake. Maybe I should retreat.

Eventually, he stepped onto the pier and got closer. Our eyes locked, and then the lines around his mouth softened.

"Hello," I said.

"Oh! Allie. My God, girl. I couldn't tell who it was. Good job on the disguise."

"Not my idea. I should be trick or treating with this getup."

"I'm glad you're here! Did you see the others yet?"

"I met Pedro and Mateo and spoke to Ian and Lucas. Guess I'll be on one of their boats."

"Yes, I'd love your company, but as you heard, I have to follow separately."

Apparently, apologies weren't necessary. He'd moved on. I would too. Then Carlos offered his condensed version of their plan.

All five of us would head toward Melinka Island near the entrance of the Corcovado Gulf. He said we would not make it to the island, but there were some rich feeding grounds along the way nestled between smaller, more unknown islands. I would travel with Ian and Pedro, Lucas and Mateo would follow, and he would be last—but far behind.

I didn't ask questions even though I had a million. I was scared to death and scared of death but did my best to hide both.

After his brief explanation that had nothing to do with my role, he ushered me to join the others. Departure was fifteen minutes away.

"This is it, Allie," he said, offering a cool embrace. "We'll get them now."

I wished I believed him.

When I returned to the dock, Ian was still running back and forth, loading last-minute items and shouting off instructions. His Spanish with them was too hurried for me to follow. Great, all I knew is that somehow I was supposed to pose as a whale researcher. *Fantastico*, I thought. Everyone's life depended on my acting skills.

Ian helped me board the *Mar-E-Sol*, a catchy name for our little vessel, that translated meant ocean and sun. He showed me a piece of equipment that resembled some old seventies tape recorder.

"It's an old tracking instrument that doesn't work. You'll be fiddling with it to keep the *Aguja* crew distracted long enough so Carlos can pass on a southern route."

"Sounds complicated," I said.

"I'll walk you through it. Don't worry."

I'd heard that a few too many times now but kept silent.

Minutes before departure, I descended into the tiny cabin, where I stayed clear from the guys as they pulled in ropes and prepared equipment. At best, two adults or three small children might fit inside this matchbox. Along with a spattering of holes on the ceiling and walls, I observed numerous wires, twisting like intestines throughout the claustrophobic space. Two electrical outlets awkwardly centered above the rusted sink didn't look trustworthy even under the calmest of ocean conditions.

In the center of the floor lay a red cooler, just like the one my mom had. My mind drifted to the summer picnics we shared. She often wore the same pink short-shorts and always brought a jug of a special lemonade I wasn't allowed to sample.

After we pulled away from the harbor, Ian joined me, offering a basic 101 on the antiquated communication equipment. Noting my silence before, during, and after the tutorial, he assured me more times than necessary that everything would be fine. He was about as convincing as most politicians.

We motored out, slowly at first. The diesel engine spewed thick billows of smoke that clung to us like magnetic glue. It was not a quiet boat. Lucas wasn't far behind, and, of course, we couldn't see Carlos since he was heading in the opposite direction.

Despite a patch, a handful of ginger candies, and an aspirin, within five minutes I was heaving over the starboard side, praying no one could see me. On such a small boat, that was unlikely. At least, afterward, I felt better. Almost normal.

The moist air that splattered against my face was exhilarating. It didn't feel cold, but then I was wearing an Eskimo jacket that resembled a spacesuit. Fifteen minutes after leaving the dock, the sun rose slowly, surrounded by streaks of orange and red that brightened the high clouds above.

"Look! There she is," said Ian, pointing east. My heart fluttered briefly, hoping to see Millie. But instantly I returned to project reality to see *La Aguja*—a monstrous commercial fishing vessel painted charcoal black like a seabound Darth Vader. I noticed "it" (not "she," as I refused to use the female pronoun for something so threatening) did not move. We were ridiculously close. That was definitely not one of the boats that attacked the Captain and me.

I would have remembered it.

"It's not moving," I said.

"No, but I'm not surprised. Remember, I told you we'd be passing her in the channel. Well, we're doing that now. Time to get ready."

I raised my binoculars. Several men were moving about on deck. I couldn't make out what they were doing, but they looked busy.

"It's massive," I said.

"Maybe seventy to eighty feet. In a few minutes, we're going to increase our speed. We'll give her a wide berth, but we'll have to get closer. They need to see you. Ditch the jacket. I'll give you a thumbs-up, and that's when I want you to go on deck, walk to the bow with your notebook in hand, and feign a serious discussion with Pedro. Point to the ocean, shake your head, and look at your notebook or the fake sonar machine. Use your binoculars if you want, but don't look their way. You need to represent someone who is seriously on a mission."

"Well, I am."

"True but not the one we're trying to sell."

"I don't have a notebook."

"I've got something you can use. We have you covered, girl."

"Uh-huh. Thanks. I think."

He patted my shoulder before leaving to talk to Pedro.

I walked to the helm, notebook and binoculars in hand. My acting debut lasted no more than five minutes. When I returned to the cabin, I felt damn proud of myself.

Ian increased our speed. We glanced at one another, sharing a look of nervous anticipation. It didn't take long. The bait worked. *La Aguja* began to move. Armando and his crew started to follow us, but there was a big gap.

"Allie, come here, Carlos is on the private VHF."

"Hola, Allie. You read? Over?"

"I'm here. I did it, Carlos. They're behind us."

"Yes, I saw a large boat on my radar. I thought it might be *La Aguja*. Thanks for confirming. I'm heading out now. I should be able to catch up with you by eleven. Tell Ian to reduce his speed another ten knots. I don't want you reaching the destination too soon."

We continued slowly for another hour. Ian said we would reach our destination in twenty minutes. It was ten thirty. I opened the bag Parker had packed and offered Ian half my sandwich.

"Nah, I'm good." Turning his head, I heard him whisper what sounded like "Uh-oh."

"What?" I asked.

"They're gone."

I walked back to the stern. He was right. No sign of *La Aguja*. "They were just there," I said. "Weren't they? When did you last see them?"

Ian shook his head. "Not sure. Not more than fifteen minutes. After we entered this channel, I knew we couldn't stay close enough to see them every minute. I'll go call Carlos."

"Good idea," I said.

While I scanned the waters looking for *La Aguja*, a general malaise in my head moved slowly toward my gut. I hoped it was seasickness or the onset of a cold, but I knew better. I'd felt this before. Twice. The first time was the day I met Miguel at the airport before the fateful trip south. The second time was the day the Captain and I set out to see whales and ended up as bait. Both times, the discomfort began before any indication of things going wrong, which led me to attribute the discomfort to something I'd eaten. This time, I knew better.

Ian didn't take long to return. And when he did, it was obvious he didn't have good news.

"I just tried calling Carlos. His radio is out," he said before rambling off instructions to Pedro.

"Lucas is still back there," I said. I just caught sight of their boat.

"Yes. We've spoken off the main radio channel. He said it was odd. *La Aguja* disappeared from their view too. He said he never saw them turn."

"That's strange. I don't think they could have hidden that monstrosity."

"Yes and no. I think I know what happened. When we first entered the channel, there was a hidden passage on our starboard side. At first I didn't see it because I was focused on following our route. I bet he moved in there, waited until we both passed, and went back. I can't believe I wasn't more careful."

"Don't blame yourself, Ian. We were all onboard. Besides, maybe there's a logical explanation."

"This happened after our communication with Carlos. I don't know how he could have picked up that channel, but the timing seems remarkably consequential."

"You think something happened to Carlos?"

"I'm hoping it's an equipment error, but if they hacked our radio system, he could have been attacked."

As we turned around and picked up speed, fear left me struggling to breathe, along with all the reminders of people hurt or killed under my watch.

Finally, we located Carlos's boat. As we approached, Ian slowed down and then cut the motor once the hulls were side by side. He yelled Carlos's name.

Waves slapping underneath us made the absence of other sound unnerving. Occasionally our boat tapped Carlos's. I waited for him to appear. To wave those big hands and tell us everything was under control.

"Carlos," I screamed, scanning the area for signs of foul play.

After latching our rope onto the metal cleat on Carlos's boat, Ian tightened his life vest and crawled onboard.

CHAPTER 47

⟨≈≈≋≋≋⟩

Not again. An unwanted flashback of the incident that killed
Captain Jack sent tremors through my chest.

Finally, Ian emerged. He pointed to the cabin, letting
us know Carlos was inside. By the grimace on his face, I knew
something had happened. He yelled to us, but we couldn't make out
what he was saying because of the swells smacking the underside
of the boat. I ran to the cabin so I could call over the marine radio.

He answered immediately. "Allie, he's been shot. Hit in the
shoulder and losing a lot of blood. Call the Coast Guard."

I wasn't surprised he'd been shot but was surprised they only
hit his shoulder. I told Pedro to make the call while I prepared to
move toward the bow, where I could climb onto the port side of
Carlos's boat. Nobody would be able to help me, so I made sure I
had a firm grip on the gunwale as I moved from one boat to the
other. Each step seemed to be a greater challenge with the growing
swells. If I took a wrong step, I could end up in the Pacific.

When my two feet landed on Carlos's boat, I took a deep breath
before shuffling down the stairs to the cabin. Ian had placed a blanket over our friend, and my eyes went directly to a patch of dark
brown on the area covering Carlos's shoulder. The spot, a rusty
shade of brown, was spreading. Carlos's eyes were open. I thought
his lips twitched when he saw me, but maybe I imagined that. Ian
instructed me to keep pressure on the wound while he went on deck
to watch for Lucas and Mateo and the Coast Guard.

Nancy Rhodes

Carlos suddenly groaned.

"Don't try to talk," I said. "Just rest."

He mumbled some form of acknowledgment.

"You're going to be fine. Help will be here soon." My words sounded fake.

"Let me prop up your head," I said, tucking a sweatshirt underneath. He blinked simultaneously with both eyes. I stared at him, and he did it again.

"I know you want to say something. It can wait. You need to rest. You can tell me…tell us everything later."

He blinked his eyes three more times. His head moved slightly. Then another groan. His mouth opened. "Arman…"

"Armando. Yes, that's who shot you."

Carlos nodded slightly before his eyes rolled high and his lids closed. His breath slowed in speed and intensity.

"Carlos! Carlos, wake up!" Thinking that he might slip into unconsciousness, I popped up so fast I hit my head on the cabin ceiling. The pain radiated down my neck.

I walked out of the cabin and yelled to Ian to return quickly.

Once aboard, Ian pointed to a closed cabinet. "I need gauze and a strap or some form of tourniquet."

"It's locked!" I said.

"*Arriba!*" He pointed to the top of the cabinet.

I grabbed the first aid kit and handed Ian the roll of gauze. While I kept an eye on Carlos's chest, praying for each new breath, Ian got busy removing the soaked wad of paper towels from Carlos's upper arm and rewrapping the wound with clean gauze. Then he pulled his sweatshirt off to remove an undershirt, which he moistened and used to stroke Carlos's forehead.

"Let me do that, Ian. You should put that sweatshirt back on."

As I gently wiped Carlos's forehead, I began to note the color leave his face.

Lucas and Pedro arrived only a few minutes later. Lucas jumped onboard, arms full of supplies including a few clean cloths and a bottle of pills.

"Can't get any real help around here," he said. "The Coast Guard won't be able to get here for at least another thirty minutes. We'll have to go to Quellón, and I think we should take this boat."

Ian mumbled something to Lucas in Spanish. They exchanged a despairing glance.

The plan was that Lucas, Ian, and I would take Carlos on his boat to get help on shore. Pedro would take *Mar-E-Sol* back, but Mateo would stay put on his boat until he connected with the Coast Guard to cancel the distress call.

Lucas volunteered to navigate while Ian and I stayed next to Carlos. My hands, locked around Carlos's wrist, counted each heartbeat.

CHAPTER 48

⎯⎯⎯⎯⎯⎯⎯⎯⎯⎯

Carlos ended up in the same hospital where I'd been two months prior. I'd forgotten how small it was. I hadn't forgotten the stench of bleach and urine.

Ian and I stayed until half past midnight, leaving when one heavy-set female nurse politely kicked us out. She said they'd removed the bullet, and his prognosis was favorable. But he was heavily sedated.

Ian dropped me off at Parker's. She was still awake, so I stayed up longer than I wanted to, filling her in on all that occurred and his current condition.

"I know you didn't want to do this, Allie," she said, staring into my eyes with more compassion than I deserved. "I'm sorry it turned out this way. I bet you're discouraged."

"It is beyond discouraging. It's maddening. But for now, I'm exhausted and am going to bed."

Even though my eyelids closed as soon as my head hit the pillow, my brain did not. I fell asleep insanely too close to daylight.

Parker's phone, in the other room, woke me.

"Oh, that's good news," I heard her say. "Is he awake?"

After a pause and several uh-huh's and *biens*, she said, "Thanks, Ian. Yes, of course, I'll let her know."

I grabbed a long flannel robe from the closet and hobbled into the living room. "News?"

"Yes. Ian said that Carlos woke finally, but he is groggy. Ian suggested waiting until after eleven to visit. You should go back to sleep."

"Thank God. That's great news."

"So you're heading back to bed then?"

I turned around. "I'll try."

Parker nodded as she turned to the kitchen, most likely to bake something that would soon fill the home with a rich, sweet aroma. With or without whiffs of yeasty sweetness, I'd never fall back to sleep.

I brought my old whale journals to bed and read them. One after the other. I wasn't prepared for the level of darkness that set in. Was this the last straw—time to call it quits? Go back to California, or some foreign land where nobody knew me?

Pulling Parker's rose-patterned quilt across my chest, I reminded myself of all the good people I'd met in Chile. Those who helped me, expecting nothing in return, including Carlos, Ian, Lucas, Parker, and the Captain.

Then there was me and my propensity to give up. To run when things got ugly. To hide when things got uncomfortable. My list was long. Many, too many, relationships, a few chances of marriage, having kids, giving up on getting a master's in social work while settling for a crappy job. And the biggie—giving up on finding Miguel, the impetus for leaving the United States and returning to this tiny stretch of country that outlined the Pacific like an exaggerated apostrophe.

Quitter. Quitter. Quitter!

I grabbed my cell phone and called Jeff. It'd been about two months since we'd spoken. He answered immediately.

"How are you?" I asked.

"Good, but I only have a few minutes to talk. Remember, one of us still has a nine-to-fiver. What's up?"

"Jeff, I miss you."

"You mean you need to vent?"

Smiling but wanting to cry, I agreed. "Everything I do or try to do gets fucked up. I don't know what I'm doing."

"Talk to me."

"I wouldn't even know where to start with all that's happened recently."

"Uh-oh. Well, Cinderella, this sounds like more than a ten-minute conversation. But I'm listening."

I took a breath and crammed the last few months into fifteen minutes.

"So why have the whales become so important to you?" he asked. "Weren't you there to settle things with what's-his-name?"

Fair question. After all, it was idealistic to think my contribution or efforts could save even one whale. And lately, all I did was get people injured. Or killed.

"Jeff, I came down here to find Miguel, but you knew that, didn't you?" Not waiting for the reply I expected, I kept talking. "But now, I don't give a rat's ass about Miguel. I should care. I mean what happened cursed me for so much of my life. But you know when I see these whales, things feel different. I can't explain it. But now, I'm scared. Everything is telling me I should quit. But I want to do something right. I want purpose in my life."

"Who is telling you to quit?"

"The poachers. First the threats to you and your family, then the attack on the boat and Captain Jack's death. And now, well, yesterday, we were out at sea, and Carlos was shot."

"Shot? What the hell are you doing down there?"

"It's complicated."

"No shit. So…Carlos—is that the guy you met when you first went down?"

"Yes. He'll be okay. He's in the hospital, recovering."

"What happened?"

"We were looking for whales…well, for the poachers. We had this big master plan to trap the man thought to be the leader. Not sure what happened. But the men we were following suddenly turned back and attacked Carlos. He was alone on his own boat."

"Allie, you have to get out of there. Whether they're after Carlos or you, seems like this is way too dangerous."

"But you don't understand. If you could only see these whales. They get to you. Once you see them up close, it's life-changing. I just wish…."

"Wish? I don't think you have the luxury of wishing anything. Please tell me you'll get on the next plane and get your ass back here!"

"Oh, Jeff, I shouldn't have called you. Look, you're right. There is a level of danger, and yes, I'm scared. But I can't quit now. I can't give up. Like you said, I just had to vent. I think I knew all along I would have to continue. I'm sorry. This probably doesn't make any sense, and I don't expect you to understand."

"I'm trying to. But I also know how you get when you make up your mind about something. This worries me. I just hope you'll be more cautious if you're going to stick this out."

"Of course."

"Well, I'm officially late, and the new boss isn't too keen on me as it is. I've got to go, but I'll leave you with one thing. Admittedly, I'm saying this against my better judgment, but there's one thing I know about you, Allie, and that is you're a hell of a strong woman, even if you don't see yourself that way. You are resilient. I also know you're a bit stubborn, which means you don't let go of things that are important to you. If this is that important to you, stick it out. Help this Carlos dude. Screw Miguel and whatever shit-ass thing he did to you. That's in the past. If you can save a whale or two, then do what you need to do. Or at least have a great love affair with that Carlos guy once he's healed, so you can come back happy."

I had to laugh. So typical of Jeff. "It's not about that."

"Uh-huh. Yeah."

Jeff's daughter suddenly screamed in the not-so-distant background.

"Hey, I'm sorry, but Kira's having a tantrum. Cereal is flying like B-52s across the kitchen floor. And Maggie's gone to work, so I've got to get this kid to day care and get to the paper before they fire my ass."

"Jeffrey?"

"Yes?"

"Do you really think I'm strong?"

"Babe, you are Wonder Woman on steroids. But right now you're a pain in the ass."

I laughed louder this time. Then I hung up.

He did it again. God, why couldn't I find someone with Jeff's sensibility, Miguel's sex appeal, and Carlos's selflessness wrapped up in one educated, addiction-free, tall and fit body?

I shook my head. *Whales, Allie—whales*!

CHAPTER 49

arlos got out of the hospital the next day. Three days later he returned to sea. He said he had to get back out there to catch Montero.

I wasn't invited. I felt the heaviness of exclusion.

Later that evening, Parker settled me down. Wine, cheese, and her jovial spirit did the trick. She explained the inner workings of the fishermen she'd come to know, semijoking that their minds and egos worked as one.

Men, she reminded me, don't process experiences like women do. They tend to want to get out and do something. While it wasn't the first time I'd heard this Venus-versus-Mars rationale, Parker's explanation helped shake my self-absorbed, poor-me attitude.

Ian called me that night. Also trying to offer consolation, he said that he didn't expect they would find Armando. He felt certain that demon was long gone but wanted to support his friend. Swallowing my disappointment, I told him he was a good man.

I spent the day walking the city, checking out the library, schools, and parks and passing a multitude of coffee shops, hostels, and restaurants. When I got back to the harbor, dozens of *lanchas* littered the docks. The low tide exposed ripples of mud, slivers of driftwood, an array of broken shells, and numerous globs of jellyfish. I lost track of time, having left both my watch and phone at Parker's, but by the rumbling in my stomach, it was past lunchtime. I found a pub with enough people inside to convince me to enter.

A young waitress delivered my *empanadas de marisco* along with the bill.

I ate slowly and then lingered, not feeling ready to return to the house.

"¿*Desea algo mas*?" the girl asked. Her anxiousness annoyed me. Was it because I was a gringa that she wanted to push me out as soon as possible? I bit my tongue.

"No," I answered, pulling out my credit card.

"Miss, sorry. Only cash," she said pointing to a sign above the bar that I regrettably hadn't noticed. Their credit card machine was out of order. The sign looked worn, so whatever the issue, it had been a while.

Trying my best to hide my frustration, I turned my attention to scouring the interior of my wallet and day pack. The stray coins and two small bills didn't come close. I stuttered my best attempt an apology in Spanish.

"You are American, no?" she said.

"Yes," I said, wondering if this would increase my liability.

"Where are you from?"

"California," I said, fighting back words like shit, crap, and stronger expletives. I didn't really want to do this small-talk dance. Not now. Not ever. I just wanted them to fix their damn credit card machine. I held back and forced myself to smile. This was not the time to make enemies.

"I like California," she said, pulling out a chair to join me, oblivious to her other customers. "I spent six months there as an exchange student."

"Where?" I did appreciate a fellow traveler. So, yes, I could be civil.

"San Diego. I love it! Very beautiful town. I am attending university now but hope to go back after I graduate."

"That's brave," I said, extending my hand. "I'm Allie, by the way."

I was beginning to like her despite my situation. I wanted to tell her what we had in common, how I moved to Chile when I was about her age…but decided to skip it. This wasn't about me. Except, however, paying the bill, which was only the equivalent of a buck fifty.

"I'm Ana," she said, reaching for my hand. "No worries, Miss Allie. You can pay another time. Are you going to be in town for a while?"

"Yes, I'm staying here, so I'll come back tomorrow with the cash."

"You stay at Hotel Paradiso?"

"No, I'm staying with a friend."

"*Que bueno.* This is a nice town. Many good people."

"Yes, it is. If Parker—that's my friend who's given me a room—if she can loan me her car, I'll come back tonight before you close."

"*Perdone*, did you say Parker?"

"Yes. Why? Do you know her?"

"¡*Por Dios*! She's my auntie!"

I asked her if she meant a blood-related aunt versus the customary practice of referring to a family friend as "*tia.*"

"Yes, she's my father's sister. Well, she was. My father died several years ago."

"Oh, I'm so sorry."

"Yes, only fifty-nine. I know Parker is much older. She was his half sister. Same dad, different mom."

Realizing a couple at a nearby table was ready to order, she said, "I better go. Please give my best to Parker. I haven't seen her since… well, in a very long time."

"I will, Ana. And I'll see you soon with the money. I don't want you to lose your job!"

"It's okay. My mom owns this," she said waving her hands in a wide sweep. "She needs me here."

I looked around, hoping to offer my apology directly to her mother.

"She's not here right now, but you don't worry about the money. *No hay apurro.*"

"That's nice of you. But I wouldn't feel comfortable with that. *Nos vemos.*"

"Okay. *Chao*," she said, her dark ponytail swaying from side to side as she hurried to the next table.

I TOLD PARKER ABOUT ANA OVER A SECOND DINNER THAT NIGHT. She had the food ready when I walked in the door, and I didn't have the heart to tell her I'd already eaten. One thing I'd learned about Parker was never to refuse her food. She took it personally if every morsel didn't disappear from your plate.

"I didn't realize she was grown up," Parker said in an uncharacteristically cool tone.

"Ana is attending college. She spent six months as an exchange student in the States. So, her father was your brother?"

"Marco, he was my half brother. We weren't very close, only lived together for about a year when I was thirteen and he was four. We exchanged Christmas cards and talked now and then. But I hardly had any contact with his wife, Ana's mom. I heard she ran the restaurant, but, well, *no me gusta*—I mean—I don't like eating out. Such a waste of money."

Sounded like there was more to that story, but I didn't press her. After several minutes, Parker put down her spoon.

"You know, Marco was an active fisherman. We only fished together a few times, but I knew the crowd he hung out with. In fact, he had some encounters with whales—big whales, apparently. Or so he said."

Her eyebrows suddenly rose into her hairline. She looked away.

"Parker? What is it?"

"Many years ago, several years before he died…." She stopped midsentence.

"What? What happened?"

"One time—this might have been when Ana was a baby—he invited me to go crabbing with him. After returning, we sat on the dock. He'd brought beer, so we hung out. After a few beers, he got chatty."

She stopped. Her eyes drifted again, like she was looking for someone. Or something. "I'm sorry, Allie."

"Sorry? Sorry about what?"

"Sorry I'd forgotten this. We have to tell Carlos!"

"Tell Carlos what?"

"I just remembered something. An important story Marco told me some time ago. At the time, I thought he'd fabricated the whole thing because he did have a reputation for spinning tales."

"What story?" I said, really wishing she'd get to the point.

"He talked about some guys who were killing whales."

"Really? What did he say?"

"Well, this was over ten years ago. Marco had just seen one of the biggest blue whales ever. He was excited about it, but like I said, I wasn't buying his story."

"Parker! You keep mentioning his story! Please explain what you mean." My breath shortened as my knee took on an independent gymnastic routine.

"Yes, well, if I remember this right, he said after they saw that whale, a friend of his told all the guys on the boat that there was a group of men from Chiloé bragging about their Moby Dick skills. Marco said they had some kind of ties to the government. He suspected it had to do with the environmentalists' movement to close salmon fisheries because of the toxins spewing out of the hatcheries and poisoning blue whales. At least a dozen were found stranded along the coastline."

Parker paused, as if pulling details of this serious conversation from some long-buried memory.

"Yes, I remember now. Marco said that his friend told him that the government wanted the problem to *go away*. I don't know. It doesn't make sense, but I guess—if any of this was true—the government wanted to make it look like the blues had left so the fisheries could continue without opposition. Seemed so far-fetched, I dismissed it as something some bored old fishermen whipped up after too many beers."

"Carlos now thinks there's no involvement with the government."

"We'll talk to him tonight. Maybe you could ask Ana's mom, Sra. Pacelli, when you go back. He was her husband."

"Do you know when Carlos will get back?" I asked.

"He's probably just now getting off the boat. I've saved him some soup, so it depends if he comes straight here or goes home to shower first."

We ate the rest of the *casuela* in silence. Finishing the last few spoonfuls, I heard a car pulling into Parker's gravel driveway. I ran to the window.

"It's Carlos!" I said, happy that he skipped the shower.

CHAPTER 50

Carlos was familiar with the salmon farm theory but had never found sufficient evidence. And while he hated the Pinochet dictatorship as much as anybody, he couldn't believe that the regime would hire poachers to kill whales to protect a salmon farm.

"Either this theory is completely bogus," he said, "or we're only hearing part of the story. We do need to check it out. I'll go with you to the restaurant. I'd like to meet Ana's mom."

Looking at my watch, I said, "Do we have time? When do you think she closes?"

"Probably late. Let's go."

Parker shifted in her seat. "Carlos, *debes comer primero.*" (You should eat first.)

Winking at me, Carlos agreed to eat a small bowl as long as she understood he'd have to eat quickly and run.

On our way to town, I asked Carlos how his day went.

"Therapeutic in a distracting sense, but pulling crab pots isn't my thing. I'm ready to go back to whales. Back to saving species, not killing them."

"I know. And I've been thinking about that. I want to help."

"Good," he said, taking his eyes off the road to flash me a somewhat sinister-looking grin.

"What's that mean? Do you have a plan? A project, perhaps?"

"Something like that," he sneered. "I'm sorry. I know I have no right to ask this of you. Not after everything that's happened."

"You're the one who got shot. What do you need me to do?"

"You remember the package?"

"How can I forget? Why?"

"I need to get my hands on it. We're so close now. But without those records, we still can't prove anything."

"Huh? I thought you had it."

"Did but don't. I left it in El Toyo. I was really worried about being followed and felt I couldn't risk taking it with me. I left it at the house after Karina moved in. I asked her to try to get it back to Jorge or hide it if she couldn't locate him. Thought it'd be safer there."

"So why didn't you ask Karina about it?"

"I was going to. I called her a few weeks after I left, but then she told me she had stage three breast cancer. She'd just found out and was freaked out. I couldn't bring it up."

"Oh, that explains why she looked so bad when I saw her. God, I'm so sorry! She's so young. Have you talked to her at all recently?"

"Couldn't. Tried a few times, but the number was disconnected."

I wondered why she would have canceled her phone. I shook my head.

"So you need the package?"

"Yes, we have to get our hands on it. The sooner the better. I was hoping you could get the papers from El Toyo."

"You want me to head up north? Wouldn't it be better if you went? She barely knows me."

"I can't go back there. People in that town know me too well. Word will get out. I don't know if the Montero cronies are still in that area, but I don't think it'd be wise. Remember, that's where it all began."

"How am I supposed to get the papers?"

"Go back to the house. Speak to Karina. You'll be able to do that more tactfully than I ever could. But Allie, if she's not home, I'll need you to go into the house and get them. I mean, we don't really know what's happened to Karina. And we don't have much time."

His words hung in the air. Was he thinking she'd died?

"This sounds complicated. Don't you have them saved on a disc?"

Stupid question. He wouldn't be asking me if he did. But I didn't know what to say. Here I was, once again, faced with something so completely out of my comfort zone. I might as well jump from the Eiffel Tower.

"No disc. No copy. None of us trusted technology. That was our mistake—paper only. We especially need that song sheet."

"Blue Song?"

"Yes. You remember."

"Of course. It was a beautiful song title. I was disappointed I never got to hear the song."

"Sorry to burst your bubble, but I'm not sure there was ever an actual song. I think Jorge thought there was—or could be, with his help—otherwise he wouldn't have gone to the conservatory that day. If there was a song, then a code was somehow embedded in the song sheet. There should be something that points to the locations where they've killed the greatest numbers of whales. It may contain information detailing future targeted sights."

"Carlos, this is crazy. Are you sure about this?"

"Only somewhat. But regardless, the papers are important. The sighting reports alone, even the names, won't be enough to indict anyone. Names were probably falsified, and I'm not sure any attorney or anyone on the Whaling Commission could take action without something more specific. So that's why I'm thinking the key has to be in that 'Blue Song' sheet."

"So," I said, looking out the window at the orange hues of sunlight disappearing beyond the horizon, "what if you're wrong about government involvement?"

"I don't follow."

"I'm afraid of retaliation. I can't shake what happened here in the seventies."

"Allie, remember what I told you—we're not under a dictatorship. Our plan, once we have solid proof, is to take our cases to the

Nancy Rhodes

Whaling Commission."

"What if someone connected with the poachers finds out?" I asked. "We know they would retaliate."

"The Whaling Commission will handle this carefully. I know who to talk to so word doesn't leak out to the wrong people."

Feeling a surge of heat, I cracked the window.

Carlos turned off the heater and momentarily took his eyes off the road. "It's raining."

"Right," I said, twisting the window crank back up. "What about Jorge? What's his involvement? I still keep coming back to the fact he didn't want the cops to have the papers."

"I think it was more about who he did want than who he didn't."

"Meaning you?"

"Exactly."

I watched him run his hands around the steering wheel. Nice hands. Strong hands. "Have you heard from him recently?" I asked.

"No, but that's not unusual. We've gone months without contact. Don't worry so much, gringa. Jorge is on our side. That man loves whales more than anyone I know."

"Not more than you."

"Maybe not."

"Do you think we are still being watched?"

"It's possible, but we haven't seen any signs of that."

Sighing, I shrugged. "That's not reassuring."

The wind and rain howled as we approached the street where I'd found the pub.

After Carlos parked, he looked at me and said, "I know it's a lot to ask, but you're the only one who can pull this off. You two got along, right?"

"Well, as I said, she looked terrible—very thin, bags under her eyes. But yeah, she was friendly enough. If she's not there, what do you propose? That I break into a house sealed with security bars across every window?"

"Good point. We often left the back door open, but no guarantee she would. Hopefully, she'll be there."

"And you think the song sheet is going to be on her coffee table, waiting for my sweet little self to confiscate it?"

"No, smart-ass. You'll have to look for it. When I was there, we kept all our important papers in a small box tucked underneath the crawl space door in the bedroom closet. She may have moved it, but that house isn't exactly a mansion. It can't be too hard to find."

I looked at Carlos. "I've got to be honest—this is way beyond my comfort zone."

"Understandable. Come on, my friend, let's go talk to Sra. Pacelli."

I prayed Ana's mother could reveal something helpful, something that might eliminate the need for a trip back to El Toyo.

CHAPTER 51

Sra. Pacelli insisted we call her Alexandra. After introducing myself and Carlos, I handed her the money for my meal, including a generous tip.

"Thank you," she said without glancing at the bills. "It was kind of you to come back. I'm so sorry about the credit card machine."

"Is Ana here? I'd love to say hello."

"No, she's off now."

"Alexandra," I said, looking around at the small crowd. "We were wondering if we could talk to you about your husband, Marco."

"Has this something to do with Parker?"

I noticed a level of discomfort that I'd seen in Parker. Carlos and I looked at one another. If there was some family riff, I had no intention of putting my spoon into that custard.

"Not directly," I answered. "But we do have a question about something your husband once said to Parker about whale poachers."

"Oh yes," she said, looking relieved and pointing to a table near the back. "Let's sit over there."

Carlos asked her a couple of questions about the place as we took our seats. Eventually, Alexandra more or less confirmed what Parker said but didn't add any useful information. I wondered if we'd wasted our time.

She offered us drinks, which we declined. I saw Carlos eying the bar, knowing he'd love a local beer, but we'd agreed earlier to keep our visit short.

"There is something you should know," she said rather suddenly. "It seems Parker hasn't told you much about my Marco, her half-brother?"

Carlos scooted his wooden chair closer to the table.

"No, not much," I said. The truth was I found it strange she'd never mentioned having a brother until I met Ana.

"They never were close, but they had a bad fight. Sadly, it was the night before his heart attack. He died before I got him to the hospital."

"Oh, I'm so sorry," I said, trying to erase a vision of her driving frantically to the hospital while her husband took his last breath. I wondered if she blamed Parker for his death.

"What was the fight about?" Carlos asked.

"Carlos! I'm sure that's not our business," I said, trying unsuccessfully to tap his shin with my foot.

Alexandra shook her head. "It's okay. It's a fair question. I never wanted to talk about this," she said pausing briefly to take another breath. "But maybe it's time."

"It's okay," I said, now feeling Carlos's foot hitting the tops of my toes. This game of footsie communication had to stop.

"I don't know if it will help you, but it sort of relates to whales… well, really a painting of whales. The argument was about an oil painting that their father had owned since they were kids. Marco asked Parker about it after their father died. He said that their dad had promised it to him. He was pretty stubborn or insistent that Parker give it to him.

"But Parker was furious that he had the nerve to ask about it before their father's spirit had gone to the afterworld. So she refused to give it to him then and later when she emptied the house. Of course, not long after Marco passed, she returned the damn thing. Well, she didn't. She had a friend bring it."

My eyes scanned the walls.

"It's over there, behind you, Allie. Behind the bar."

As I stood, she added, "I still don't like it. I never wanted to see it again, but Ana loved it and insisted we put it up. She said it'd be good for business."

I smiled, not knowing how to respond.

Alexandra ran her hand through her thick, short hair. "It's been there collecting dust for many years! My Ana said it would bring us good luck. How ironic! But she didn't know. I never told her that ridiculous painting probably killed her father."

Not knowing how to respond, I fought the urge to get a closer look at it. But Carlos, Mr. No Filter, did just that. I cocked my head, glancing at her in a silent apology. She patted the top of my shoulder gently.

"Go ahead, *mi hita,* go look. I'm not so angry now." Pausing, she pushed a strand of hair from her face. "He did, after all, have a bad heart and refused to diet or exercise."

At first glance, I dismissed the painting as another exaggerated attempt of depicting a turbulent ocean, overdramatized with thick smudges of blue and gray. My sister, a self-proclaimed connoisseur of original oil paintings depicting oceans, rivers, or lakes, had many of these garish paintings inside her 3,600-square-foot home.

Carlos raised his index finger and pointed to the very edge of where the ocean met the sky.

"Yes!" exclaimed Alexandra. "*Ballenas.*"

They weren't obvious, but as I leaned forward, I saw the arched backs of two whales, painted with streaks of charcoal gray. The images were like the rest of the painting, without sharp detail, like looking at something with the wrong prescription lenses.

"Interesting," I whispered.

"You don't like it either," said Alexandra.

"I didn't mean…."

"Don't worry, my dear. I'm not attached to it. I enjoy observing people's reactions to it. Some hate it. A few like it. Most have no opinion one way or the other."

Carlos cleared his throat. "Well, I like it. I like it a lot. It is a bit impressionistic, but the way one has to look deep into the painting to see the whales in the turbulent ocean speaks volumes to one who has spent two decades trying to do just that."

"You should have it then," she said, shocking us both.

We turned, mouths agape. Carlos stammered with his response, a slight pink peering through his olive-toned cheeks. "Oh no, I did not mean to suggest anything."

"Of course you didn't. But we are going to fix this place up a bit. In fact, in a month or so, we're going to paint it, replace chairs, that kind of thing. It's time for this to go. The sooner the better. It does need a new frame. As you see, it's oxidized a bit."

"What about your daughter?" I asked. "You said she didn't want to part with it."

"No. She's moved on. Believe me, I've asked her. Now she likes that modern stuff. Splotches and cubes and lots of color."

Carlos took a step back. "I was admiring it, but I don't have a place for it. Thank you though."

Alexandra dropped her head. "Well, there's only one thing to do. We should give it to Parker."

"Of course. That's perfect. We can bring it to her if you'd like," I said.

"*Si, si*, that would be great. Take it tonight. Please."

Carlos lifted the painting from the hook and gently placed it against the bar.

"I guess we should be going, Carlos," I said, slinging my weathered day pack across one shoulder.

"There is more to the story," she said. "If you can stay a bit longer, I think you might want to hear this."

"Yes, certainly," I said, looking at Carlos, who nodded in agreement. We returned to the table, carefully leaning the painting against the table legs.

"About a week before this stupid fight," she said, her voice quivering slightly, "I was behind the bar cleaning up glasses. It was just before closing."

She took a deep breath as if finding the courage to continue. "The door opened, and three *carabineros* came in asking to speak with Marco. I know the local police well. Most of them come here for nightcaps or food, but I'd never see these men before. They asked if they could speak to my husband. I didn't like the looks of them, so I told them he wasn't available. They demanded I find him, that it was important and urgent. So I said that I'd check again upstairs. I took off my apron, my hands shaking so much I had trouble undoing the tie. Then I slowly walked up the stairs, intending to warn Marco and help him hide."

She sighed.

Carlos shifted in his seat, extending his legs from beneath the table. "So what happened?"

She leaned forward. "He wasn't there! And I knew he'd been up there. I was so confused, because if he'd come down, I'd have heard him. I called out his name. I looked under the beds, in the bathtub, closets, everywhere! It wasn't until I turned to go back downstairs that I noticed the upstairs window was open. Later he told me that he'd heard the men. He was confident that they weren't really police and had no intention of talking to them."

"What did you tell them?" I asked.

"The truth. That he wasn't there and I didn't know where he was."

Carlos looked at the painting and then back to Alexandra. "Did Marco ever explain why they were looking for him?"

"He told me we were not going to talk about it. And when Marco didn't want to talk about something, we didn't talk about it. He was old school, you know. Macho, I think is the word you use for this."

"Didn't that bother you?" I asked.

"We'd been married a long time. Some things are better left unsaid or, in this case, unknown."

After removing the painting and saying our goodbyes, we headed back to Parker's. We both agreed they had an unusual relationship, finding it difficult to believe that she wouldn't want to know why some cops were going out of their way to find him.

When we arrived at Parker's, I asked Carlos if he was going to give her the painting right away.

"I'll bring it in," he said. "We don't need to say much."

"Keep it simple?"

"I can do that."

"I wish we could ask Parker if she knows something more about Alexandra's story."

Carlos shook his head. "Remember. Simple."

"Yeah, yeah. Okay. Let's head in."

Parker barely reacted to the painting. At one point, she said something about the frame. She liked the frame, rust and all. I was tempted to ask her about Marco, but one look at Carlos reminded me to keep my mouth shut. Besides, he was her half brother, and they weren't close. She probably knew nothing.

"Parker, I'm going to walk Carlos to his car. I'll be right back."

"I'm off to bed, kiddo. *Buenos noches.*"

As we walked to his car, I gathered my courage. "I've made up my mind," I said.

"Uh, okay?"

"I'll go to El Toyo."

Carlos turned. We were so close that for some stupid reason I expected a kiss. I wanted a kiss.

I didn't get a kiss. But he thanked me. And with it, a smile—a genuine smile that, in that moment, was enough.

CHAPTER 52

While I worked on my plans to return to Santiago and El Toyo, Carlos put together a team for a one-week trip to look for blues. He contacted a biologist, a photographer, and three well-experienced seamen. I couldn't hide my envy. I'd rather be losing my cookies in the deep blue seas than trying to steal a music sheet from someone's home.

Fortunately, Parker had the wherewithal and time to help me plan my trip. I could take one long bus ride to Puerto Montt or travel by ferry, small plane, and larger plane. Since sitting on one bus for all those hours sounded excruciating, I chose the latter. I'd start with a five-hour ferry ride to Chaitén. Since Chaitén was the third of my three targeted areas, I liked this option. Plus, we'd pass through the scenic channels of the Chiloé archipelago. From Chaitén I would fly on a twin-engine plane to Puerto Montt, where I'd have to spend the night before catching a two-hour flight to Santiago.

She warned me that at this time of year, there would only be one ferry a week, and with inclement weather, trips might be delayed or canceled. I told her I had lots of time. For once in my life, I would practice patience and flexibility. Besides, I wasn't all that anxious to reach my destination.

The ferry left as scheduled. And, thankfully, the ocean was calm and clear for the first two hours. We passed several islands. I sighted a couple of whales spouting, but the height of the spray was far too low to be coming from a blue. A few other passengers saw it, reacting with the typical whale-sighting enthusiasm. I smiled when one older woman enthusiastically asked if I saw the whale, extending her binoculars my way.

"That's okay. But thanks."

I returned to my hard Pullman seat. Maybe I'd become a whale snob, but honestly, if they weren't blues or smaller whales that breached, spy hopped, or nestled close to the boat, I'd just as soon be inside the cabin trying to get warm.

I didn't exactly love the plane ride to Puerto Montt. Never having been in a plane holding less than a busload of people, I wasn't prepared to feel every air pocket. And while I still got sick on boats, I preferred ocean travel to air travel any day.

The bed in the small motel near the Puerto Montt airport was soft and bumpy but still greatly appreciated. I buried myself beneath the thick wool blankets, not once worrying about spiders or bedbugs. I had to wake early for my morning flight to Santiago. Fortunately, it left on time, so I expected to be in Santiago somewhere between noon and two, depending on Santiago traffic from the airport.

Even though it was spring, the layer of smog covering Santiago was as menacing as any summer day. I wasn't happy being in a large city—especially this one. After renting a car, I drove toward Providencia to look for an affordable and hopefully inconspicuous motel. Fortunately, off-season rates meant I didn't have to stay in a flea-infested hostel.

The next day, I called Jeff. It was comforting to hear his voice again. I wasn't exactly forthcoming with details concerning my departure from southern Chile, but he was used to my unexplainable activities. After a brief discussion about whether I would be returning to the States soon, he mentioned my sister was trying to reach me.

"Sarah? What about?"

"Don't know. She was vague. But you should give her a call."

"Do I have to?"

"God, you haven't changed."

"Beg to differ about that, but as far as talking to Sarah, you're correct."

We bantered like our usual selves for nearly an hour. In the end, I assured him I'd call Sarah sometime. But frankly, with what I had to do, Sarah the snake would have to wait.

The house in El Toyo looked tragically worse than the last time I'd seen it. The boarded windows and missing lock on the gate were indicative of no tenants. I prayed that didn't mean Karina had died. An old bicycle lay against one side of the house, its tires flat and chain turned brownish-orange. A basket clung to the front bars, filled with layers of decomposed leaves. A miniature compost bin.

I walked up the fragile steps and tapped on the door, at first gently with my knuckles, then with my fist.

"Anyone there?" I said, looking around in hopes no one on the street was watching. "Hello?" I yelled, unabashedly conspicuous.

After several minutes I left the front porch and walked to the side of the house. I hadn't gone but ten steps when a eucalyptus root seemingly grabbed my foot, sending me off balance. My knees took the brunt of my landing, although my right arm hit the edge of a rock and decided to bleed. In trying to stand too quickly, my right knee hyperextended. Some great spy I'd turned out to be.

Worried the pain would intensify with time, I hobbled back to an upright position, dusted off my pants, and walked slowly toward the back porch. Thistles and overgrown shrubs had grown high. The outbuilding Carlos mentioned was only a few steps past the porch.

One glance and I knew no one would stash important records inside this unlocked, piece-of-shit shed. The room was less than eight feet square. A few barren shelves lined one side. A rake hung from a hook. No signs of loose floorboards. I turned to leave. *A rake? Really?* While it wasn't uncommon to leave a rake behind, what caught my attention was that it looked new. Very odd, considering the shape of everything else. Even the Jumbo Supermarket price tag was unscathed.

I left the shed, my pain intensifying with each step. The back door was, of course, locked. Tilting my head upward, I noticed a small window above the door. But the problem was access.

And my knee.

Sporadic-yet-sudden twinges of pain traveled the length of my leg in protest. Blood had seeped through my jeans. I didn't want to look at it. Nor did I need to. I knew that inflammation was increasing the size of my knee by the way my skin pushed against the denim.

Tired, I leaned against the house, afraid if I sat again, I would never get up. Wishing I had cell service to call Carlos, I took a few breaths, trying to center my thoughts. Breaking a window wasn't an option. Like many Chilean homes, every reachable window was protected with thick iron bars. I looked again at the window above the back door, my only hope. But how? It had to be at least twice my height.

I gave serious consideration to abandoning this ridiculous mission. After all, someone could show up at any time. I did not want to spend my next birthday in a Chilean jail.

Fuming over the wasted effort, time, and money to come this far, I consoled myself that if I wasn't in as much pain the next day, I'd try again. Maybe Karina would be there. Not likely, but maybe. Maybe I could bring a ladder.

Two steps into my exit, my leg gave out. Completely. I landed on my side as a searing pain traveled south. Finally pulling up my pant leg, I confirmed that my knee had doubled in size. Standing took some ingenuity because of the increasing pain in my arm. Eventually I managed to get up onto my right leg.

I was able to hop but found the effort gave me vertigo. I looked around the side of the house, calculating the car was at least three hundred hops away. Glancing back at the shed, a mere ten hops away, lay my new cane. The rake.

When I pulled the rake off the hook, I noticed a strange metal band at one end, an aftermarket thing. Probably something someone haphazardly added for whatever reason. I turned the end with the steel teeth upward to use as a walking stick. After hobbling out of the shed, the hardware piece at the bottom of the rake handle got stuck in a hole in the ground, muddy from yesterday's deluge.

"Come on! Seriously?" I screamed. This final blow of frustration threatened to unleash an epic stream of tears. I didn't want that. I didn't like crying.

Using my good arm, with a lot of effort and failed attempts, I finally wiggled the rake from the mud. In the process, the strange piece of hardware came off, which led to the unfortunate splitting of the rake and me falling face-forward to the ground. The mud and dirt seeped into my clothes. After my pity party, I pulled myself together with equal measures of self-talk and fake courage. I needed to get going even if it meant crawling. The sun was dipping behind the distant mountains and hills, and I didn't want to be stuck there after dark. Rotating onto my stomach, I spotted a shiny object laying near the rake. Reaching forward, my arm coated in mud, I extended my fingertips. It was a key. A house key. I now understood why the rake split so easily. Someone had previously made the cut in the handle to stash the key.

"Hell of a hiding spot," I whispered. And despite the pain, the blood, and the sinking sun, I smiled.

CHAPTER 53

The key worked. And while it took me a while to climb onto the porch, a surge of hope empowered me to hobble around inside the house. Unlike the exterior facade of neglect, the interior showed signs of life—a few pieces of furniture, dishes on a counter, and a pot on the stove top containing remnants of tomato sauce splattered across the rim. A filthy dishtowel, still moist, hung from a hook by the sink.

The furniture I'd seen before hadn't changed. I took that as a good sign. She hadn't moved out. I just prayed she wouldn't catch me busting into her home. Not exactly a bond builder. Despite the increasing pain in my knee, I had to hurry. No telling when she might return.

I didn't see a desk or any obvious hiding places. Remembering what Carlos had said about his stash place, I entered that bedroom where once upon a time, I'd spent the night after the rock attack. I found the loose floorboards and quickly pulled a couple of slats out. Several spiders, lots of dirt, and rat poop. No papers. Then I opened the hall closet only to find a short stack of faded, brown towels on a shelf. I scoured the kitchen, every cupboard, every drawer.

Besides the usual clutter, dust mites, and loose papers, the only item of interest was a piece of paper folded to the size of a business card. When I opened it, I saw a note from Carlos to Karina, written in 2009, telling her how much he enjoyed their hike and hoping they could have dinner someday. While my brain wanted to process

Nancy Rhodes

what that might have meant, I reminded myself that this was not the paper I had come for.

Limping around the kitchen, I stopped to catch my breath. As I rolled my neck to ease the tension, I noticed the small window above the kitchen door. Squinting against a stream of light entering a gap near the top of the frame, I spotted an oddly placed piece of wood laying on the ledge.

I grabbed one of the two kitchen chairs and moved it below the window. Using my good leg, I hobbled up onto it, and then stretching my body as tall as possible, I was able to touch the edge of the board and toss it to the floor. With the board gone, I saw what looked like a scroll. Unable to reach it, I had to get down again to get the board, which meant having to use my bad leg way more than I wanted.

Back on the chair with board in hand, I pushed the scroll off the ledge.

"Victory!" I shouted as I watched it fall to the floor.

Slipping off both rubber bands, I determined that this was exactly what Carlos needed. Gently lifting each page, I saw maps with scribbled notes across the margins. Besides Spanish words I didn't understand, there were colored symbols and characters that might as well have been written in Egyptian hieroglyphics.

Had Karina hidden this? Did she know it was here?

Despite the growing spasms of pain, my lips crested into a grin. Evidence. This could be the evidence we needed. But unfortunately, my moment of glory ended abruptly with the sound of tires crunching across the driveway. Whether or not it was Karina, I was an illegal intruder and could not explain my way out of this. They would have seen my car, but being a rental, I felt confident they wouldn't know it was me.

I recognized Karina's voice but couldn't hear what she was saying. Then I heard another voice, this one loud and unfamiliar. They were along the side of the house, presumably heading to the shed for a key that was no longer there. Very soon they would know something was amiss. I didn't have much time. As their footsteps neared the back of the house, I turned the deadbolt on the front door.

Dear God, it was stuck! Jiggling the lock back and forth, I didn't know what else to do. I tried thinking of an excuse for breaking into their home. Nothing came to mind. As their footsteps landed on the steps to the back door, the latch finally twisted open. If I was going to escape, I had to run, but my left leg wasn't liking it. Feeling my tendons shred with each step, I clenched my teeth to hold back the gasps of agony rising to my throat. Half running, half hopping, I was certain I'd never felt this much pain. I would have happily amputated the limb if given the choice and the tools.

As my hand touched the car door, a man stepped out of the house and began shouting. I didn't understand his Spanish, but there was no mistaking his mood. I hoped Karina might come out and rescue me from this guard dog. When Mr. Furioso left the doorway running, I threw my body inside the car, locked the door, and started the ignition. Glancing quickly at my rearview mirror, I saw that he had turned around. A brief moment of relief fell short when I saw he had keys in his hand and was running to his truck. As I started to drive away, Karina came outside and caught up with him before he got into the cab. I watched him shove her hard to the ground.

I wished I could have helped her. Instead I forced my foot down on the gas pedal, leaving an unruly cloud of dust. Rocks and gravel rumbled beneath my car in protest. I'd gone only a block when I saw his truck push through my dust cloud.

Highway...I have to get to the highway. Once I reached it, I would have a better chance of outrunning him. His truck was old and probably a stick shift, giving me and my new-model rental car an advantage. I left the gravel road and picked up some speed. In the meantime, I had to navigate a narrow road with unfamiliar turns. In between the turns, I glanced back. This only increased my anxiety, because the distance between his truck and my car was lessening by the second.

I remembered an intersection that led to the highway and hoped it was coming up soon. Then I would punch it. The stranger's truck was only two car lengths away with no one between us. A speed limit sign appeared from nowhere and disappeared. My guess is I was traveling some fifty miles per hour, only double the limit.

Just as his car approached close enough to see his unshaven, irate face, the intersection came into view. *Shit!* I would have to slow down; one does not plow through a four-way stop sign in the heart of a small town. But I did consider it, at least until I noticed a couple of middle-aged women approaching the intersection with a herd of small children. Okay, not a herd, but a bunch. Like four or five.

Although facing unknown personal consequences, I couldn't risk running over a kid. Besides, whoever this crazed bully was, he couldn't be stupid enough to hurt me in front of an audience. When I was a quarter of a block from the intersection, the menacing white truck pulled up behind me. My hands shook so hard I clung to the steering wheel like it was a life raft.

I couldn't look at him. I turned my gaze to the four little tots. The smallest, a girl clad in pink everything, looked about two years old. A woman, either an older mother or a young grandmother, struggled to hold the little princess's hand as the girl fought for her independence right there on the curb. My foot let off the gas. In a moment of perfect divinity, when my car was only a few feet from the crosswalk, the princess in pink broke free from her captor and collapsed on the sidewalk, face down, arms and legs flailing wildly in a full-fledged temper tantrum.

Oh, sweet child, I adore you, but I must do something that your mama isn't going to like. I cranked the steering wheel to the left and pushed the gas pedal to the floor, speeding through the intersection, my heart racing. When I looked back, the woman, whose face had turned crimson, waved her hands in my direction with utter—but warranted—displeasure. Meanwhile, another woman stepped into the intersection and extended her hand at the approaching white truck in a firm *you-better-stop-asshole* gesture.

Entering the two-lane highway, my hands eased their deathly grip from the steering wheel. A quick rearview mirror peek led to a long exhale. No white truck in my wake. I drove a good twenty miles before I was able to stop checking the mirror every thirty seconds.

Just outside of downtown Santiago, I pulled off a tree-lined road next to a park where a handful of children were kicking a soccer ball. The neighborhood was newer, the homes large, all with perfectly manicured front yards. After cutting the engine, I leaned down to pick up the scrolls, my hands trembling like willow leaves in a windstorm.

The first page was the oceanic map I'd seen inside the El Toyo house. Then I found five sheets of paper rolled inside the map. With pages strewn across my passenger seat, I took my time examining each one. When I got near the end, I noticed a song sheet. *Bingo.*

At the top, centered in bold, black full caps, was the title "Blue Song." Never having played an instrument or invested the time to study music, I assumed it was a song sheet, but honestly, I had no idea if I was staring at music or hieroglyphics.

After several minutes, I noticed some odd symbols. Turning the page sideways, I found notes written in a minuscule font. It took me a while to make sense of it, but eventually I figured out that the notes correlated with either a latitude or longitude number. Some symbols implied directions such as *F* (forte) for north, the sharp symbol for east, and so on.

This was a map. A very important map. I rolled the pages together and tucked them under my seat. Driving back to the hotel, I blasted the radio, singing whether I knew the words or not.

When I got to my hotel room, I locked the door and called Carlos.

"Carlos, I've got—"

"—Rebecca! How nice of you to call!"

Rebecca, right. Realizing I'd spaced out on precautionary measures, I stumbled into feigning a fake voice. "I've got that desk for you, the one from Marcy," I said, floundering for words.

"I know. That's great. I appreciate that. Yes, okay then. I will get that from you later."

"Uh, sure. This one is a *good* one."

"Look, um, I'm tied up now. But how about you show it to me when you're in town?

Really? Was his phone being tapped? I presumed he was telling me we couldn't risk talking until I returned. How disappointing! I was so anxious to tell him that I got the papers.

Waiting two days for the next flight tested my patience and left me with far too much time to think about what might follow now that we had the proof Carlos wanted.

Is this enough evidence to stop the poachers? Then what? Could I let go of finding closure about Miguel before returning to the States?

I decided to make the best of the two days. My recent visits to Santiago hadn't been the most relaxing. Besides, October, as I remembered, generally was a nice time to be in the city. The equivalent of April back home, the temperatures were often mild with less rainfall.

But, of course, the next morning, it rained. Plans to go to Cerro San Cristobal were abandoned, replaced with ideas of a cozy movie theatre. My choices consisted of an animated children's movie or a horror flick. I chose the latter, which had no English subtitles.

Day two, however, was a picture of springtime perfection without a cloud in the sky. I left my room around ten in the morning and took a cab north of town to the base of the Cerro San Cristobal, where a steep funicular on noisy tracks took people to the top in only a few minutes. I wished I could have hiked or even bicycled like so many others were doing, but the bum knee wouldn't permit it. While in the queue to purchase a ticket, I met three energetic and friendly youngsters who came from Taiwan. We shared a gondola, which turned out to be one of many highlights of my day. Their English was perfect, their sense of humor off the charts.

I'd been to the top before but never on such a beautiful day. A few months later in the season and these views would be lost, shrouded by heavy smog, a blanket of gray obliterating the cordillera peaks, leaving only vistas of city buildings and urban sprawl.

I hobbled up several stairs and walked around a path, taking in the views of the mountain range. Flowers were exploding in bright colors all around me, blending with carefully planned terraced evergreens and a few towering palms. Glad I'd remembered to bring cash, I purchased an ice-cold *mote con huesillo* drink—a traditional beverage made with dried peaches, cinnamon, and a whole lot of sugar.

Between the sugar and sun, my joy was so complete I managed eight magical hours without thinking about whales, music sheets, or threatening poachers trying to kill me. I concluded my afternoon in a small and trendy bar that made the absolute best pisco sour.

CHAPTER 54

When I boarded the plane in Santiago, my hobble was so apparent that several people offered to help with my carry-on. Because the scrolls were tucked inside of it, I politely declined. Three times I told people that I was fine. Another lie and probably an obvious one, since by the time I got to my seat, sweat covered nearly every ounce of my ragged old body.

Upon landing in Puerto Montt, I stayed aboard until everyone else exited. A young female attendant stopped me before I got to the exit door. "Looks like you could use some help," she said. "A passenger left this on my last flight. You're welcome to it," she said, handing me an aluminum cane. "Not sure if it will help."

"That's kind. But I don't think I can manage that."

"Well, I can carry your bag," she said, looking apologetic as if she'd caused my injury.

"No. No thank you."

The cockpit swung open, and a handsome, dark-skinned pilot at least ten years my junior looked my way, then addressed the attractive and much-younger attendant. "Problem?" he asked curtly.

"No, Captain. Just helping this passenger. Her leg is, uh, *como se dice herido*?"

"Oh no, I'm fine," I interjected. "But thank you both."

"Is someone meeting you, Miss?" the captain said, checking out my left hand, presumably the ring finger. If he hadn't been such a damn flirt, I might have allowed myself to feel flattered.

"Yes. My boyfriend."

"Thanks for flying with us," the attendant said, nudging her body closer to the pilot.

"Hope to see you again," the pilot echoed. His lips parted in a lopsided grin while his arm nudged ridiculously close to the attendant's breast. These two needed a room, and I was in the way.

Scumbag, I thought, my bag flopping against my hip as I hobbled down the airplane steps. I hoped she wouldn't fall prey to his exploits. Another Miguel-versus-Allie story in the making.

By the time I got inside the terminal, tears joined the sweat dripping down my face. Admittedly, I had a low tolerance for pain, but this was a test I didn't want to take. A test I was failing. I turned back to see if anyone could help me. Nausea threatened to send me to the ground. I needed help, and I needed it immediately.

Many painful seconds later, I saw Carlos, barely twenty feet away, hands stretched out, as if ready to catch me on my way down. I couldn't believe he'd come to Puerto Montt to meet me, having to endure the long-ass ferry ride and the small plane ride from Chaitén.

"Carlos!" I yelled. "What are you doing here?"

When our eyes met, he shook his head. Just a little. A subtle warning. Then he gently took my arm, leaned in, to kiss my cheek. His lips lingered as he whispered, "Careful what you say until we get in the car."

"You have a car?"

"Rented one. And from the looks of things, it's good I did. What the hell happened to you?"

"A fall. Get me to the car quick. If I don't sit soon, I'm going to get very intimate with the ugly beige carpet beneath our feet."

He took my bag in one arm and used the other to support me. Once we got outside, he found a bench where I would rest while he got the car. As I waited, I saw Mr. Pilot and Miss Attendant pass through the minimum security area. Once out, her arm snuggled across his waist while his right hand grabbed her derriere.

Nancy Rhodes

Several minutes later, I heard a honk and watched a small Fiat pull up to the curb. Carlos got out and helped me off the bench. When we got in the car, I kept shaking my head. "This is insane! You came from Quellón—all this way for me?"

"Of course. I was concerned…and anxious."

"But it's so far. The ferry ride, the plane—did you spend the night here in Puerto Montt?"

"I've been here a couple of nights. I had some other business. After our week-long excursion, which basically was a waste of time and money, I heard about a marine biologist here who might have some thoughts or suggestions on what's been happening. I'm so sorry I couldn't talk to you by phone. I've been so anxious to hear what happened! Did you get them?"

"Yes. The papers, the song sheet. I think it's all there. I can't wait to show you. Shall I show you now?"

"It is tempting, but I can't stay parked here. Plus, the sooner we get out of here, the better."

"Makes sense. But I can't wait for you to check it out."

Looking over at my leg, he said, "That looks painful. What happened?"

"Ugh. Stupidity."

As we drove away from the airport, I told him what had happened at Karina's—the break-in, the strange guy, and my risky getaway. He asked questions. A lot of questions.

I grew tired.

"Enough about me," I added, noting he'd grown sideburns. "Did you say your trip wasn't successful? Does that mean you didn't see whales?"

"We saw whales but not many blues. Covered some of the areas where you and I'd been. Didn't see Armando either. He's disappeared. At least from the ocean. Anyway, enough of that."

"So we're headed to the hotel?"

"We will, yes. I left my stuff there. But we need to get you to a doctor. That knee needs some attention."

"Oh—I don't…" my voice trailed. I was too tired to argue. And while I hated the idea of having to see a doctor, the potential for getting painkillers was tempting.

"No arguing, *amiga*. I know a clinic that's not far from here. You're not going to find an orthopedic doctor in Quellón or anywhere on Chiloé Island for that matter."

At some point, I fell asleep.

⸙

"Allie, wake up. We're here," Carlos said, gently rubbing my shoulder.

We pulled into the front of a small clinic. After an hour's wait, they took X-rays. The bad news was I had fractured my kneecap in two locations. The good news was that the fractures were not displaced, so surgery wasn't required.

With Carlos at my side to translate, *el doctor* Oswaldo Piñera explained treatment. Carlos said, "He says it's critical you stay off the leg. He's going to get you crutches and some meds. Wants to see you back in two or three weeks."

"How long on the crutches?"

Carlos asked Doc Piñera and then turned to me. "He says a minimum of five weeks with no weight bearing."

I looked at Carlos, then at the doctor. No way in hell I would wait that long.

After the doctor left, I turned to Carlos. "Five weeks?"

"They are probably erring on the side of being overcautious. But just don't push it."

"Yes, boss. By the way, thanks for everything. I still can't believe you went all that way to meet me at the airport. I think I was too out of it at the airport to show my appreciation. How did you even know I was on that flight?"

"I figured you'd be heading home immediately after your call. It's not like there are many flights from Santiago to Puerto Montt. I can't wait to see what you brought back. Sucks what you went through to get it."

"Well, speaking of…it's in that oversized blue bag that's under the table over there."

Carlos put his index finger to his lips, signaling me not to say more. We waited as two nurses walked past our room.

"The nurse told me you need to schedule your follow-up."

"I don't need to—"

"Yes, you do. I'll bring you back when the time comes. Let's get that appointment scheduled and get the hell out of here."

After he wheeled me out of the clinic, I waited in the late afternoon sunshine while he walked to the parking lot, holding my bag. The bag.

As Carlos helped me into the rental car, I thought I saw a small sedan, dark blue—maybe black—drive by slowly. The darkly tinted windows seemed out of place. Not a car I'd expect to see in a small town in southern Chile.

"Carlos—" I said, as he helped me into the passenger seat.

"What?"

It disappeared. *Allie, you're too paranoid. Not every dark vehicle with tinted windows belongs to gangsters.*

"Sorry, nothing."

"You okay? Want me to put your seat back?"

"I'm fine. It's just a bad knee. I'm not crippled, you know."

He rubbed my shoulder. "Of course."

"But thanks," I said, smiling back as he helped me into the car.

With my eyes closed, feeling the gentle sway of the car, I began reflecting on how much I admired Carlos. He was an extraordinary individual. He'd been so patient and kind. Through everything. And I had faith in him. With what I brought back and the connections he had, we could get the killers away from the whales. I wanted, needed, to believe the remaining blues would be safe. Or at least safer.

Ship strikes, military sonic testing, and global warming would continue their destructive paths unless or until people across the globe stepped in and demanded change. I'd taken so much for granted. Never had even given much thought to ocean creatures, big or small. So much I didn't know about. So much to learn.

"Watcha thinking, *amiga*?"

"What a good friend you've been. I can't believe you left Quellón and came here to meet me."

"No problem. You deserved it. You've been through a lot. Do you have any idea who that man was? The guy who chased you?"

"Nope. He knew Karina, but he didn't treat her very well."

"I don't like the sound of that. Especially after dealing with cancer. I'll try harder to get in touch with her after we get back."

The road narrowed as we approached a less populated area. A few minutes later we pulled in front of a one-story, flat-roofed motel.

"This is the place," said Carlos. "I know it's not the Hyatt, but it's cheap."

Thinking it wasn't even close to Motel 6 standards, I said, "It'll be fine."

"You okay sharing a room? There are two beds."

Smiling, I nodded. "Yes. But you've been warned, there's a chance I snore."

"Then you can sleep in the bathtub."

"You'll need to help me in—and out—of it."

The laughter and banter continued as we made our way to the room. Once inside, we briefly passed through the awkwardness of sharing a room. I was happy for sweats, because no way did I want him to see me in my old daisy-and-daffodil nightshirt. We flipped a coin to decide which bed, and I was pleased to end up with the one closest to the bathroom. Carlos fell asleep first. I tossed for at least another ten minutes before succumbing to the land of slumber.

WE LUCKED OUT ON TIMING THE NEXT MORNING AS THE FERRY ride from Chaitén to Quellón was departing early, but we had enough time to return the rental car. The passage, while still five hours, felt like a vacation in Carlos's company. Besides an abundance of whales including one blue, we saw dolphins, sea lions, and even a pair of black-neck swans. My stomach stayed content, never once hinting of nausea.

We grabbed a cab and rode in silence for a while, listening to the rain hit the windshield with such intensity the wipers were useless. My mind wandered. I desperately wanted to peek inside Carlos's brain. What did he think of me?

Sneaking glances, my mind drifted until I found myself imagining what it'd be like to sleep with him. We'd never spent so much time together, and although there'd been no hint of romance, suddenly I craved intimacy. I pictured our curves fitting tightly as one, like pieces of a puzzle.

"Allie," he said, startling me to reality.

Feeling like my face had gone pink, I said, "Yes" without looking his way.

"I know you're not happy about your knee and having to be inactive while it heals, but damn, girl, you did it. That took a hell of a lot of courage."

I didn't feel deserving of praise after all that'd happened to others because of me, but I mumbled a thank-you.

The taxi driver, an older man with a bald patch shaped like a horseshoe, glanced in his mirror and smiled. I looked away. He turned his focus to the radio, turning up the volume. A monotone voice rumbled through the muffled speakers. I understood nothing.

Carlos pulled a small notebook from his satchel. I lowered my window a crack to smell the approaching shore.

His well-intended compliment stirred up a myriad of images of people I'd lost. First my parents. Then Captain Jack and even the memory of Carlos bleeding on the boat. He hadn't died, but maybe he would. Maybe he was next.

Then another image filled my head. This one more vivid. The newspaper photo of Miguel's wife and daughters. Such a beautiful young mother with her two little princesses. Smiling. A photo probably taken by Miguel. They too had died. Gone because of me. Dead because their lying, horny father chose me over them.

Carlos was wrong. Courage was not stealing some papers from a house. If I had courage, I would have strangled Miguel when I saw him on the airplane. I wouldn't have let him slip out of my hands. Again.

CHAPTER 55

Carlos had the cab drop me off first but accompanied me to the door. He said something about a good night's rest. Parker helped me into the living room after inviting Carlos to stay for dinner. He told her about the cab out front, adding how we'd had a long day and he was ready to go home. Of course, I interpreted that as he was tired of my company.

As Parker left to make tea, I saw the whale painting on the floor, leaning against the back of the sofa. Thinking she was going to at least get a frame out of it, I felt my spirits lift. Once she joined me, I gave her a condensed version of my exploits. Then I asked her about the painting.

"It'll take some work. Frame isn't in the best shape, but it's so unique. The intricate lines and patterns around the corners. This could be over a hundred years old. I'm thinking of restoring it."

"And the painting?" I asked, yawning. "What will you do with it?"

"I don't know yet. Do you want it?"

"No thanks, but I'll check with Carlos later if you decide not to keep it."

After several yawns slipped from my mouth, Parker offered to bring me ice for the knee. "Might be good before you nod off."

"Sure, thanks."

I was asleep before she returned.

I FELL INTO A ROUTINE OF ICING, GENTLE STRETCHING, AND short walks over the next few weeks. Carlos came every few days but was distant. I tried not to take it personally, but with too much time on my hands, I often failed.

One morning, about three weeks after my return, I found Parker at the kitchen table with pliers, a hammer, and a painter's knife splayed on the table.

"I've done it," she said boastfully, holding the frame above her head.

"It's beautiful. What will you do with it?"

"I'm not certain. I have a watercolor that an old friend painted for me years ago. I may use it for that."

Noting something else on the table—a drawing, perhaps—I joined Parker. "What is this?"

She picked it up. "It looks like a map of some kind, but I don't know. It was tucked behind the painting and the matting. What do you make of it?"

The paper was thin and yellowed and the ink so faded that many of the lines of the map had disappeared. I moved the paper closer to my face.

"I have a magnifying glass if that would help."

"Yes," I answered, listening to Parker rummaging through kitchen drawers.

With magnifying glass in hand, I placed the map on the table. "Well, it's somewhere in Russia. Look here," I said, pointing to an area near the southern coast, not far from China and Japan. "It says 'Sea of Okhotsk'" I said, pointing to a group of islands.

"Why would someone have put it inside a frame?"

"No idea other than obviously to hide it or safeguard it. Was there anything else?"

"Yes, but I have no idea what it is." She handed me a small piece of lined notepaper. It didn't seem as old as the map.

"Gibberish, right?"

"Probably—might be Russian, but don't know. We'll show it to

Carlos."

A few days later, Carlos returned. After showing him the papers, he said, "You're right. These are map coordinates. It is written in Russian, and I've no idea what it means."

Parker handed Carlos a mug. "Just brewed," she said.

"Thanks, Parker. I can't stay long, but I appreciate it."

Looking back at the map, I pointed to a large island not far from Japan.

"What island is this?"

"That's Sakhalin," said Carlos. "Russia's largest island. Huge population."

"Is the map worth anything? It looks old," said Parker.

"I wouldn't know without taking it to an appraiser, but it's not in very good shape. I can show it to a friend who can give us an estimate if you want."

Parker nodded. "Sure, that'd be nice. A few dollars wouldn't hurt."

<hr/>

THAT EVENING I SUFFERED ONE OF MY WORST HEADACHES EVER. Dinner consisted of Motrin and black tea. I crashed early. After much thrashing and tossing of pillows, I fell asleep despite the saturation of caffeine in my system.

Crazy dreams filled my head, each one filled with people I either liked or loved. In the first dream, I sat on the edge of a large boat decorated with hundreds of tiny, blue sparkling lights. I wore a long, black dress more appropriate for a funeral, but the mood was festive, not somber. I saw friends from my childhood. Friends from California. And all my new friends—Carlos, Parker, Ian, and even Captain Jack. A dozen or so people surrounded me, clinking tall champagne flutes in celebration. Then everyone circled me, taking turns to hug and congratulate me.

Then an odd silence. I looked at my friends. Their heads were bowed. Suddenly they began humming a song. I loved the melody so much I started crying. And from nowhere, Karina appeared. She began singing, her voice similar to Judy Collins. Everyone joined her. I didn't know the words, so I moved my lips just to fit in. But Karina was wearing a black bikini, exposing insanely skinny arms and legs. Then she held her index finger to her lips, signaling me not to say anything.

And then, as dreams do, the scene changed. Carlos and I were on the bow of an enormous sailing ship, his arms wrapped around me. He pointed to a blue whale that uncharacteristically breached high above the ocean surface. Carlos started to sing the same tune my friends had hummed earlier. With his strong arms, he pulled me a few steps back and insisted I sing too. He said I had to help. I didn't know what he meant. His voice was perfect. I worried that if any sounds escaped my throat, the whales would leave. I would break the spell.

On the beach, everyone sang the "Blue Whale" song. Distant whale chants joined their voices. A choir of whales in perfect harmony.

Then a new scene. Carlos hugging and kissing me. His lips tasted like cream soda.

CHAPTER 56

Parker was a great nurse and an even better companion. But as weeks passed and days grew longer with hints of summer, I grew restless. Carlos didn't visit as often. He'd been at sea nearly every day since I returned, trying to find whales and searching for Armando.

One night, when he joined us for dinner at Parker's, he confessed that his desperation for answers led him to consult a psychic. I had a hard time hiding my shock and skepticism but asked him if it was helpful.

"Helpful? I'm not sure if I'd call it that. I'm still not a strong believer in this kind of thing. If anything, she left me with more questions."

"What did she say?" I asked.

"Well, a lot. She said that water was a strong force in my life, that it was my element. I had no idea what she was talking about, but I figured she was a con. I mean, most people know I love the ocean. Then she started explaining the five element symbols, something about how water represents emotion and wisdom. That lost me. I just wanted to leave."

Taking a bite of Parker's homemade flan, I turned to Carlos to ask him if he did.

"No, Allie, I didn't leave. The psychic suddenly got personal. She said that this present force was like a riptide threatening to pull me under. She said I had made progress with my fight to find resolution to strong currents pounding my soul." Carlos stopped to finish the wine in his glass, glancing directly at me as he paused.

"She warned me that I might be heading too fast and too hard into the current. When I asked her what that meant, she said something bigger—or stronger—would present itself unexpectedly. If I didn't want to be pulled under for good, I should step back."

Parker and I glanced at each other. This was creepy shit, and I wasn't sure I wanted to hear more.

But Parker was curious. She asked if that was everything.

"I asked this woman if I would ever get the answers I needed. She told me some answers would come but that lessons were more important than answers."

"Got to admit, Carlos, I don't get it," I said, shaking my head. "So tell me, have you received any spiritually directed answers yet?"

"No, and I'm not ready to quit. I know it sounds like *una locura* (crazy thing), but I can't stop now. We're close. I know it. And I don't want to share or expose the evidence you collected until I'm a hundred percent certain there's nothing that could prevent definitive action against everyone involved."

"I wish I could join you."

"Hopefully soon. You're making good progress."

Yeah, I thought. I could walk from my bedroom to the kitchen with only a minimal limp. Yippee.

ONE AFTERNOON WHILE PLAYING CHESS WITH PARKER, I HEARD the unmistakable rumble of his car approaching the house.

"Carlos is here," I said. I jumped up so fast my knee jolted like the tendons had disconnected from the surrounding muscle, a reminder that my knee hadn't progressed as much as I'd hoped.

Parker got up too but only after calling checkmate.

"Again? You kill me, Parker. Maybe one of these days you'll let me win."

Laughing, she opened the door.

His steps were light, his smile huge. I recognized the bag he carried, and immediately my stomach gurgled with anticipation of some fresh-caught abalone for dinner.

Looking at my knees, he said, "Look at you! Walking without crutches!"

"Yep," I told him, "it's been more than three weeks. I called the doctor, explained I couldn't travel back to Puerto Montt, and he said if I was careful, I could start weight bearing. You brought us *locos?*"

"Yes," he said, moving his other arm forward, "and champagne!"

"Something tells me we have something to celebrate."

He smiled. "We do."

After Parker prepared a plate with rolls, cheese, avocado, and a few cookies, we moved into the living room where she settled into her favorite chair. Carlos and I sat on the sofa. He poured the bubbly while I handed out plates.

"Ready?"

"Hell, yes!" I said, taking off my sandals and tucking my good leg crosswise under the other.

"Two days ago we spotted an unfamiliar fishing vessel. Apparently it belongs to Armando. I guess he has a fleet."

"Seriously? Did you catch him?"

"Hear me out, Miss Impatient. We started taking photos as we approached his vessel. When we got within forty meters, we cut our engine and drifted in. Then," he said, pausing, "well, we just couldn't believe our eyes. As if on cue, two blues spouted right next to his vessel. His crew—we counted five—lined up starboard to watch. They seemed unprepared. As you know, it's not typical for blues to swim that close to shore. We were able to approach Montero without detection. We hid behind a cove and waited, scopes and binoculars in hand.

"His men behaved so recklessly," Carlos explained. "Two grabbed spears. One actually tripped over something on deck. I don't know…maybe they'd been drinking. A fourth man began yelling from the upper deck. We couldn't make out his words but saw his hands waving chaotically. He clearly wasn't happy with the crew and wanted them to do something. Well, then the three on deck picked up harpoons."

Hoping dead whales weren't a prelude to some happy ending, I bit my lip and waited. Carlos was quite the storyteller, but I wished he'd get to the point.

"Don't worry, they didn't use them. But I was concerned. Especially when one of the men pulled out a gun, possibly an M16. He shot a few rounds but didn't hit any of the whales. We got everything on film."

"What now?" I asked.

"We're ready to contact the Whaling Commission. With this film, the 'Blue Song' sheet, and records you brought back, along with Parker's documents found hidden in the frame, we have enough to turn everything over to the authorities."

"Did you see what Armando looked like?" I asked.

"Not sure. I couldn't see much looking in the viewfinder. But I'm hoping the photos, once enlarged, will be clear enough to confirm identities."

Parker let out a sigh but nervously began twisting the ends of her braid. I looked at her. Then I looked at Carlos.

"What?" he said.

"Do you know if Armando is at the top?" she asked.

"Not sure, but the Whaling Commission will find out if someone's above him."

"I don't think you should do anything yet. Especially if he's not the lead man."

"Parker," he said, "we have no one else to turn to. It's time. I'm certain. You know me. This isn't something I've rushed into. I've waited years for this. Years!"

Parker cleared her throat. "Time is pointless. Time is but a sphere, passing and continuing, and totally out of our control."

"Cut the philosophy, Parker. Give me another idea. Tell me what else we can do."

Stunned by his tone, I stared at the floor. Only once had I seen him this edgy. My body sank into the cushions. *Stay out of it, Allie.*

Parker responded calmly. "We need to find out who is behind this, and I strongly suspect it goes beyond Armando. If we can find out why, we'll find out who. The Whaling Commission doesn't have the resources to investigate who's at the top."

Carlos didn't agree.

I downed the last of the bubbly from my glass and rose to my feet.

"You don't need to leave, Allie," said Carlos. "Parker knows me well enough now. She doesn't get offended if I don't agree with her."

Parker nodded. "True, but I'm telling you that your plan is too dangerous. This will further anger the mob. Armando is not smart enough to be at the top, and, seriously, if he gets captured, someone will retaliate. If you proceed now and get the commission involved, it could result in more dead whales before they even begin to prepare a case."

"I know the commission," he responded. "We need their help, and I trust them. You mean well, Parker, but this time I think you're wrong. We've got to go ahead. Now."

Parker said nothing more. Battle lines were drawn.

After an awkward silence, Carlos said goodbye without offering the customary departure kisses. I wondered if this wedge between them was deeper than either could admit.

After he left, I returned to the kitchen and found Parker leaning over the sink, emptying half a bottle of expensive bubbly down the drain. I tiptoed away and returned to my room, feeling the grief of two stubborn but well-meaning friends torn apart.

CHAPTER 57

W hile this wasn't the first time I'd walked a tightrope between two estranged parties, the strain was affecting my sleep. And my headaches returned with a vengeance. Parker, despite her comments about not being affected, withdrew and became sullen. Carlos stopped coming around.

I considered moving out. When I suggested it one day, Parker looked significantly hurt.

"I'd miss you, Allie. I really would. This will pass soon. I'm a bit disappointed that Carlos is being so impatient and stubborn, but I'm not angry. I guess this is hard on you, knowing how much you like him."

"It is awkward," I said.

"He'll come around. But, well, if you need to go, I won't hold you back. I know you spend a lot of time at that flat of his, so if you want to live with him, go for it. But don't leave because of our rift."

"Oh, I wasn't thinking of living with him," I said, hoping she saw through my lie. "I'll stay with you, Parker."

ALTHOUGH CARLOS CONTINUED TO KEEP HIS DISTANCE FROM Parker, he and I met frequently. One day he picked me up in an old Toyota, a car he had just purchased.

After a couple of weeks, I got my knee back. I started jogging, which I hated but figured I had to do something to combat the new roll of belly fat from Parker's cooking. The only thing I liked about running was it seemed to clear my head.

Carlos spent a lot of time working with an attorney who eventually led him to the head of the Whaling Commission. Carlos didn't discuss the details, but I knew that with the support of authorities, they were closer to capturing Armando Montero.

"What if Parker is right and Montero is not at the top?" I asked, one rainless afternoon after packing sandwiches for a hike. The trailhead was still another half-hour drive.

"I thought we weren't going to talk about that stuff. This is our fun day, right?"

"Yes, soon. But answer my question. I can't have fun until you do."

"Okay, bossy pants, I'll answer your question. Hopefully just this one. Right?"

"Um, maybe."

With hands on the wheel and looking straight ahead, Carlos did a few neck rolls to release tension. "If Armando is not at the top, we're hoping he'll lead us to whoever is."

"Does the commission understand how dangerous he is?"

"I can see I'm not getting out of this with only one question. But, yes, they definitely do. Which is why we have to involve the authorities. They know Montero attempted murder."

"Correction. Not attempted. Don't forget Captain Jack."

"Right. Sorry. But unfortunately, there's no proof of that. Don't worry, the plan is to end this. To get Montero and whoever else. But we can't do it without government resources."

"And you think that's safe?"

"My attorney, Randall, looked into the fishery in question and found no ties to the government. Some of the money has been hidden in secret accounts in the Caymans, some in Europe, and a few smaller accounts in the States. Not the way our current government would act. Randall suggested possible ties with Japan or Russia."

"Russia, once again."

"Yes, it's one of many possibilities. No surprise, given their history. While Japan is getting away with whaling in the name of research, Russia's exploits are more clandestine.

"But killing whales in Chile for Russia? Doesn't make sense. Sounds unlikely and risky."

"I agree, but it's a start. Randall said the government has resources we'll never have. If we want Montero and his cohorts put away, we have to involve them."

I nodded but wasn't convinced.

"You can't share this information. Not even with Parker."

I wondered if he would have felt that way before the misunderstanding.

"Allie?"

"All right. Okay, I won't say anything to Parker. But geez, Carlos, you know she can be trusted! I wish you two would just get over this, whatever it is."

"It's not about that. I do trust Parker, but it is just better we don't involve anyone else."

Sounded like a line of bullshit.

"When is all this going to happen?"

"Soon."

"What do we do in the meantime?" I asked as he pulled off the road near our trail.

"We continue what we've been doing, looking for blues. The more we stay close to them, the less chance anyone will pursue further attacks. But we need to be careful in case we're being watched."

Closing the car door, I pulled my hair back into a short ponytail. "Got it. Thanks. Okay, let's go on a hike."

Laughing, he put his keys into a small backpack. "About time."

"Smart-ass," I said, looking ahead at narrow trail along a swollen river.

<hr>

A WEEK LATER, SOMEONE FROM THE INVESTIGATIVE TEAM

called Carlos. Four crime members connected to Armando Montero and his mafia were apprehended. What should have been good news wasn't. They did not get Armando. This wasn't enough. Not even close. His cronies wouldn't rat.

The morning after Carlos called with this disheartening news, I had been enjoying warm, fresh-baked muffins with Parker when, out of the blue, she stated, "It's happened." She pushed the article below my face.

"Yes, I heard from Carlos last night, but this information was not supposed to get out." The article was vague and located in the back of section B, but sadly, the wrong people would see it.

"You must have known this was coming down."

"I'm sorry. I wasn't told much but…well, it was a sensitive matter."

"I just hope I'm wrong."

"Wrong?"

"About retaliation. I hope you won't head out for a while, especially not with Carlos. That bullseye on your back is larger than ever. Especially since Armando is still out there somewhere."

"I can't promise that. We have so much to do. In fact, yesterday we spotted Millie again. She's been coming in closer. Carlos thinks she might be ill or injured. She's not taking any deep dives, been hovering way too long near the surface and staying closer to shore. Not normal and not safe."

"You saw Millie?"

"Yes! She actually wanted to be close to us. We could almost touch her."

Parker picked up our breakfast plates and washed them in silence. I couldn't tell if she was more worried about Millie or us. I patted her shoulder gently, silently thanking her for caring so much.

DESPITE PARKER'S WARNINGS, CARLOS AND I CONTINUED GOING out almost daily. Ian, who had returned to Quellón and was temporarily working for a local fisherman, joined us when he could. But we didn't see a lot of him. Since whale watching season was around the corner, we knew he wouldn't be sticking around for long. Plus, rumors were floating about that he had a new girlfriend.

One day in late November, Parker handed me an envelope postmarked from California without a return address. I hadn't received any mail the entire eleven months I'd been away. I tore it open with all the patience of a seven-year-old on Christmas morning. Inside was a piece of binder paper containing a short paragraph in Sarah's perfectly concise handwriting:

I tried calling you, but the number I have is disconnected. Guess you prefer to continue living your separate life. Fine. But I've had two calls from some guy named Miguel Aguirre. Please call him, as I don't appreciate getting his phone calls and have no way of calling you myself.

At the bottom of the note was his phone number, an international number.

"Thanks, Jeff," I muttered. He was the only person who knew Parker's address and the only person who would have given my sister a way to contact me.

I tore off the corner with Miguel's phone number and tucked it under some papers in the single drawer of my nightstand. Maybe I'd call him but on my time, not Sarah's. The rest of the notepaper landed inside my wastebasket.

CHAPTER 58

My cell rang just before midnight. It was Carlos.

"*Hola*," I said. "What's up?"

"Sorry to call so late, but we have a problem. A whale stranding a few hours south of here. I could use your help. If you think you're up to it."

"Sure. I told you the knee's fine. What time?"

"Four. I'll pick you up."

"See you soon," I said, yawning and looking at the time.

Although I was able to get back to sleep, the alarm clock jolted me awake three hours later. I pulled on my oldest, least favorite jeans, the ones that fit too tight in all the wrong places. Work clothes. Necropsy clothes. I'd helped Carlos once before and swore never again. In my opinion, performing a necropsy was the most disgusting, putrid job known to mankind. Yet here I was dressing in various layers of secondhand clothes in case I got coated with whale guts.

I grabbed the pink day pack Ian had given me about four months earlier. When he offered it, saying someone had left in on his boat and never claimed it, I snarled my nose in disgust. Besides being my least favorite color, I found the large block letters that said "THINK!" extremely obnoxious. But I used it. A lot.

Vanity aside, it was a good-sized pack, large enough to hold my camera, a couple of apples, a notebook, and even my sweatshirt. At the last minute, I grabbed my parka, not expecting to use it since the days had been warm—even at the coast.

Driving along the two-lane, windy road, I practiced some breathing techniques to calm my nerves. I'd learned this simple technique years ago at a calming seminar offered by the newspaper. I guess they thought it would increase productivity. I found it a waste of time, perhaps better suited for newspaper reporters than salespeople.

"Exactly where are we going?" I asked.

"The notice I got indicated the stranding was on the southern end of a beach called Playa Negro. I haven't been there before, but I understand it's a small public beach with limited access."

"Will we need to hike in?" I asked, staring at my rubber boots.

"Doesn't look like it. There may be some dunes. I couldn't get a read on the place from the internet."

A half hour into the trip, we lost the radio signal. Carlos grabbed an old cassette and popped it in the player.

"Riders on the Storm" filled the car. I'd forgotten the beauty of the beginning of that song with gentle rain and thunder preceding instruments and vocals.

"Such a classic," I said. "Are you a Doors fan?"

"Big time. How about you?"

"Yes, actually I am. Or at least I used to be. I kind of stopped following them after Morrison died."

"I hear you. Do you have any of their records?"

"Four of the six produced before he passed."

"Lucky you!"

With the wind whistling through a crack in my window, we stopped talking and started singing. My pitch was off, but I didn't care. The music settled my nerves, and I began to feel more upbeat, reminding myself that we'd made good headway with recent whale sightings. And while I wasn't looking forward to smelling and maybe even cutting whale flesh, it felt good that Carlos had asked for my help. Time and whales had brought us closer.

THE PARKING LOT WAS SMALL BUT EMPTY. NOT THAT I EXPECTED a crowd at six thirty in the morning.

"I think that trail goes down to the beach," said Carlos, pointing to an area barely resembling a path.

I got out and put on my sweatshirt. The wind was picking up. Typical for the beach but early. Usually, we could count on a few calm hours after sunrise. Looking up, I saw a thick layer of stratocumulus clouds.

"Do you think it'll rain?" I asked.

"Probably not. I wouldn't bother with the parka. Just one more thing to carry," he said, glancing at the contents scattered about in the hatchback. I looked at all his necropsy tools and shuddered with uneasy anticipation. He had brought gloves, goggles, dissection trays, scissors, forceps, scalpels, and Ziploc bags, and those were just the things I could see.

The trail meandered over a few small dunes with beach grass reaching to my thighs. It was hard to navigate in my oversized, secondhand boots. When we finally got through to the beach, I caught the stench. That undeniable smell of rotting carcass that sent waves of nausea through my body. The smell of death.

"I see why it's called Playa Negro," I said, looking across a large stretch of black volcanic sand.

Once we reached the sand and started walking, we saw the carcass far down on the opposite end of the beach.

"A blue. For sure," said Carlos, picking up his pace.

We walked in silence. My hair kept flipping into my eyes from the wind, which unfortunately pushed the stench directly into my face. I couldn't keep up with Carlos. When he'd gone half the distance from the trail to the surf, he stopped, mumbling something under his breath. After I took a few more steps, I heard him the second time.

"Millie."

"No. That can't…" I stopped myself. I knew he was right, but I wanted to be wrong. Denying it wouldn't undo the truth or the tragedy. Her enormous body lay motionless near an incoming tide.

We continued walking toward her. Our pace faster. Our mouths shut. Our hearts severed. When we got within sixty feet of her corpse, we stopped. Predators, mostly gulls, covered her back, their squalls drowning out the pounding surf. Carlos's footsteps slowed as he pulled his ball cap low. I assumed he wanted to hide his emotions, his vulnerability. My friend had seen a lot of beached whales, but this was personal. To make matters worse, the scavengers and lice had consumed quite a lot of her flesh. She'd been there awhile.

When he got to her side, he pulled out a measuring tape. Before anything else, we had to take measurements. "Let's get started," he said, looking up at the sky.

Business, I thought, *straight to business*. His way of dealing with loss. The darkening clouds made me wish for my parka. But he was right about getting started. We had a huge job ahead of us.

Carlos had taught me a lot. I understood the importance of science, why we needed to recover what we could to learn more, not just about Millie but about the species. Carlos once said that finding a beached whale, while unpleasant, was considered a scientific goldmine. It didn't happen often. I wished it hadn't happened to Millie. She deserved to die peacefully and sink to the bottom of the ocean. Food for millions.

I'd learned that with any necropsy, retrieving the lens is necessary to determine age. And knowing the animal's age is crucial to more than just understanding the animal's health. Age statistics assist in numerous aspects relating to marine biology and population of the species. The other tasks that I would intentionally forego would include cutting into her skin and blubber to obtain samples of her liver, kidneys, and heart. And maybe her ovaries. Unfortunately, she'd been beached for at least a week, so besides predators eating away flesh, her internal organs may have broken down significantly, making it harder to determine the cause of death.

While all this science puddled inside my brain, I couldn't get past the horrific reality that this was Millie. Carlos had suspected she wasn't doing well when he last saw her, but this came as a shock. At least to me.

Pressing my right hand against what was left of her dorsal fin, I fought against the sour stench. My gloved hand moved upward, scanning her flesh for clues. Following Carlos's advice, I started with a more general scan while my nose and lungs adjusted to the smell. Later, I'd return for a more thorough inspection of her flesh.

Eventually, I made my way to her head.

When my hands passed the ventral grooves and reached across her blowhole, I stopped immediately.

"Oh shit!" I yelled.

One of Millie's eyes was gone. The torn flesh had to have been from a harpoon. As I slowly walked around her corpse, I found evidence of other wounds, both harpoon and gunshot.

"Carlos," I yelled, running around to where he stood, pulling a bone saw from his pack.

"I know. I know."

"You knew and you didn't think to say anything to me?"

"I should have. I'm sorry."

"God, this is, is so…"

"Ruthless?"

"That's one word."

"I'm glad she didn't bloat. All the gases inside a whale usually cause massive bloating. Not a pretty sight and occasionally dangerous. Legend has it that they can explode."

"Explode?"

"Well, it may be more fiction than fact. But I would not want to find out."

"Do you think this is the payback Parker warned us about?"

"Hope not. Look, don't think that this isn't bothering me. It is. But we have so much to do. Hours' worth. And if these clouds let loose, it's going to get real nasty. "

I knew he was right, but my heart didn't operate like that. Discovering your favorite whale dead was tragic enough, but to realize she'd been slaughtered, that her life had been cut short in such a horrific manner, was something I couldn't process. The first time I did a necropsy, I suffered a predictable mix of dark emotions. But this was Millie. And despite everything I'd witnessed since returning to Chile, the brutality was incomprehensible.

While I walked around her ninety-foot corpse, dodging dozens of stubborn predatory birds, feelings of bitterness overtook feelings of grief. Rain was now imminent, and with the wind gusts, I regretted leaving the parka behind. But it would take fifteen to twenty minutes to retrieve it. Watching Carlos in action, I knew I had to help him and help him now. It was only rain. I wouldn't melt. We had a job to do.

Donning face masks and gloves, we worked in silence. Carlos performed the more serious tasks including cutting thick, rectangular squares of blubber for tissue and organ removal. I continued to look for evidence of ship strikes, disease, parasites, and unusual skin discoloration. I took notes. Detailed recordkeeping during a necropsy was critical. Usually I'd write copious notes, making a separate page or two for questions, to avoid interrupting Carlos. But because it started raining, I kept my note-taking to a minimum, writing only specifics like location, size, and suspected causes for the smaller lesions. Carlos would handle the harpoon and gunshot wounds. If he needed a photo, he would call me.

After a grueling two and a half-hours, I needed a break. My knees were stiff, my neck tight, my shoulders frozen, and my air passages were screaming for a break from the stench. I grabbed my pack and walked halfway back to the beach grass, south of the trail. Since Carlos was on the other side of Millie and probably in deep concentration mode, I said nothing. I wouldn't be long.

Finding a sturdy log large enough to plant my butt down, I took the pack off my shoulders and removed my gloves. I pulled the camera halfway out of the pack to review the photos Carlos and I had taken of Millie. It was a little tricky with the rain, but by keeping it partially inside the pack, I could see the screen without getting it wet. The photos weren't spectacular, but they would work. When I was done, I put the camera back inside and reached for my apple.

I looked at the waves. If I stared straight on, I could see the ocean without seeing Millie. But occasionally my eyes went back to her corpse. The incoming tide brought waves closer to her head, a reminder that I should be working, not taking a break. I looked away. Maybe just five more minutes. Maybe ten.

Pulling off my boots and socks, I squished my toes into the wet sand. Therapy. Beach therapy. Carlos wouldn't mind. I looked north, toward the trail, and thought I saw a couple of people coming down from the trail, but it was so far away, I wasn't sure. It wasn't a beachy kind of day, so I shook my head.

The wind now sent sheets of rain into my face. I turned my body against the force, wrapping my arms around my torso. Downwind I watched a flock of sandpipers scurrying back and forth, in and out of the shoreline, their beaks pecking into the sand. Then they took flight, soaring and swooping up and then down, flying in graceful formations yet creating dizzying patterns with their sheer numbers. Grateful for the restoration of peace and this visual reprieve, I tossed my apple core and decided to get back to work.

CHAPTER 59

After I straightened my knees and bent down to reach for my boots, I saw the two people I had seen earlier. Two men. They were coming our way. I wondered if they needed help. But a few minutes later, I saw one man held something that resembled a gun. I rubbed the moisture off my eyes to focus. It was roughly the size of a television remote but resembled the shape of the revolver my mother used to keep under her bed. As they got closer, it became obvious they weren't coming to ask for a tidal chart. The lead man's movements sent nervous tremors down my spine. I couldn't see the other walking in his shadow. I wondered if he too had a gun.

"Get down!" Carlos shouted.

I dropped to the sand.

Lying on my stomach, my hands over my head, moisture immediately seeped through my sweatshirt. Something large and pliable was under my stomach, something oozing a different kind of moisture through my layers. Curling to one side, I grabbed the object with my bare hand. Bile filled my throat. The object was a piece of Millie's flesh, probably carried and dropped by a bird. Vomit landed across my arm and on the ends of my hair.

Carlos was partially hidden behind Millie's backside. I thought about running to him but couldn't muster the courage. Besides, what would we do if I did make it? Carlos didn't have a gun, at least not on him. Where could we go? The southern end of the ocean abruptly ended with a steep wall of unclimbable terrain, and the grass and dunes would be impossible to cross swiftly without a trail. The ocean was closest, but no chance in hell we'd survive the strength or cold of Mother Ocean. I scooted my body back until I was able to lie behind the log.

Carlos inched his body to the backside of Millie's fluke. Soon he would be more visible. I presumed he planned on running to join me, which was not a good idea. The area between us was too open. I shook my head, trying to tell him not to risk it. I didn't want another death on my hands. Especially not his.

The lead man's pace slowed, his eyes scanning the beach as he walked somewhat unsteadily across the lumpy pockets of wet sand. Perhaps he knew Carlos was here. Perhaps Carlos was his target. I wasn't sure if someone could shoot from that distance, but I didn't want to find out. While my adrenal glands argued between fight and flight, pounding heart palpitations reverberated like crashing cymbals inside my skull. I had no idea what to do.

Physically and mentally tired of hiding face-first in the sand, I crawled out from behind the log and stood up. Random thoughts passed through my head. Maybe I could talk to them, let them know we're harmless. Maybe I could de-escalate the situation, whatever the situation might be.

"Allie," I heard Carlos say. "Don't!" Then, trying to whisper, he told me to drop down and run for cover behind Millie. I assumed if I could hear him, so could they.

I looked at the men. I looked at Carlos and Millie. The men were so damn close. My legs wouldn't move. I didn't want to turn my back on these guys. It would take the leader less than thirty seconds to tackle me, but, of course, he'd probably shoot me long before that. Carlos obviously wanted me to hide with him. But I didn't want to. I'd been hiding all my damn life. While this was not the best time to attempt some badass act of bravery, I didn't want to hide. I didn't know what I'd do, but I needed to do something soon.

Peacekeeper. Not something I'd ever been good at. And at this particular moment, if I failed, I would die. Then again, I understood I might die no matter what I did.

The leader slowed his pace. God, he was a big man. Wide, tall, with stocky arms and thick legs. I could see his face now. He looked familiar, but I didn't know why. A face full of hatred and meanness, a multitude of pockmarks and permanent lines etched deeper than scars around his eyes and jaws. A tattoo of an unfamiliar symbol covered half of his oversized neck. I dug my bare heels deep in the sand. When I stopped moving, so did the man behind the leader. The leader turned and said something to him, shaking his head and waving his hands in what looked like a motion of dismissal. Neither moved, but from my viewpoint, the man in back didn't seem to agree with the man upfront.

While all of this may have occurred in less than a minute, the next moment fell into a timeless quagmire. The second man removed his raincoat hood and looked at me. Intently.

I stared back.

With gut-wrenching disbelief—much like the horrendous moment I stared at my TV watching one, then two planes dive into tall skyscrapers—I whispered his name.

Jorge. Jorge Montero.

Standing before me was the man I met on a Santiago street two days after my return to Chile. The man I'd once felt sorry for. The man who tossed a revealing package of codes and maps into my hands. Someone we thought was making it his life goal to save whales—even creating a song to raise awareness and money for the cause. Why? Why was he here?

My eyes shifted back to the gunman, who bore a strong resemblance to Jorge. Same nose, similar chin, and dimple. His deep-set eyes were similar in shape but more intense. Eyes that beneath the murky sky appeared as black as coal or tar or the sand below my feet. But this man was older than Jorge. Most likely not brothers. Maybe the gunman was Jorge's father or uncle. And then I remembered.

A few weeks into my knee recovery, Carlos brought me a photo of Armando Montero that he printed off his computer. Despite the poor resolution, the face in that photo matched the gunman. Same dark eyes, same bloated cheeks speckled with pockmarks, and same tattoos covering his entire neck.

So here was Armando Montero. We had spent so much time searching for him, but in the end, he came to us. He got us when—and where—we were vulnerable. I had no doubt that this was the asshole responsible for Millie's death. He probably inflicted the lethal wounds himself.

Armando must have known her body was on this beach. He probably faked the stranding report.

I desperately wanted to tell Carlos that this was Armando, but the wrong people would hear me first.

Jorge stood motionless, his body stooped, hands stuffed inside his raincoat pockets. He seemed genuinely surprised to see me, but maybe I was wrong. Obviously, I'd never been a great judge of character. He shook his head—a quick, almost undetectable, movement. After a few seconds, Armando turned and took a few steps back to talk to him.

In that welcomed millisecond, I bent down and grabbed my pack. The pink pack with the word THINK emblazoned in big, gold letters. Recognizing the irony of the message, I nearly smiled. Quickly I twisted my torso to hide the pack behind my back. Then I stood still. I couldn't let them see my fear but had no idea how to look courageous. My sweat glands were active despite the cold. My hands, legs, and heart shook in rapid succession.

Jorge turned. To my surprise, he started walking in the opposite direction. Armando yelled at him, but Jorge ignored him. Armando threw his hands up in disgust. Then he turned back and resumed his slow steps toward me.

He raised his arm and pointed the gun.

Something shifted inside of me. Like a settling of nerves. I didn't have time to diagnose this strange and unexpected feeling.

Maybe it was bravery. Maybe desperation. Whatever it was, I'd never experienced it before.

I took a step forward. Then another.

Once again, Carlos shouted. I couldn't make out his words. He probably thought I'd lost my mind.

But I hadn't. I'd found it. I'd finally found it.

"¡*Párete, gringa!*" Armando said. This I understood. He was ordering me to stop.

"*Tengo algo importante,*" I said, telling him I had something important and hoping to sound believable.

"*Mujer,*" he said, "*nada de lo que tienes será importante. Especialmente tu vida.*" I understood. Nothing I had was important. Especially my life.

My teeth clenched tight. This asshole killed Captain Jack. And Millie. I didn't give one shit what came out of his mouth. I was not scared. I was determined. I took another step forward.

"Allie," Carlos yelled, this time loud enough to be heard. "Don't!"

Shaking my head and feeling the heaviness of the pack on my right shoulder, I casually reached with my left hand to touch the underside of the pack. A plan. I had a plan. But if my plan didn't work or if I waited too long, I wouldn't stand a chance. I wondered what it would feel like to take a bullet. I hoped it was fast. And I hoped it would give Carlos time to escape. If Carlos survived, the whales would have a chance. My death would provide all the necessary proof.

Sounds faded from my consciousness as if Carlos, Millie, the ocean, my past, and future fell into some deep vortex. But with this shift came a new clarity. I would do this. Regardless of the outcome.

My feet disappeared in the sand one at a time as I continued inching closer to Armando, our bodies fifteen or twenty feet apart. His eyes looked like they might explode from his ugly face. He could have shot me, and it would have been over. But, apparently, he wanted to drag this on. Perhaps he got off on prolonging the moment, prolonging my end. Frightening the hell out of me, or so he thought. So typical of a psychopathic tyrant, desperately longing for control to satiate his ego.

Taking another step, Armando yelled, "*Mujer. ¡Al suelo!*"

No way was I going to drop to the ground.

"Gringa, why you wanna mess with us?" he said.

I said nothing but felt blood surging into my limbs, causing an internal shaking that I prayed wasn't visible.

Standing with his legs wide apart, he said, "You a big problem. But problem going away."

I took a deep breath, wondering if it'd be my last.

Continuing forward, Armando said, "You a spy from your country. We know. You not get out of this, woman. Even if you beg."

I had no intention of begging. *Why does he think I am a spy?*

Armando moved the gun to the right, then back at me. Twice. Through the corner of my eye, I saw Carlos approaching. I imagined Armando's little brain trying to decide who posed the greater threat, who to take on first.

"Leave her alone!" Carlos shouted. "She had nothing to do with the whales. Nothing!"

In the time it took me to exhale, Armando returned his aim to me. I stared at the muzzle. A big round O was now a couple of feet from my face.

"She dies. You second, amigo."

I was his first choice.

Now, Allie. Now!

Everything happened so fast. My right arm grabbed the shoulder strap of the pack. I knew it'd be heavy, especially since it was soaked. Then I heaved it with every ounce of energy left in my body. My aim was perfect. As the gun slipped from his grip, Armando stepped forward to catch it. But somehow, be it an angel or luck, a nice little sand hole met with his left foot, sending him tumbling. I had just enough time to run forward and grab the gun.

I stepped back for balance. He got up immediately. I raised my arm to aim, but he lunged forward. I swung my arm—the one with the gun—to the right. Fueled by rage, his movements were unsteady. His hand missed the gun and flew into my chest. His disgusting, murderous hand touched my body.

I pulled the trigger.

The blast was so close to my eardrums my head went numb. I watched his body fall to the sand, blood spurting from his chest. He squirmed, his shoulders twisting right and then left. He moaned, crying out Jorge's name. The sand around him turned rusty brown. Strangely, the sight of all that blood didn't bother me. I continued to watch as the color gradually drained from his face.

The gun was still warm. My finger slid back to the trigger. Maybe this whale-killing asshole was still alive. No matter. Dead or alive, Armando Montero deserved another bullet. The first was for Millie. This one, for Captain Jack.

Suddenly something—someone—whacked my arm, causing me to drop the gun. I turned, expecting to see Jorge, which of course made no sense.

It was Carlos. "Stop," he said, wrapping his arms around my torso. "Enough," he said, softening his voice. "It's over. Look at me."

I killed a man. I didn't want to look at him.

I looked up the beach. Despite the distance, I heard Jorge holler a loud, mournful "Papi!"

"That's Jorge," I said, nodding toward the trail. "Armando was his father."

"Unbelievable."

We watched Jorge turn, then run, and disappear into the dunes.

Carlos continued to hold me. "Are you okay?"

I killed a man.

"Allie?"

"No. I mean yes."

But I just killed a man.

Seconds passed. Then minutes. I felt my chest move. One big breath. Then another.

"Carlos, I killed him."

"You had no choice. He would have shot you."

"I don't know. I don't know anything."

"You did what you had to do," he said. "Breathe. Keep breathing. I'll hold you as long as you need me to."

My body rocked forward, then back. Over and over. Then my knees weakened, sending me to the sand. Carlos sat down behind me, his arms wrapped around my waist.

"You're shaking. We need to get you warm. Let's go back to the car."

"No."

The thought of moving, of doing anything, felt impossible. My legs were lifeless. My head buzzed with noise. And the ringing in my ears hadn't stopped.

"Okay. We'll wait a bit."

I looked at the ocean. The sky. The rain had stopped.

"I still can't believe Armando was Jorge's father," said Carlos. "All that time I knew him, he never spoke of his family."

I had nothing more to say.

Minutes passed. I had no idea how many.

Slowly some sounds returned. Birds. Predators. I hoped they would choose the man's body. Not Millie. And I heard the waves again. That steady pattern of waves rolling in and out, hypnotic and steady.

Carlos dropped his hands. I realized what a comfort his touch had been. He stood up.

"Will you be okay if I run to the car? You need your coat, and I need to get the phone and call the police."

"Uh-huh."

"I wish you'd come with me. I'll help you walk."

"I'll stay here."

He didn't push it. As the sound of his boots landed heavily in the sand, I watched him slowly break into a run. I turned my head. Behind me lay the big whale that had once changed my mindset about animals. A whale so spectacular in both size and beauty I knew when I saw her that I'd do anything to save her species. And there, a few feet to my right, lay the corpse of the man responsible for her death.

In what felt like seconds but probably wasn't, Carlos returned. "They're on their way. Here's your coat."

"Uh-huh," I said as he knelt beside me to guide my arms into the sleeves.

Turning from Carlos, I looked at Armando. *That strand of hair is out of place.* My hand touched his cold forehead.

Carlos grabbed my hand.

"Don't!"

After getting me to move a few feet away, Carlos sat me down again and caressed my arm. The same arm I used to touch Armando. He leaned forward and gently swept away strands of hair now covering my face. He tucked them behind my ears, under my hood. His movements were slow. His face, sad.

The whiny squawk of a seagull swooping down near the corpse acted as a catalyst for unleashing my emotions. A low rumbling of sound came from my throat. What followed was something from my gut. A wail so loud the nearby birds once again took flight. I was left without air. I couldn't seem to find the next breath. Maybe I would suffocate. That would be nice. No more fighting. Maybe I could join Millie, ride on her back, and be carried out to sea.

"Allie!" Carlos shouted.

I wanted him to go away.

"Look at me."

When I didn't respond, he slapped my face.

The sting was real. Not enough to leave an imprint but enough to get my attention. After touching the afflicted cheek, I looked at this man who for some reason cared about me. He grabbed my hands and pulled me to my feet. We began to walk, my feet moving parallel to his. Then he wrapped his arm around my shoulders and guided me to a log close to the dunes. He sat me down with my back to the ocean. Turned, so I could no longer see Armando. Or Millie.

Nancy Rhodes

"What happened?" I cried.

"A tragedy. A really horrible thing that I wish I could reverse. But it's over."

"No. No, it's not."

He didn't argue, but I did. I wanted a fight. "You know," I said, "they weren't acting alone. Armando was just a soldier. A pawn."

"You're probably right, but don't think about that now. The police are coming. They'll take care of everything."

His words had a funny echo. Every word reverberated like he was in a tunnel. Maybe I was in a tunnel. Or a cave. No, no I wasn't. I was on a beach poisoned by death.

We sat there for a while. Staring at the dunes. Not talking, then talking.

"I knew Jorge," he said. "He really cared about the whales. I don't think that was an act. Perhaps his father abused him. Maybe he had no choice. I don't know. But I'm sure he didn't know that he was coming out to help his father kill us."

I shook my head. "How did Armando even know we were here?"

"I don't know. Maybe spies. Maybe phone taps."

My brain replayed everything that had happened. An unwanted replay.

"I just killed Jorge's father. What if Jorge wants revenge?"

"You did it in self-defense. I saw what happened. You don't have to worry about Jorge."

"What about the others? The mafia?"

"They'll be caught."

"Bullshit. Armando said he thought I was a spy!"

"I guess because of the papers. Jorge must have known his father was involved with the killing of the whales. Now that I think of it, I bet when the police were chasing him that day you were in the city, he was more afraid of his father finding out than he was about getting caught with a little weed."

"This doesn't make sense!"

"No, you're right. But now the authorities can take over. They'll get answers."

I didn't believe him.

Moments later, we heard the sirens approaching.

"I'll go meet them," he said. "Stay here."

As he walked toward the men descending upon the beach like a TV SWAT team, my brain hit replay again and again.

The five uniformed police questioned Carlos. They all looked at me. The murderer. Maybe they would lock me up.

In North America, the police would've immediately questioned me. Shock or no shock, cops in the United States wouldn't let someone go without a statement. So I was surprised when several minutes later only one of them followed Carlos to meet me. The others walked toward Armando's body. They should have gone to Millie first. She was the only victim that mattered.

"This is Officer Robles, Allie."

I looked up and nodded. Officer Robles looked too young for his uniform. But he offered a gentle smile. A compassionate smile.

"*Habla Español?*"

"She only speaks a little," said Carlos, before my lips moved to respond.

Looking at Carlos, Robles said something about getting a statement later. He offered to drive us back.

Carlos shook his head and told the man we had our own car.

They shook hands. Carlos helped me off the log. Glancing back at Armando, I said, "He murdered my whale."

Carlos leaned into my body, pulling back my hood. He told me not to say anything else. Robles thanked Carlos, shook his hand, and left.

We started to walk. One step after the other. Leaving Millie, leaving the body of a man I'd just killed.

When we reached the trail, I felt the wetness of my jeans. And despite the dry parka over my wet clothes, I felt cold like I'd never felt before. *I might never feel warm again*, I thought.

Finally, back at the car, Carlos opened the door for me. I thought how much a life can change, sometimes in minutes. When we'd first arrived at this beach, I'd been so excited. So damn excited about helping Carlos with a stranded whale.

As if that was such a big fucking deal.

CHAPTER 60

Carlos turned on the engine and set the heater to full blast. We backed out slowly.

"You feel the heat yet?" he asked minutes into our trip.

I nodded yes.

"I won't pretend to know how you feel."

"Good," I answered.

"I'm so sorry, Allie. This is my fault."

"Stop the car."

"Wha—?"

"I'm going to be sick."

Immediately he pulled the car to the dirt shoulder. I opened my door before the tires stopped. After two rounds of dry heaves, the third was successful. After wiping the grossness off my sleeve, I returned to the car.

Turning on the ignition, Carlos asked if I wanted water.

"Nope."

"What can I do? Can we talk about it?"

"Nothing and no."

"It might help."

"Carlos, please. I can't think right now. I need quiet."

"Right. Let me know if it gets too warm in here."

I nodded.

He respected my request for the next half hour or so. But when a South Andean deer suddenly darted in front of the car, he yelled an expletive in Spanish. He braked so hard my body flew into his.

"Sorry! Are you okay?"

I wasn't, but I nodded. I couldn't wait for the drive to be over. I couldn't wait to hide in my room.

"That was strange. They're on the endangered list," he said in almost a whisper.

Like the whales, I thought.

When we finally arrived at Parker's, Carlos guided me out of the car. I thought about protesting but didn't have the energy. My legs felt like cinder blocks.

Parker met us at the door. Her mouth formed a big O when she saw me. She seemed to be looking at my legs a lot. It wasn't until I got to my room and she peeled off my soaked jeans that I understood why. Stains covered both pant legs. Blood. It wasn't Millie's.

They must have given me something strong. I remember the pants and a shower but nothing after that.

When I first awoke, sometime the next afternoon, I looked at the walls around my bed. Could it all have been a nightmare? I looked at the floor. No bloody jeans. No dirty clothes anywhere. But then I saw the backpack. Someone had put it on the small chair in the corner of the room. From where I lay, it didn't look wet or bloody. I had no intention of getting out of bed to check it. I preferred the bad dream theory, even if I knew it wasn't true.

I WAS LATER TOLD I SPENT TWO FULL DAYS AND NIGHTS IN BED. The second night was much like the first. Lots of drugs. No memory.

But on the third night, the terrors began. My head was filled with visions of Armando. Armando alive. Armando dead. I dreaded going to bed because of the nightmares. Carlos gave me some sleeping pills, obviously weaker than what I'd had the first two nights. I began doubling and then tripling the dosage. My goal: comatose. If I ended up dead, that was fine too.

Nights were a bitch, but days were worse. Because that's when

I thought about Millie.

I knew she was old, but she didn't deserve to die like that. The horror of seeing the empty eye socket and other big harpoon and gunshot wounds haunted most of my waking hours. I tried replacing those images with the happier memories, like the first time I saw her. But without fail, the happy memory would slide into darkness as I recalled the day she tried to warn us about the incoming attack that killed Captain Jack.

I imagined it would take months for Millie's body to be picked apart by predators. A few times I thought about returning to the beach. Twice I got dressed, and once I even called a taxi. When he arrived, I climbed inside, and while he waited for me to announce my destination, I lost my nerve. I feigned sudden nausea and paid him a handsome amount.

The news leaked despite efforts to keep the story out of the press. While I was still in my semi-comatose state, an article appeared on page three of the local paper. Fortunately, I didn't see it until several days later. The story was brief, full of exaggerations, and not at all to our liking. Where or how they got a photo of me remained a mystery.

Gradually I resumed some basic activities with Parker and occasionally Carlos. They were careful to skirt away from any topics that could remind me of that day. But everything did.

Unfortunately, the rest of the world wasn't so polite.

Parker was more successful than Carlos at fending off interview requests. Interrogations were another story. Whether it was police, lawyers, or maritime agencies, an uncooperative spirit wasn't an option. At first, Carlos bore the brunt of the inquiries, but soon I became the focus. I was, after all, the person who killed Armando Montero.

The media gobbled up the story. Journalists, especially the less ethical, spewed a full spectrum of speculations, ranging from the polluting fishery theory to vague illusions about an international crime ring. Photos of whale meat sold at fish markets in Japan with the headline "DEADLY DELICACY" popped up in a local tabloid.

After a week, Carlos and I started sneaking out on early morning walks, occasionally stopping at a bakery or store for a treat. We did our best to avoid reporters, but occasionally they'd sneak up from nowhere, shoving those large, obnoxious microphones into our faces and asking their ridiculous questions.

With mixed feelings, we waited for news about Jorge. They would catch him. Carlos and I were fairly certain that Jorge had not been part of his father's exploits. But we didn't understand why he'd accompanied his father to the beach.

The rift between Parker and Carlos passed. Carlos acknowledged that Parker had been right about retaliation. I overheard them discuss the Monteros and various ideas about what the authorities should or should not be doing.

On the days I didn't walk with Carlos, I sought comfort under my blankets, trying to somehow process and recover from the nightmares and recollections of what later we referred to as "the beach day."

Generally, after a sulk fest, I'd look for things to do. Sometimes Parker and I worked on puzzles or crosswords. If the weather kept us indoors, Carlos, Parker, and I played old board games like Monopoly. We created our own rules, making it easy to become major real estate giants, dissolving our cares into a fantasy world of giddiness and greed. Without this, I would have sunk into a dangerous, if not deadly, pit of despair. Between never resolving or working on the Miguel crisis and the nightmares of beach day, I struggled with understanding the value of living. My friends worked hard at finding ways to distract and entertain me.

One afternoon in December, Carlos and I met on Parker's porch to enjoy a particularly gorgeous afternoon by working together on a challenging crossword. We were discussing different possibilities for a word that implied greed when suddenly the screen porch flew open. Parker rushed toward Carlos, house phone in hand.

"It's that female inspector—Gloria something," she said, with an unusual display of excitement.

"Can't it wait? We need a break. It's been five weeks. There's nothing else to say."

"You better take it," she said.

Carlos sighed, then put the call on speaker, our standard protocol so both of us would receive the same news at the same time. But, more often than not, such calls would be a waste of our time—an unwanted interruption. On several occasions, we made sarcastic faces to each other while the well-intentioned party rambled on about their latest theory.

Carlos said hello, his tone not exactly warm and friendly.

"This is Inspector Lorentelo," she said in perfect English. "Sounds like I'm on speaker."

"Yes," replied Carlos. "Is that a problem? I have Allie here, Inspector. I hope this can be brief."

I scowled. He returned my gesture with a wink.

"*Diablo!*" I mouthed quietly.

"Yes, of course," she replied curtly. "I thought you would like to know we just heard back from Sr. Renski at the Puerto Montt Whaling Commission office."

Carlos and I exchanged glances. Neither of us had heard of anyone named Renski.

"Renski?" asked Carlos.

"Yes, Renski. He is staying in Puerto Montt, but he's actually from the Cambridge headquarters of the International Whaling Commission."

She had our attention. We hovered together near the phone, our eyes twitching with nervous curiosity.

"Jorge Montero has been detained along with one of his uncles and three others."

"Was there—"

"Excuse me, Miss Bennett, please let me finish before you ask further questions."

"Oh, uh—okay," I said, rolling my eyes as I looked at Carlos.

"Your testimonies, along with the reports and map you turned in, were helpful. Sr. Renski was impressed."

I waited. I had a million questions. While I was pleased that Parker's Russian map had contributed to the case, I wanted to know more. I wanted a word-by-word replay of everything Renski had said.

"He concluded that they have sufficient evidence to have the Monteros prosecuted. The Chilean government has offered to cooperate."

"Not liking the media coverage?" said Carlos.

"Exactly," she responded. "And if you agree to testify, I will inform you what we've learned since his apprehension. Due to the seriousness of this case, we cannot leak any information unless you are directly involved in the trial."

Testify? Relive this nightmare? In court? Risk my life again?

I shook my head. Carlos dropped his left hand onto the lower part of my thigh, deepening the pressure.

Removing his hand, I prepared my refusal.

Carlos, intentionally ignoring me, replied, "Of course we will."

I opened my mouth to protest. Carlos put his hand over my mouth.

"Miss Bennett, do you agree?"

Heart bouncing chaotically inside my chest, I looked again at Carlos. He removed his hand and watched me. He would let me speak. He had to.

The skin that Carlos had touched suddenly felt cold.

"Do you need my answer now?" I asked.

"The sooner the better, but I can wait. The proceedings won't begin for several weeks, maybe longer. But I won't be able to share any more details until I'm assured you'll testify."

Carlos put his hand over the phone. He leaned into my ear and whispered one word.

Millie.

The struggle between heart and brain reached such an impasse, I fell silent. Seconds, maybe a minute, passed in which no one spoke.

After a loud sigh, Ms. Lorentelo said, "Shall I call you at another time perhaps?"

"No," I replied, inhaling what I envisioned as my final breath of courage. "We'll cooperate. We'll testify."

Carlos looked at me with such an exaggerated smile I wanted to laugh. "Yes, yes, we will," he said.

"Excellent," she replied with an unusual display of mild enthusiasm. "I'll set up a meeting with Sr. Renski and call you with the details."

Four days later, we met Inspector Renski in a small, barren office provided by local authorities. The room, no bigger than my bedroom at Parker's, was hidden on the third floor of a mostly inactive city building. Renski was young, probably late thirties or early forties. His brown hair, neck length, was layered perfectly, framing a long, narrow head. Round, John Lennon-ish glasses lay on the bridge of his nose. I felt disappointed by his looks. I wasn't sure why, but I'd imagined an older, dour sort of fellow. He spoke deliberately, showing no more emotion than my beloved ex-boss Ms. Baker.

After introductions, we were led to a pair of non-cushioned wood chairs opposite an old metal desk. Sr. Renski reminded us that everything he was about to tell us was highly confidential.

"Mr. Costanera, Miss Bennett, do you swear not to share the following information with anyone?"

Feeling like I was already on trial, I nodded.

"We are recording this meeting, so I will need your verbal responses."

"Yes, of course," Carlos said.

"Yes, I agree," I echoed.

"Thank you," he said.

He didn't take long to get to the point. "Armando Montero and his brother Javier Montero, along with another group working in southern Argentina, have ties to a mafia ring based in the Mediterranean. As you may have suspected, they were working closely with the Russians. While the slaughter of the Chilean blue whales wasn't huge, their plan was."

I wanted to object. Not huge? Upwards of a dozen dead blue whales? I didn't need another knee squeeze to know I should hold my peace.

"The southern Pacific waters were their test market. And not just for blues. Gray, minke, and humpbacks were on the list. This was," he paused to clear his throat, "a global plan."

"May I ask a question?"

"Of course, Miss Bennett."

"Why? I mean, a plan to obliterate all marine life? It doesn't make sense."

"What we've determined thus far is that while they planned to profit from black-market sales of whale meat, their goal was larger. They wanted to eliminate certain marine life from popular areas because of potential objections to increasing the number of industrial fisheries tenfold or more."

Carlos's mouth dropped. We looked at one another. I mouthed, "Tenfold?" and he nodded. Already the fisheries were poisoning the ocean. This could cause irreversible damage to all marine life.

Before either of us could speak, Renski continued. "Russia is currently the ninth leading producer of fish in the world. They want to be number one. It's already a two-million-dollar business, but they want more."

"Are you talking about salmon?" asked Carlos.

"Mostly salmon," he replied. "But also whitefish, flounder, carp, and char. Wild fisheries and aquaculture. Both present problems, especially if they're not scrutinized and regulated. Mass numbers of any animal in a small area breed disease and pests, especially sea lice. And waste handling is often less than adequate, resulting in toxic waste piling up on the ocean floor. This can seriously affect bottom-dwelling animals and plant life. Entire species may become extinct. Scientists are just beginning to understand all the dangers of these fish farms. The side effects of antibiotics used on their fish is a huge problem."

"Not to mention all the foreign pathogens entering our water system," added Carlos. "I've heard that a lot of aquaculture practices involve using chemicals to produce a larger volume—chemicals that will likely affect the food chain."

"Correct," said Renski, glancing at his watch.

"That's tragic," I said. "Money and power. Forget the planet."

Renski looked at me.

"Miss Bennett…"

"Call me Allie, please."

"Yes, well, Miss Allie, we are grateful for what you've done."

Grateful that I killed someone?

"Your actions—yours also, Mr. Costanera—played a crucial role in what's been an extremely long investigation."

"Investigation? Whose?" I asked.

"The IWC."

"Long? How long?" asked Carlos.

"Upwards of ten years."

Carlos and I again exchanged glances.

"Do you have any more questions?" asked Renski, glancing at his watch yet again.

"Yes, I have a few. What about Jorge? Was he involved in this?" I asked.

"I believe he's been cleared."

Carlos smiled. "Good to hear."

"So," I said, feeling the hardness of the chair seep from my butt up to my spinal cord. "How long will the trial take?"

"I don't know. It could take weeks, months, possibly even a year."

"A year? I am only in Chile temporarily. I may not be here."

"You should stay in Chile until the trial is settled. I don't know how long, but we'll keep you informed."

"Can I leave the country before the trial starts?"

"Yes. You are a witness, not a suspect. We will give you a week's notice for the trial. Keep that in mind if you travel."

"Yes, sir," I answered, my mind whirling.

Carlos stood up, thanking Renski. And after a few handshakes, we departed.

Once out the door, Carlos turned to me. Tears dampening my cheeks, I leaned into his chest and wrapped my arms around him. We silently held each other in a drab, cement floor hallway until Renski exited his office, cleared his throat, and passed us in silence.

In the car, Carlos grabbed my hand. "It's almost over."

I nodded, staring right back into his watery, bloodshot eyes. "We still have the trial. A long trial."

"We can do that."

"Speak for yourself."

"It's time you start giving yourself credit. You can do a trial."

I sighed. He was probably right. Compared to staring death in the face and killing a man, a trial would be a piece of cake.

"I'm relieved about Jorge," Carlos said.

"Me too. But this must be hard for him. Will you contact him?"

Carlos scratched the side of his head, long hairs falling from his loose ponytail. "I'm not sure. It might be best to give him time. Considering…"

I saw his discomfort at the slip. *Considering I killed his father*. I let it go. I was getting better at that.

"Let's go home," he said. "Maybe douse ourselves with sparkling wine."

"Can we share this info with Parker?" I asked.

"We're not supposed to, but I'm planning on it. They'll never know."

I wasn't sure if his bubbly suggestion was intended as a celebration. Thinking about a long trial and having to relive the events of the past year did not feel like cause for celebratory libations. Alcohol for mind numbing, perhaps.

When we returned to Parker's, I considered excusing myself. I wanted quiet time alone to process all we'd just heard as well as what I'd committed myself to. Some thoughts needed sorting. Like why did I suddenly yearn to be back on California soil? And

Carlos—did I want more between us? Or was I afraid of more? Or did I simply prefer to explore a solid relationship with myself, without distraction?

Once we stepped indoors, the overwhelming scent of empanadas not only filled the room but permeated through my nose, straight to my empty belly. Parker's famous empanadas, both the beef and onion and the three cheese, surpassed any I'd eaten on either side of the equator. She didn't make them often, so when she did, it was cause for celebration and binging.

After not one but three empanadas and a glass of *vino tinto,* it felt like a pack of stones had been lifted off my back. When Parker brought out a bottle of pisco for dessert, my arm needed no twisting. After several shots, I was dancing. We were all dancing. We danced to a variety of music from Parker's vinyl collection. After Carly Simon and the Eagles, we danced to music by artists I'd never heard of. Then Parker asked if we were ready to dance La Cueca.

I nodded with some reluctance but also respect. La Cueca was a national dance, celebrated throughout the country by young and old, affluent and poor, at rural country farms and heavily populated plazas. It was also the first—and only—dance my mother taught me. She began the practice on my fifth birthday, right after our first visit to Chile. It became a ritual on every birthday until I turned thirteen and told her that I never wanted to hear that type of music again.

Lacking actual handkerchiefs, we grabbed paper tissues as substitutes. Once Parker dropped the needle on the record, we began poor imitations of the jovial interchange of movements. This traditional dance was a parody of the courtship between a rooster and a hen, but after several pisco sours, my movements fell into something between The Bangles "Walk Like An Egyptian" dance and Michael Jackson's moonwalk. So much for lusting chickens.

As the evening wore on, my feet ached from dancing on the wooden floor. When sharp spasms shot through my toes, I collapsed on the sofa. Carlos followed. Parker danced alone in a world of her own and happy for it. Sometime after midnight, she finally stopped too, plopping her sweaty body between us.

Carlos closed his eyes and drifted off, a soft snore occasionally sneaking its way through his nostrils. He was drenched in sweat, lips softly slanted into a peaceful pose. Something had changed in him. I could see it even in a state of slumber.

I'd changed too. But I wondered if old insecurities might return, especially when faced with a trial and having to relive the past year. I knew I should be feeling nothing but contentment since, at least for now, the remaining blues wouldn't be harpooned for selfish exploits. But true joy felt about as attainable as a chocolate cake on the highest shelf of the tallest cupboard. Unreachable. At least, without extreme effort.

CHAPTER 61

⁂

Decomber and the long days of summer were upon us. I couldn't believe almost a year had passed since I quit my job. Fortunately, the media had moved on to other stories and left us alone. With two extensions of the trial date, I had lots of time for reflection.

What an incredible, tragic, and life-changing year it had been. I never resolved the issue with Miguel and finally stopped blaming myself. He didn't fill my head as often, and when he did, I found ways to let go before anger found its way back to my heart. But with each passing day, my yearning to return to California increased. I missed Jeff. I missed the coffee shops. I missed hiking the trails of Mt. Tamalpais and Mt. Diablo and visiting old hippie shops in Berkeley. Sometimes I missed the crazy bustle and frenzy of people with too much on their plate.

I even thought about Sarah. Maybe it was time to accept my sister as who she was rather than who I expected her to be. I also wanted to find a job I actually cared about. *What do I care about?* Whales. Sea life. The ocean. Yes, I wanted to live closer to the ocean. I would sell my suburban home and find a place near the coast.

I knew this inventory of my life and intended changes might be a bit extreme, but if I learned anything through the challenges of the past year, it was the brevity and unpredictability of life.

I tried balancing all the sitting around and contemplation

with walking and jogging. One day after a longer-than-usual run, I noticed Carlos's car out front. Smiling, I waved as he came out to greet me.

"Hi there!"

"Well, you look cheery," I said, offering the customary kiss to both cheeks. *God, he smells delicious!*

"I've got some news about Karina."

"Well, you're smiling, so it must be good."

"She's in remission! I finally got in touch with her again. I had to call three different people to track her down."

"That's great news!" I considered warning him that it hadn't been that long and might be premature to get excited but decided to keep negative thoughts to myself for a change.

"She said she's been trying various alternative treatments and that even her oncologist is surprised at how well she's doing."

"Curious, did you ask her about the guy who chased me?"

"I didn't have to. She was upfront with that at the get-go. His name was Alex Danute. She admitted she'd started dating him but hadn't known him long when he moved in and started bossing her around. She said after she saw how he reacted when you broke in—not her exact words—she kicked him out. It wasn't easy. He was stubborn as hell, and eventually she had to get the police to remove him. Turns out the jerk had a standing warrant for spousal abuse and drugs."

"Is he locked up?"

"Yes, and—by the way—I asked Renski to check him out."

"And?"

"No connection to the poachers."

"So he was chasing me because I broke into the house?"

"Something like that."

"Well, that's great news about Karina. Maybe I can go see her before…"

"Before what?"

"Oh, well, before too much time passes."

I wasn't ready to tell him I wanted to return to the States. That could wait for another day. But by the way he looked at me, I suspected he already knew.

⁂

OUR LIVES WERE PEACEFUL, AND CHRISTMAS WAS NO DIFFERENT. We decided to forgo presents, opting for a long hike and a casual meal that Parker, Carlos, and I made together while consuming numerous glasses of wine. Carlos was in charge of salad; Parker, a traditional turkey and yams; and me, lasagna.

I'd spoken with Jeff the day before, giving him another update and providing only the details the attorney said were okay to share. He didn't like that I withheld so much from him, so I agreed to call him once a week. He talked about his family and an upcoming trip to Hawaii to celebrate their tenth anniversary.

Early afternoon Carlos and I took a break from kitchen activities and decided to call Ian. The minute he answered the phone, we sensed something was up, something that made his voice rise with a joyful pitch we hadn't heard in a while. We suspected it had something to do with his new love, Catalina. He confirmed our suspicion by telling us a wedding announcement would arrive soon. Ian shared that besides her beauty and intelligence, she held similar values, especially about environmental issues. I felt joy—and envy—that he found his soulmate.

"A wedding!" I exclaimed like I'd never been to one before.

Parker returned from the kitchen. "Turkey's out but needs to sit a bit."

"Good," I said. "The lasagna won't be ready for another half hour."

"Well," she said, "I'm going to take a rest. What were you saying about a wedding?"

"Oh, Ian and Catalina. The invite is on its way."

Parker smiled. "Good for him. Although I'm not much on weddings. Big waste of money."

"Bah humbug!" I said, gently jabbing my elbow into her side.

"Well, hope they keep it simple. Save their *dinero* for adventuring somewhere they've never been."

Carlos nodded in agreement.

After Parker closed her door, Carlos refilled my glass. "I presume it will be in Italy. Do you think you'll go?"

"Depends when, but I don't think so."

Carlos cocked his head. "You know the trial won't start for another two or three months."

"Not that. I have been thinking about going home. Stay there until the trial begins."

I watched the smile drop from Carlos's face and wondered if I should have saved that announcement for another day.

"Time to face reality," I added. "Whatever that is."

Tossing his head back, Carlos said, "Reality? As in a US of A reality?"

"I've been thinking about the life I left behind. Whatever it was. Or is. I left so much in limbo."

Carlos glanced toward Parker's room. He removed the band holding his ponytail, gray curls falling over his shoulder. "Come here," he said patting the space next to him on the sofa.

"I don't take orders."

"Right. Shame on me."

We both stood our ground. But only for a few seconds.

He put his arm out, palm up. Then he stood and met me where I stood. I accepted his warm hand. We stood inches apart.

His hand stroked the side of my face. "I was kind of hoping you'd stay."

"Kind of?"

"Smart-ass."

"Carlos…"

"Uh-oh. That tone…this doesn't sound good."

"Well," I said, "I need to tell you something."

He looked at me. "I want to say something, but—"

"Go for it," I said, curious.

"Well, this is where I tell you that I like you. I like you a lot. And I'd really like to get to know you outside of the drama we've been through, outside of the whales, and any other causes that may grab our hearts."

I didn't expect that. And I didn't know how to respond. So I didn't.

"Maybe," he said, "we could travel, go exploring somewhere. Or just hike. Or even hang out here, maybe plant a garden or something."

I had to laugh. "Plant a garden? Here?"

"Give me a break. I'm nervous. Or desperate."

Despite his flattering offer of domestic bonding, I shook my head. "We still have so much ahead. The trial."

"The trial," he said, his smile gone. "Yes. But it won't last forever."

"Thank God," I said, feeling like I had so much to say and, at the same time, nothing at all. "But after the trial, well, we'll see. I mean I want to go slow before jumping into anything else."

"I get that, Allie. It wasn't a proposal."

"Of course!" I said louder than intended. "I didn't mean…"

"You're blushing."

"Stop it. You'll make it worse. Besides, I still have a house in the States. And my friend Jeff. And my sister."

"A house that's leased, a man who's married, and a sister you never speak to. Fess up, *amiga*, is this about that man you told me about? What was his name?"

"Miguel. I may still have some doubts about him, but I can't change the past. I didn't tell you all of it, but if he did what I thought he did, then I've accepted that he'll face his own hell sooner or later. I'm done with paying for something I had no control over. No, it's not about him. But I do want to make amends with Sarah. She is all I have left, family-wise."

"You have a family here."

"That's sweet. You're right. I do adore Parker, and I like you too. A lot, actually—if you couldn't tell. But I still have things I need to work out. I would like to head home next week, come back for the trial, and after that—I may return to the States. I don't know."

He wrapped his arm around me.

"We don't have to figure it all out today," he said "But I hope somehow we'll continue together. However that will work. For both of us."

And then Carlos leaned forward, perhaps intending to give me a tender peck, but his lips landed closer to my ear than my lips.

"Oops," he said.

"Oops," I confirmed, smiling.

I wondered if I'd lose him by returning to California. I wondered a lot of things. But my doubts were brief, disappearing under an inner voice beckoning me to trust my gut. Whatever might happen or not happen back home with Sarah, Jeff, and the house wasn't an issue. I was learning to walk away, learning not to be swayed by the expectations of others. Learning that as exciting as Carlos's attention and attraction might be, I could give myself time.

"Can I kiss you again? I promise my aim will be better."

"Of course," I answered, closing my eyes, telling myself a little consolation kiss couldn't hurt.

His lips met mine. They were so warm. This kiss was different. Our tongues met, only briefly—stopped by the creak of Parker's bedroom door.

"Oh, excuse me," she said, turning around.

"Get back here," I demanded. "Christmas dinner is ready!"

"Are you sure? Looks like I might have been interrupting."

Carlos and I looked at each other and then laughed.

"Parker," I said. "It's Christmas. My lasagna will have black frosting if I don't get it out of the oven. Let's eat!"

CHAPTER 62

To close the hellish year of 2012, Carlos, Parker, and I gathered again on New Year's Eve. Before our meal, we bowed our heads to share mutual reflections and appreciation for our beloved lost friends—Captain Jack and Millie. We agreed that while 2012 could be remembered as our worst year ever, it was also our best. By the time we finished dinner, we agreed to spend the rest of the evening celebrating our success in helping to protect the remaining southern hemisphere blue whales. Carlos opened a special bottle of brandy that he'd been hoarding for years.

"You two go ahead. I've got to make a call," I said.

Neither inquired about who I was calling. Maybe they thought I'd be calling Jeff or even Sarah now that I started talking about her again.

After reaching the folded paper tucked far into the pack of my nightstand, I dialed. He answered on the second ring.

"Hello. Who is this?"

"Miguel, this is Allie."

A deep sigh muffled through the speaker. "My God," he said. "This isn't what I expected on New Year's Eve. Or ever."

"Yes, about that. I'm sorry I didn't call sooner. Sarah told me you were trying to reach me. Should I call another time? Tomorrow?"

"No, this is fine. I'd never sleep if I had to wait another day. So, yes, I spoke to Sarah a few months back. I really have wanted— needed—to get in touch with you."

"Okay," I said, holding my breath.

"So how are you? And where are you?"

"I'm in southern Chile," I answered, wondering why the formalities and what was so important that he'd track down my sister. "I'm doing fine. What about you?" Every neuron shouted to me that this was a mistake. That I should hang up.

"Good," he answered quickly. "Much better. I had some rough months, but I'm doing well now."

If he only knew. His idea of rough probably meant his latest girlfriend found somebody else.

"So why did you need to talk with me? Sarah told me you contacted her." I was done playing nice girl. He didn't deserve my patience.

From his end, another sigh. A cough. Smoker's cough, probably. Then he spoke. "They've been found."

My first thought, ridiculous as it might have been, was that he was talking about whales. But that was my life, not his. I was preparing to ask who. He couldn't be talking about his wife and daughters' bodies. Even Miguel wouldn't bring that up with me. Not now. Hopefully not ever. Plus, I really didn't want to imagine what a sea-soaked corpse might look like after three decades.

He broke the silence. "Alive."

"W-what?"

"They didn't drown. Allie, my girls—they're alive! My wife had made it all look like an accident. Like a murder. It turns out I wasn't the only one having an affair. But that bitch, that whore, she stole my girls. Moved to Puerto Rico, changed her name, and robbed me of their childhood."

He was crying. Miguel never cried.

"What hurts the most is that she lied to them about me. They grew up thinking I'd abandoned them."

I had no words. Even he didn't deserve that.

"You there?" he asked, taking a breath between sobs.

"Yes, oh my God, Miguel. This is unbelievable."

"You probably mean that literally, coming from me. After all that I kept from you."

"No, don't go there. Not now. I do believe you. I'm just so, so sorry. Sorry for you, sorry for what I thought."

"I can't blame you, and I don't. I was a total ass back then."

"How'd you find out?"

"My girls called. God, was that a shocker! At first, I thought it was a scam. But eventually they told me what'd happened. Sandra, their mom, died about six months ago, and they were cleaning out some of her things. They found a bunch of old letters and love notes from different men. They also came upon a large stack of receipts and reports from an investigator. Someone she hired to keep tabs on me. This made them curious, so they called the guy and told him their mom had died. After several meetings and having to pay him off, he filled in the holes, so to speak. They still weren't sure if I was the asshole she made me out to be."

"Miguel, that's insane. And sad. I can't imagine what this must have been like for them and for you."

"Uh, yeah. Understatement. Our first conversation started awkward and slow, but we talked for two hours."

"Have you seen them yet?"

"Oh yes! I went to see them—they both live near Los Angeles—just days after they called. And soon they'll be moving here to Costa Rica. Both of them! One is married—Marissa—and there's a grandbaby on the way. Marissa's husband was totally onboard with the move. He's a tech guy of some sort who can work from anywhere. My other daughter, Michaela, well, she's still figuring out life. A bit like her old man, sadly. But much brighter, way smarter."

"I am really happy for you."

"So what about you? When I saw you on the plane, you were talking a lot about whales. How's that going? I don't remember what you told me."

"I—I don't think I told you much. But yes, I got a bit involved in some whale, whale…"

"Whale what?"

"Research. It's kind of a long story."

"Well, a good one, I hope."

"Eventually it will be. Anyway, I'm glad things worked out. And I wish you and your girls a great 2013."

"You too, Allie. By the way, do you have someone in your life now?"

I paused. "Yes, I do. Not married, but life is good. Well, my friends are waiting, so I'll let you go. Again, sorry I didn't call you back earlier, but I am truly happy for your news."

"You can call me again, you know."

"Thanks. We'll see."

Hanging up, I smiled. Even though I had let go of the angst caused by his betrayal, this provided unexpected closure. Tossing his phone number into the garbage, I reveled in a whole new level of gratitude. Had it not been for Miguel, I wouldn't have gone to Chile. I wouldn't have met Carlos or Parker, Ian, and Lucas, and God bless him, the Captain. Soulful people—people who preferred oceans to city centers, boating to parties, landscapes to shopping malls. People who fought and risked their lives to save a few whales.

I walked into the living room, finding my two dearest friends in deep discussion about whether Carlos should buy a property near Parker's that would soon be on the market.

Carlos looked at me. "Everything okay?"

"More than okay."

Handing me the brandy snifter, he tossed his head back. "Well, here's to being more than okay!"

"And here's to a New Year," I said, raising my glass.

Wine glasses clinked together in solidarity while Parker's old clock ticked peacefully into a new year.

Nancy Rhodes

ACKNOWLEDGMENTS

I begin with acknowledging my mother, who enthusiastically read many of my childhood stories and even typed a few to send to *Reader's Digest* or God knows where. I doubt she knew how much that early encouragement fueled my desire to keep writing, but I hope she did. Mom won't see my first published novel, but she did witness my first publication. Seared in my heart is her enthusiasm over the little pocketbook collection featuring my story on the cover. As I recall, she had that issue of *Thirteen Stories* on her coffee table for a few years. Whether or not she put it there just for my visits matters not.

Presently, I am grateful to many for their support and assistance.

The first to read some of the early pages of *Blue Song* and provide feedback was coworker Larry Peltz. We worked at a newspaper in the advertising department where some of the ideas for this novel sprouted, although no characters in this story were based on coworkers, friends, or family.

I also thank early manuscript readers from the Coastal Writers group led by Karen Nichols, especially fellow whale enthusiasts Sunny and Rod Hatter, who inspired me to volunteer with Whale Watching Spoken Here.

Speaking of whales, thanks to Oregon State park ranger Luke Parsons and his wife, Mindy, for reading a "Millie" scene and to Luke for the education he provided each year during the Whale Watching Spoken Here training program.

A very special and gracious thanks to *mi amiga* Terri Deits for her passionate encouragement each time I emailed random pages. Terri accompanied me on the stunning (but turbulent) whale watch trip in Monterey where I took the cover photo.

Warm appreciation and thanks to writer, editor, and teacher Mike Foley, whose classes and editing kept me going and growing.

I also am grateful to Brooke Shafer and Kerry Hanson for reading segments and offering their support. Many thanks to my son, Brian Romanoff, and neighbor, Jan Walters, for helping me with details relating to "the big scene." I still laugh at the image of Jan and me standing in the street outside our homes, Jan holding a television remote at a specified distance to help me determine how close someone must be for a gun to be visible.

I want to extend my deepest gratitude and thanks to Barbara Giles, who read and provided editing suggestions for the entire manuscript. This book would not have moved forward had it not been for her selfless investment of time to read and reread so many pages, so many times. Thank you, Barbara, for your dedication and a keen eye for details.

Enormous thanks to editor Catherine J. Rourke for her wisdom and support and to the entire team at Luminare Press.

Also, special thanks to my Chilean friend Alejandra Romanoff for her tremendous help in turning my Spanglish into Spanish.

To everyone who has offered me encouragement, support, ideas, and help of any kind, *un millón de gracias.*

Made in the USA
Middletown, DE
29 June 2021